Prai

What do you get when yo_____th
an unyielding and intriguing_____t's
what this is. *Virginia* is a tale of the beginnings of relationships between
those who lived on America's shores and those who came from across the
sea. Not only is this a tender love story but one of danger and adventure.
Highly recommended!

> –Michelle Griep, Christ Award-winning and bestselling author

McNear's *Virginia* quickly draws readers into the what-ifs and lore of
what became of the first English child born in the New World. Not to be
missed, this haunting tale captivates from beginning to end.

> –Jennifer Uhlarik, author of *Sand Creek Serenade*,
> a Will Rogers Medallion Award Winner

With a powerful knack for laying open the hearts of her characters,
Shannon McNear presents what may be my favorite installment yet in her
gripping Daughters of the Lost Colony series. *Virginia* is a story of epic
proportions that traverses the gamut of separation, sorrow, revenge, and
beautifully—redemption. Exploring the question of whether anything we
have done or suffered is wasted, *Virginia* offers an emotional experience
you won't soon forget.

> –Naomi Musch, award-winning author of *Polly–Apron Strings,
> Book One* and *Courting the Country Preacher–
> Four Stories of Faith, Hope, and Love.*

In *Virginia*, Shannon McNear deftly draws readers back into the world
of the former Roanoke colony members and the Kurawoten and other
native peoples they encountered. She masterfully captures the essence of
both European and Native cultures and portrays how, by blending their
differences through their shared humanity, the two peoples could well have
developed a close-knit community. While this can be read as a standalone,
I recommend reading *Elinor* and *Mary* first to get a clearer picture of how,

by God's grace, such a community might develop. McNear creates an appealing vision indeed!

–J. M. Hochstetler, author of *The American Patriot Series* and coauthor with Bob Hostetler of the Northkill Amish Series.

Virginia is a richly woven tale, full of the details you expect from a top-notch historical fiction writer. Shannon McNear chooses women from a dimly known time and brings them to life in a vibrant way, not shying away from the issues they would have faced or from matters of faith.

–Lynne B. Tagawa, author of *The Shenandoah Road: A Novel of the Great Awakening.*

Shannon McNear's *Virginia* is a mesmerizing blend of historical intrigue and lyrical storytelling, weaving together the rich tapestry of Virginia Dare's imagined fate with captivating authenticity. This novel is a must-read, transporting readers to the mysterious and enchanting world of the Outer Banks with every beautifully crafted page.

–Jenelle Hovde, Historical Romance author with Guideposts Fiction and Tyndale

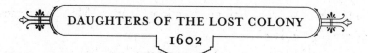
DAUGHTERS OF THE LOST COLONY
1602

Virginia

*A Riveting Story Based
on the Lost Colony of Roanoke*

SHANNON MCNEAR

BARBOUR
PUBLISHING

Virginia © 2024 by Shannon McNear

Print ISBN 978-1-63609-927-9
Adobe Digital Edition (.epub) 978-1-63609-928-6

All scripture quotations, unless otherwise noted, are taken from the Great Bible (and updated with modern spelling), https://studybible.info/Great.

Scripture quotations marked ESV are from The Holy Bible, English Standard Version®. Text Edition: 2016. Copyright © 2001 by Crossway, a publishing ministry of Good News Publishers. The ESV® text has been reproduced in cooperation with and by permission of Good News Publishers. Unauthorized reproduction of this publication is prohibited. All rights reserved.

This book is a work of fiction. Names, characters, places, and incidents are either products of the author's imagination or used fictitiously. Any similarity to actual people, organizations, and/or events is purely coincidental.

Photograph © Rachael Fraser / Trevillion Images

Published by Barbour Publishing, Inc., 1810 Barbour Drive, Uhrichsville, Ohio 44683, www.barbourbooks.com

Our mission is to inspire the world with the life-changing message of the Bible.

Member of the
Evangelical Christian
Publishers Association

Printed in the United States of America.

Dedication

For my own daughters—
all strong young women who regularly remind me of my worth.

Blessed be the God and Father of our Lord Jesus Christ!
According to his great mercy, he has caused us to be born again to a
living hope through the resurrection of Jesus Christ from the dead.
1 PETER 1:3 ESV

OTHER BOOKS BY SHANNON MCNEAR

The Cumberland Bride (Daughters of the Mayflower)
The Rebel Bride (Daughters of the Mayflower)
The Blue Cloak (True Colors)

Daughters of the Lost Colony

Elinor
Mary
Rebecca
Virginia

Dear Reader,

Nestled within the legends of the Lost Colony, Virginia Dare has become iconic in her own right. As the first English child born in the New World who then disappeared into the mists of history with her parents and community, she could hardly avoid such a fate, but it reached a fever pitch with the 1901 narrative poem of Sallie Southall Cotten. According to Cotten's poem, Virginia grows up as part of Manteo's tribe, beloved by all, and as a young woman finds herself caught between love for a Native chieftain and the jealous affections of a powerful Native witch doctor. When she refuses the witch doctor's attentions, he turns her into a white doe. Her love's quest to restore her humanity goes awry, and she dies in his arms. Though ultimately restored to life, she survives only as the White Doe, which legend says still haunts the region.

This myth, seen as extolling Virginia Dare's unsullied whiteness and maidenhood, was taken up in the 1930s by a group of white women seeking to block Black women's right to vote. This in turn led to the name of Virginia Dare being used as a modern-day banner of extreme right-wing white supremacy. When researching for *Elinor*, I stumbled across a particular website and could hardly believe that certain things are still believed, much less written, in our day and time.

I cannot find words strong enough to disagree with the thinking represented by that website. If the real Virginia Dare survived childhood—and I think it very possible she did—then I'm sure she did indeed lend whatever genetic strength she had to the people of Croatoan Island and by extension the First Peoples of North Carolina, and eventually the modern-day residents of Hatteras. May this story be a tribute to her, and to them—to what is likely our country's first and possibly only English and Native blended community.

This book can be read alone but is best enjoyed as a follow-up to my previous stories, *Elinor* and *Mary*. Since book 3, *Rebecca*, is unconnected to this story and set another five years in the future, either *Rebecca* or *Virginia* can serve as the last in the series.

For those who happen not to have read the earlier stories, a glossary and a cast of characters are provided at the end, defining historical and Native words and explaining the historical context of people, people groups, and places.

As always, thank you for taking this journey with me!

My most earnest regards,
Shannon

Part One

Chapter One

Spring 1602, Cora Banks

Mama was still the most beautiful woman in the community. A little wild she was, or so the English women regularly whispered, many of them still all bound up in their boned bodices and kirtles, tattered though they were. But who could blame her, being a survivor of captivity and wife to the stern and wild Suquoten man responsible for both snatching her away and bringing her back?

'Twas was still the stuff of romantic legend more than ten years later.

Virginia Thomasyn Dare, affectionately known as Ginny to family and the community, watched the way the other women subtly deferred to her mother in matters both small and great. The men as well, if it came to that. Mama attended council as often as she could, often with a babe in arms, which no one minded. All the Kurawoten women did, and most of the English. And enough time had passed since their crossing that the English nearly stopped commenting on how strange it was that the women held leadership positions as strongly as the men. After all, Manteo, the Kurawoten who had been to England not once but twice, may be Lord of Roanoke and Dasemonguepeuk, as well as leader of the English, but his mother was still *weroansqua*, or chief woman, of the Kurawoten themselves.

Ginny rolled her eyes every time the subject was brought up. It made her feel both restless and irritable inside whenever they talked of the old country and its ways. True, the tools and devices they had brought were wondrous—although the limitations of such were beginning to show after so long—but how pitiful must their homeland of England be if they did not properly value their women?

"'Twasn't like that," Mama would protest when Ginny would ask her about it. But then she would only shake her head when pressed to explain.

At the moment, the discussion centered upon the question of whether to return to Kurawoten Island. Some had gone back a few seasons past. Others felt the mainland offered more in the way of good living. Several swung between that and the protection the island offered from their enemies.

Ginny found it all just dreadfully dull.

She caught the eye of Henry Harvie, seated halfway around the council circle. Though the bulk of his bark-brown hair was caught back in a tail, he sported a thin roach standing upright from forehead over the top of his head, mimicking the Kurawoten men—and none could gainsay him, since Georgie Howe, English himself but married to Manteo's oldest daughter, had taken to dressing his own hair in that fashion years ago. The spiky crest of hair bobbed when Henry's gaze snagged hers, and his eyes widened, then he winked. Ginny sniffed and turned her attention back to the conversation. Best she feign interest than let him tempt her to sneak off into the forest. Henry was once one of her best playmates—they were born, she'd been told, less than the span of a day apart—but he'd gotten passing strange since her body had crossed the threshold of womanhood. He fancied himself a young man already, despite retaining a gangly frame and the high voice of childhood.

If anything, his voice had gotten squeakier of late.

Still, an escape into the surrounding forest and waters might be preferable to a slow death by tedium here. It wasn't as if this were anything but council—she'd never dream of slipping out from church services. And others came and went as needed.

If anything important happened, Mama would tend to it, along with Papa Sees Far.

With slow, casual movements, she unfolded from where she sat next to Tirzah Chapman, whispering that she'd return soon, and picked her way through the gathering. Outside, a light rain pattered, and she nearly went back in. The town lay mostly deserted, however—a few chickens scratching in the dirt, heedless of the drops falling on them, and hogs grunting contentedly in their pen under the trees—so after the barest hesitation, she took off.

She waved to the guards at the gate. Where should she go, river or inland? She angled toward one, then the other, reveling in the wind against her skin, the strength of her slender legs as she ran faster.

A figure loomed out of the shadows, keeping pace with her, then another. Henry had followed, and Redbud, one of the Kurawoten lads. A laugh burst from her lungs, but then she had to give all breath to the race. She would not be bested by these two, neither of whom had gone through *huskanaw* yet.

Mama was sure to scold once she returned, but first she would wring every drop of joy from the outing.

The marshy forest was alive with spring. Birdsong and flowering trees—dogwood just opening while the one that lent Redbud his milk name, with drooping clusters of tiny pink blooms, had begun to fade. Squirrels scampered away from them, and at one point Ginny leaped, squeaking with surprise, over a black snake sunning itself.

They came at last to one of her favorite places, where an earthen bluff overlooked the bend of the river and the mouth of a smaller creek. Here she could tuck herself into the exposed roots of a great oak and watch the water and all manner of wildlife that dwelt there. Thankfully the spot was yet dry, for she must try to mind her shift, or Mama would have even more cause to scold if she soiled it overmuch. The boys followed her down into the hollow, their breathing too loud even though she was sure they tried to be quiet, and they found places on either side, near her but not touching.

Below them, the creek slid away into the wide river, which sent small waves ashore with a gentle shush. Birds' cries echoed, first geese then a single osprey. A fish jumped. The tall trees lining the far banks stood cloaked in mist.

"Think we'll see any *wutapantam*?" Henry asked.

"Only if you are quiet," Redbud said. "But you never are."

"Hey!"

Ginny nudged him. *"Ehqutonahas!"*

Henry made a sound in his throat. "Why is the Kurawoten word for 'hush' longer than the English one?"

Because the Kurawoten tongue—and in many ways, their culture—was more elegant than the English. But Ginny would not be caught saying so.

"The Kurawoten are more graceful and beautiful," Redbud said. "The English are loud and obnoxious."

She would not agree with that either—not aloud, anyway.

A snort this time. "Your mother is married to an Englishman."

"And you see how he mostly takes the Kurawoten ways."

"Ehqutonahas!" Ginny said again.

Across the creek, a white heron landed and dipped for fish. This time, they were quiet, or mostly so. Enough at least that a young buck, its growing antlers thick with velvet, ventured to the water's edge for a drink. Ginny held herself still, and wonder of wonders, so did the boys.

A second creature stepped from the shadows—this time a doe, her coat so pale it shimmered. Ginny and the boys caught their breath, nearly as one.

Speaking of graceful and beautiful. . .

The buck lifted its head, water dripping from its muzzle, ears twitching. The doe followed suit. For a moment, the entire world was silent.

A rustling, accompanied by muted footfalls, swelled to fill the quiet. In a flash, the deer wheeled and bounded away.

It was Ginny's turn to freeze. Both boys looked around, eyes wide, and Redbud silently eased upward enough to peer over the edge of their hiding place. Heart pounding, she did the same, and likewise Henry beside her.

A brace of warriors ran past in single file, remarkably quiet for their speed and accoutrements. Bows slung across their bodies, as long as each man was tall, bundles of arrows and other provisions rolled and hung at their lower backs. Wicked-looking wooden cudgels. All faces painted black and red, with a profusion of feathers and other ornaments arraying their hair, ears, and necks. Warriors who were clearly not Kurawoten, nor Cwareuuoc, nor any other people she was familiar with.

And she most certainly should not be caught out here, away from the town, with naught but a pair of silly boys to defend her.

Shouts of alarm broke into the council discussion, followed by the sounding of a trumpet. One long blast, then another. Heads went up, faces turned this way and that, and cold shivered through Elinor from head to toe.

She knew what that call meant. They all knew.

Over the heads of the assembly, Sees Far met her eyes and, with the barest nod, ducked outside. A painful drumbeat beneath her breastbone kept time with her thoughts—Sunny and the boys should be safe at the house—but what of the two youths she'd seen slip out after her too-comely elder daughter?

Gracious God in heaven. . .

Her heart could not finish the prayer. She could only address its recipient over and over as she climbed to her feet and picked her way through the thinning crowd, hand against her rounded belly.

Sunny met her halfway across the green, golden braids a-flying and linen shift fluttering as she dived into Elinor's embrace. The top of the girl's head came nearly to Elinor's nose already, but she buried her face into Elinor's shoulder as if she were still a tiny child. "Mama!"

The two boys trailed behind and threw themselves against her skirts, one on either side, likely for no other reason than that their sister did.

"There now," she soothed, touching hair and shoulders, "all will be well."

15

Mouse tipped back his head, dark eyes wide and black hair glistening even without direct sunlight. Owlet remained glued to her knee, not looking up.

"I'm not scared, *Nek*," Mouse said, and straightened as if to prove it. "But it was a long council meeting."

A smile tugged at her lips. "Of course you are not, my brave young warrior." First child of her union with Sees Far, the boy carried more than his share of his father's spirit. She angled her body toward the meeting-house, tugging them with her as one. "But we must go back in for now and let *Nohsh* and the other men do their work."

Ginny sank back into hiding below the edge of the bank, heedless now of the mud and dirt on her linen shift. Henry and Redbud dropped beside her.

"What now?" Henry whispered, eyes wide.

"Where are they going?" Redbud asked.

Her heart pounded so, she could hardly breathe—or think. "The town?"

Redbud grimaced. "We cannot go back."

"But we should warn them," Henry said.

"Can we outrun warriors—?"

Ginny's decision was made in an instant. She could run—oh aye, and they all knew the secret ways between this hiding spot and the town. Even as the rustle of the war party faded into the forest, she pushed up and out of the hollow then sped away, her *mahkusun*'ed feet carrying her through the brush.

She ducked under vines and leaped over fallen logs and small streams. The boys were hot upon her heels, but she didn't look back.

Near the town, just short of where the brush and trees had been cleared for fields, she slowed and took shelter behind a great oak. The strange warriors they had seen now circled the outside walls, half hidden as she was.

Too late. She sank down, all her strength gone like water spilling from a skin. Her breaths came in short bursts. She blinked and scanned the forest. The boys peeped from behind a bush and a tree, about half a bowshot away. Henry's face was a pale blur, and even Redbud's face lacked its usual color.

They beckoned furiously to her, but her limbs would not move. Yet neither could she remain there.

With the sounds of struggle muffled by the walls of the meetinghouse, Elinor gathered the children close and kept her voice steady and calm as she told the story. "And Jehoshaphat inquired of the Lord, 'How then shall we meet this enemy?' And the Lord answered and spoke unto them, 'Set the priests and Levites before the army and have them declare my glory and praises. Then stand still and see the salvation of the Lord.'"

Distant shouts and the report of guns—they still had a few working firearms after all this time, with shot and powder made from resources found here in the New World—floated to their ears. The children had held their questions to listen.

"Will God indeed fight for us here?" Mouse asked, dark eyes bright.

That one longed to be out there at his father's side, she knew, and she smiled, caressing his hair and that of several other children in turn who sat nearby. "He will. And however the battle goes, we will trust Him."

"Should we also sing?" a girl asked. The next-to-youngest of Georgie and Mary, that one, called by the milk name Firefly.

"Singing is a brilliant idea."

She led them in a stately hymn:

Even from the depth, unto Thee, Lord,
with heart and voice I crie:
Give eare, O God, unto my plaint
and helpe my misery.

Manteo's mother and the other women drew near to add their voices, and soon the entire meetinghouse rang with the sweet notes rising and falling, giving voice to their plea for the Lord's intervention.

Sees Far trusted Elinor to remain safely inside the walls and tend well to the children. His only concern was whether those walls were secure enough.

He knew too well the look and feel of a raid. How strange to think that at a certain time past, it was him out there, taking part in an assault on this very town—the same raid that garnered him Elinor as a captive.

Twelve turnings of the leaves, it had been. He could scarce believe it so long.

Was this the work of his fellow Suquoten? Were any of Wanchese's sons old enough to seek vengeance? Such a thing was not improbable. They had all half-expected such an attack, after Sees Far's former friend met his end attempting to take Elinor a second time. A quite ignoble end for a warrior who had once sailed to England and back alongside Manteo before turning against the *Inqutish*.

Sees Far gathered his weapons, fastened on the lightweight armor made of bound reeds, and joined the others at the wall. What a mismatched group they must appear, with some clad in the iron armor they'd brought over *yapám* with them, some in the traditional gear of the People, and others in tunics of stiffened wutapantam hides. But they were of one heart and mind when it came to defending their own.

Sees Far climbed the ladder to the lookout platform and peered cautiously between the spikes of the palisade. The fields lay bare, all yet in the early stages of being cleared and planted. In the woods beyond, here and there a face peeped out, painted black or red, heads adorned with feathers of various plumage.

"Mangoac," he said. "Warriors of the west. Those who will pretend to trade but always seek the weaknesses of others, to make war upon them."

"Sounds like others we have known," one of the Inqutish muttered.

Sees Far did not bother to favor him with a look, but several of the other men murmured their protest.

Still, it was truth that some were enemies, no matter how one chose to view them. A strong and powerful nation were the Mangoac, holding the inner lands and feared by all—even the Powhatan.

This day, most definitely arrayed for war, and in no mood for trade.

They held back, watching, doubtless having tasted of gunshot. Did they surround the town, or was their approach solely from this direction? Could he and some of the others sneak out and circle around behind them?

They must try. He gestured to Manteo, standing nearby on the platform, and made his way down again. Manteo's visage grew more furrowed as Sees Far outlined the suggested plan, but then he gave a quick nod, his *wassador* necklace glittering with the motion. He divvied up the men, assigning some to hold the wall, some to guard the entrance, and some to slip out through the back side. He and Sees Far would lead those going out, along with the English who were the truest shots.

They came under fire almost immediately. He let loose an arrow, then two, while three of the English crouched and returned a volley with their guns. The others ran for cover of the woods, at an angle from the arrow fire, then he and the others joined them, bent and huddling.

There the fight began in earnest.

Sees Far returned arrows with as much heat as they came. In the din of battle, he thought he heard singing intermingled with war cries, but dared not stop to pay heed. He and the others pressed on until their assailants scattered into the woods, some this way and others that. He motioned for his men to follow, split them into two groups, and led one toward the river.

"Smoke!" came a cry. "They've set something on fire!"

Not the town, surely? He whirled, looking around—as they all did—but when he spotted the rising smudge, it was in the direction of the river and not the palisade. The smoke thickened as they ran faster.

"'Tis the pinnace!" another called. "They've set fire to the pinnace."

The sounds of fighting grew closer—yips and howls from Native throats, the roar of guns, and the shouts of the English. Ginny dragged in a breath and, shaking, forced herself to her feet. Henry's and Redbud's eyes were so wide she could see white rimming them.

It was now or never. She had to try—

She launched herself across the space. A shout sounded from behind her, but she was almost to the boys—almost—

Rough hands laid hold of her, lifting her off her feet. Her world tipped and tilted, and her gut slammed into a war-painted shoulder, driving the breath from her body.

Henry and Redbud shrieked in protest—at least, she thought those were their voices, quickly growing more distant as her assailant rushed through the forest, but never completely fading away. Were they being carried off as well?

God—God in heaven, hear our cry!

But her assailant did not stop running.

Had she brought this misfortune upon them by determining to escape the boredom of a council meeting, thus shirking her responsibility to her younger siblings—not to mention the community?

God, if 'tis so. . .I am deeply sorry.

And. . .I'm so sorry, Mama!

Chapter Two

A t last, when Ginny was sure she would shame herself by losing the contents of her stomach over her captor, they stopped—but 'twas only to be set roughly back on her feet, hands tied in front of her, then prodded with gestures and words to run alongside. And this time they did not stop, except for a brief mouthful of water, until the sun was slanting behind the trees ahead of them.

In a hollow surrounded by mossy boulders, her captors built a small fire then set to examining each of the boys before turning their attention to her. Fingering her hair, the braid half-frayed now, they leaned close, touching her skin and peering into her eyes. Then they made motions toward her clothing, but she stood frozen until one of them approached with a sharpened rock, as if to cut the front of her bodice. She pushed him away, but someone caught her skirt from behind and lifted it high. With a cry, she lashed out in that direction as well, earning several laughs from all around.

Her ears burned. A hundred different conversations flowed through her memory, of Timqua and Mary and the others discussing the possibility of being taken captive by rival peoples, and how a woman should comport herself in such circumstances. Of Mama's tight-lipped observances of her own experience.

She turned a slow circle. Did they merely want to be reassured that she was female, or was there more to their sudden fixation on her raiment?

A warrior of uncertain age, his head bristling with a dozen or more turkey feathers, gestured again to her bodice.

Better that she untie it and have a chance at wearing it again.

There was a yank on her shoulder, and a rip. She whirled again, peering behind her. "Now look what you've done!"

Another wave of laughter. With shaking hands, she tugged at her laces. A man's hand swooped in and, with a flick of his stone blade, cut what she was trying to untie. Another squeal escaped her as the rest of her clothing seemed to simply shred away. . .

And then she was left bare, trying to cover herself with her arms.

Out of the corner of her eye, she could see Henry and Redbud struggling furiously against their captors while at the same time trying not to look. Rough hands turned her this way and that, with a babble of discussion about her apparent assets—or would that be the lack thereof? She was still quite slender, compared to two or three of the slightly younger girls at Cora Banks.

A gruff voice cut above the others, and one man swept a cloak-like garment, woven of rabbit skins, around her shoulders. He spoke sharply to the others, chin jerking upward, eyes glittering. A word or two that sounded suspiciously like protest, then the other men backed away. Or mostly so. She was herded to a place near the fire and handed a piece of roasted meat.

Across the fire, she met Henry's gaze—wet and sorrowful. Her own eyes stung in response.

She shouldn't care. The girls and women of the Kurawoten still, after ten years and more with the English, often wore only a skirt, especially in summer and while working. For that matter, she'd spent her share of time as bare as she was made—but this was different by far.

At least they'd allowed her to cover herself again. She fingered the weave of the cloak. In Kurawoten society, before the majority of them had become followers of Christ, such a thing would have denoted special status. What was it? She seemed to recall that it was—aye, that was it, the position of priest. Her gaze sought the one who had given her the garment, although 'twas difficult telling the men apart, save for patterns of war paint. There, a little way around the fire, his face black even in the flickering light—but his glittering eyes upon her, watchful in return.

A chill swept her. If only she could fold in upon herself and disappear inside the soft warmth.

"You are not one of us. You will never be one of us."

The words echoed in his head, years past now, but they swirled through his thoughts, taunting him at particularly trying moments.

Yet here he was, dressed and painted and armed as one of the Skaru:re, running along as one of the war party.

Accepted.

Trusted, even.

Life among them had not been one of ease, especially not in the early years—but it was good.

A great honor, it was, to have been included in this war party. The planning had been discussed for many a year—to strike the settlement of the foreigners who had been accepted by the foolish Kurawoten. The Skaru:re knew what it was to welcome strangers only to be turned upon and their hospitality scorned. For the foreigners to use kindness in the most bitter betrayal. It did not matter if these were from a different nation and claimed to be enemies of those who had been before—the outcome would be the same.

The guns of the *Inglés* had driven them back, yet they'd carried away two striplings and a young woman. At least one of the striplings was Kurawoten, but the other had the look of someone born to those from over the ocean. Though both hair and eyes were dark, arguably not as black as Native born, his locks held a definite curl, and despite tanned skin, his features were finer.

Rather like his own, he knew.

The girl, however—she left no doubt. Hair of a shade he recalled being described as *flaxen*, with eyes as blue as the sky above. A simple shift made of woven fabric rather than deerskin. Her age seemed indeterminate until they stripped her of her garment, and then the high, pale rounding of her breasts proclaimed her budding womanhood.

She bore the indignity more bravely than he'd have expected, which led to Blackbird providing her with a skin cloak. Likely she remained unaware that this was the first token of being claimed as his, but that would come later.

Ginny had not returned. Nor had Henry or Redbud.

Elinor's heart lay leaden in her chest. She'd known it could bode no good when her elder daughter had slipped out of that council meeting, with the two lads following straightaway.

And—the pinnace! Just as the town had decided at long last to return to the island, their chief transportation was damaged, perhaps forever.

The men clustered together, talking and gesturing and shaking heads over the matter. To be fair, they were also discussing the dilemma of three of their youths being caught outside the walls and carried off by an apparently beaten but swift enemy.

She'd already sent Sunny back to the house with the little boys, with instructions to begin preparation for supper. The other women agreed nearly without words to combined efforts to feed everyone tonight, so Sunny need only bring the basket of *apon* they'd cooked that morning—if any yet remained. Still, Elinor should not leave her to it, in the event the boys had gobbled it all during the meeting. Seeing to her family's nourishment needed no thought, however exhausted beyond words she might be with worry for Ginny and the lads.

She plodded in the direction of the house. Her firstborn, taken by the People. Just as she herself was, all those years ago. . .

Pulling in a ragged breath, she forced her thoughts toward prayer. *Gracious God in heaven, go with her and be her strength, as You were mine!*

Abruptly, her knees gave out and she sank to the ground, covering her face and huddling over a belly too big for such things. . .but she could go no farther.

Sobbing took her. "I—cannot—face this, O God. I cannot. 'Twas one thing to be taken captive myself—another to have to watch while my daughter is taken." A wail threatened to break free. "Especially after—having seen her father fall as he did."

She bent farther, crushed beneath the memories.

"Elinor!" A blade flashed. Deep red spilled over his armor. . .

"Elinor!"

Strong but gentle hands took hold of her. She straightened, looking up into the face of the one who had stolen her away.

Stolen at first in body. . .later in heart.

A pang rippled through her at the love and concern in those dark eyes. The arching brows knitted in worry.

Too much knowledge etching his strong features.

"Elinor," he murmured and knelt with her.

"My—daughter," she squeaked.

He gathered her close, his chest rumbling with a word that assured her he felt her pain. *I love her too.* And she knew it was so. Knew he loved Ginny as his own.

"*Kuwumádas*," he said then. *I love you.*

She could only weep.

It was too much. It was all too much.

When it seemed the worst of Elinor's tears had passed, Sees Far lifted her into his arms and carried her toward the house. The other men watched from a distance. "Meeting after we sup," Roger Prat called.

A handful of the other women were waiting when he reached the house, busy at various tasks. The smell of cooking filled the air. Timqua met him at the door, her expression grave. "Take her up and tend her. We will see to all else."

Another woman, however, Alis, one of the Inqutish, trailed him up the stairs, bearing a cup of something steaming and probably restorative. Elinor's eyes fluttered open as he tucked her into the bed, and the woman bent close with the cup. "Do you drink a little," she murmured, and Sees Far supported Elinor as she sipped. When she turned her face away with a little head shake, the woman waited until he settled Elinor and then handed him the cup. "You as well."

He drank—sweet and strong, not quite as bracing as the hours-long infusion the People often brewed, but of the same leaf. "Thank you," he said, and she dipped in response.

"I'll bring more presently."

As she withdrew, he cuddled in next to Elinor, who burrowed against him but did not speak. He knew by the rhythm of her breathing that she remained awake, and so he stroked her hair and held her close.

"I will go to the meeting," he said at last, keeping his voice low. "No doubt we will talk of pursuing them."

Elinor shivered. "I do not wish you to go. What if—what if I lose you as well?"

He sighed—but quietly. "We will talk," he said again.

With renewed weeping, she pressed closer. He held her until Timqua came, bearing a platter with bowls of food. "Come, sister," she said, "you must eat. For your little one if nothing else."

She sat up stiffly and eyed the array while Sees Far's stomach contracted, but he waited for her to select something first. She shook her head. He set a morsel of broiled fish on a piece of apon and held it near her mouth. Her lips quirked, and the blue gaze flashed to his before she opened her mouth and took it. Tears welled again in her eyes, but she did not refuse more.

He fed her patiently, steadily, until she shook her head again and lay back down, and then he finished off what was left. He smoothed a hand across her head before rising and gathering up the dishes to return below.

The children spilled into the room, clamorous. "Ehqutonahas!" Sees Far said. "Nek is resting."

"Nay, let them come."

To his surprise, Elinor was pushing herself upright again, reaching out an arm as the two boys leaped upon the bed, Sunny following with more reserve. Elinor gathered them all into her embrace, sniffling as she kissed and nuzzled them. Her renewed weeping stirred Sees Far's distress—but then he understood. The children's presence comforted her, a reminder that not all was yet lost.

He needed that reminder as well.

He soon left Elinor in the capable hands of the women and joined the men at the meetinghouse. He entered midargument about whether or not the pinnace could be repaired.

"A long task does not mean it cannot be done," Captain Stafford said. "And Chapman is well skilled."

"But will it be seaworthy? We've already waited fourteen years, and no one has returned."

Manteo waved a hand, and the others finally quieted. Hair threaded lightly with silver though his body lacked no strength, the Kurawoten *weroance* lifted a pipe with smoke trailing from the bowl. "We will first take the *uppowoc* and think about this matter. More than ever we need to behave as men and not unruly children." He favored them all with a small smile.

After a few pulls, he lowered the pipe. "We have long discussed returning to the island. Many things have delayed our doing so—not the least of which was my taking a wife of the Cwareuuoc. If I must stay behind and join her people so the rest of you are free to go—"

A murmur arose at that, but with another smile, he held up his hand again then passed the pipe to Roger Prat, who took it with a short nod and puffed thoughtfully.

Sees Far nodded his approval. Best to let age and wisdom speak first. The younger men leaned forward, containing their impatience toward that gesture—among them, Sees Far's protégé and Manteo's son-in-law, Georgie, now a man full grown, who wore the beard of an Inqutish yet arranged his hair as a warrior of the People.

Prat lowered the pipe to his lap. "We have several concerns at hand. The first is the defense of our people. The second is provision for our people." His eyes swept the group. "Third is the question of whether our three youth who have apparently been taken can be retrieved." Here he cut his gaze to Manteo, who gave the barest bob of the head, an ambivalent gesture, and to Chris Cooper, who only huffed and folded his arms. "The spring crops are already growing, but we yet have seed for the next two plantings. If we sent one party to survey the situation at the island, with another to pursue our attackers. . . ?"

He passed the pipe to the next man, who puffed once, twice, before handing it off again. "I've nothing to add to the discussion yet."

And so it went, with each man offering a similar comment or expressing agreement with what had already been spoken.

Georgie, however, held the pipe for a moment after a single puff then looked around. "What hinders us from pursuing them right away?"

Sees Far allowed a little smile, as did several of the other men. Georgie was the one who, so many turnings of the leaves ago, had delayed returning from huskanaw in order to attempt fetching back the rest of the captives taken during the raid in which Sees Far had acquired Elinor.

Manteo smiled as well, with much affection. "Besides nightfall?"

A collective chuckle circled the group. Georgie did not smile in return but leaned forward with his elbow on his knee. Manteo's expression softened, gaining an edge of sadness. "Have patience, my son."

The bond between these two ran deep, none could doubt. And if there was anyone Georgie would listen to—besides Sees Far himself—it was Manteo. Not only because Georgie had Manteo's daughter to wife, either.

"It is a risk to go after them," Manteo continued. "These people do not share our tongue. And we know less of their ways than of those who took Elinor and the others." He flicked the briefest glance toward Sees Far.

"You mean, of where they ended up," Georgie said, and Manteo nodded.

"I know she is as your own sister," Manteo said, more quietly.

Georgie tucked his head. "'Tis not only that. Although, aye—when Elinor herself tasked me with looking after Ginny all those years ago, I suppose I have never forgotten." He looked up again, his blue eyes sharp. "But 'tis not only Ginny. The thought of Henry and Redbud also being lost, and our making no attempt to retrieve them, sticks as a fish bone in my throat."

"It is a wonder, perhaps, that such a thing has not happened before—at least not since Elinor and the others were taken." Manteo exchanged a glance with Roger Prat. "We have held ourselves strong as a people while here at Cora Banks. Beechland has also held strong, and flourishes. To expect that our enemies would not at some point rise up and try that strength would have been unwise. But to immediately chase after is also unwise, and taking the time to talk and plan does not mean we do not grieve the loss of those who were taken."

Georgie gave a slow, thoughtful nod, then passed the pipe.

Night had fallen by the time Sees Far returned to the house. The inside lay dark but for a fire, where Elinor sat waiting. Wrapped in a blanket and hair braided over her shoulder, she rose from her chair and padded across the floor to him then leaned into his embrace. "The children?" he wondered aloud.

"Mary took them for the night." She let out a long breath. "How went the meeting?"

"Well enough. Plans are being made for pursuing Ginny and the boys. And other things," he added after a moment's hesitation.

It did not go unmarked. Elinor lifted her head to look at him. "A move back to the island?"

He gave her the barest nod. As he suspected she would, she slipped out of his embrace, putting her back to him as one hand came up to her forehead. She turned a circle before swinging to face him once more. "Why now? They should have followed through on that five years ago. We should have—" She dropped her hand and turned another circle.

Sometimes when she was in such a frame of mind, it was better to catch her in close and hold her until the tempest passed. Other times, letting her fume and pace was the best course of action. He judged this to be the latter and, folding his arms, merely watched her.

She strayed to the fire then whirled toward him again. "I know you will but remind me of why we did not."

He nodded again, gravely.

"Because of the Spanish."

"*Kupi.* We not only sighted their ships, but they came ashore to look at where the town had been, on Roanoac."

Her expression, despite being wreathed in shadows, shifted in a way that assured him she recalled well the agony of their decision to remain where they were. In addition to the English dread of the Spanish, enough whispers of their doings to the south and west had convinced all that the Spanish were indeed still a threat and would remain so for some time to come.

Elinor's shoulders drooped. "Clearly, there is no place for us which is thoroughly safe."

"*Mahta.*"

She closed the space between them and sagged against him. He drew her in, his chin resting on the top of her head.

"Whether here or there," he said softly, "we trust the good God and seek His leading."

She nodded, head still resting on his chest. "I am trying—to trust Him. But this—this seems passing difficult—"

He tightened his arms around her. His own heart ached, fiercely so, for Ginny's absence.

"I know too well there's little hope of getting her back," Elinor went on, weeping now. "I keep thinking of—of Emme, and of Libby, and our captors' decision to marry them off. 'Tis too far a stretch to think that can't, or won't, happen to Ginny."

Her words were, unfortunately, too accurate for him to argue with. "And yet, if God. . ."

She shook her head and kept weeping.

Chapter Three

G inny woke with a start to grey dawn and men's voices speaking a tongue she did not understand.

Her whole body hurt. She couldn't remember ever feeling this much pain at one time.

She still wore the rabbit-fur cloak. Clutching it about herself, she rose cautiously. Henry and Redbud were awake already, sitting over by the fire. Henry caught her eye, nudged Redbud and pointed, but earned himself a cuff from one of their captors. His head went down again.

She cast a glance about her. None of the men said her nay when she sidled out to the brush to see to her needs, but they did sharpen their watch. She finished, went down to the stream to wash, then hesitantly made her way to the fire. One of the men handed her a chunk of roasted meat.

Abruptly, the fire was doused, the boys were hauled to their feet, and Ginny was prodded into motion.

At least she still had her mahkusun. They held firm despite alternately wading through swamp and clambering over rocks. The sharp fear of yesterday faded into a dull ache, with the occasional spasm of homesickness and missing Mama and her siblings. The question of whether she would ever return pulsed through her—and of whether it was even possible to escape.

Mostly she was simply weary.

"Hurry up, Mud Crawler!"

He let his only response be a smirk, since he was not by any means falling behind. The young warrior—no older than himself—laughed and turned his attention back to the path.

"That one," grumbled the older warrior behind him, "needs to think far less of himself."

He allowed himself a silent chuckle this time. In truth, he did not care. The others could heckle all they liked—he'd well proven himself beyond anyone's doubt. *Guh-neh*, they called him. The Eel. He would not let that trouble him. He still knew his true name—the one given at his birth—even if he walked now as a warrior of the Skaru:re.

Even if he felt Skaru:re in all the ways that mattered.

They entered another swampy pool. Ahead of him, the girl stumbled—likely a root or log—and the cape swung about her, baring a lean but muscled thigh. She'd still not complained or faltered, though he could see she'd not the energy of day's beginning. Recovering, she chose her footing more carefully but still glanced about—including a look over her shoulder. He ducked his head. Better not to betray himself yet.

The striplings also did tolerably well. The Kurawoten lad, no one could be surprised at, but the Inglés? The other warriors muttered that they'd expected him to wilt the first day. Instead, he strode along, attempting to make conversation with the warriors nearest him.

That one would do well. . .provided the Skaru:re did not decide to make a sacrifice of him.

He hardened his heart against that thought. No concern of his what they did with captives. He must focus only on minding his own behavior.

The sun stood overhead before their captors called for a halt. Ginny trudged into the bushes as was customary then sat down to rest however long she might have.

Henry crouched next to her. "How fare thee?" he asked, poised and ready in the event one of their captors decided he shouldn't speak with Ginny.

"I am well," she responded. "And you?"

He bobbed a nod. "I'm trying to learn as many of their words as possible."

Redbud appeared on her other side. He nodded at her cape. "The man who gave you this—he is *quiakros*."

Ginny blinked. "A holy man? I thought so."

"*Hai!*" One of their captors stepped closer, scowling through his now-smudged war paint, and gestured vigorously at the boys.

Exchanging looks, they rose and moved away from Ginny. She suppressed a sigh. The man in question strode closer and peered at her. For a moment she held his gaze—dark and glittering, perhaps even concerned, but of a certainty far too intent. Swallowing, she looked away, tucking her feet up under the edge of the cloak.

A thought struck her, chilling her to her very middle. She had always been told that men of Tunapewak—the People—did not hold with forcing themselves upon women. But—what if that was not true of all the Peoples?

What if that was not true of these men?

It was the first time she'd shown a glimmer of fear. Guh-neh wished for about the space of a heartbeat that he could reassure her. But in truth, she had much to be afraid of as a captive. That he knew all too well.

Blackbird watched her, drew a deep breath, then, gesturing, told her to get up, but not unkindly. She shrank a little at first before gathering herself and rising. Chin lifting, she glanced around then fell into step with the others as they moved out.

Blackbird glanced back, saw him, and waited for him to approach. "She shows strength."

"I observed it as well." He thought of inquiring after Blackbird's intention but held his tongue. The older man would tell him if he wished.

"That one may make someone a good wife," Blackbird said, his eyes slanting toward him as if gauging his reaction.

As he thought. He kept his own expression blank. "Certainly she would draw attention with her hair and eyes. I cannot say whether that would be a thing to be desired."

Blackbird laughed, his face creasing with the worn war paint. He let a small smile curve his own mouth in response.

Sees Far took only those who were Tunapewak or who dressed similarly enough to pass as one. Two days they had tracked the Mangoac war party, and that not easily.

Halfway through the second day, they found the remainder of a fire and a camp. Georgie was the one who spotted a single shred of the light cloth, *linen*, such as Ginny's dress was made of.

Their hearts all fell at that. But there was no blood, no sign of great struggle.

They sorted out, between all the different footprints, that there were many men, one small pair of mahkusun that would be Ginny, and then the lads, both barefooted.

"Ginny stood here, likely slept here, then left with the others down this path."

All footprints led, eventually, away from the camp then ended at the edge of a swampy pool. Sees Far surmised their trail pointed west, and so he led them on, slogging through the soupy wet.

At the far edge, they fanned out until footprints were again located and then carried on from there.

Only one of their party spoke the tongue of the Mangoac—an older warrior who gladly joined when asked. They would all go, Sees Far thought, for their love of Ginny—and Elinor. By now he had been with the Kurawoten long enough to recognize their great regard for the one he called wife. Their jealousy of him had all but faded completely by now, a fact of which he was grateful.

In truth, he did not know whether having the man along would be of help. Whether they had any true hope of retrieving the three. But they could not simply give up the search either.

Five days, or perhaps six—she had lost count. Walking and ofttimes running, from first light to dark twilight, through swamps and deep forest, across rivers, and at last to higher ground where streams burbled over moss-covered granite. A wonder of trees and plants where spring continued to awaken the land, and mighty oaks and pine stood guard, but the former without the graceful drapings of feathery grey she was used to seeing.

Five long days of her fears rising, heart beating so fast she thought it would crawl up into her throat and choke her, then sinking again and collapsing into ash. Was there no middle ground between abject terror and complete numbness?

She kept expecting to wake at any moment and find she'd been dreaming.

They arrived at last at a town nestled among low hills, overlooking a creek that spilled across rocks into a wide, shallow-looking pool. A shout went up, and a crowd gathered to greet her captors—then they pressed in on Ginny. Poking, patting, tugging at her hair and the cloak so scarcely covering her. Exclaiming over her hair and skin and eyes.

She gritted her teeth and forced herself to endure it all without response as the boys suffered a similar examination. Papa Sees Far and the others had spoken so often of Mama's bravery in captivity. She must be brave as well.

Nearby, with a sharpened rock, they were cutting off the boys' hair. Several women fingered hers, but the holy man who had given her the cloak was suddenly there, and an argument ensued. At last, when the boys were already in the pool being scrubbed down, they simply pushed her toward the water, snatched her cloak away, and subjected her to the quickest, coldest, and most unpleasant washing she could ever recall. Afterward, the cloak was put around her again and they were herded up the hill to the town proper.

There, she and the boys were made to sit down by one of the fires where women were busy cooking. Their manner of dress reminded her much of the Kurawoten and neighboring peoples—soft deer hide, fringed and ornamented, covering from navel to midthigh. The occasional tunic with one shoulder bare. Ears and necks and arms richly ornamented with shell, bone, copper, and what appeared to be colored gems. Arms and legs and sometimes faces adorned with skin markings. Most striking was the women's hair—arranged familiarly enough, but with some sort of red dye worked in.

A chorus of long, shrill cries went up, and accompanied by drum and song, their captors fell to dancing in a wide circle around Ginny and the boys as others built up the fire and raised a spit for roasting a deer. She folded herself small. As accustomed as she was to the day's-end celebrations of the Kurawoten and the dancing the English had oft remarked as outlandish—nay, as much as she loved it, all of it—this was different. Fiercer. Darker, though the sun stood high yet.

Oh Lord, have mercy. . .protect us!

These people were not the gentle, gracious islanders she had known all her life.

When their captors tired of exulting over their victory, the holy man approached and beckoned. She glanced about. There was no recourse here but to follow. He led her to a small house, standing among others, where an old woman waited. The man spoke, gesturing between Ginny and the house. The old woman studied Ginny for a moment then set to scolding—it could be nothing else, for he actually looked chastened. After impatiently motioning for them to follow her, she ducked inside the house, where she dug in a basket and drew out a wad of deerskin.

With a word, she handed it to Ginny then gestured down her body. Ginny shook out the item. 'Twas a tunic, tattered but still serviceable.

The old woman gestured and spoke again, more sharply. Did she expect Ginny to change right there, in front of the man? She glanced up at him, and he huffed but turned his back. Ginny quickly doffed the cloak and wriggled into the tunic. It came barely to the top of her thighs, but the old woman also handed her a worn skirt, which she quickly tied in place. The old woman nodded.

'Twas a comfort to think that, apparently, the granny of another nation felt she needed to be decently covered as well.

The old woman held the *waboose* cloak out to the man, but he made a dismissive gesture and left the house. The old woman snorted and tossed it to the side, onto a mat. She limped over to where a pot stood by the door then spoke again and motioned—the pot, Ginny, outside.

She wished it. . .emptied? Filled? With water, perhaps?

The woman lifted the pot and shoved it into Ginny's hands. Ginny sniffed it cautiously. A water vessel, most likely. Outside, then, to fill it.

She stepped back into the sunlight. Which direction was the stream? The swirls on the rim of the pot caught her eye, and with a fingertip, she traced the designs, both like and unlike those used by the Kurawoten, and the glaze—

A blow landed across her shoulders. Ginny bit back a yelp. The old woman scolded, gesturing toward—well, what Ginny hoped was the direction of the stream.

Shifting the pot against her hip, she set off. Sure enough, there it was. She trudged down the slope to the stream's edge.

She wandered upstream from where others busied themselves washing or simply splashed about. Finding the clearest stretch of water, she knelt and filled the pot then lugged it back up to the town. The old woman stood at the brow of the hill, hands on hips, watching, her lean, oiled skin gleaming in the sun. As Ginny neared, she scolded again, beckoning, and led off, slightly hunched and half limping.

Did the woman have no family to look after her? Ginny hefted the filled vessel, but carefully, and followed after.

Though small, the woman's house was neatly tended. By all appearances, though, she was the only resident. So strange, since all the older folk Ginny knew had younger family living with them. Several of the older women also dwelt together, and likewise the older men. Ginny set the pot down where the woman indicated and then stood waiting quietly.

She was not disappointed. The woman gave her a basket of corn—the multicolored *pegatawah* grown across the New World—and, with a string of words, pointed out the door then mimed grinding with both hands. Ginny dipped her head and ducked back outside.

And whatsoever ye do, do it heartily, as though ye did it to the Lord, and not unto men.

Was that from one of Master Johnson's sermons or from Mama's reading of Scripture? Whichever, Mama had quoted it many a time, reminding Ginny and her siblings that neither parents nor community had final authority in their lives, so it was not them they should ultimately seek to please.

. . .knowing that of the Lord ye shall receive the reward of inheritance, for ye serve the Lord Christ.

Could she do that here, captive of a people whose tongue she could not understand?

Lord, help me. Give me Your grace and favor—and understanding!

Grinding was tedious but not difficult. Ginny might be slender, but she knew her own strength. She would seek to serve the old woman as if—as if she were Ginny's own grandmother.

Her resolve lasted but a few hours. By evening, she had nearly crumbled to tears under the old woman's demands and ill temper. Perhaps 'twas the woman's aim, after all, but Ginny stubbornly swallowed them back and tried yet again to comprehend what she was being told. At last the old woman threw up her hands with an exclaimed "*Ah!*" and pointed at a mat laid in the corner. Not knowing what else to do, Ginny sat down, and the woman nodded vigorously then mimed laying her head on her hands. Ginny lay down. The woman huffed and walked away.

Ginny rolled over and let the tears come.

Would Papa Sees Far and the others try to find them? Or was she here forever?

'Twas suddenly difficult to imagine the possibility of returning home. Mama had only done so because Papa Sees Far had stayed with her the entire time she was a captive. The others—she'd heard the miraculous nature of their rescue, and even so, the two girls who had been taken with Mama never returned. Would Ginny meet a similar fate?

And why—why would God indeed not consign her to such, since 'twas her foolishness to begin with that led to them being taken?

Out of the growing dark came a rumble—the thud of drums accompanying voices. A chill swept her, and she curled up more tightly.

Ginny slept at last, and the next morning, the old woman seemed to have a little more patience. She indicated the waterpot and said a word, pointing out the door. Well, that was an easy enough task—both common and familiar, fetching water as she had the day before—she could hardly spoil it.

Could she?

At least she also had proper clothing. It was one thing, she decided, to be working in the field, or even washing at the river, and to strip naked or mostly so with the other women and girls—women she knew. 'Twas another thing entirely to be an oddity in an enemy nation, where everyone stared at her, wanted to poke and prod at her with no regard to her person or dignity.

Slaves have no status, she recalled Mama saying.

The old woman followed after and watched without comment as Ginny once again made the trek down to the stream. Several children splashed about in the shallows, laughing and shrieking. They paused to stare at Ginny and point. Bypassing them, she flashed a smile but tried not to be too obvious. 'Twas one of the details the older Kurawoten women included in their instructions regarding survival as a captive. One must accept captivity, they said. Returning to one's own people was too rare, but women were usually given a decent chance to make a life if they kept their heads down, did as they were bid, and drew no more attention to themselves than they had to.

Ginny thought herself biddable enough. Mama never voiced such fault with her or even was as stern with her as she saw other mothers—at least the English mothers. Kurawoten mothers were indulgent almost to a fault. She smiled a little. That was, at least, until their children reached the edge of adulthood, and then they were expected to step into that role without hesitation or complaint.

Being taken captive, however, was a different sort of circumstance.

"Strangers have come, asking after the captives."

Blackbird beckoned to Guh-neh then turned toward the scout. "Have they followed us all the way from their town?"

"That appears to be so."

"They are a war party?"

"No, but they present themselves as a delegation. They wish to parlay."

The men exchanged glances and burst out laughing. Guh-neh, as always, observed but kept quiet.

"How should we reward their courage? With arrows and fire and death?" the scout asked.

"I think we should hear them out. It could be amusing."

Blackbird led them outside the town to meet the delegation, such as they were. A strangely mixed group, they wore paint, but not necessarily for war—at least, it was in no such pattern that he recognized. Mostly an even red or deep brown.

One of their party, however, bore the curiosity of blue eyes. The Skaru:re glanced among themselves again and then at Guh-neh, who had not missed the oddity.

An oddity he shared.

Speaking through a barely comprehensible translator, the strangers asked to see the three captives. A young woman, they said, and two striplings not yet gone through huskanaw. The Skaru:re feigned ignorance. Captives? Why would we take captives?

The strangers grew restless. They offered to trade—foodstuffs, beads, metals.

Only a life would suffice for a life, was the answer given.

The strangers exchanged glances, and the pale-eyed one stepped forward, holding out open hands, apparently offering his own life in exchange.

Blackbird made a dismissive gesture. No need for all that.

Another stranger spoke with urgency, hardly giving the hapless translator time to keep up. "Why did you make war upon us? Strike in a way that endangers not only our lives but your own? How have we wronged you?"

Blackbird drew himself up. "Have you not angered the spirits of the land and turned them against you for harboring the pale ones? They are surely no better than others who came and pretended friendship, only to use our people harshly. They must be driven back into the sea whence they came, or their blood offered to water the land."

The other Skaru:re nodded emphatically and gave a deep shout, their assent to the priest's words.

The stranger's face hardened. "We will have our children returned to us."

Blackbird's mouth spread in a mocking grin. "Your children should hope to mingle their blood with ours and be honored in it, since that is the only way they will continue to live and breathe. Return to your town and be content with that."

At last they took their leave, faces grim.

"They show wisdom," one of the other men said. "Our numbers are too great for them."

"Or cowardice," another said, snickering. "Were they men, they would seek honorable death in the attempt to retrieve the children of their town."

And so back to their own town they went.

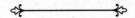

"The blue eyes of the one," Sees Far said. "Was he of the Inqutish, do you think?"

They'd withdrawn some distance from the Mangoac town and found a place to make camp. With dried fish and pegatawah to hand, they needed no fire, but crouched under cover in the twilight.

Sees Far's thoughts had been busy, and he was reluctant to speak their fullness.

Beside him, Georgie shook his head slowly, sobered and looking much burdened. "Spanish, or perhaps French. I've heard tell of attempts at settling to the south. None ended well." He drew a deep breath, held it. "Were we fools for attempting this?"

The other men leaned in, listening.

"It may have been foolhardy," Sees Far answered at last. "But the good God showed us the path. And we know the three still live."

While scouting the perimeter of the Mangoac town, they had caught glimpses of the boys and Ginny but were unable to get close enough to speak with them. Though the town had no palisade, the surrounding fields and glades were well watched, and Sees Far had discerned the time not right for open attack.

"Need we give ourselves to more prayer for how next to move?" Georgie asked.

Sees Far released a quiet sigh. "I have been thinking. That blue-eyed one. . . I feel in my spirit that he is important in some way. That God will use him."

Around him, eyes widened, then narrowed.

"What then are you saying? That we should simply leave them here and return home?"

He gave a slow nod.

Georgie sat back, spitting a curse. Others responded similarly.

"You may gainsay me," Sees Far said. "I am no weroance, to tell you what we must do."

"Mahta," Towaye said from across the circle, "but Manteo set you over the party, and we know how often the good God has used you and spoken through you. We can wait and watch through the night, and all of us pray, before we decide."

"I think we need not wait," Georgie said. "As much as I like it not, I feel the rightness of Sees Far's words in my own spirit."

Chapter Four

G inny set the waterpot down and looked to the old woman, who
regarded her with a thoughtful expression. At last she patted her
chest. *"Keh-squa-reeh."*

Was that a name or a mode of address? Ginny pronounced it carefully
back to her. "Keh-squa-reeh."

The woman then went around the room and spoke other words.
Some were simple and easy enough. Others held subtle intonations, like
a rolling of the tongue or a nasal inflection that Ginny found hard to
mimic, but she kept trying.

The old woman's frustration grew once more until she threw up her
hands and stomped out of the house. Ginny sighed.

"I cannot teach her!" Grandmother Dove fussed. "Either she is too simple
of mind or she has not the ear. What kind of people are these white faces?"

Blackbird scowled. "It has only been a few days. You must have
patience."

Grandmother Dove made a scoffing sound. "Patience so that—what?
I may hand her over to you to warm your nights? How does that help me,
alone as I am?"

They turned as one to Guh-neh, where he worked an arrow and
mostly ignored the conversation until now. He stilled, glancing from one

to another, feeling like a rabbit caught under the gaze of a wildcat.

"You are of the white faces," Grandmother Dove said. "Can you speak her tongue?"

Could he? In the mists of his far memory, he seemed to recall such lessons. "*No hablo Inglés*," he muttered without thought, then shook his head.

Blackbird's gaze narrowed. "I will bring the other two captives, and you shall try."

By all the stars in heaven, no. But the holy man was already in motion, and he was bid follow.

Blackbird explained the problem to the elderly men tasked with minding the two striplings—older warriors still hale enough to chase after them if needed. One shrugged and pointed at the Inglés lad. "That one is learning quickly enough. But if you think it would help the three of them adjust—"

The other peered at Blackbird. "You do not intend either for a sacrifice?"

"I have no plan for it unless they somehow fail to prove themselves."

Off they went, then, back to Grandmother Dove's. The girl cried out and greeted the boys with obvious gladness but then hesitated, glancing at the others.

Blackbird nudged him forward. He stepped closer, clearing his throat. "*¿Hablas español?*"

Both the Inglés snapped to instant attention, the girl releasing a gasp, and the boy's eyes widening. Their gazes fastened on his. Oh aye, they saw now.

His eyes were blue.

His skin bore the same dusky shade as the other enemy warriors, as well as markings on his arms and legs in various patterns, and he attired himself and arranged his hair so as to be a perfect imitation of them. But even indoors, his eyes were blue as the sky. Nay, bluer. Ginny found herself leaning a little closer, studying them.

But—he could not possibly be English, could he?

Henry took a step, sliding between them. "You are Spanish!"

The young man's gaze left hers, and he gave a single, grave nod.

"But—but—how. . . ?"

" 'Tis clear enough *how*, Henry," Ginny hissed. She slanted a look at Redbud. He'd caught up with the significance of it and actually appeared a little pale beneath his Kurawoten-dark skin. "The question is, when? And what happened to his people? Is he—was he—a captive like us?"

An expression of exasperation rippled across the young man's face, and his eyes closed for a moment. He shook his head and said something to the older ones, and the one she knew as the holy man gestured and replied with clear emphasis. The young man sighed and glanced among the three of them again. "I—no speak—good Inglés."

He grimaced, but Ginny gasped again. "Oh! But it is something to work with, at least."

She offered a smile, meant to be encouraging, but he swiped a hand across his face and turned a little away.

"I am Henry," her almost-brother offered.

The young man refocused on him and repeated the name, then laid his hand on his chest and said, "Felipe."

Was that hesitation before he spoke the name?

Henry pointed at her, then at Redbud, and said their names.

Felipe. She thought she recalled a king in Spain by that name. She also was named after a monarch, though more indirectly. The Virgin Queen, Her Majesty Elizabeth of England.

She stepped up beside Henry. "How old are you?" she asked the young man.

His gaze flickered, and he shook his head again.

"How many years?" She pointed at herself. "I am fourteen." She held up both hands, fingers splayed, then her right hand only with the thumb tucked. "Fourteen." She pointed at Henry and Redbud. "Fourteen as well."

Felipe only gazed at her steadily, either not comprehending or—nay, she'd wager it was refusing to answer, given the shift of his expression, like he was calculating. Instead, he pointed at her and Henry. "You—and you—Inglés. Him?" He pointed at Redbud.

"Kurawoten," Redbud answered smoothly. He swept a hand to include the room. "And you? Mangoac?"

Felipe glanced at the others.

The holy man nodded, his face impassive.

"Skaru:re," Felipe said.

'Twas a curious name, one she'd not heard before, but it struck a measure of dread into Ginny.

A look of open pain crossed Felipe's face. "I teach you Skaru:re." He gestured to the three of them.

Ginny could not help but stare at him. Was it the difficulty with their tongue that caused him such discomfort?

He grimaced. Could this be any more painful? And why had he given them the name of his birth rather than the one given him by the Skaru:re? Was he ready to be known again as Felipe, and not merely "the Eel," which invariably got twisted to "Mud Crawler"?

And the girl was entirely too pert—too winsome—to survive as a slave. It was no wonder Blackbird had his eye on her.

The stripling boys were little better, although their attention could serve them well.

He straightened, fixed them all with a stern look, and snapped, in Skaru:re, "You are captives. Obey, and you will do well. Resist, and you will only find death."

The older Skaru:re chuckled. The captives did not exactly shrink, but their eyes widened.

He repeated the sentence in his birth tongue. Still no comprehension, which he expected, but they would learn. The tongue of the Skaru:re if nothing else.

Finding the key words in their tongue now required ransacking his entire memory. Why had he not paid more attention to his studies?

"You—captive. Submit—live. Be trouble—die."

Nearly as one, their faces paled. White rimmed their eyes. But he could see the moment the resolve entered their hearts. Chins lifting, shoulders squaring, spines stiffening. A flush swept the girl's cheeks, and her eyes glittered. He bit back a smile.

Moving toward the door, he beckoned to them. "*Ga:çi.* Come."

He peeked behind once, simply to make sure they followed—which they did, looking half terrified and half entranced, murmuring among themselves. He did not stop them. For one, he couldn't deny them a bit of snatched conversation, and for another, it gave him an opportunity to listen to their tongue. *Fare ye well?* the boy called *Hen-ree* asked, and the girl reassured him that she did. He caught the words, *a strong people,* and this time let himself grin. Perhaps it would be an easy thing to win them over.

That was, as he'd been told repeatedly, the benefit of younger captives, after all.

The people of the town stopped to stare at them as he went, but he led directly to the river and turned to face the three. Blackbird and the two older warriors trailed behind.

He pointed at the stream. "*Kahyeháhre.*"

The three gaped at him, and he spoke the syllables again, more slowly, emphasizing the rolled *r* in the last. "Kah-yeh-hah-rreh." The boys attempted and did fair, but the girl faltered. He repeated the roll. The boys accomplished it immediately, but the girl tried and failed. Felipe could not withhold a smirk, and her face washed crimson.

He looked at the boys and said the word again. *Stream.* Then he stooped, caught a handful of water, and splashed. "*A:we.* Ahh-weh."

They all three obediently repeated it, then the girl said, "Water."

He nodded but returned his expression to stern. Then he pointed at the trees. "*Ure:ye.* Ooh-rreh-yeh."

Slightly better approximation this time, except for the girl's attempt at the roll. She looked clearly unhappy but still trailed after as he led them, pointing out different sorts of trees and various other features of the landscape.

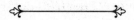

The young man—Felipe, she reminded herself—dragged them all over the town and its surroundings, drilling them over and over in the Skaru:re tongue. While he was certainly more patient than the old woman—whom he taught them to call *Gusud Urí:'neh,* which meant something like Grandmother Bird—he was also more persistent. Ginny's head ached by the time he returned them to Grandmother Bird's house. 'Twas a relief to grind corn and shape it into apon—except that they had different words for that as well, which Felipe made her repeat at least five times. *Unéheh. Kanehúche.* Now she couldn't recall which was pegatawah and which was apon.

He did shortly leave her to the task and traipsed off with the boys, who seemed thrilled with the lessons, especially Henry. Giving herself to the rhythm of grinding, she tucked her head to hide the burning in her eyes. Would they ever return to Cora Banks—to the English and Kurawoten?

To Mama, and Papa Sees Far, and her sister and brothers? And what about the baby?

A sob took her, but she pushed it back down.

Gracious God. . .our Father which art in heaven, hallowed be Thy name. Let Thy kingdom come. . .

She let the familiar words take over, soothing, comforting.

Who shall separate us from the love of God?

She bent, overcome. God was with her. His love was with her. It did not matter where she was or what happened to her.

But what might she have to endure for that to be proved?

"Just give me strength for it, gracious Father. Please do give me strength."

Granny Bird—she'd shortened the form of address in her head—gave a squawk of displeasure. "*Ah!*"

With a quick swipe of her forearm across her eyes, Ginny straightened and renewed her task.

Her thoughts still spun in a dozen different directions. Felipe. A

Spaniard! For all her life, she had heard nothing but the dread of the Spanish. Stories of their fierceness and cruelty—certainly both on the level of the Mangoac. And here he was, living up to that reputation with his mocking little smile, as if he took pleasure in her discomfiture and in her difficulty with the nuances of the Skaru:re tongue. She was furious all over again thinking of it.

She poured more kernels onto the stone and set to working them.

But if he made it possible for them to understand their captors—and be understood—that was a most unlooked-for favor.

Curiosity curled through her again. From whence had he come? And when? How many years did he have? His jaw was clean of any beard, but that might mean nothing if he plucked it as did the Native men, or shaved it. In body, he was as tall as the other men, reminding her of how Georgie and others had outstripped the height of most older Englishmen. Everyone said that because the food of the New World, and the country itself, was so much more healthful than that of England, the younger English men gained inches they might never have, had they not made the journey. . .

The very thought sent a pang through her again.

It was time to brush the meal together into a heap, add water—a:we—and shape the small round loaves for baking. That too was a task her hands knew without thought. Thankfully, it did not appear that these people prepared their bread significantly differently from those in the coastal towns.

Afterward, with the round, flat breads stacked on a wooden trencher, Granny Bird sniffed but seemed otherwise satisfied with the result. She tasted one and sniffed again. Ginny bit back a smile. Was the old woman just looking for something with which to find fault?

The old woman handed her two of the cakes then carried the trencher away. And here came Felipe again, with Henry and Redbud in tow, their heads so bare and strange looking. The jolting reminder of their status here brought another jagged ache to her heart.

In the dark of their bedchamber, Sees Far held Elinor close, savoring her warmth and the gentle movements of their child where her belly rested against him. Neither spoke. So many words had already been said, and she seemed to have wept all the tears she could for the time being as well.

He'd feared for her health when Ginny and the striplings did not return after the attack, but now she appeared merely resigned—and determined. Not unlike other times he'd witnessed her grief.

"Thank you," she said at last, "for coming home to me."

Did she not love her elder daughter enough?

Had she loved too much, as some charged, and coddled her? Was that why God allowed her to be taken away?

The questions swirled, banishing any bit of sleep Elinor might snatch after the baby's nightly dance. She rose, creeping around Sees Far with as much stealth as her bulk would allow. He still grunted and rolled over, reaching for her. A dry chuckle bubbled from her chest, despite the sorrow. Twelve years now and he seemed no less attached. But 'twas a blessing.

At last clear of the bed, she shook out her shift and silently paced, stopping at the window to peer out and listen to the night sounds. Nothing out of the ordinary. *Lord God, You see all things. Where is my daughter? Be close to her. . . You promised never to leave her. Help her to know that. Protect her. Keep her strong. Whether You choose to bring her home to us or not.*

Elinor's eyes burned. Oh, she was so weary of the tears. So weary of the sorrow and the separations. Fifteen years ago, she was on a ship, Ananias beside her, Ginny still safe in her belly. They'd many hardships and privations, even peril, between storms and stops on the southernmost isles, but their hopes for the New World rode high. And then came the horrible murder of George Howe just after landing on Roanoac. Papa's being sent away. The removal to the island of Kurawoten, a time she'd grown to appreciate—then again to Cora Banks. Being snatched away by Wanchese and his band, which, ironically, included Sees Far, who had singled her out amongst the others for reasons she would not know for months. And then Ananias' sudden, awful death before her very eyes.

That was the final thing, she supposed, that plunged her into a spiritual wilderness. Only the realization she carried yet another babe—another child of Ananias—bestirred her to dare hope again.

Dare. Another wry giggle escaped. 'Twas his surname, and her married name, and the one her eldest daughter carried according to proper English society. The play on words had always amused her, particularly given Ananias' impetuous nature.

Ginny had shared that nature as she'd grown. Always leading around the other children her age. Willing and cheerful enough to help with chores but easily bored—which was precisely why, Elinor knew, Ginny and the boys ended up being out the day the attack occurred.

What would her daughter's experience in captivity be like? Would Ginny struggle with questions of her faith and God's presence, as Elinor had?

There by the window, she sank to her knees, folding up as much as her rounded belly would allow, bent her face to her hands, and let the tears flow. *Lord. . .oh Lord.*

It was all she could articulate, but she trusted that God would hear the wordless groans of her soul.

Morning brought with it a strange calmness. Elinor might even call it *peace*, after the turmoil of her prayers the night before. Or was it just resignation?

Nay, this felt like more. But she dared not dwell upon it overlong. There were children to feed and a house to keep, both tasks that were never truly finished. Tasks that under other circumstances she might chafe under. But she knew too well, and did feel proper gratitude for it, how the presence of those children tethered her to life when she otherwise might wish to simply let go.

Besides, in the event Ginny did return to them, it wouldn't do for her to find Elinor so completely undone.

Once the morning's most immediate chores were completed, Elinor released the children to play and set to sweeping the floor. For the first time since Ginny had been taken, the sudden quiet did not reduce Elinor to tears.

Her thoughts circled back, however, to the memory of her own struggle to trust God's goodness, and the question of whether Ginny might as well. *Protect her, oh Lord—in body, of course, but especially in mind and heart.*

The motion of sweeping seemed to unfurl the prayers from within her heart.

Let her not doubt You. Remind her You are with her always, as You did me.

She thought of the girls who had been taken alongside her all those years ago. *Continue to be with Libby and Emme. Let them remain strong, and a blessing to those around them. Indeed, may all our children be a light to the neighboring peoples, wherever You've allowed them to be.*

Considering that Henry and Redbud could indeed be in more peril than the girls. . .

Please, Lord. Protect them all.

She worked the dust and debris pile toward the door, swept it outside, then paused a moment on the threshold to glance about. The usual sights and sounds greeted her, the laughter and shrieks of children, the voices of adults going about their work.

Peace and quiet, as if no ill hap had befallen them just two handfuls of days ago.

Elinor drew a deep breath, released it, then finished sweeping the dirt from the threshold and pathway.

Someone called her name from across the way, and she looked up. Several women were walking toward her, most of them Kurawoten.

She greeted Manteo's mother, weroansqua for the Kurawoten for longer than the English had been in the New World, and her daughter Timqua, in training for a similar position, who had surprised them all by agreeing to marry the town's minister, Nicholas Johnson. Both women embraced her in turn, and then Elinor gave an especially long hug to Manteo's daughter Mary, who had married Georgie and carried her youngest in the way of the Kurawoten, over her back. When they drew apart, the young woman, now a mother of four herself, smiled tremulously with tears shimmering in her dark eyes. "How fare thee, Elinor? Tell us true."

The tears did come then, and the women pressed in again, all around, weeping softly with her.

"It sore grieves us," Manteo's mother said, "that three of our children were taken—Henry and Redbud and Ginny. Her brightness is much missed, and we share your sorrow in her absence."

Elinor leaned into the older woman's shoulder. She'd not realized how bitterly she missed her own mother—gone twenty-some years now—until this moment, but she let herself be drawn in and held. Accepted the comfort afforded by this unlikely community of English and Kurawoten. Her father's vision come to life.

But oh, that it should be the absence of her own sweet Ginny that enabled her to taste it in full.

They went together to find Henry's mother, Margery, and Redbud's mother, Netah. Margery was still much distressed, but Netah gave more comfort than she received, or so it seemed to Elinor. She marveled at the Kurawoten woman's quiet faith and confidence. They, the English, were the ones who first brought the knowledge of Christ—but now these beautiful people had much to teach about living out the faith.

Chapter Five

The young Inglés boy, scrawny as he was, had a quick mind. A pity their understanding of each other's tongues hindered the flow of knowledge between them, but as spring blossomed into summer and the captives settled into their place within the town hierarchy, so grew their comprehension of the Skaru:re tongue—and his of Inglés.

It did not take long for Henree to learn enough to begin questioning Felipe in more detail about the sort of people who held them and what they could expect as captives. No surprise, either, that many of his questions centered on the girl and her expected fate.

"You have feelings for her," Felipe said to him in Inglés shortly after the questioning began.

Henree's hands clenched into fists. "Just answer."

Felipe took measure of him. Was it possible the lad had grown a bit since coming to the Skaru:re? Did his people not feed him well enough? "*Indignación* will do you no good here." He switched to Skaru:re. "You are a captive. Obey, and you will do well. Resist, and you will find only death."

The now-familiar admonition—which they recognized well even if they could not yet understand every word—just brought more stiffness to the lad's bearing. Resisting the urge to roll his eyes, Felipe folded his arms and let out a sigh as if he were wearied.

"Aye," he said, again in Inglés, "the holy man has an interest in her. That is why Grandmother Dove has charge of her, both to teach her to serve and to protect her from others who would use her ill."

Henree's face went pale then reddened. "She would be given to the holy man? Has she no choice?"

Felipe lifted his chin. "I am sure he would not force her. But there would be much, ah, *prestigio* in accepting such a position."

Redbud stood with his arms folded, looking as unhappy as Henree.

Did both lads hold affection for her?

And come to think of it. . .

"How is it the three of you were out away from your town, alone?"

They exchanged a look. Henree swallowed hard. "We should not have been. There was a town council meeting, and we had grown bored. Ginny slipped out, and Redbud and I followed. We were in our hiding place on the bluff overlooking the river when your war party ran past."

"Hmm. And you two often followed her about?"

As he expected, Henree flushed and Redbud's eyes glittered. "She is a friend," Redbud said.

"She and I were the first English babies born in the New World, and within just a day of each other," Henree said. "She is like a sister. Perhaps closer." His mouth worked—clearly his relationship to the girl agitated him as nothing else. "She is well beloved by our entire town. Her grandfather was our governor, but he may have been lost at sea. We would give much to protect her. . .even perhaps to see her returned to our people." His chest heaved. "I—I would be willing to stay and remain a slave, if it meant her freedom."

Felipe stared hard at the lad. At one point in his life, he might have known someone with that depth of concern for him—might he not?

He held himself very still and straight so as to appear completely unmoved. "I do not believe you will have that choice."

Granny Bird still kept a very close eye on Ginny on her trips to the stream for water—and if she did not, the other warriors did so. She was not entirely comfortable under their ever-glittering gazes. Some were merely vigilant, but others held open hunger.

As the heat of early summer deepened, she was directed to help the other women in the fields around the town. Their chatter filled the air, threaded with the shrieks and laughter of children. All familiar enough, except she struggled yet with the Skaru:re tongue.

There were moments when she could almost believe herself back at Cora Banks—but then she'd commit some silly blunder, and the children would laugh at her and the women scold and mock, and she'd remember she was naught but a captive and a slave in this place.

She struggled to maintain prayer—and hope. No word came from the English and Kurawoten. After growing up hearing the stories of Mama's captivity—where she was snatched away and then redeemed back by the same man, none other than Papa Sees Far—and of the heroic rescue of the others by Georgie, Two Feathers, and Towaye, well, she had expected something by now.

Would they not have come for her and the boys already? Might they still come? Had they tried and fallen in the attempt?

Wilt Thou not deliver me, oh God?

She thought of Mama's sorrow over the years at having never seen her own papa again, and it brought a burning to her eyes. Would this be her fate as well? To never again hold those dearest to her?

Despite her doubts and the laziness of her devotions, a prayer for their protection pulsed through her.

"Ho! Ginny!"

The loud whisper pried open her eyes and had her searching the bushes. There—Henry and Redbud, trying to hide but gesturing wildly.

She walked to where her tunic lay, set aside the hoe, and was still pulling the garment over her head when Henry scuttled around the perimeter of the field. "Ginny! We have to tell you—"

She huffed. "Let me at least be fully clothed?"

"My apologies." Henry's cheeks, which she suddenly noticed now sprouted incongruous fluff, stained crimson. "But we just talked with Felipe. Did—did you know you're all but promised to the holy man, Blackbird?"

A chill seized her limbs, stilled her hands in the act of pulling her dress straight. "What did you say?"

Henry struggled to get his breath, and Redbud took over. "It is true! When he gave you his waboose cloak that first night, that was him expressing interest in you before the other men, so none would touch you. So it is understood that you will be his."

It had been a while since something had caught her so completely by surprise. All the strength seemed to drain from her body.

"Felipe says he thinks you aren't to be forced at least," Henry hastened to add. "But I thought you should know."

She closed her mouth, which had somehow fallen open. "Th–thank you." A shout came from somewhere behind her, and she peeked over her shoulder. Granny Bird was beckoning to her. How the woman had let her slack off this long was a mystery. "I must needs go back to work," she said to Henry.

"That's all?" He gaped. "Just, 'Thank you, I have to work now'?"

Behind the boys, Felipe approached, his face like thunder.

"Aye. Now *go.*" They did not move, and a desperate anger spurted through her. "I have women's work to do. Mayhap had I been tending what was needful and not out running the timber, we'd not be in this muddle."

She snatched the hoe and stomped away. Perhaps her show of temper would turn the Skaru:re's wrath away from them.

It didn't stop Granny Bird from cuffing her, however, or a couple of the other women doing the same, and judging by Felipe's snarls at the boys, neither was he deterred. She merely ducked her head and shucked the tunic once more, leaving only the deerskin skirt for cover, then applied herself to the hoeing of the infant crops. But her heart ached. She missed their carefree conversation. She missed her own town and people, and most of all she missed Mama and Papa Sees Far and her sister and brothers.

Do whatever is needful to survive, the Kurawoten women had always said. Did that include becoming wife to a heathen priest? So much had been made of the Kurawoten's turn from a dark, dead religion to belief in the one true God and His Son, Jesus, and the need for those of the Christian faith to choose a spouse of the same. "Do not be unequally yoked," Master Johnson had said.

Where did that leave her, in this situation?

Not to mention the thought of submitting herself to that man in marriage, and all it entailed—she could not suppress a shudder.

God. . .oh God, help me! Do not turn away from the sound of my cries. . .

Would praying in the form of the Psalms incline His ear to her? She brushed aside the thought and hoed more furiously.

Granny Bird scolded. Though she did little of the actual work herself, she lingered at the field's edge, presumably to make sure Ginny did her share. Ginny shot her a glance, tucked her head, and slowed down.

'Twas amazing how much she could extrapolate just by the old woman's tone. Granted, Ginny knew well how critical a crop or even a mere garden was to the feeding of a family or community. Just a few severed plants might mean the pinch of bellies come winter.

She dared not look to see what had befallen the boys. They'd merely have to fend for themselves.

The hurtful words she'd flung at them, though—'twasn't untrue. The ache in her chest continued unabated. She who thought herself so obedient, yet unwilling to sit through a simple town council meeting, much less to look after the younger children while the adults deliberated. She'd once overheard Mama calling her *free-spirited* to one of the other women—a woman who had taken issue with Mama dealing with Ginny with too loose a hand. Ginny had clasped the term to her heart like a badge, reveling in the status she enjoyed with her mother, and thinking the other woman rather shrewish.

But. . .had she been right? Should Mama have been more strict with her?

Felipe lay staring into the dark.

Nothing would induce either of the lads to spill what they'd told the girl. He'd threatened and thumped as much as he could stomach—not nearly enough by either Skaru:re or Spanish standards—then had both of them dragged off by the older warriors and put to harder work than before.

Clearly they were not kept busy enough—and the other warriors were not attentive enough—if they were able to slip away and chatter at the girl.

Then the way the girl herself dodged aside and tried to tell them to leave. . . What had been her thought? Was it unwelcome news? For it seemed in the moment it surely must be, although she composed herself and returned to work, and most haughtily at that. Perhaps she was learning, whether or not she understood his constant admonition, to behave as the humble slaves they were meant to be.

He'd watched her later, during the evening dancing and prayers. Sitting folded, observing all around her, face a carefully blank mask. Blackbird nudged him later. "What should we call her?"

Felipe merely shrugged. He would not be pulled into pretending interest. Especially not with one of their chiefest holy men panting after her. Blackbird wandered away, and when the singing had faded for the night, Felipe overheard Blackbird's conversation with others. "White Doe seems fitting."

White Doe? They couldn't find anything less sentimental? She may be a prize captive, but she was still captive, at least for now. That golden hair and pale skin muddled all their heads.

He huffed and rolled over on his pallet in the men's lodge. There was something about her, to be sure. At one point, she'd looked over and caught him watching her, but rather than glance away, she held his eyes. Simply held them.

Was she brave? Or merely half-witted?

And could he pry out of her what the boys had said?

Ginny woke from a dream of a sea tempest sweeping its waves over the island to the quiet just before dawn. Well, nearly quiet. The first birdsongs rang out from beyond the town. She breathed in, held it, and let it out again.

Thank You, oh God, that there was not truly a sea storm.

Or had there been? Was she remembering something from her childhood?

She shook off the niggle of unease, but a new one took its place. A much clearer memory, from last night. Felipe's searing glare.

Was he angry about the boys speaking with her? Had he punished them sorely for it? She shuddered. Something about him inspired more fear than the Skaru:re—or perhaps it was a different kind of fear, because being able to communicate, even a little, was a strange comfort. Regardless, last night, his gaze would not let her go.

Wide awake, she rose and shook out her skirt and tunic. Granny Bird still snored on her pallet in the opposite corner, so she went out to tend her usual needs, finger-combing her hair as she walked, soaking in the early-morning birdsong.

In moments like this, she could almost believe herself home.

She walked down to the stream to wash. A few women were there already, but they looked at her then pointedly turned away. With a sigh, she braided her hair and tied it before picking her way down into the water.

Back at the house, Granny Bird was just stirring. While the older woman sat blinking at her, Ginny took up the waterpot, lifted it with a meaningful rise to her eyebrows, then trudged back to the stream. A few more were about now, but no one she knew by name. Not that she really knew anyone yet besides Granny Bird, Felipe, Blackbird, and of course the boys.

She hefted the filled jar and climbed the hill once more. A tall figure fell into step beside her, sending a frisson of mild alarm along her nerves.

'Twas Felipe, his shoulders squared and chin tilted at an arrogant angle as if she were not there. She sniffed, adjusting her grip on the jar, and kept walking.

Halfway to Granny Bird's house, he spoke, still not looking at her. "What did Henry say to you yestermorn?"

His accent was slightly better than before, but the Spanish—or what-ever it was—remained thick. So that was what he wanted to know? Well, she'd not give up the boys' secrets so easily. "No—habla—Español."

His eyes snapped to hers.

"Or Skaru:re," she added. "Whatever your attempt was at speaking."

He halted as if struck. Then to her complete shock, he laughed. She slanted him a quick glance, biting back a smile—the laugh completely transformed him—turned her back, and hastened the last few paces to Granny Bird's.

The old woman's gaze flicked from her to Felipe, and her expression melted into a grin. She spoke, her tone so full of teasing affection that it made Ginny's throat ache. He answered easily then watched Ginny as she set down the jar. Granny Bird gestured between them and spoke again.

Ginny turned, keeping her face impassive, but he chuckled again. "She say, cook for me as well this morning."

Granny Bird gestured again, smiling, pointing to the basket of pega-tawah, or as she knew it now, unéheh.

She would not complain. She would not give trouble over this. But she did not have to be cheerful. After gathering a few ears, she ducked outside to the grindstone and set to work.

Naturally, Felipe trailed after and crouched nearby.

"You could go stoke the fire," Ginny said, not looking at him.

He shrugged—she caught that much from the corner of her eye. "Grandmother is." He cleared his throat. "What did Henry say?"

Nothing if not persistent, he was. She thought about how to respond. Mayhap no response would be best. Would he shout at her, as he had the boys? Even strike her?

Did she want to risk that?

Nay, she would not be bullied. The women's injunction to *stay alive* did not include letting her captors push her around on every little thing, did it?

She ground for a little while, added kernels, ground some more. "A question for a question," she said at last, speaking a little slowly so he'd follow more easily.

His brows lifted.

"How did you come to the Skaru:re?"

He chewed his cheek then reached for a stone nearby and drew in the dirt. An outline took shape that she recognized from maps the elder English often pored over—maps of the New World. Felipe pointed at a particular feature, which could be a peninsula, or—

"*La Florida.*" The word confirmed her suspicions. "I came with my father—*Capitane*—and other *soldados.* They were killed. I was taken." His gaze sought hers, challenging, his expression haughty once more. "I am captive but become more."

He spoke again, words she now recognized as the statement in the Skaru:re tongue he'd made every day since first revealing he could understand English even a little. Slowly this time. She could almost, not quite, comprehend it all now. Then, in English, "You are a captive. Obey, and live. Be trouble, and die."

Oh. That must be the translation, or as near to it as he could manage in English.

His gaze remained steady. "This is why I tell you. *Obey.* It will, ah, go well for you."

She forced herself back to the grinding. "Your English improves."

He chuckled. Then, "What did Henry say?"

She sat back on her heels, curling her hands, dusty from the grinding, on her thighs. 'Twas only fair, since he answered her question without hesitation. She blew out a breath then bent a severe look upon him. "Is it true I am already claimed by the holy man who gave me his cloak?"

Felipe's eyelids flickered, and his lips flattened. Both movements were slight, but she had been watching carefully for them.

"Blackbird?" she pressed, and he nodded.

She continued studying him for a moment, covering for the sick swirl of her insides. "How old were you when you came here?"

His brows twitched. "I had nine winters when we sailed from home."

Nine. She thought what that might feel like—to leave all that was familiar, only to see one's father and other companions killed and then be taken by the ones who had, presumably, done the deed.

Mama had witnessed Papa Ananias' death while being carried away. Sometimes she still bore the shadows of that sorrow. How much more would such a thing have scarred Felipe's heart and soul?

Then she blinked. What was she thinking? He was of the Spanish, and now the Skaru:re. Naught but ruthlessness in either. And he did not seem particularly moved by the prospect of her being claimed by their holy man.

But then, was there any reason for him to care? She was not of his people.

She put her hands back on the grinding stone, refocusing on the task, but hesitated a moment. "I am sorry for your loss."

Was she dismissing him? Or did she truly not know what else to say?

There were so many more questions to be asked—by both of them. And he'd barely recovered enough remembrance of her tongue—what little he'd learned before—and built upon it to make conversation much more than a simple matter of pointing at things and saying their names.

Yet now somehow all he could do was sit back and watch her grind.

She stopped long enough to wipe her forehead with the back of her hand and flick him a glance. "You should leave. Granny Bird will scold. I'm not sure why she hasn't already."

He sorted through the words, then said, "What? Granny—Granny *Bird?*"

Another, longer look, but she kept grinding this time.

"No, no. It is not *bird*; it is—" He sifted his memory and came up empty. "They go *crrr, crrr—*"

He imitated their soft, whirring coo as well as he could.

She frowned, arms stilling again. "A dove?"

"Yes, that is it! *Dove.*"

She glanced over her shoulder then hummed. "Tell me again, in Skaru:re?"

He spoke the name of the old woman who had been both mother and grandmother to him and made the girl repeat it until she had improved in some of the nuances.

Grandmother Dove did come out at that, standing in the doorway of her house with a look somewhere between amusement and vexation.

Chapter Six

S ummer came blazing in full nearly before Ginny had time to think about it.

'Twasn't so bad, life here. Not all things considered. She had something of a rhythm now, seeing to the accomplishment of daily tasks, and then often Granny Dove would allow her to gather materials for the making of baskets and sit outside on the dry days weaving them. She'd first learned the methods for using both sea grasses and pine needles from the aunties of the Kurawoten, and 'twas not difficult to adapt what she knew to the patterns favored by the Skaru:re. Mama once commented that perhaps Ginny had inherited such dexterity from her papa Ananias, who had come to the New World as a skilled tile- and bricklayer. Not that Mama herself was possessed of mean ability when it came to hand and needle arts, in Ginny's opinion.

Even here, the work gave her much satisfaction. Yet the ache for Mama and Sunny and Papa Sees Far and the boys lingered still beneath her breast. The constant jolt of realizing she wasn't really home after all, after she'd been lulled into drifting along with a day's flow. It only took a word, spoken in that beautifully rhythmic but still-mysterious Skaru:re tongue, or the flash of faces that, while more familiar by the day, were not her beloved Kurawoten family. Singing and dancing that held an undercurrent of shadow, despite the wild abandon in celebrating the close of each day.

Deep, deep forests that lay far away from tide-kissed waters.

Bare glimpses of Henry and Redbud, being driven along from one task to another, often bloodied and bruised yet clearly in training by the men to become Skaru:re warriors. As Felipe said had happened to him.

And then there was Felipe—that arrogant, maddening Spaniard masquerading as one of the People. At odd moments he reminded her of Georgie, who was as fair and blue-eyed as any other English but, aside from growing out his beard like other Englishmen, kept his hair shaved on the sides and the back long and caught up in a knot as the Kurawoten men. Most of the time, however, Felipe was completely unlike Georgie, whose kind attentiveness to both Mama and Ginny and her siblings made him more like an elder brother than aught else.

Just the thought of Georgie—and his wife, Mary, like a sister in her own right—brought a thickness to her throat.

And she missed being part of the easy fellowship among the women. Ginny could observe it here, but only as an outsider. The women oft scoffed and scorned, and she still barely comprehended much of their speech. None used her very ill, except for tasking her with what felt like the most tedious of chores, and none cuffed her after that day the boys tried to speak with her.

Did they hold back because of Blackbird? She had tried not to think through the implications of what the boys had said, but the fact remained these people were not as cruel to her as always rumored to be.

Granny Dove continued to scold and admonish by turns over this or that, and to instruct on a daily basis. Ginny depended less on Felipe for translation now than in the early weeks, and she owned to mixed feelings about that. He was a comfort in his own way, true, but—oh, he could be vexing.

Most unsettling of all was how he still watched her, almost continually. Not that half the other men, whether young or old, didn't as well. Were they merely afraid she would try to escape? Or was there more to their attention? She could mark now that Blackbird's was more intentional than the others', but as he had not made any sort of move to openly express his interest, she had relaxed a bit since the boys had first revealed it to her. Or perhaps she had merely grown used to having eyes upon her wherever she went.

But Felipe—somehow it was different with him. *He* was different. She had felt that at the beginning, but 'twas an even deeper conviction now.

Yet his differences made him no less vexing. If anything, he was even more so, for the puzzle he presented.

Her fingers worked nimbly, almost without thought, until a shadow fell across her. She looked up, suppressing the urge to start at the women surrounding her in a loose circle. Their leader—or so she appeared to be, by how earnestly she chattered at Ginny—made an impressive speech then waited for Ginny to respond.

The words sounded familiar, as if she ought to recognize them, but she could make no sense of the whole. She straightened and offered a smile.

Another speech, shorter this time. Ginny smiled again but shook her head a little and lifted splayed hands.

The woman huffed and strode away while the others laughed and obviously berated Ginny.

She tucked her chin and kept working on the basket. Oh, she was weary of this.

The Skaru:re woman returned but a few moments later, Felipe in tow. *Of course.* That one listened then took his usual stance, arms folded, slightly narrowed gaze fastened on Ginny.

She'd long since ceased to be enamored of the blueness of those eyes.

"They complain," Felipe said, "that you are well accomplished at everything except speaking their tongue. Even the boys have learned to speak it."

Somehow mention of Henry, who was always prodigious at anything he learned when it came to words, and of Redbud filled her with fury. She broke into Kurawoten, because it was the finest defense she could think of in the moment. "I do not want to hear about the boys! I want to go home, where I can understand what is spoken in either tongue."

They all stared at her, stricken to stillness by her tirade. She drew a long breath and forced herself to speak more clearly, this time with words he might have a chance at comprehending. "Of course Henry would learn the tongue of the Skaru:re more quickly. He is richly gifted in that manner. I? Nay, I am better at helping and smiling and—and sometimes looking pretty."

Now why had she added that last bit?

Well, mayhap it was to draw a response from Felipe, because the shift of his expression and the quirk of his mouth were nothing if not satisfying. Although—

"Don't you dare tell them I said that."

But he was already turning away, speaking again, presumably translating her words. She sighed noisily and stared at the half-woven water grasses. A laugh rippled through the group, and she offered another, more uncertain, smile.

Nay, this was gaining her no favor.

He turned back to her, that maddening smirk playing about his own lips. "What were you speaking?"

"Kuh-rah-*woh*-tain," she said with exaggerated slowness so they all might catch it. Comprehension lit their features. She nodded. "I have spoken both that and English since infancy. But Skaru:re—it is different enough that my mind does not like the learning of it." She lifted a hand and dropped it. "I wish it were not so. I have been trying."

As Felipe translated, the women's faces turned thoughtful. At least, many of them did. Some were still scornful.

She gave a little laugh. "Does anyone here speak Kurawoten? I would gladly converse in that tongue."

All heads shook in a universal *nay*, although one or two looked as if they wished they might.

"Well, we have *him* here," she said, tipping her head toward Felipe. "Ask me anything you wish."

Chuckling, Felipe addressed the women again. And the questions came—mostly having to do with her family, how the English had come across the sea, how they now dwelt alongside the Kurawoten. Some things made her think harder—how to answer without endangering Cora Banks or the island itself, since there had been talk of the townspeople moving back. Would they care about details such as her being the first English child born on their shores? Of Papa Ananias being slain in an attempt to rescue Mama? Of Papa Sees Far's heart being changed as he grew to love Mama, so that he was the one who brought her back home? But she shared it anyway—some, at least—and wondered how well Felipe managed to translate it. Gauging the women's response—so much of the scorn melted away—it must be approaching true.

Life here was not crushingly difficult, at least not in regard to basic bodily needs. But how exceeding marvelous it felt, after weeks and weeks of no one to talk to with any sort of meaning save Felipe himself, to suddenly be heard and understood and responded to. She had prayed for comprehension of their tongue and yet struggled. So this—this felt like something of a gift.

Felipe's manner changed as well, but she tried not to think about that. Did she remind him of his own past? Of his mother and father and a home on the other side of the sea?

What was it about this girl? She could not even speak the Skaru:re tongue, and yet she commanded the attention of this entire gaggle of women.

Of course, he was partly to blame. If he chose not to translate her words as precisely as he could—perhaps if he slanted her responses—but he could not bring himself to dissemble so.

Nay. He was too confounded honest to do anything but relay inquiries and replies back and forth as directly as they were given.

The Inglés girl was nothing short of enchanting, and the Skaru:re women were certainly captivated. There was nothing old women—or men, and he'd observed this at home in Spain as well—loved so much as gossip and news, and she was the embodiment of a completely different world for them. And while the Spanish had left nothing but a bitter taste in the mouths of the Skaru:re, word of the English was mixed. Some said the English were as bad as the Spanish for treachery and killing, while others claimed otherwise.

This willowy, golden-haired maiden, however, seemed far removed from all of that.

The Skaru:re women were not entirely distracted from their original purpose. One finally posed the question Felipe had been half dreading but knew was on all their minds. Did the girl not have need yet to visit the women's house?

The girl laughed a little, pink sweeping across her cheeks, and shook her head. "Not since before I was taken captive."

The women hummed and chattered over that. Could it be she was with child?

Felipe speared the girl with a glance and asked her.

Pink turned to crimson, and her blue eyes widened. "Nay. I have never—just, nay."

He could believe that, somehow, but the other women? Silence fell for the space of a pair of breaths, and then exclamations and laughter all around.

The girl stood, stiff, her gaze darting about. He could not resist prodding her just a little. "Not even with Henree?"

Fury swept aside embarrassment, and he braced himself for the onslaught—but it did not come. She grimaced—and he could swear she growled—but otherwise she did not move.

"Do not think I am unused to the teasing over that—or him," she said. "But we are too close in age. I have done *huskanasqua*, while he and Redbud have not."

His curiosity was piqued. "Hus—"

"Huskanasqua. Or huskanaw for the boys. It is the ceremony marking the crossing into womanhood or manhood, which the English learned from the Kurawoten."

"Ah. Aye. The Skaru:re do similarly."

Even stranger. To think any of the peoples from across the sea—those who claimed to be, what was it, *Christian*—would adopt a practice of this land.

"There is a story behind it, though," she went on. "Our people, the English and Kurawoten together, have made it uniquely ours, and it is carried out in a way that honors Christ as well as traditions of the People."

He felt his jaw sagging. Was such a thing possible?

And. . .how long had it been since he had even thought of the one called *Christ*, much less heard Him spoken of?

But there was no time for reflection. The Skaru:re women were clamoring with more questions.

One stepped forward and produced the fragments of the dress the girl had worn when they'd taken her. "What is this material, and how is it made?"

"Too bad the men tore it all to pieces," another of the women said. "I would have liked to see the garment in whole."

With a soft cry, the girl took it from them. He relayed what they sought, and she knelt, laying the pieces out and rearranging them until they formed a rough outline of the dress she had worn.

"There," she murmured, sniffling.

Was she weeping?

A gust of—something—swept through him, sharp sorrow borne on the memory of a sweet-faced woman imploring Papá not to go and certainly not to take Felipe. A woman who wore just such a dress as an undergarment, and little sisters who did the same.

He reeled back a step.

The girl was in the middle of trying to explain fiber and weaving. The women looked as if they might actually be following. He tried to insert relevant terms—linen, flax, spinning, looms—but his Skaru:re failed him. Then he considered equivalent processes—the making of cording for bows and such, and the weaving of baskets and mats. The image of the rabbit-skin cloak that Blackbird had thrown about the girl flashed through his thoughts as well.

Drawing the women's attention, he explained it more quickly and smoothly. Just as they'd woven strips of the soft, furred hide into a large, workable garment, and as they did much the same with grasses or strips of bark for other things, so the cords made from fibers of certain plants could be woven together. The fabric of the girl's garment was also made of a plant, beaten out, and twisted into a much finer cord.

A chorus of *aah*s broke out among the women. He explained shortly to the girl what he'd just said, and she grinned, her blue eyes sparkling, the same shade as the sky above them. The sunlight glinted gold off her braid and the loose waves framing her face.

No. He would not be drawn in by her. He would *not*.

The women took the girl then and led her to where they were working fibers from *cunewahskri:yu*, a broad-leaved plant with a milky sap that butterflies loved. The present process would result in a twine or cord, very useful for all sorts of things, but the girl began fiddling with the fibers, twisting them between her fingers, presumably to see how fine a thread she could produce.

"The pinnace is a dead loss," Captain Stafford said.

The words fell softly, like water dripping into a half-empty pail. *Plink, plink, plink, plink.*

Or like stones into the deep dark of Elinor's heart.

"We will continue to consider ways to salvage some portion of it," he went on. "Chapman is confident he may yet be able to do so—but as far as being able to save it in whole?" He spread his hands. "We will have to carry what we can back to the island without it."

It shouldn't matter. They had boats—the *kanoe* of the Kurawoten, both great and small, more than capable of carrying them all back across the Sound. Perhaps the pinnace would have helped with the larger things, the disassembled houses and such, but they could make it work.

Truly, it only meant the final move would take a little more time than they'd hoped. But that meant more time for Ginny and the boys to find their way back to Cora Banks—or for a war party to go back out to fetch them.

No one is going to fetch them. Not against the Mangoac.

Sees Far had not said it like that, not in so many words. But was it not truth? Did not the Coree and Newasiwoc also say so, in essence?

Meanwhile, word had returned from the island that things were going well and those who had returned before were flourishing. Why would the others not follow? And yet they continued to deliberate and halt between two opinions.

Her heart felt so, so very leaden. The softly moving roundness of her belly, even heavier.

Beloved Lord and Savior, how much more can we endure?

The council meeting concluded with no real conclusion. Supper was served at large and eaten and a handful of songs played and sang after, but few joined in the customary day's-end observance. At last they gathered, those who were left, for the offering of prayers.

Then it was herding the children back to the house, little Owlet riding on Sees Far's shoulders, Mouse pestering Sunny, who scolded back as if she were the mama herself.

A role she'd taken more and more since Ginny's disappearance.

Lord. . .oh Lord. . .

Back to tears and the inarticulate prayers. Perhaps those were the best and most honest, after all.

They all settled into their beds in near darkness, one by one snuffling or sighing off to sleep, Sees Far last of all, curled against her back. The cadence of his breaths eventually soothed her enough that she was close to dropping off as well. . .

Faint cramps rippling low in her belly brought her to awareness. She drew a lungful of air, held it, then let it out again.

'Twas time. Another little one would soon make his—or her—appearance.

Four times of awaiting this woman to give birth. The first was Sunny, Elinor's second child by Ananias, and thus only the last three were his own children by blood. Yet the wonder never paled—and he hoped it never would.

A daughter this time. Such a tiny, scrunchy, sweet face, topped with a shock of dark hair and eyes that blinked slowly into his. Sees Far cradled her close and felt his heart bursting with love and joy.

Elinor smiled sleepily. "Would that Ginny were also here to welcome her."

"We will make the welcome all the more joyous on her behalf." Sees Far bounced his arms ever so gently, and the little one yawned.

A daughter. He had another daughter. Because those first two were as much the children of his heart as this one.

Great God, protect her! Protect us all. . .

He would not tell Elinor yet, but Chris had given him the word while she was in travail that as soon as she'd regained her strength, they'd be next to pack and sail across the Sound to the island. With everything in him, he longed to be leading a party back over to the Mangoac—Skaru:re, whatever—and retrieving Ginny and the boys.

Protect them—and if You will, bring them back to us somehow.

Chapter Seven

A fter weeks and weeks of mysterious absence, her woman's time caught up with her at last.

Granny Dove escorted her immediately to the women's house and instructed her—to be sure she knew, Ginny reminded herself wryly—in the digging of a shallow bowl-like hollow in the floor then directed her to sit over it. For once, Ginny found it a relief to just rest and do next to nothing for the next few days. The bleeding had hit with a bit of a vengeance.

The other women present peered at her but did not speak. She let out a long sigh and closed her eyes. 'Twould not matter, anyway, when her understanding of their tongue was still worse than a child's. A child, in fact, would do better.

"It is time at last! Once she is finished with her stay in the women's house—"

"We still have not determined whether she would be suitable as wife for a holy man. It would be one thing if another took her, but for all that she's claimed to have grown up amongst the People. . . Have you seen her disdain during our evening dances and prayers?"

"And she still refuses to speak our tongue, or even to make a reasonable effort to learn it."

"Blackbird can teach her what he wishes her to know." Knowing laughter followed.

"Do not be simpleminded in this. She is—you see how she charms all those around her. And that's even with the Mud Crawler translating."

More chuckles. Rolling his eyes, Felipe laughed along. Some things he'd never outgrow.

"Why does Blackbird even want her, anyway? She is ugly."

"She's only of a different shade. Like the White Doe we've named her after."

"Well, it's ugly."

"Beauty is in the eyes of the one who sees," Blackbird intoned between bites of roast deer. "And she may have trouble speaking, but she is brave." He sucked a piece of meat from between his teeth. "Brave mothers make for brave sons."

They all made sounds of assent. It was true enough.

"Still—pah! One of the white skins."

Felipe could feel the sidelong glances his way, but he kept eating as well.

"We can do nothing else but continue to make use of the Eel as we make final preparation. Under close watch, of course."

Of course.

"What if I refuse?" he said, unable to keep all the sauciness from his tone.

They laughed, as he hoped they would.

"Blackbird takes the girl to wife and that is that."

Felipe pretended to think upon it. "Is she not to be given a choice?"

Muted chuckles. But they were pondering. Blackbird leveled his gaze upon Felipe. "I am not an unreasonable man. But neither am I hard to look at. Am I?" he asked the group at large. He grinned as they all avowed he was not. "She will be made to see the sense of it. What status she will gain as my wife."

Fair enough. At least from the view of a Skaru:re.

It was no different in España, either.

The girl's face flashed in his memory, upturned, smiling, blue eyes and golden hair bright in the sun. Would it crush her to become a Skaru:re wife, or would she adapt and find her own joy in it?

It was of no account either way.

But she was someone's daughter—someone's sister. . .

It was of no account. She was of the Skaru:re now.

The discussion and banter continued, flowing around him.

"The women will take her to the river and perform the necessary washing, then she will be given new clothing and pronounced one of us." The older holy man, Strong Oak, nodded at Felipe. "He will translate if necessary. But let this be done."

"Let this be done," they all echoed.

Felipe mouthed the words, but his voice stuck in his throat.

Her week being finished, Ginny was all too happy to slip down to the river and bathe. She lingered, letting her hair and body soak in the cold current, then wrung out her tattered tunic and skirt and put them back on, ignoring the feel of the wet deer hide against her skin.

Granny Dove was nowhere to be found when Ginny reported back to the old woman's house. No matter. She'd find something to occupy herself. She knew the routine by now, and if nothing else, prepared food would be welcome.

She tossed a few ears of pegatawah into a basket and carried them outside but had barely begun the grinding when approaching voices and footsteps drew her attention.

A whole mob of women marched toward her.

What had she done this time?

She sat back slowly. They surrounded her, chattering, gesturing for her to get up. "But—unéheh—"

Granny Dove was there too, speaking in what she was sure was meant to be soothing tones, also gesturing her up. And away, so it turned out. They half pushed, half led her back through the town and to the stream's edge, then down into the water. "But I just bathed—"

They tugged at her tunic, not ungently. She decided quickly on cooperation, however, rather than face a possibly rent limb. Then as one woman began to sing and the others joined in, they subjected her to an even more thorough scrubbing than when she first arrived—sand and a bit of rough, twiny fabric. Ginny grimaced but otherwise forced herself to submission.

Do whatever is necessary to survive. . .

Head to toe, they were nothing if not thorough. At last, though, they led her back to the bank, instructing her to stand on a wide, flat rock. There they rubbed her down with more of the rough fabric then applied an oil that shaded her skin to something very close to theirs, giving especial attention to her face, neck, and ears. A pair of beautifully ornamented and fringed doeskins was draped about her hips, and they combed out her hair, rubbed it thoroughly with the red dye, and dressed it as well, twisting the sides up into knots and pinning them with various ornaments. Chains of copper, pearls, and precious stones were hung about her neck, and a short cape woven with feathers of varying colors and sizes. Ginny fingered it, admiring the shimmer. How many different species were represented here, and which ones?

But what meant all this preparation and display? Her heart began to pound in a most uncomfortable manner as suspicion grew. She'd not allowed herself to think about it at first.

Their efforts completed with a finely wrought pair of mahkusun, the women all broke into song again and nudged her up the hill.

An array of warriors greeted them at the top. They gave a great shout then formed two columns for the women to walk between into the town proper.

Each beat of her heart was nothing short of painful now.

He watched her face as she drew nearer, surrounded by the singing women, appearing composed but for her rounded blue eyes darting this way and that. And very bright they were against her oil-darkened skin.

She was splendid, and Blackbird would doubtless be pleased.

An ache bloomed in Felipe's chest.

Her gaze snagged on him then, widening yet more, pleading. But he drew a breath, straightened, and did not move from his place in line. Then she was led past, on toward the center of the town, where Blackbird himself waited.

Felipe and the other men gathered in behind the women, forming a double escort to the proud plumage of the once-captive but now-adopted girl. Did she yet comprehend the honor being shown her? If not, he'd be compelled to step up and explain it to her.

An unwonted dread tugged at him at the prospect.

The women brought her to within a few paces of Blackbird, surrounding her behind in a half circle as the men did the same behind the women. The singing ended abruptly. As already arranged, Felipe stood where he could observe both the girl and Blackbird and intervene if necessary.

And intervene, he likely would.

The feathers and fringing of her skirts betrayed her tremors. White clearly rimmed her eyes now.

Blackbird spoke. "You, child of the white skins, have been brought in to the People. We call you White Doe, now and henceforth. And on this day, after your cleansing from your womanly blood and the blood of the white skins, I have chosen you to be my woman."

He extended a hand, but the girl did not move, except for her trembling becoming more pronounced.

Blackbird dropped his hand to his side and shot Felipe an irritated glance. "Tell her."

Felipe stepped even with the line of women and, catching the girl's eye, repeated what Blackbird had said as nearly as he could in her tongue. Blackbird reached out to her again.

Tearing her gaze away from Felipe, she drew in a long breath and shook her head, faintly at first, then with more emphasis.

A distant shriek split the air. Over on the other side, Felipe caught a glimpse of Henree being dragged away by a pair of men. The woman next to him huffed. "They were supposed to be kept well busy, helping tend the feast."

The girl shook now from head to toe. "No," she said, then again. "No. I cannot. I'm sorry—"

Against the growing thunder of Blackbird's face, a babble of voices rose. "You cannot? Why? Ungrateful girl! Does she not know what she refuses?"

"Hsst!" Blackbird made a cutting gesture and silenced them all. He beckoned to Felipe. "Explain more. Help her understand."

Felipe had never seen the man look so genuinely distressed. He turned to the girl. "Will you sit down? Let us talk."

A handful of deep breaths, and the roundness of her eyes lessened a little. She sank to the ground, and he crouched beside her. When Blackbird would have hovered, Felipe made a gesture and said in as calm a voice as he could, "Also sit. It may ease her fears."

The holy man did not look happy, but he did as asked.

"First," Felipe said, "they chose this name for you some time ago. White Doe. And Blackbird has indeed been waiting until your time in the women's house proved you were not carrying another man's child. It is the way of the People."

She spared Blackbird but a glance. "I have heard of such things."

"The Kurawoten do not the same with captives?"

A small sound bubbled from her throat. Was that a laugh? "The Kurawoten have forsworn taking captives since they came to Christ."

He sat back. "Truly?"

"Truly."

"What does she say?" Blackbird prompted him.

"She is explaining that she does not know the customs behind the keeping of captives because the Kurawoten have given up such things after deciding to follow the God of her people."

It was Blackbird's turn to rock back in shock. "But—is that not the same God of the Español? And they also take captives!"

Which was exactly what made this matter so curious. "So it is said—that it is the same God. But there are differences in how He is worshiped between her people and those I came from."

He frowned. "How so?"

Felipe looked at the girl, shoulders now sagging and her head resting in her hand, elbow propped on one knee. "It is too much to explain here and now."

Did those differences have anything to do with her reluctance to be given to Blackbird?

"It may take several days of talk," he added.

Blackbird waved a hand. He clearly had no patience for such things, especially not when he had expected to be taking a wife before this day's end.

Felipe turned back to the girl. "Are you completely unwilling to be his wife?"

She peered across at the holy man. "He is not. . . He does not know the true God." A hesitation. "Does he?"

He shook his head a little. So he was right. "And if he could be persuaded to do so?"

She released a bitter chuckle and straightened. "Am I to be given a choice?"

His own throat burned like ashes. "Truly, I do not know."

Her eyes came to his. "Please do not force me."

He made himself take even breaths—in and out—then turned to Blackbird. "She is asking that you not force her."

A growl from the holy man. "Are we not sitting here speaking?"

A smile teased Felipe's mouth, but briefly. "He is trying to have patience," he told the girl.

She did not look comforted.

"So, you had no husband among your people. Were you promised or even attached to anyone?" he probed. He knew Blackbird would ask that next.

A sharp shake of the head. "I always wished to take my time. To choose carefully." Her eyes fluttered closed. "I suppose that no longer matters."

"Well." He set his hands on his knees. "Blackbird has great respect and status among the Skaru:re. He is not cruel, unlike others I have known." Felipe was suddenly grateful none of those lingering nearby could understand him. "You will be well cared for—you and any children you bear him."

The girl shivered, though Felipe thought she tried not to.

"What are you saying to her?" Blackbird grouched.

"I am trying to explain to her how desirable a choice you are amongst our people," Felipe answered.

Blackbird lifted his eyebrows.

"He has also praised your courage," Felipe said to the girl.

She sniffed.

Why did it even matter to him if she chose this willingly? An unreasonable frustration rose up within him, and he could not keep the edge from his words this time. "You are captive. These people are your home now. He is offering you your own house and elevation from the status of slave. Why would you refuse?"

She met his gaze directly now, and to his horror, tears welled up and spilled. "The Kurawoten women always told us girls if we were taken, we should do whatever was needful to survive. I have survived already. But—this? It is the last thing I have say over, I suppose. If 'tis foolish, then so be it. But I will not go willingly to that man's house—or bed—today." Her chest heaved. "I will *not*."

It was his turn to huff. "There is much to admire in your spirit. But the Skaru:re are bound to crush it."

More tears fell, but she held herself proudly. "I do not care."

"You will," he said very quietly.

One of the women stepped forward. "What is the delay? Why all the talk? Let us be done with this!"

The others' voices rose around them. Blackbird shot to his feet, arguing with the women, and several of the other warriors stepped forward.

The girl curled in on herself, still weeping. Felipe stuffed down a sigh and rose as well, waiting for a moment when he might be heard.

"Cease!" Blackbird said at last, and the tumult began to quiet. "This is not how our people conduct themselves! Speaking all over each other rather than waiting our turns, indeed."

The others fell silent, and for a moment Blackbird gazed on the girl at his feet, a scowl darkening his features, then gestured with a sweep of his arm. "Go, all of you. See to the feast. Bring us food. And someone bring drink." To Felipe, "Tell her to come with us into the shade. There is no sense in staying here."

Felipe touched her shoulder. "Come, White Doe. Let us go out of the sun."

She slowly unfolded, peered at him, and then glanced around before accepting his hand up.

"There will be food—" he began, but Blackbird interrupted, snarling.

"What is this? You touch this woman before me?"

"I—" Felipe had to think a moment before realizing what he had done. "No. I was only helping her to her feet. It is a gesture of honor, a small honor only, amongst our people."

Blackbird's expression darkened further. "You both are not of those people any longer. Do you forget you are now Skaru:re? Next time she can get up on her own. You do not touch!"

Heat flared through him. He could only nod wordlessly.

"Now, come!"

Felipe held out an arm for the girl to walk before him. She hesitated, gaze sliding toward Blackbird. "Where are we going?"

"I told you, out of the sun." He tipped his head more emphatically.

She went, thankfully, this time stopping only at the doorway to Blackbird's house to angle Felipe another look.

"I can make you no guarantees," he said. "But Blackbird has been, to my eye, a fair man."

The girl bobbed a nod and went in.

Inside, Blackbird himself laid out several mats in a rough circle, sat down upon one, and indicated the girl and Felipe should do the same. Several others filed in—some of the chief men and women and their attendants. Some began rolling up the mats on two sides of the house, so as to let in a bit of breeze.

The girl settled herself primly, once again composed and alert. The oldest of the chief men lit a pipe, and others followed suit. This seemed to calm the girl somewhat. Perhaps this at least was familiar to her.

After puffing for a time at his pipe, the eldest chief gestured and spoke. "What then is the difficulty here, Blackbird?"

The holy man still scowled, even after tobacco, his eyes on the girl. Felipe quietly translated the question for her.

"She is captive," the eldest chief went on, "yet if we adopt her, then she is a Skaru:re woman and has a choice. Is this not so?"

One of the clan mothers lifted her hand. "That depends upon whether we decide her adoption depends upon her acceptance of the marriage."

Blackbird's brows drew together even more fiercely. "Are we not a reasonable people?"

"Reasonable, yes, but she is a captive."

The tension returned to the girl's body as she grasped the flow of the conversation through Felipe's translating.

"Have you sought the will of the spirits in this?"

Blackbird's baleful glare would have frightened any lesser person. "Of course." He waved a hand. "The girl came to us, unlooked for. Perhaps it was in a moment's impulse that I gave her my cloak, but I have prayed and fasted and sought the spirits since then." He looked at White Doe again. The frown did not ease. "I had not expected this part to be so difficult."

"Hmm." The clan mother also looked at the girl and addressed her. "Why do you refuse our holy man?"

Felipe relayed the question. She fidgeted only a little, her gaze flicking about. "First, he did not ask."

The clan mother's head bobbed. "You were washed and prepared and brought to him. He held out his hand to you. That was asking."

The girl's chin came up slightly. "But also, I may only give myself to a follower of my God, and he is not."

As he translated, the assembly sat back, most deep in thought, but some clearly offended—not least of all, Blackbird himself. "Why is your God better?" he asked.

White Doe swallowed then drew in a breath. "Because He came as a man and died to be our sacrifice, so that we need no longer pray and sacrifice to the old gods." A murmuring rippled through the others, but she went on, "And then He defeated death itself by coming back to life, and dies no more."

That did it. All the venerable chiefs were in an uproar. Cries of shock, expressions of scorn. "We heard of this from the Inglés all those years past—the Español also believe it, but look at them—"

The eldest bid them all quiet once more, and they returned, disgruntled and sulking, to their pipes. Blackbird stared at the girl as if she were not sane—perhaps even not quite human.

A trickle of sweat ran down Felipe's back. He could see the girl's face glistening with it.

"I propose," the eldest said, "that White Doe be given a time of courtship. Blackbird will seek to win her in all the ways a Skaru:re girl should be won. At the end of that time, she must give the words in our tongue, with no one needing to translate." He sent a hard look toward Felipe. "And if she refuses his suit, then she will return to being a mere captive and will serve our people the rest of her days."

Chapter Eight

The wind off the water was sweet and fresh, cooling Elinor's cheeks. Little Berry lay tucked against her chest, shaded by a lightweight blanket—much like her eldest sister had when crossing these same waters from the north, on her first journey to Kurawoten. A smile curved Elinor's mouth at the memory. Sunny sat directly in front of her in the kanoe, holding Mary and Georgie's youngest, while Mouse and Owlet had been dispersed between others—likely the wisest choice, to keep the children well watched as they paddled across the Sound on their return to the island.

Sees Far sat just behind her, paddle in hand, with Chris behind him, and Mary and Georgie in front. Their kanoe rode the waves easily, but it helped that the water was calmer today than it had been at other times. Mary insisted on paddling with the men, and the four of them were determined to make at least as good a time as they'd have made sailing.

It felt to Elinor like they were flying.

She closed her eyes and tipped her face into the wind. Already she could smell the sea. 'Twas a strange balm to the aching of her heart at having to leave Ginny and the boys behind.

Father, thank You for letting us return to the island. Please grant that we all arrive safely. Preserve all of us who have come to these shores. Especially preserve Ginny and Henry and Redbud—oh Lord, strengthen them in both mind and body, and keep their hearts safe in You! Surround them with Your presence. Help them not forget who they are in You.

She prayed again for Libby and Emme, the girls who were taken with her so many years ago and then left behind.

If it pleases You, Lord, to leave Ginny and the boys with these other people. . . Lord, please help me to find comfort. Grant me Your peace.

Tears ran down her cheeks and dried with the wind.

Above all, however. . .protect her. Please. . .please protect her.

They had released her at last, after what seemed hours of talk, interspersed with much food and strong, sweet drink. Barely had she escaped Blackbird's house before a bevy of women surrounded her again, this time to collect the gorgeous feathered cape and all the ornaments they'd so painstakingly covered her with. At last only the skirt was left. "My dress?" she asked, gesturing down her body, and they only shrugged. Had it been left at the river's edge? She darted away, not waiting to see if they intended to divest her of her last shred of dignity.

Great, heaving sobs bubbled through her by the time she reached the stream. She glanced about—there, in an unrecognizable heap at the base of the rocks where they'd made her stand. Then she left the beautiful skirt on the rocks and, for the third time that day, went back into the water, the poor, tattered deerskin garments in hand.

Feet braced against the current, she ducked under and stayed as long as she could bear. Up—a gasp of air—then under again. Oh, if only she could stay and let the shush and gurgle of the water lull her to sleep. . .

Up, and she swiped back her hair as her lungs worked like bellows. Some of the red dye had washed out, but not all. The shadows were growing long, the sound of singing insects throbbing in the still-warm air. Her breaths slowed, approaching normal, and then she broke once more into weeping.

"God—oh God—"

"I warned you the Skaru:re would break you."

A ragged, guttural scream tore itself from her throat as she whirled and fell back into the water, chin deep to cover herself. There he stood, not five paces from the edge, the last rays of sun edging his features, the high cheekbones and narrow nose and chin too sharp to be Tunapewak. The crag of his brows cast his eyes into shadow, but she could tell he watched her.

And too intently by half.

"Go *away!*" she shrieked.

He appeared completely unmoved. "They have tasked me not only with teaching you their tongue now but with making sure you do not escape. Or do yourself harm. And with the other women weary from their efforts to make you presentable—" He lifted a hand and let it drop.

The cold of the water drew a shiver. "So I must endure his wooing and accept him, regardless of what I wish?"

Felipe remained quiet a moment. "Is he so repugnant to you?"

She gaped at him. How could he not understand? Was he truly so dim-witted?

He stepped nearer. "Is it that he is Skaru:re? Would it be different were he Kurawoten?"

"I—nay!" She shivered again, gulped a breath. "Might you turn around so I can come out of the water and dress? I promise not to drown myself or run away." The words were hardly comprehensible, she was sure, from her shaking so badly.

He sighed but turned as she had requested. Her feet would hardly carry her out of the stream as she slogged ashore, keeping her eyes on his shoulders, the tunic and old skirt clutched to her chest. There was barely enough space between them to shake the garments out and put them on, but somehow she managed it.

"There," she panted when she had finished.

He swung back toward her, the deep blue of his eyes suddenly visible—and quite vivid. "I ask again," he said softly. "Is he so repugnant? Are you so determined to refuse him?"

"I have determined nothing." She wrapped her arms about herself.

"Well. You must receive his attentions, at least. Give consideration to what lies before you." He sniffed. "You could do worse."

But she didn't want to merely settle for "not worse." She wanted the genuine love she'd seen between various couples at home. She wanted—oh, the romance between Mama and Papa Sees Far. The playful passion she'd witnessed between Mary and Georgie.

"Are you hungry?" Felipe asked.

She shook her head, but in truth, her middle felt hollow and her limbs still quaked. She simply wasn't sure she could keep anything down.

"Come," he said, using the Skaru:re word. "Let us go back to Grandmother Dove's house. You should rest."

She walked beside him, arms still folded, and noted with dim amazement that he matched his pace to hers.

"Do you have a woman?" she asked. The thought had just popped into her head.

He twitched but kept walking. "No."

"Anyone in mind?"

"No." This answer came more swiftly.

"I presume you are of age to be allowed to think of it?"

His face jerked toward her. "I am fully a Skaru:re warrior and well able to provide for a woman and children, should I so choose, if that is what you are asking."

"I was just curious," she said.

He shooed her inside Granny Dove's house, which was empty at the moment. "I will bring you food," he said, with a sternness belied by the words and action. "You should try to eat."

She watched him go. Why was he such a puzzle?

And more importantly, why did she care?

Why must she be so winsome? So accursedly sweet that, in such a moment, she would suddenly inquire after his familial status?

It wasn't as if he hadn't already considered seeking a woman. Several of the Skaru:re girls were likely enough. And many were happy to offer themselves for much less formal arrangements, none of which he had accepted. After a few refusals and questions about what was wrong with him, they now mostly steered clear of him.

He'd pondered often on the matter, and he didn't think it was due to their Skaru:re-not-Español otherness. The women of this land were comely and desirable—almost too much so. His father had his scruples—at least, Felipe thought he did—but the other men partook of the Native women's charms almost without hesitation. Some of them went so far as to claim women as wives. Felipe even recalled christenings and marriages solemnized by the priests who accompanied them.

He'd no call to hold back simply because he was different. But it was enough of a question—well, there was a reason he'd asked White Doe what was behind her reluctance to accept Blackbird.

Feasting was still taking place over at Blackbird's house. Felipe slipped in at the edges, gathered up a little of everything—what was it she'd eaten the most of before? It would benefit no one if she refused to eat. He managed to be away again without anyone's notice.

When he arrived back at Grandmother Dove's house, he found the girl curled up on her mat against the back wall, asleep. Her hair spilled across the mat, still damp and darkened from the bloodroot they'd used, and delicate lashes lay against her cheekbones. With all the guardedness out of her expression, she looked simply childlike and. . .sweet.

Well, perhaps not completely childlike.

For a moment—only a moment—he let his gaze trace her slender curves, draped in deerskin, then he set down the wooden platter and cup near her head and went back outside. With a long sigh, he sat down and leaned his elbows on his upraised knees.

It promised to be a long summer. Please God—whether the one of his childhood or those of the Skaru:re, he did not know—that the girl would learn the tongue more quickly now and make her choice for Blackbird and free him of this accursed duty.

He must have dozed, for when he roused to the sound of approaching footsteps, the night had much deepened. Blackbird came to a halt before him.

"She sleeps," Felipe said.

The other man sighed. "Today has been much distressing."

Felipe had no response to that.

"Come. We must go see to that boy."

Climbing back to his feet, Felipe winced. What would Henry's fate be for daring to cause trouble this day? If they hadn't punished him already, Felipe would be surprised.

Sure enough, they found him trussed and guarded as they would a new captive, face and body bearing several bruises. He sat up, blinking against the torch Blackbird borrowed from one of the guards, fear and defiance at war on his face.

Blackbird surveyed him for but a moment. "I see they spared your life. That will not be the case if you interfere again." He wiggled his fingers at Felipe. "Say it again in his tongue."

Felipe crouched. "Did you understand?"

Henry swallowed. "Partly."

Felipe translated, and the boy's gaze cleared.

"How is she—Ginny?"

"Well enough." Felipe sat back on his heels. "The marriage did not take place. She is to be given a time to be courted in the way of the Skaru:re. Then she will choose between Blackbird or remaining a slave to the end of her days."

Henry's eyes widened.

"See then—save your indignation. Another such outburst will endanger both of you." Felipe glanced about, but the Kurawoten lad was nowhere in sight. "All three of you, mayhap. Do you understand?"

A slow, deep nod was Henry's reply. Felipe rose to his feet.

"Be the man I know you nearly are. For her if for no other reason."

She woke to the twittering of birdsong at dawn. Memory returned in a hot rush, and as she sat up, her gaze caught on the food and drink placed near her head. She lifted the platter and sniffed, tasted, then wolfed down several bites. Oh, but she was hungry. The drink was strong and sweet, clearing the last of the cobwebs from her head.

She set both platter and cup aside, empty. Granny Dove still slept nearby.

Felipe must have left them last night after she'd fallen asleep. She hardly recalled lying down. The weariness overwhelmed her so sharply, she couldn't stay upright. A flutter curled through her middle at the thought of his presence there while she slept, completely unaware.

She thought of Blackbird scolding him after he'd given her a hand up. But then Felipe was tasked with watching her? They must trust him. Or was there more behind their decision to assign him as her guard? She could think of nothing significant in the moment.

She rose and moved the platter and cup to beside the door then took up the waterpot to fill and begin her usual morning routine.

Just inside the doorway she stopped. If Blackbird truly meant to court her, what could she expect? And when? There seemed to be no one in sight, however, so she should be safe enough going to the stream—

She went to take a step and nearly fell headlong. A little squeak escaped her as she fumbled with the jar, and a muffled *oof* came from the very solid body she'd thumped into that was lying just outside the house.

Felipe, wrapped in a deerskin—or at least he had been until she'd startled him awake—surged upward, arms flailing and the cover going in all directions. Blue eyes glared into hers.

"You must sleep here as well?" she asked, aghast.

His only reply was to bare his teeth and rake a hand across his face.

A laugh escaped her. She could not help it. "But why? Are they so concerned I'll run away? Or—"

"Or harm yourself? Such things have happened for lesser reason."

Ginny did not want to contemplate whether she understood being desperate enough to attempt such a thing.

He shook out the hide and dropped it against the side of the house. "Come. Let us get water. There is much to do today."

She sighed noisily, took a better grip on the pot, and marched toward the stream. So much for a peaceful morning.

After fetching water, washing themselves up, and partaking of the morning meal—Blackbird thoughtfully sent leftovers from the feast for that—Felipe selected two bows, both his tall hunting one and a smaller one for training, gathered sufficient arrows, and led the girl just a bit upstream. "Something Blackbird has tasked me with is seeing to what you are able to do. As a wife of the Skaru:re, you will be required to teach your own small children, sons especially, how to draw a bow—"

Eyes flashing and mouth set, the girl took the training bow from Felipe's hands, drew an arrow from the quiver at his hip, then stepped a pace away. With an ease and form that bespoke long practice, she nocked the arrow, drew back, lifted the bow, and shot. The arrow embedded high in a nearby sapling.

She shoved the bow at him. "Aye. Kurawoten mothers do the same. And we were all taught to shoot, not just the boys."

Felipe rubbed a hand across his mouth to hide a grin. Perhaps White Doe should not be given a bow and arrows of her own. At least not until her allegiance was proven. "Very good," he said, then repeated it in Skaru:re and pulled out a second arrow. "Again. This time, name your target first."

She fitted the arrow to the string then scanned the treetops. "Do we need food?" she asked, nodding toward a squirrel scampering a short distance away.

"We can always use food."

Lifting the bow, she tracked the creature's movement, then—

Thwack, and the creature fell to the earth. They both moved forward, and where the squirrel lay, impaled by the arrow, she knelt, setting aside the bow and reaching presumably for his knife. He gave it without hesitation.

She made quick work of making sure the creature was indeed killed, but her sniffling betrayed her.

"You weep for the animal?" he asked.

She hesitated, cutting free the arrow. "I am reminded of someone whose Kurawoten name meant 'squirrel.' She. . .is as an older sister. A very dear friend. I miss her."

He took the arrow from her, and she picked up the carcass by its back legs.

"Who do you miss?" she asked.

He looked up and found himself caught by the earnestness in her sky-blue gaze. A dozen or more faces flashed in his memory.

"Your mama?" she prompted, and he nodded.

"Who else?"

"Papá, of course." He took a breath, and it hurt. "My younger sisters. Grandmamá."

There were others he could not name, or he could not find the words to explain what they had meant to him.

His father's entire company.

She rose and set off walking, but slowly. "How long until I stop missing them?"

It was the first sign she'd given of any sort of resignation to being here. For some reason, it only deepened the ache in his chest.

"Perhaps never," he murmured.

Ginny wasn't sure what else Felipe had planned before she'd so rashly shown off her skills with the bow, but he led her back to the town in silence and much sooner than she suspected he otherwise might. They returned to Granny Dove's house to find three women sitting outside with the old woman, all sipping tea, and all of whom at Ginny and Felipe's approach rose and began chattering. One lifted the skirt Ginny had worn the day before, and another a pair of the necklaces. Felipe quieted them, listened, then turned to Ginny. "The garments and ornaments are yours, gifts from Blackbird. And they wish to help you dress your hair and present yourself as a young woman of the Skaru:re, so to ready yourself for his visit."

Ginny had to close her gaping mouth. Shifting from one foot to another, she lifted the squirrel carcass, still dripping a little. "What should I do with this?"

The women clucked and scolded. Felipe smiled crookedly. "I will skin and dress it for you." At Granny Dove's chirp, he added, "She said she will be glad to roast it, and—" There was a brief exchange between him and the old woman, during which he pointed at Ginny and dipped his head as if assuring her that aye, Ginny was indeed the one who shot the creature. "And she thanks you for the meat."

Felipe set off in the direction of the stream, and the three women herded her after him, still chattering and scolding. He turned, walking backward, the smirk full blown now. "In the future, you will do well to remember that hunting is men's work."

Heat rushed through her. "You're only chapped because I shot so well."

He laughed then trotted away.

One of the women poked Ginny, spoke what was clearly a question, then pointed between Felipe and Ginny. "*Enh?*"

Her cheeks were burning. She could well guess the tenor of that inquiry, and shook her head.

Another lengthy lecture. By then they'd reached the stream's edge, Felipe continuing on downstream, and she was only too happy to wash up from the squirrel.

Once again she submitted to being dressed, oiled, and ornamented. The women led her back to Granny Dove's, where Felipe was just handing off the cleaned squirrel and its skin.

And there Blackbird was waiting as well. Ginny could tell he had taken extra care with his appearance. She held herself still under his scrutiny and made herself look at him with fresh eyes as well. He was not so old as she'd perhaps first thought. His limbs were all straight and strong, his body lean and well proportioned, his face unlined. He wore a full array of feathers stuck into his hair, which was pulled back and knotted at his nape in the customary manner of the men. The sides had no doubt been freshly shaved yesterday, in preparation for. . .

For what had been intended as their wedding. She felt her heart drop, remembering. Comprehending. It could not have been easy or comfortable for him.

He was not unhandsome, and in many ways reminded her of Papa

Sees Far and Manteo. But what she had said about him not following the one true God yet held true.

What if his heart were to change?

Come to think, Papa Sees Far had started out as an enemy. As Mama's captor. Then he had fallen in love with her, even while he was still her enemy.

Blackbird offered a hesitant smile. She tried to respond, but it felt far too wooden.

Chapter Nine

B lackbird had invited her for a walk. Naturally, Felipe was required to tag along.

She was dressed to perfection, if more simply than the day before, with her hair knotted soberly back, leaving her neck and shoulders bare, save for the necklaces.

Not that he'd noticed.

She held herself with calmness and grace, walking beside Blackbird upstream, conversing with the help of Felipe's translation. So far that consisted mostly of discussion about features of the land, the different birds and wildlife they saw, and trees and plant life. The girl—*White Doe*, he reminded himself—dutifully repeated words and phrases and smiled with obviously forced politeness but spoke little of her own.

It was strange and not a little amusing to watch Blackbird have to play the suitor. Felipe could see the man's rising frustration at the lack of discernible progress or depth in the conversation. At last he turned to Felipe. "It has been too many summers since I have done this. Am I neglecting something?"

Felipe coughed in an effort to stifle a laugh. Unfortunately, Blackbird recognized it for what it was and scowled more fiercely.

Felipe considered White Doe for a moment. He knew for certain that such reticence was completely unlike her. Dozens of questions likely bubbled under the surface. It was simply a matter of drawing them out.

"What would you ask Blackbird?"

She fidgeted, glancing away and drawing her arms over her chest. "Am I permitted to ask whether he already has a woman and children?"

Felipe bit back a grin. He walked her through saying the Skaru:re words: *May I ask—women and children do you have?*

Blackbird's expression shifted to relief and chagrin, and he turned to answer her. "Two women, each with three children. They live for now in other towns, with their families."

She digested that. Felipe thought she was trying not to look dismayed, but her brows came together and stayed there.

Not quite a scowl. He was impressed.

At last she bobbed a nod. "Have you any other family here?"

Felipe guided her through the Skaru:re, and this time Blackbird actually smiled. "The one you know as Grandmother Dove. She is my father's mother."

"How did you come to be one of the holy men?"

"I was chosen as a boy, and the visions I received when crossing into manhood confirmed it."

"And what are your duties in that position?"

Blackbird was fairly preening now. "To conduct prayers and sacrifices. To teach the proper ways of seeking the spirits' favor. To seek the spirits for myself and the people."

"Hmm." She tipped her head, an oh-so-courtly motion.

"And what of your people's holy men?" Blackbird asked.

A smile flitted across her face. "It is the same. Except our belief in which God to serve is different."

Well played, little White Doe.

Blackbird's chin came up, and his mouth curved in response. "Perhaps we can talk more over food and drink?"

She gave that little dip again. Blackbird's gaze flashed at Felipe, glittering.

Her gut sloshed like a basketful of rocks as they walked. Would she even be able to eat?

'Twas a strange repetition of the day before—only this time 'twas only her and Blackbird, with Felipe between. She felt no sense of immediate peril, but her skin prickled with the awareness of the man's intent.

And he wished her to be his third wife? 'Twas bad enough, him not being a Christian.

She'd not be guilty of being on anything but her best behavior, however, or of not comporting herself with dignity. Was she not the daughter of Elinor and Ananias, and the granddaughter of Governor John White?

A platter of bread rounds and roasted meat was set before her. A pot of squash stewed with corn followed. Ginny offered a smile and thanks—in proper Skaru:re, at that. She was learning at least a little.

Surprising that he'd not required her to do the cooking, but that would no doubt follow.

After sating his initial hunger, Blackbird sat back. "Explain again about your God."

She did so, letting Felipe walk her through the Skaru:re words. If nothing else, it gave her practice in the cadence and pronunciation.

Was this how Mama and the other adults felt about learning Kurawoten at the beginning?

Blackbird's smug expression did not change. "This thought of a God who becomes man, dies, and comes back to life. It is—"

Felipe struggled to translate the word Blackbird spoke next, and for a moment he and Ginny went back and forth on whether Blackbird meant ridiculous, insane, or merely simpleminded.

She would have to remember not to use that word. Wrangling over the tongue did not quite diffuse the sting of his intent.

"Others have thought so and then had their hearts changed later," she said.

More wrangling, during which she snapped at Felipe, "If I could simply tell you and have you tell him, 'twould be easier!"

But he only smirked and answered, "But you would be slower to learn the tongue. And is that not one of the conditions?"

A soft growl escaped her, and he laughed outright.

Blackbird's gaze flickered between them, and he asked another question, more imperious.

"What is the difference, then, between the Inglés and the Español?"

She and Felipe looked at each other. Would Blackbird have patience for this part of the discussion?

"The English and Spanish have been bitter enemies," she began. Felipe translated, not forcing her to say the words too this time. "My elders would say that the Spanish have an unparalleled thirst for conquest, and an equal amount of savagery in carrying it out."

"But the Inglés have the same," Felipe returned.

"Not all English," she said.

Blackbird windmilled a hand and said what she was almost certain was, "Keep going!"

"It is more, however. The Spanish hold to the Roman Church, which adds any number of idolatries to the pure doctrine of Christ and redemption."

Felipe gave her a long look then shifted and relayed her words—or tried, for many *ah*s were interspersed throughout his translation.

Had she made his hackles rise with such a confrontational statement? But 'twas no different from what Master Johnson and others had said over the years, with much more passion.

"Idolatries?" Felipe said.

"Is there such a word in Skaru:re?"

"I told him the Inglés believe we put other things before God."

Her turn to wave a hand. "That isn't quite accurate. I mean, aye. But it's the observances that are specifically attached—you must pray to Mary and the saints, you must say the rosary, you must do penance—"

"And the Inglés attach nothing to their devotion? They are not guilty of their own idolatries? Why, King Henry setting up his own church just

101

so he could trade out wives—"

"And my family left England to escape the corruption of that church!"

Blackbird's laugh rang out. She and Felipe turned almost as one.

The older man spoke, and Felipe answered. Ginny used the moment to collect herself. The sharpness of her and Felipe's contention both surprised and rattled her.

Yet what could she say that would soften her argument and still be true to her understanding of Scripture?

She bent her head and rested her forehead against her fists. Breathe in, breathe out. *Lord. . .oh Lord God. . .*

It was so easy, growing up. Most everyone believed, and the few who might not have didn't make a great row about it. The neighboring towns always listened to their explanations about God with at least politeness if not great interest—but then, led by Manteo, they had a way of explaining that Ginny seemed to fail at.

She wanted to be able to explain. How was it honoring to God to do otherwise? She suddenly understood the elders' insistence on discussing their deepest beliefs.

All her life she'd heard the stories. Their coming to the New World, they said, 'twas more than uprooting in body and soul and trying to make a home in a completely different country. There was a clash between old ways and new ways, between old gods and the one true God, a conflict not just of thought and ideals but of spiritual forces. How many times had she heard Master Johnson and others read the verse about not wrestling with flesh and blood but with principalities and powers? And yet. . .she had never truly comprehended.

She looked up to find both Blackbird and Felipe regarding her with curiosity and not a little concern.

If she understood Scripture, then neither of these men was her enemy.

But what did that mean for the situation she found herself in?

She still could not give herself in marriage to Blackbird, not unless his heart was turned to Christ.

And Felipe—did he carry an awareness of the faith he had been brought up in? Or had he abandoned the Spanish beliefs of the Roman Church?

"What did I miss?" Her voice came out as a croak.

Felipe cleared his throat. "I was telling him how we may follow the same God, but we sharply disagree on how to serve Him. As you and I made so clear."

Ginny nodded. "That is a fair enough assessment."

Blackbird spoke again. Felipe translated, "How is it this matter prevents you from becoming my woman?"

She sifted through all she had been taught. The term "unequally yoked" came to mind, but there was no equivalent in the ways of the People.

" 'Tis—light. And dark." For each, she laid one hand, palm up, on either knee. "The one true God is light, and in Him is no darkness at all. We belong each of us to the dark until we come to Him. So for one of the light to marry one of the dark—" She winced. It sounded arrogant even to her own ears. "I can think of no other way to explain."

Felipe relayed it, and a frown gathered on Blackbird's face once more. "So you think you are better than I? That your people are better than ours? This explains much."

"Nay, it is not like that—" It was exactly like that for some, she knew, recalling what the elders had taught about the English who had come before them, and their mishandling of the Suquoten and others. "Aye, there are some who view it that way. Some of the English. I would guess many, or most, of the Spanish, given how they treat the peoples of this country. But most of those in my community? Nay. Most emphatically not. We see all peoples as made in the very image of God, whether or not they know him yet as God. They are worthy of our respect." She blew out a long breath. "We have not always behaved as though they are. More shame upon us for that."

Ginny lifted her head and watched Blackbird as Felipe finished translating.

"It does not mean, though," she added, "that we do not share what we know of God and hope for eyes to be opened and hearts changed."

He stared back at her, mouth hard.

"I think he did not appreciate that 'eyes opened and hearts changed' part," Felipe said.

"'Tis true," she murmured.

He rolled his eyes and turned back to Blackbird. Whatever he said broke the older man's mood and made him laugh again, and the two of them bantered for a few moments.

Ginny's cheeks went warm. "Why do I feel like I was the butt of that?"

Felipe laughed. "Because you were."

Her turn to roll her eyes. "Boys. They truly never grow up."

Felipe kept pace with the girl on their way back to Grandmother Dove's.

"You're still smiling," the girl said. "What did you say to Blackbird?"

He laughed ruefully. "Whether he was certain you were so worth his trouble."

She huffed. "And his answer?"

" 'Ah, someone must bear the hard tasks.'"

Felipe did not tell her the next thing Blackbird had said: *At least she will not be dull to live with!*

An understatement, that.

"You're doing it again."

He gave her a sidelong glance. "What?"

"Smiling. Nay—grinning, in truth."

And she was of a certainty not smiling along with him. When he did not respond, she tucked her chin and stayed silent as well until they reached Grandmother Dove's.

He dropped to sit against the wall and closed his eyes.

"What are you doing now?"

"Resting." He cracked an eyelid. "You are exhausting."

She folded her arms across her chest and lifted her chin, glaring.

A sigh escaped him, and he sat straighter. "What is it?"

"How am I, a Christian, to reconcile myself not only to his unbelief, but to be his third wife?"

Felipe blinked.

She waved a hand. "Such things may be done amongst the People, but not ours. Not mine."

He huffed. "I do not have an answer for you. Look, it will take some time. Mayhap your heart will change before then."

Her expression hardened.

"Mayhap *his* heart will change."

"As in, he may decide he does not want me after all?"

Felipe studied her. "No, as in, he decides to follow your God. Would that not help the matter?"

To his faint surprise, she tucked her chin, now looking at her finger-nails. "No woman wishes to be in line after others."

He supposed he could understand that. Still. . . "You have only two choices in this matter. Reject his offer and remain a captive. Or accept it and content yourself with not being the center of his attention for always. You may be glad to have him absent."

She did not respond to his wry smile. At last, with a long sigh, she squared her shoulders and went inside.

The echo of his words pinged against his own heart. Perhaps he should not have said them—at least not in that manner. She'd have to toughen considerably, however, to survive here.

Still, his rancor sat heavy in his gut.

And it wasn't so much that he was tired. He craved time and quiet to think about what she had said. *Idolatry.* Was that what the English truly thought of the Holy Roman Church?

He remembered both grandiose cathedrals with soaring ceilings and humble chapels with barely a bench to sit upon. Paintings and sculptures of people with grave, reverent faces. The smell of incense. The thrum of chanted prayers. Crosses bearing the figure of the bleeding Christ. The taking of small, dry, flat bread and sips of wine and being told they were the body and blood of Christ. Myriad observances meant to bring them closer to God.

A God he'd given little thought to in his years here. Suddenly, this slip of a girl had brought it all to the forefront of his mind again, and because Blackbird found it of interest. . .

He huffed again and sat up. In truth, the observances of the Skaru:re felt much the same. A bare handful in either Español or Skaru:re lived and breathed enough devotion to inspire others to follow. Blackbird represented one such here, and a few of the priests he recalled from his childhood, among the Spanish. Oh, and Mamá, certainly. Papá too in his own way, although arguably his greatest passion was winning another segment of the New World for España. But he would have avowed that merely an extension of his devotion to God—to see other peoples brought in under the sheltering wing of the church.

The girl—White Doe—might also represent such devotion. Although he had caught a glimpse of something he might term a more martial spirit, at least were she a man and not a woman. It did remind him a bit of Papá.

And oh, if that was the sort of spirit the sailors and soldiers of España had encountered in the Inglés, then no wonder the Armada met with defeat.

He must guard himself lest he find his own ship going down in flames.

She'd forgotten.

How sweet were the sea breezes. How restorative the very sunlight.

They arrived well into evening, and Elinor had more or less fallen onto a pallet and knew no more until the sun came peeking through matted walls. The other women greeted her joyfully, and after an unhurried breakfast, she tied little Berry against her chest and went for a walk. At the top of the familiar low hill, she found a resting place on a fallen oak, settled Berry to nurse, and simply watched the not-so-distant waves on the ocean side of the island.

In the beginning was the sea. . .

She smiled softly. 'Twas a common enough refrain in the early years—but another thing she'd forgotten until now.

Tipping her head, she soaked in the rays filtering through the treetops onto her face. What a gift, to be back here.

Berry broke off from nursing and squeaked. Elinor lifted her to her shoulder and patted. And what a gift, this little one. Who knew, when Elinor first made this journey, that she would find, aye, love and comfort after the loss of Ananias—and in such a one as Sees Far. Son of the great weroance, Granganimeo. She kissed the tiny, downy head of the newborn bobbling on her shoulder. She—mother to the granddaughter of Granganimeo! This child represented, as her sons did, the melding of English blood with the New World. A wonder and a marvel.

Papa would be overjoyed.

The sorrow still pressed in at the edges, of course. She would always miss Ananias. She would always wonder what had become of Papa. And she was not the only one to feel it. When Margery Harvie had caught sight of her last night, she'd come running to embrace Elinor, and they'd wept together over having to leave the mainland without any hope of recovering their children.

Either of them—the first girl, the first boy, to be born of the English on these shores—and now lost to the wilds of the land's interior.

Redbud's mama was more philosophical about the entire thing, but Elinor knew she grieved as well. When it had come time to leave Cora Banks, the Kurawoten woman had decided she could not bear leaving, so she and her English husband chose to stay behind.

Elinor understood that. Had been tempted to dig in her heels as well. Ultimately, it was the desire to give the other children the opportunity to experience the freedom of island life with its abundance of fish and other foodstuffs that decided the matter for her. It could not be called safer, all things considered, but she was so weary of the constant vigilance against enemies to the west of them at Cora Banks.

Papa had once said that all life was risk. That he would rather venture all, even if it meant facing death, to pursue whatever challenge God set before him, than to moulder away at home and miss the thrill of new sights and experiences. Part of his appeal to her and Ananias for accompanying him on the voyage fifteen years ago was that he wished not to be separated from her for so long. How great the irony, then, that they'd all eventually decided to send him back to England to champion for their support. Yet there seemed no other decision to be made at the time.

Perhaps Papa could have stayed, and the end result would have been the same—and then he would be here to enjoy the fruits of his labors.

Elinor squeezed her eyes shut. How fiercely she still missed him. Yet she had learned over the years, 'twas needful to put Papa firmly in God's hands—and leave him there.

She needed to do the same with Ginny.

The thought struck hard, driving the breath from her lungs. *Oh Lord— most gracious, almighty God! Have I failed to trust You with my daughter?*

Chapter Ten

Weeks went by, summer deepened, and the first of the pegatawah grew tall. As the ears ripened, the Skaru:re prepared for a festival. Ginny found herself caught up in the busyness and excitement.

At least, she should be caught up in the excitement. Her understanding of their tongue had increased enough for her to have simple conversations with the women. She kept busy caring for Granny Dove and making baskets. And though Felipe and others continued to watch her, they hovered less these days than before.

Except in regard to Henry and Redbud. She'd caught their gazes a few times from a distance, but at the first sign of intent to go speak with them, had been sharply prevented from doing so. Felipe had given her a stern look. "Do not. I have reassured Henry of your well-being and warned him not to endanger you. You must do your part as well."

He and the other Skaru:re were most determined to treat her as a full-fledged member of their society now, it seemed. And that included having nothing to do with lowly slave boys.

In a few weeks, summer would begin its ponderous turn toward autumn, and she and Henry would mark the anniversary of their birth. At home there would be a celebration, but here in exile, none could even be sure of the day it came.

Henry had grown quite tall the last few months. Still gangly as ever, but the nearest she could tell, he had at least a hand on her now, although he was not yet the stature of Felipe or Blackbird.

And that one—her stomach soured at the mere thought of him. Of the impending decision she must make. Further conversations over spiritual matters led only to frustration and the same arguments, over and over. Blackbird appeared determined that she would accept the Skaru:re view of the world. Felipe, equally so to discredit the English mode of worship. If their probing had accomplished nothing else, she'd been forced to dig more deeply into her own reasons for holding to the faith of her fathers—but she was failing miserably at communicating any of it.

In the meantime, most of her prayers consisted of simple pleas for mercy and aid. And how tempting it was to believe that God was not listening, much less actually coming to her rescue.

Blackbird visited almost daily, accompanied by Felipe. If the weather was fair, they would walk, and if not, she and Granny Dove were expected to entertain them indoors with whatever food and drink they had to hand. And talk—always talk. Felipe had complained of Ginny being greatly wearying, but in truth? She felt beyond the limits of her own strength in this.

Was she meant to be as Esther in Scripture, given through no will of her own to a heathen king who had many women at his disposal? And if so, did that mean the great God had a plan to use her in some mighty way? She could scarce conceive how it would be so.

On a hot, sunny day, with the entire town abuzz with festival preparations, Blackbird invited her to stroll upriver in the cool of the forest. Ginny observed by the way he held himself that much was on his mind, though he spoke but little as they set off.

As always, Felipe trailed them, closely enough to translate if needed—and he was needed far less of late. Another thing to twist the dread more deeply.

She released a little sigh. The treetops were full of birdsong—sparrows, redbirds, and the harsh scold of a bluejay. Somewhere out of sight, squirrels chittered. Delicate blue and yellow flowers dotted the stream's bank. Were her company more pleasing, the day would be nigh on perfect.

110

With no warning, Blackbird spoke. Ginny stopped to hear Felipe's translation.

"What is it you wish in a suitor?"

Her heart thudded painfully. She'd nearly understood the words as Blackbird had said them—and that did not bode well for her having much more time.

It was a question he'd posed before.

Another sigh escaped her. "Love," she answered, nearly without hesitation.

Down came Blackbird's brow. Frustration, or ire? Ginny steeled herself for either harsh words or an actual blow. It had been a while since she had tested the limits of his restraint.

But the Skaru:re turned and, bending swiftly, plucked a flower, a cluster of tiny yellow blooms on a long stem. He handed it to her, and his response held a note of sorrow.

And again she understood much of it.

Felipe cleared his throat, looked at the ground, and finally said, "If what he offers you is not love, he does not know more how to demonstrate what he feels for you."

The ache deepened. This Skaru:re warrior-priest loved her? Or believed he did?

And yet. . .she could not return the feeling. Nor could she explain why.

She felt the weight of Felipe's gaze upon her as she searched Blackbird's expression then glanced down, twirling the flower stem between her fingers. "What of the two wives he already has?" she whispered.

A quick exchange of words, and Felipe turned back to her. "He asks, can a man not love more than one woman? Yet you would indeed be favored above them."

Blackbird's eyes glittered. Ginny felt all the strength leave her limbs. What response could she make to that?

Suddenly, the younger man snapped something to Blackbird then strode away, deeper into the forest. Blackbird gaped after him.

"Felipe!" Ginny called after him. "You cannot just leave us here!"

He twitched, throwing a glare over his shoulder before breaking into a run.

Blackbird sighed. "Come," he said in Skaru:re and, beckoning, set off for the town again.

Felipe knew his abrupt abandonment would not go unremarked. In the moment, he cared not if Blackbird beat him for it later, but by the time he made his way back to the town, the burst of emotion that had driven him into the woods had cooled enough to let fear edge in.

He'd seen others punished for much less.

Yet he could bear it no longer. Having to be the intermediary for Blackbird—and not for just any girl, but this one. And then for her to bring up love? No—a thousand times no. He simply could not.

Love. What complete nonsense! And yet Felipe felt the tugging of his own heart. A great swelling of longing that he dared not allow to spill over, much less give voice to.

Blackbird waited for him just outside the town. Felipe slowed his steps as the older man crossed the space, features distorted by a fierce scowl. Blackbird shoved him, then again. "What did you mean by leaving us like that?"

Felipe straightened and met him nose to nose. "When all this is done—or perhaps sooner—I want a woman of my own."

Blackbird's eyes widened. At last he gave a slow smile, too knowing and sly. "Ah, so that's how it is."

With a laugh, he clouted Felipe on the shoulder and walked away.

Felipe's breath escaped him in a rush. That was entirely too easy.

"One more sleep until Green Corn Festival," Granny Dove said.

Ginny smiled, nodded, and repeated the Skaru:re words.

Apparently, she'd erred in encouraging the old woman, for Granny

Dove cackled and added, "Soon—you and Blackbird." She gestured between Ginny and the direction of that one's house.

For the past several days, alongside the other women, they'd cleaned and inspected earthenware pots and prepared food. And now the pegatawah was ripe, and tomorrow was the set day.

Curiously, Felipe had left off his efforts to assist her with—or more like, bully her into—learning the Skaru:re tongue. Neither did he accompany Blackbird on visits, as that one continued bringing her small gifts and attempting small talk. There had been no more walks, however, because of preparations for the festival.

Come to think of it, since that last walk when he'd left her and Blackbird so abruptly, Felipe had not even spoken directly to her.

Did he judge her ready for Blackbird to further press his suit? Because she was not.

Please, merciful Father. . .

The heaviness in her gut smothered any further prayer.

The morning of the feast day dawned clear and beautiful. She rose with the first birdsong, as always, and went down to the stream to wash and fetch water. A few other women were there, talking and laughing. Everyone needed an early start to the day's work.

Ginny left her waterpot and slipped away into the brush for her personal needs. She was just making her way back when she heard, "Hsst! Ginny!"

She stopped and peered through the dense bushes. "Henry?" she whispered.

He eased into view, looking about, then beckoned her closer.

"What are you doing here?" She knew her voice was sharp, but—oh, it was good to see him.

And he was definitely about half a head taller now. His hair was growing out, sticking about wildly, but his brown eyes were desperate. "How fare thee?"

"I'm well, Henry. Truly. And you?"

He grimaced. "I— It could be worse, but—" He seized her hand.

"Come with me, Ginny. If we all work together—you and I and Redbud—we can slip away. Tonight, even, maybe during the dancing—"

"What are you doing?" a third, rather deep, male voice asked.

She and Henry both started violently—and there stood Felipe.

"Of course it would be you," Henry snarled, just as Ginny was letting out her breath.

Felipe stalked closer until he was nearly nose to nose with Henry. "Do you *want* to die?"

Henry's mouth sagged. "No. I just—"

"You 'just' what? Do not say it was to inquire after White Doe's welfare. You can see clearly, every day, that she is cared for." He leaned in and, when Henry stepped back, stayed apace with him. "What you were doing is not thinking, with this plan of running away. It is folly. You will only get yourself—and White Doe—killed. Do you want that?"

Henry shook his head, slowly at first, then more firmly.

"No? Then *cease.* Now." Felipe cuffed Henry's shoulder with enough force to make him wince, then started to turn away.

"Mayhap 'tis better than having her serve as wife to *him*," Henry muttered, rubbing the spot.

A cry escaped Ginny's throat, and Felipe rounded on him again in an instant, seizing him by the shoulders. "Do—not—speak—that," he said, punctuating each word with a shake as if Henry were a child. He tossed Henry away then sucked in a deep breath through his nose. "I like it not either."

An ugly chuckle escaped the younger boy as he picked himself up. "Oh, I'm sure you don't."

"Henry!" Ginny exclaimed.

He looked at her but said nothing. Felipe, however, shifted a step nearer again, eyes narrowed. "And what do you mean by that?"

Henry stretched his shoulders and straightened the deerskin kilt about his waist. "I think you know."

Ginny took in Felipe's clenched fists and hardened features and Henry's uncharacteristic sneer. Without thought, she put a hand on Felipe's chest, pressing him back, and faced her childhood companion. "Henry. You must stop. God will take care of us—we need only trust Him. Please don't stir up any more trouble."

Henry eased away, but he spat a laugh. "Trouble? Is that all you can say about this?"

It was so eerily like that one day in the field when he and Redbud told her of Blackbird's intentions. She frowned.

"What is it, Henry? We were friends. What has you so discomfited?"

He dragged in a breath, and for a moment, she thought he would weep. "Friends?" The word came out as a squeak. "Surely you know, Ginny—you can't help but know—I always hoped there would be more. And when you didn't marry right away after huskanasqua, I thought mayhap you would wait for me—" Another noisy breath. "We'll be fifteen in a few weeks. Is that not old enough for you to even consider—"

Felipe shouldered between them. "You should leave. Now. Go back to whatever work you have been tasked with. I will not be responsible for what should befall you if Blackbird discovers you in this place or hears you have said these things."

Henry gulped, searching Felipe's face and darting a glance at Ginny before taking the young warrior's word seriously at last and beating a path through the forest.

Throat clogging, Ginny sank against a sapling and closed her eyes.

Hands brushed her upper arms then released her. "Are you well?"

She peered up at him—the angle of the sun on his features, the glimmer of his dark blue eyes. "I did not know," she whispered.

One brow ticked upward. "Does it change anything?"

Did it? She found herself shaking her head. "Nay, but—" Covering her face with her hands, she gulped several breaths.

Oh Henry. . .

She pushed herself upright and hazarded another glance at Felipe. "Thank you."

He frowned. "For what?"

"For not pummeling him into complete dust." She started walking

115

back toward the town and stream then stopped. "Will you tell Blackbird?"

Mouth tight, Felipe shook his head.

Felipe stood still, taking deep breaths, and let her go. He'd not be seen leaving the forest with her, not after the past handful of days.

He would not tell Blackbird any of it.

Nor would he tell her that he knew exactly why Henry had taunted him.

He pitied the boy—so hopelessly enamored of the girl—and he could not blame Henry for it, not one whit. When she'd put her hand on his chest—

Felipe had not intended to be following her, or even looking after her, but when she'd lingered too long in the brush, he couldn't ignore the uneasy feeling tapping at his spirit. And of course, there was Henry, trying to persuade her to run for it.

He couldn't blame them for that, either. But he knew too well the consequences for those attempting escape.

On the other hand, the last thing he wished right now was to draw attention to anyone who might be perceived as any sort of rival to Blackbird. The holy man was already frustrated enough—partly from his lack of progress with the girl, and partly at being left to fend for himself in courting her these past few days. But now Felipe would need to watch her even more closely.

Ginny's heart still ached and her thoughts still spun as the festival officially began.

She and Granny Dove stood with others in the town center as the first prayers were offered by the eldest of the holy men. While everyone around her joined in, Ginny closed her eyes and composed her own silent prayer of thanksgiving. *Thank You, oh Lord God, for all You provide. Thank*

You for preserving the boys and me here. Continue to protect us...

And thank You for Felipe. May we all grow in Your grace, here or otherwise.

Granny Dove nudged her. Blackbird was taking his place in front of everyone, fully ornamented and skin shining with fresh oils—everyone had dressed in their best on this day—lifting his hands and intoning another prayer. Ginny swallowed.

He cut a fine enough figure, but knowing where such devotion was aimed? She could find no comfort or admiration in any of it.

And may he come to know You, Most Glorious One.

At last this portion of the festivities ended, and the drumming and singing began. Ginny let Granny Dove drag her away to help finish tending to the feast. The rush and bustle of it all—checking foods to be sure they were cooked, laying things out on platters or scooping them into bowls—did distract her somewhat.

Until someone stepped close and she looked up to see Redbud.

Gracious, but he had also grown taller than her these past months! The familiar angles of his beloved Kurawoten face, sharpening now to manhood, brought a burn to her eyes.

His gaze caught hers intently. "Just so you know, none of it was my idea. But if you are interested—"

He swiped a pair of apon from the platter in her hands and strode away, leaving her to gape after him.

She'd barely had time for a breath before Felipe slid in next to her. "What was that about?"

"Gah!" She nearly dropped the platter. Before one more person could sidetrack her, she wove her way through the crowd and set the platter with others on a row of mats laid out for that purpose. Once again, Felipe hovered at her elbow. "What is it?" she snapped at him.

"What did the boy say?" Felipe asked.

A dull throb pulsed between her temples, in time with the drums nearby. "A greeting between old friends, nothing more. I'm forbidden from receiving even that?"

And then she saw Blackbird, just a few steps behind him, watching them both. With a huff, she turned and fled again through the crowd.

Others could attend the food. She'd had enough for a few minutes.

Though the temptation to keep running was strong, she made for Granny Dove's house, where she dropped to her mat and curled up tight. Her thoughts were too snarled even for prayer.

Felipe stopped just short of the house, close enough to watch but not close enough to overhear if she was weeping.

He did not want that rending his heart as well.

Blackbird started to move past him, but Felipe held out a hand. "Give her time."

The older man's brow crinkled. "She should be out celebrating with the rest of us."

"She grieves her people." It was the best reason he could think of.

"Still?"

"Yes. You know she is yet young."

Blackbird gave the barest nod. "My patience is wearing thin," he said at last.

Felipe considered that. "Perhaps you should go visit one of your wives while you continue to wait."

The older man's mouth curved a little. "A woman who welcomes me would be a refreshing change."

He sniffed, stood for a few moments longer, then walked away.

Felipe went to sit against the outside wall of the house. He strained to hear, but only silence greeted him from inside. Of course, it might be difficult to hear anything over the sounds of revelry in the town center.

At least here he could mostly shield her from Henry and Redbud.

As if the thought had summoned him, a shadow appeared from behind the next house over—and stopped. Henry stood glaring at Felipe.

He smiled and lifted his chin, just a little. He shouldn't provoke the lad even further, but somehow he couldn't help it.

At last Henry left, and with a sigh, Felipe leaned back, still keeping watch.

Dusk neared, and the smells of food wafted through the town. Should he rouse the girl or simply go fetch her food? A scuff and a sniffle from inside the door drew his attention, and he looked up to see her standing there.

"Have you been here the whole afternoon?" she asked, her voice thick with sleep—or tears.

"Aye." He rose and beckoned to her. "We should go eat."

She rubbed a hand across her face. "I should go wash first."

He stayed at her side down the hill to the stream and waited while she went out into the bushes and back. "You'll not slip away while I'm not looking?" he asked beforehand, and she only rolled her eyes at him.

Even so, he kept ears and eyes open, and when she came padding back, an odd relief swept through him. He tipped his head toward the festivities, and she followed without a word.

They wove through the crowd, found food, and withdrew again to the edges to eat. "Do you wish more?" he asked when she'd finished.

She shook her head.

He brushed crumbs from his hands and kilt. "We should join the dancing."

Her face hardened. "I cannot bring myself to dance in honor of pagan gods."

He studied her and noted the sudden shimmer of her eyes. "Did you dance among the Kurawoten?"

A tear spilled over, and she brushed it away. A quick, hard nod.

"You could dance here and let it be for them. For the God you do know, in your own heart. Could you not?"

Her gaze came to his, widening.

"Come. Let us both dance to the God we were taught as children."

Chapter Eleven

G inny could not move. Could hardly breathe, and yet. . .
Dare she refuse the challenge in his eyes? To make of this celebration something no Skaru:re or their false gods would be able to take
from her?

Lord, is it an acceptable offering to You if the others here intend it as some-
thing else?

The drums and voices tugged at her, and when Felipe again tipped his
head, she nodded.

They made their way to the edge of the dancing circle. Her feet had
already found the rhythm, a slow shuffle at first, then a steady stomp.

Oh. . .she had missed this.

A laugh bubbled out of her as her hands came up.

For You, oh Lord, only for You! For the joy of life, and in thanksgiving for
all the blessings You have afforded us—even if these people do not recognize You
as their true God.

She started to close her eyes—but could not lose her place in the
shifting crowd of dancers, so she tipped her face to the sky.

Let me speak of You—let Your face shine upon me and give me Your favor
even in the midst of my enemies. Bless and preserve all those I love. And please
help Henry and Redbud walk true as well!

Her thoughts drifted back to Felipe's words. Did he believe, or was it
merely nostalgia for her sake?

Help him, oh Lord. Help him believe! Return his heart to You—or bring it to You now, if he did not understand before.

Somehow, just watching her kept his own feet in motion.

And he could do naught else but watch her.

At some point he caught a glimpse of Blackbird talking and laughing with one of the Skaru:re women. Was he planning to take solace elsewhere tonight because of Felipe's earlier suggestion? It was of no account if so. Men and women did largely as they pleased regardless of marital ties.

Felipe half expected him to come out of the gathering and claim the girl on the spot. The way she seemed to gather all the light to herself—the transformation from the look of stark terror at his invitation to dance, to purposeful motion, tentative at first and then with joy and abandon. Blackbird never did so, however. Felipe himself felt like a moth to a veritable flame. He thought he saw Henry and Redbud as well, their expressions dark with jealousy and alarm, but those two he could do nothing about, except stay close to the girl.

And stay close he did, matching her step for step, unable to keep his own laughter back in response to her delighted giggles. Their gazes met in the firelight, then she tipped her head back again, her hands fluttering.

Was she in truth worshiping and praying, as he had encouraged her, to the God she professed to believe in?

Are You there, oh God of my fathers? Do You see her, how completely mesmerizing she is? And. . .do You see me here?

He could not account for the unlooked-for joy sweeping through him in the moment.

Much later, as the town quieted and people sought their beds, he and White Doe carried food and drink back to Grandmother Dove's house and sat outside to partake. The old woman padded to the doorway, squinted at the two of them, sternly warned Felipe to be pushing her to better use of their language but to be quiet about it, then went back in.

White Doe's hair had fallen from its fastenings and lay all around her shoulders. She made one attempt to put it back, but gave up and returned to nibbling at her bread. Between bites, she waved the half-eaten round and cleared her throat. "You spoke of us both dancing in thanksgiving to the God of our childhood. Do you still believe in Him?"

Did he? He chewed thoughtfully. He'd not thought so, after so many years with the Skaru:re, but watching her this night? He could, again.

"In all our talks about the differences between the English and Spanish," she went on, "and how the Roman Church differs from what I was taught. . . Blackbird wants to convince me that the gods as he understands them are the proper view, but you? You always defend the Roman Church." Her eyes sparkled in the moonlight. "So what exactly is your belief?"

He could do naught but shrug.

"Mama used to say," she said softly, "that one has difficulty truly knowing God is there until He proves Himself in a very specific, real way." She sipped from her cup of strong, sweet tea. "I think she must be right. For them, 'twas safe passage across the ocean. Finding refuge among the Kurawoten." A deep breath. "Coming home again after being taken captive."

"Is God only real if He does those things?" Felipe thought the question sounded mocking even to his own ears, but something in him wanted to know. "If you perish at sea or are slain by foreigners or are taken captive and live out your life as a slave, does that prove He is indifferent? Or powerless? Or is not at all?"

She nibbled at the bread again. "Some would say it does beg the question."

"What would your mamá say? Or the others?"

"That He is God, regardless. The good things we enjoy, the little miracles that come, they come because He is good and loves to bless us. But the lack of blessings does not prove His absence or lack of care."

"That may be wisdom," he said after a moment.

She laughed, as he hoped she would, but then sobered, peering upward. "But here we are, on the edge of the world, caught in a struggle between the old gods and—who they would argue is a new God but in truth is the eldest and only." Her chin tucked, her lashes falling. "There are days when I wonder if any of it matters. Yet I know it most assuredly does."

He swallowed the last of his bread and licked his fingers. Even now he could hardly take his eyes from her. "You should sleep."

She quirked him a smile. "You never replied to my question."

"I am still thinking upon it," he answered, meeting her gaze as directly and honestly as he could.

" 'Tis fair," she said with a little nod. Then, "Do you think Henry and Redbud will try to sneak over here tonight?"

He snorted. "Without a doubt. Which is why I am not leaving."

And so they talked on into the night, until the moon had begun to dip behind the trees and White Doe yawned more often than not.

Felipe came awake suddenly to her weight against his shoulder. He shrugged to push her upright. "Hie—none of that. You must go to your bed."

"Wha— Oh." She blinked then smiled sleepily.

He was on his feet in a moment, looking around before turning back to her, stepping away to put distance between them. "It is no light matter. Blackbird nearly rent me asunder that once when I offered you a hand up, for touching you. Were he to see this—"

She climbed to her feet as well, eyes wide and suddenly alert. "Yes, I remember he scolded you about that."

"Aye. And I am meant to be guarding you, not—"

He drew in a breath that was like fire all the way to his gut.

Not courting you for myself, he'd nearly said.

She just looked at him, so lovely and sweet in the moonlight, it made every beat of his heart a lingering hurt.

In truth, he was not sure he could bear watching Blackbird make good his claim upon her. Even had he a woman of his own.

"Thank you for insisting I dance," she said. "Sleep well."

And with that, she slipped inside.

Felipe let out a hard breath and sank down against the wall once more.

The boys did not return that night. Ginny didn't see them for several days, in fact, and fear plagued her that they'd been found out and punished again—or worse.

To her surprise, Blackbird was also missing from the town. Felipe told her in passing that he'd gone to visit his wives, and then he was barely present as well.

She missed Felipe, fiercely. Of course, she still missed Henry and Redbud, but not nearly as much. Henry's grand revelation the day of the Green Corn celebration had blunted her affection somewhat, and she'd already grown accustomed to seeing them only from a distance. But Felipe, now—*ugh*! How had he become such a part of her everyday routine that she expected him to be there on every hand, regardless of what task she set to?

In the meantime, conversation with Granny Dove and the other women was suddenly so much easier. The old woman went to cackling over something one morning as Ginny saw to the cooking, and with a jolt she realized she'd comprehended what was said. *See, we do not need Guh-neh to help us go about our work. You are Skaru:re!*

She was Skaru:re now. Her heart sank.

Would Blackbird insist on completing his courtship upon his return?

She lifted her head. "Granny, must it be Blackbird I marry?"

The words were all mangled. The older woman's eyebrows lifted. Ginny huffed and tried again. She knew it came out something like, *I marry not Blackbird?*

The confusion cleared, and Granny Dove cackled again. "You serve me—always?"

"Certainly. Aye," Ginny muttered, and went back to cooking.

Her eyes squeezed shut. Who would she choose, if she could? Was she not merely a silly girl? Henry's declaration pulsed through her. Nay, not him—and too much remained unsettled elsewhere.

Elsewhere, of course, meaning a certain vexing Spanish-Skaru:re warrior.

Too many questions lay unanswered between her and Felipe. And above all, she wished she had not entertained even the merest shred of thought of him to begin with.

A handful of days in which to do nothing but roam and hunt a little seemed luxurious compared to the tension of the past weeks.

Blackbird had come to him the morning after the festival. "I go to visit my wife in the nearest town and will take the white-skin boy with me." When Felipe hummed in response—not intentionally—Blackbird fastened him with a stern look. "What is it?"

"Watch him closely."

"What has he done this time?"

Felipe gave a humorless chuckle. "Nothing yet. Going with you may be a good thing."

Blackbird rubbed his chin. "I saw that he and the other boy still watch White Doe too closely. Which—what was that, last night? You bringing her to the circle to dance?"

So he had taken note, after all. Felipe shrugged, feigning unconcern. "She wished to give honor and thanksgiving to her own God for the harvest."

The older man gave him a hard look then grunted. "Continue looking after her. And I would like her to be ready to receive my proposal when I return."

Of course he would. Felipe would be sick of waiting as well.

Except. . .except if it were him, and he had any hope of this girl setting her affections on him, he'd be willing to wait however long was necessary. And she would be worth that wait.

Look after her. Well, he was trying. But also avoiding her because he was beginning to not trust himself. Not after spending half the night dancing and talking with her.

How was he going to navigate the days—the months—to come?

And her question kept pulsing through him. *Do you still believe?*

It wasn't as simple, however, as just believing. Was it? When he'd been so long removed from the auspices of the church, so far from the sacraments. If he was unable to attend mass or receive the Eucharist—they'd allowed him to receive Confirmation before he sailed with Papá and the others, charging him to comport himself as a soldier in Christ—and thus unable to partake in the grace of God, then where did that leave him?

No, one did not simply "believe in God." And for her and the boys who were taken with her, being separated from their Christian community meant they were in the same situation as Felipe.

And perhaps all life did, all things considered, come to the same place. Felipe had a difficult time being completely convinced, after becoming one of the Skaru:re and learning to regard them as worthy in their own right, that not being in Christ meant consignment to perdition out of hand. Especially when many of these people were kinder in heart and held honor and integrity in higher regard than some of his father's compatriots and, from what he'd been told, much of the English.

Then again, maybe they were all equally deserving of hell.

He took a deer, a small buck with velveted antlers, and carried it back to the town. Grandmother Dove would appreciate—no, he would not take it to her, not with the certainty of having to speak with White Doe. He would present it to some of the other town mothers and make sure they shared with Grandmother Dove.

Aye, that was a good plan.

At the edge of town he approached the women working in one of the fields—they had Redbud with them, tasked with the heavier work—and handed over the buck. Then he returned to the woods.

Redbud followed him. Felipe let him trail after for a time then rounded on the lad. "Will you pester me about the girl as well?"

The Kurawoten lad scratched his nose. "Perhaps. I do wish to know if she's well. And when Blackbird returns, what will happen? Will he bring Henry with him?"

Felipe blew out a long breath. "Blackbird has not said aught. He is visiting one of his wives."

Redbud gave an uncertain nod. "Best perhaps if Henry is kept out of trouble here."

"Aye." Felipe squinted at him.

"Are you hunting?"

"Aye."

Redbud surveyed the forest around them. "I miss hunting. And ranging about."

Felipe propped the end of his bow upright before him. "Should you not be helping with the field?"

"The women said I could accompany you."

"Huh. Such trust." A smile curled his mouth, and Redbud grinned back.

They set off, and Felipe was pleased to see how silent Redbud kept in their passage. He took another deer, this time a yearling, which Redbud carried back to the town.

"How long has Henry harbored feelings for White Doe?" Felipe asked as they went, since they no longer had to be completely quiet.

"White Doe? Oh, you mean Ginny." Redbud laughed. "Everyone loves Ginny." He sobered a little. "I suppose Henry has always felt he should be her first choice, since they were firstborn of the English and all. But even I can see she views him only as a dear brother."

Felipe grunted. "Will he at all abide it if she chooses Blackbird?"

"Mmm. I cannot say."

"Will you abide it?"

Redbud's gaze slid toward him and away. "I suppose, if I must. But it is a hard thing for her, to have to choose a man who is not Christian. . .and who already has two wives. It is—unfair—to those of us who have none."

Felipe tried to ignore the burn growing in his chest. "And did you hope she might choose you?"

Redbud's cheeks darkened, but his expression did not change. "Everyone loves Ginny," he said again, but more softly.

He certainly could not argue with that.

The Kurawoten lad eyed him suddenly. "If the situation were different, and Blackbird were not courting her, I might suggest she consider you."

His knees nearly buckled. What was this infernal weakness plaguing him? "Do not even speak of that," he snapped.

"Nay?" Redbud's brows arched now. "Do you fear she would not accept you because you are Spanish? Her mother married a man who was once an enemy. I think—"

"Do. Not," he growled. "Do not think, do not speak."

Redbud regarded him for a moment then laughed—entirely too long and too heartily.

"Have no fear, my Skaru:re brother," he said at last. "I will keep your secret. Even from Henry." He hummed for a moment. "Nay, especially from Henry."

"Good," Felipe said gruffly, when he could speak. "Now, are there any other women you might recommend as wives? Surely you have marked some during your time among the Skaru:re."

Ginny had the hardest time keeping track of days here. The English were the ones most concerned with recording the passing of time, with minutes and hours, with days and weeks and months. The Kurawoten seemed to just—know. She knew of none who made use of calendars the way the English elders did.

She'd long since lost count of how much time had passed since she and the boys had been taken captive. A whole season, certainly.

Mere days since the Green Corn Festival and Blackbird's departure the morning after. Was it six, or seven?

After completing the early chores, she settled in, just outside her door, to work on the covered basket she'd had in progress of late. Today she might finish the body of the basket and begin the task of edging the rim, if she had no interruptions.

Some sense of awareness prickled her skin, and she looked up to see Blackbird striding toward her.

Well, she couldn't count on no interruptions.

He looked freshly washed and oiled, his expression open and hopeful. A smile tipped his mouth as he approached. She nodded once in acknowledgment.

Her stomach curdled. *Oh Lord, please help me!*

Blackbird stopped a couple of paces away. He indicated the basket. "Your work seems to be going well."

She thought she'd caught his meaning, or most of it, and nodded again, more hesitantly.

He launched into a longer speech, this time accompanied by sweeps of his arm and a hand pressed to his chest and then extended to her.

She caught a few bits. "I return. . .wife. . .you my favorite, I love above all."

Her pulse beat too quickly. "I—I thought—"

She closed her mouth, cheeks burning. The words had come out in the wrong language entirely.

She was supposed to have time. He should not be trying to do this when she didn't yet understand their tongue fully enough to respond.

His hand dropped, his face hardened, and he shouted over his shoulder, "*Guh-neh! Come!*"

Felipe came slinking out from behind one of the nearby houses, as if he'd known and was just waiting.

Why had she expected otherwise? 'Twasn't like Felipe sided with her in this—but she'd somehow forgotten.

He'd waited just out of sight, where he could hear the conversation and be on hand if Blackbird needed his assistance—and sure enough, Blackbird did.

The man's visit to one of his wives seemed only to sharpen his desire for the girl. Felipe suppressed a grimace and walked out where he could be seen.

White Doe set aside the basket and scrambled to her feet. Her face was pale beneath her tan. "I cannot think of the right words!" she cried. "I should not have to make my decision before I can reply in the Skaru:re tongue."

Felipe regarded her as impassively as he could. "You might as well be ready, given that you seem to understand well enough what he said to you."

Her chest heaved. "Do I? What did he say?"

A thin smile pulled at his mouth. "What do you think he said?"

She flushed crimson this time. "Essentially that he has come back from seeing one of his wives but I am the one he favors—and loves."

Felipe folded his arms across his chest. "As I said, you understood."

Tears welled in her eyes. "I am not ready!"

He fought the urge to swallow or grimace. "Will waiting any longer change your answer?"

She sucked in a breath. The wetness poured down her cheeks. "Nay."

"Well, then." He tipped his head toward Blackbird, standing there in a similar pose, his face stony. "Give him your answer and be done with it."

High time that the decision be made and put behind them. Perhaps then he could truly get on with his own life.

White Doe tore her gaze from his, squared her shoulders, and swung to face the warrior-priest. In halting Skaru:re, punctuated by soft sobs, she told him, "I am sorry—accept I cannot—good man you are but your woman I cannot be."

Oh. This was not at all what he had expected.

Blackbird's chest slowly puffed as he drew a long breath, his expression now somewhere between ice and sharpened obsidian.

White Doe wrapped her arms about herself and shrank back a step. "I know—I now stay captive."

Blackbird shook his head, slowly at first, then with more force. His arms swung to his sides, fists clenching, his teeth bared. White Doe dropped her head yet still watched him.

"*Ah!*" Blackbird released a roar then rounded on Felipe. "This is your fault! You somehow turned her against me."

"I did not!" Felipe held himself still. "I have done all I could to persuade her that she should accept you, that you are a worthy choice."

Blackbird leaned closer. "How do I know that for certain? You might be saying something else entirely when speaking that infernal pale-skin tongue." He whipped a glare toward White Doe. "The Green Corn Festival. You danced with her. Laughed with her. Do not think I missed that."

Felipe held out his hands now, still endeavoring to appear calm. "None of that was for my own sake. Only for yours."

"Tell me you do not also wish to take her as your woman."

He faltered at that. "I—would not. You claimed her first."

Blackbird's fist met Felipe's chest. "But if I had not?"

Felipe glared as well. "How am I to reply to such an unfair question? You gave her your cloak that first day. Have we not all respected you in that? Do we not all give you respect in your place as speaker to the spirits? And were you not the one who showed me kindness when first I came here, helped train me to be Skaru:re and a warrior?"

A crowd was gathering. Grandmother Dove stood near White Doe, looking torn—which surprised him. The elders and others edged closer then made way for the chief man and clan mother.

"What is the trouble here?" the clan mother said.

Blackbird flicked a hand toward White Doe. "The girl has refused me. And it is all because of this one." Stepping back, he gestured toward Felipe.

She arched her brows. "Oh? And what do you reply to this matter?"

"White Doe has refused him, true," Felipe said, "but she is also distressed that he did not wait until she was learned enough in our tongue to answer well."

"She answered well enough in our tongue," Blackbird growled. "And she does not need full knowledge of it to be my wife."

Some of the onlookers laughed, but the elder woman only shook her head. "You cannot force a girl to accept your suit. If she prefers to be a slave, what is that to us?"

"Let us ask her if she needs more time," the chief elder of the men said.

Felipe turned to her, and he asked first in Skaru:re, then English, "Would your answer change were they to give you more time?"

The tears welled again, and she shook her head. "I am sorry."

"This is his fault," Blackbird spat. "See how she looks upon him with tenderness? He has pretended to help me in wooing her but has drawn her to himself all along."

"I did *not*," Felipe said.

Another chuckle rippled through the crowd.

"I already said to Blackbird," he went on, raising his voice, "that we marked his claim upon her from the first day, when her clothing was torn and he covered her with his cloak. I have respected that. I—" Somehow he could not breathe properly. He grimaced and surveyed the crowd, gulping for air. "I cannot help I was the only one with any knowledge of the captives' tongue. I have committed no dishonor, to Blackbird or anyone else."

"Hmm." The clan mother considered him, then Blackbird, before addressing White Doe. "Whom would you choose, were you free to do so?"

"That is of no account!" Blackbird said. "Her only choice was to be either my wife or a slave—nothing else."

The clan mother bent a look upon him, and Blackbird subsided a little. She turned back to the girl.

Felipe knew too well by now what the shifting lines of White Doe's face meant. He repeated the elder woman's question, but softly.

White Doe's eyes came to his—pools of blue, like the summer sky reflected on water. The entire gathering seemed to hold its breath.

Her lips parted then closed again and firmed. She shook her head. "I—not say," she murmured in Skaru:re.

The crowd erupted. "You see her look!" Blackbird bellowed.

The clan mother waved, and relative quiet settled again. She chuckled. "I see two youths who would perhaps be very pleased with each other, but Guh-neh defers to you, and she has not spoken thus. And I am only an old woman." She shifted to face Blackbird more fully. "Do not let your pride rule you here. She is but one girl."

"A girl I claimed, but who has refused me—because of that one." Once more he threw a gesture toward Felipe. "See how he has repaid the kindness I showed him since he was brought here as a child."

"What do you want, then, Blackbird?"

Rage distorted his features. "I want to see him burn. Let his blood run as a sacrifice." The murmuring rose around them again as ice swept through Felipe's veins. "If I cannot have her," Blackbird declared, "neither will he!"

"You are much overwrought, Blackbird," the chief elder said.

"My honor has been insulted," he snapped. "And you know it is within my right to demand a sacrifice. We have clearly been too mild with our captives—Guh-neh especially."

Some nodded and voiced their assent. The elders rubbed their chins or tapped their cheeks and looked at each other.

Felipe drew in a breath, felt the sharpness all the way to his gut, and let it out again. This surely could not be happening.

Chapter Twelve

W as she understanding aright? Was what she thought she saw unfolding before her very eyes the truth of the matter?

She clutched Granny Dove's arm, but the old woman only shook her head and covered Ginny's hand with her own. Mere paces away, Blackbird frothed and some of the crowd had begun to be stirred up as well, while the council looked variously resigned and reluctant.

Felipe stood in their midst, pale beneath the sun's bronzing, chest heaving a little, but otherwise quiet. His chin lifted, and his gaze found hers again through the crowd, then with a new look of resolve, he lifted his arms, wrists held together, and muttered something that sounded suspiciously like, *So be it.*

Someone produced a thong and bound his wrists, then Blackbird and some of the others hustled him away.

A cry tore from her throat. What were they doing? She darted forward, pushed her way between lean, oiled bodies until she'd reached Felipe's side. "Why have they bound you?"

His gaze was oddly soft. "Blackbird thinks I have turned you against him. They have determined to make me a sacrifice to appease his honor."

And there was Blackbird, trying to push her back.

"What? *No!*" She fought loose with another scream then wedged herself between them, facing Blackbird. "If anyone has besmirched his honor, it is me. And I—" She gasped for breath. "I should be the one to die. Not you." She looked up at Felipe, over her shoulder. "Tell him."

The crowd had grown still for a moment. Felipe's eyes met hers, the deep blue of twilight.

"Tell him!"

"Why?" Felipe wondered. "Why would you offer yourself instead of me?"

"Because—" She wanted to weep and shriek and fling herself about, but with a hand across her face, forced herself to composure. "Because my faith is settled and my eternal fate secure. Yours is not."

His gaze widened.

"Say it is not so!" she pressed.

He shook his head a little, nostrils flaring. "You cannot know that."

"I can. The entire Scripture speaks of confidence in the finished work of Christ. We can add nothing to it. I trust in Him, so—" Despite the weeping that somehow would not cease, she held her arms up before Blackbird, as Felipe had, and spoke carefully in Skaru:re. "Me—for him. Take me instead."

His eyes glittered, brow lowering again. "You would gladly die rather than be my woman?"

God, give me courage!

"I would die—for him." She gave a single hard nod toward Felipe.

With a growl, he struck her across the face then seized her arm and dragged her toward the town center.

Behind her, someone was putting up a terrific fight—was that Felipe? *Please, Lord, let him do nothing rash. . .*

As they reached the bonfire already being built up where another had burned just days before, a new voice rose above the others. "Ginny! *Ginny!*"

She squeezed her eyes shut. Oh. . .not Henry, not now.

Then he was there as well, demanding—his command of Skaru:re was so much better than hers—wait, what *was* he demanding?

The crowd had stopped to murmur again. Blackbird looked fit to slay anyone within reach. But Henry stood before him, tall and slender, dark eyes full of desperation but not, somehow, as he had been days ago. Ginny thought she glimpsed here the man he might be with more years and growth.

And what were those words coming from his mouth?

Very much like what Ginny herself had just offered.

Me. Take me. Release them. Have I not also given you much trouble?

She collapsed, sobbing. "Oh Henry, no! No, no, no. . ."

What was the young Inglés doing?

Still bound yet desperate not to lose sight of White Doe, Felipe had dragged three or four men along in his pursuit of the crowd. And suddenly, there was Henry, standing before the fire with arms outstretched.

Blackbird grimaced. "What mean you, 'take me'?" He looked at one of his fellow holy men and the other warriors flanking them. "Are all our captives just so eager to die? Have we struck them one too many times in the head?"

Subdued laughter met his words. "Slay them all, perhaps?"

Blackbird firmed his mouth and drew a long breath, nostrils flaring. "No. Just one. We will take the English."

Henry stood proud and calm as the crowd pressed in to seize him. Felipe strained to catch sight of White Doe—there she was, on the ground. As he was pulled forward into the chaos, he angled toward her and dropped to his knees beside her.

"You will watch!" Blackbird shouted, glaring down at them. "Watch or your lives are also forfeit."

Felipe leaned in to communicate the words to White Doe. She lifted her head, aghast. "You must," he said, low but emphatic. "Do not let his sacrifice be in vain. If ever you loved him—as a brother or otherwise—show courage."

He could feel her trembling where their shoulders touched. With no one attending at the moment, he worked loose the knots at his wrists with his teeth.

Another glimpse of Henry through the now-frenzied crowd showed bruises marking the boy's face and rivulets of blood tracking down his body from dozens of small cuts. And yet he did not cry out, but looked almost—joyful.

How? How could that be?

Felipe could not reconcile what he was seeing with the fury he'd witnessed in Henry just days before. He was reminded, then, of the stories he'd been told from boyhood of various saints—those who had become martyrs for the faith, elevated by holy deeds and their ultimate willingness to lay down their lives for Christ. But Henry—this was not that—was it?

Beside him, White Doe rocked, sobbing, eyes glazed with weeping yet valiantly still open.

It was awful. The blood ran more freely, and at last, with cords at wrists and ankles, they suspended him over the fire, where he did at last cry out.

Or was that—a song?

White Doe began to sing as well, tremulously at first then with more strength. Their voices rose together, ragged at times but somehow triumphant.

Felipe could only gape with amazement. He was sure others were as well.

The flames roared with sudden fierceness, and above them rang Henry's voice—a clarion call, inarticulate yet victorious. Chills lifted the hair on Felipe's scalp and swept his entire body.

And then the boy fell limp.

A pair of hands grasped Felipe's shoulders. He nearly yelped—but it was Grandmother Dove, bending over him and White Doe. "Up! Both of you, come with me!"

He did not hesitate but leaped to his feet, helped White Doe to hers, and, gripping her forearm, dived through the crowd with the old woman guiding them.

Faces turned their way, but Grandmother Dove scolded and waved, and somehow they were allowed to pass. She led them to her house and inside.

White Doe collapsed to her knees, weeping. "No, you must get up!" Grandmother Dove shook her, and the girl stared for a moment with no comprehension in her eyes. "Quickly now. Take what you can." She seized a small covered basket and shoved it into Felipe's hands, then White Doe's footwear and what looked like the old tunic. "Put these on," she told the girl, "and hurry!"

While White Doe did so, the older woman rummaged again, found a carrying pouch and waterskin, and shoved them into Felipe's hands. She met Felipe's eyes. "Blackbird may stop at shedding the boy's blood, but he will not forgive. You and the girl must go—now, and far away. Do not return."

"Grandmother," Felipe breathed. "Will they not punish you?"

Her face creased in an uncommon smile, and her hand came up to stroke his cheek. "I am old. You and the girl are not. And she has been helpful and kind when she need not have been. You also. Go then, and live, both of you."

His eyes were stinging. "And what of Redbud?"

Grandmother Dove rubbed her chin. "I will see that he gets away as well."

He tucked the basket under his arm, took White Doe's hand, and, after scouting outside the house, led her away at a run.

She was still weeping. How could she not?

Henry. . .oh Henry! How could you do this? And why?

A part of her wanted to stay, to throw herself into the flames as well. After all, their being captive was her fault to begin with. But somehow her limbs obeyed Granny Dove's frantic exhortation, and though stumbling at times, her feet matched Felipe's pace as the greater part of the town's inhabitants were lost to bloodlust and the fury of jealousy.

My fault. . .all my fault. And now Henry was dead.

They made it, unchallenged, to the edge of town. Felipe paused to look around then led her out past one of the fields to where two deerskins were stretched, drying. He plucked both from their pins and rolled them up, and this time took her hand before setting off again at slightly less of a run than before.

Some distance away, they stopped. Felipe bent, hands on his knees, catching his breath. Ginny dropped to the forest floor and curled up on her side.

God. . .oh God, I dreamed so often of escaping—but not like this. Never like this!

"White Doe. Are you well?"

A single sob jagged through her. "Do—not—call me—by that name."

Silence, filled by the sounds of the forest, then, "What should I call you?"

She shoved herself upright and swiped a hand across her face. Felipe crouched a pace or so away, peering at her.

He looked as broken as she felt.

"Do you not even recall my given name?" She hated the whine in her voice.

His gaze dropped to the ground for a moment. "Jin-nee?"

"You do remember." She drew up her knees and wrapped her arms about them. "It is properly said *Ginny*. Or Virginia. What the English call this land."

He nodded as if familiar with it. "Virginia," he said, his voice so deep and Spanish accent yet so thick, it sounded foreign.

But it was her true name.

Burning filled her eyes, and she squeezed them shut.

"Virginia. We must keep going."

How strange to hear no trace of the mocking tone she'd grown so used to these past months.

"I know," she whimpered, rocking a little. "I know."

Awful images flashed before her—Henry bleeding. . .Henry writhing in the heat, even as he lifted his voice in a hymn. . .

Arms came about her, gently, almost tentatively. She could not help leaning into the shoulder offered and weeping harder.

"What about Redbud?" she asked through the tears. "Do we simply leave him?"

"Grandmother Dove promised to look after him," Felipe said. "I think he is able to find his way home if need be, aye?"

She started to nod, then— "What else did she say to you?"

His arms loosened, and sitting back a little, he looked away. "She said Blackbird likely will not forgive. She wished us to go and not return."

Ginny could only blink. "But—why?"

His eyes came back to hers, red-rimmed and haunted. "For the kindness you have done her even as a captive. For—for the affection she bears for both of us, I think. She is afraid Blackbird will still want blood."

"So what now?"

He rose and held out a hand to help her up. "Do you not also wish to go home? But for today, we should simply put distance between us and Blackbird."

Home.

What a thought.

And at what price.

In the beginning was the sea.

Elinor recalled the constant tossing of the waves while on board the ship. Comparing her belly to Margery's. Laying their babes side by side, after birthing not even a day apart. "What good friends they shall be, growing up!" Margery crowed.

Elinor laughed. "And perhaps more. But only as the Lord wills."

And now both of them were gone, taken at the same time. The hollow ache inside Elinor never quite went away. She could see by the expression on Margery's face that she felt the same.

The island was lovely—comforting and refreshing in so many ways. And yet. . . The absence of Ginny and the boys was as palpable as a missing limb. Some nights she slept well. Others, she woke in the dark and felt a pressing need to pray. Henry especially had been on her heart the last few days, him and his family. She knew Margery was grateful for the health and safety of the children born after Henry, just as she herself was for the children she bore after Ginny, but those blessings did not diminish the loss. None could ever replace another in their hearts.

So she prayed, almost without ceasing. Some days, nearly without hope. Yet she couldn't *not* pray.

Over and over she had to remind herself to commit Ginny to the Lord's hands. On some days she even found a measure of success at leaving her there.

Just days ago, Master Johnson had called for a special prayer meeting on behalf of their captive children. Elinor had found solace, at least for the moment. But each day thereafter, the peace eroded until she'd lie awake late into the night, or awaken in the wee hours, plagued by questions and cares. Mornings brought new strength, or perhaps 'twas merely the necessity of pushing through each day to tend her other children.

On one such morning, she had gone out for a very short walk to the eastern ocean side, but while passing through the forest, she thought she heard the sound of weeping. She stopped to listen. Aye, that was crying, for certain, almost covered by the shush of waves ahead of her. Should she intrude. . . ?

Tucking baby Berry closer in her wrap, she turned aside. The sobbing was clearer now—and then she spied Margery, huddled at the foot of an oak, hands over her face.

Elinor eased herself to the ground beside Margery and put her arms around her. "I know, my friend. I know."

Naught else seemed fitting in the moment.

Gauging the angle of the sun, Felipe led off then peered back over his shoulder.

Virginia. Of course she would be named after the country itself—or the English word for it, at least.

She picked her way after him with grace and nimbleness, despite clutching the rolled deerskins to her chest and despite the tears continuing to pour down her cheeks. He could not begrudge her mourning. The day's events had cascaded too suddenly for mortal belief.

Should he have foreseen Blackbird's abrupt plunge into fury? The Skaru:re holy man had been patient and kind enough with Felipe. But a particular sort of pride was at stake here, with White Doe—Virginia—which Felipe understood. It was why he'd held himself back from allowing himself to even think, much less do, any of what Blackbird had accused him of. Why he'd been so careful to try to aim her attentions and affections in the Skaru:re's direction.

The memory of Henry flooded in. The younger boy's fury as he faced Felipe the morning of the Green Corn Festival. Before that, his eagerness to learn the Skaru:re tongue. How watchful he always was of Virginia.

His insistence on taking Virginia's place. *Her* insistence on taking Felipe's.

It should have been me.

Her words haunted him. *My faith is settled and my eternal fate secure.*

Not a breath of hesitation.

How could she be so firm in her confidence, even so far from the sacraments and graces of the church? She'd gone on to speak of—what was it?—the *finished work of Christ*. What exactly did she mean by that?

He nearly turned to ask, but there would be time enough for conversation later.

In the meantime—should they continue forging through thick forest and undergrowth, or find a deer track to follow? If Blackbird and the others were inclined to track them—or Redbud, for that matter—they probably left more sign in unbroken brush than an established path. On the other hand, they stood in greater danger of meeting other people on a path, and then they would be expected to stop and talk and explain who they were.

And that begged the question, would Blackbird and the others be inclined to pursue them? Would his anger be satisfied with Henry's death? It could, indeed. Since coming to live with the Skaru:re—actually before then, when Papá and the others still lived and traded with the local peoples—he had witnessed countless times when someone's rage flared without warning, the offender would suffer a beating or worse, and then the matter would be considered settled.

Blackbird had said he would be satisfied with the sacrifice of one, even if that one had not directly offended in this case, or at least not in the way Blackbird was aware. But depending upon how deeply he felt the insult, would he change his mind?

Felipe could definitely see Blackbird changing his mind on account of this girl.

Another glance back. Her head was bowed, the golden hair half escaped from its braid. She stumbled but recovered then gazed off into the forest, looking lost.

He could not stop and comfort her again—at least not yet. No matter how strongly he wished to do so. They had to keep moving.

Go, Grandmother Dove had said. *Go and live.*

The basket held a dozen rounds of corn bread, no doubt baked that morning. Not less than two days' worth of food for the old woman, and yet she'd offered it to them and made sure White Doe—Virginia—had shoes and a tunic.

The day passed in a haze. Ginny kept her feet moving, as Felipe had urged her, and the tears kept flowing. Sometimes it was only the wetness pouring down her cheeks, and sometimes soft sobs overtook her.

She never knew a body could weep so and not simply shrivel and die.

'Twas small comfort that Felipe said Granny Dove promised to help Redbud escape as well. She could scarce believe the old woman had helped her and Felipe. In truth, she could find little gratitude at the moment that they'd not also been slain.

Well, that was not completely so. She was grateful for Felipe's life being spared. But hers?

This was her fault. Not Henry's. Certainly not Felipe's.

They came upon another stream, and Felipe made her drink. She found herself gulping greedily, but that only fueled a fresh wave of tears. He sat her down next to the stream and put a round of bread in her hands.

Amazement and confusion put a brief halt to her weeping. "Where did you get this?"

He pointed to the covered basket, which she realized at last was the one Granny Dove had used to store the day's food. "Eat, if you please," he said.

Firmly, yet also with that strange new gentleness.

She didn't think she could, however, and started to hand the bread back. He crouched before her. "I do not tell you not to mourn. But do not fail to honor what Henry has offered for you by refusing to eat when we have it."

Concern shimmered in his blue eyes.

With a small nod, she took a bite. The tears flooded back. The taste of life and nourishment—of which Henry would never again partake...

Felipe's hand brushed her arm. "Was Henry firm in his faith?"

Her gaze sought his again.

"As you said you are. Was his faith as secure as yours? I must believe so, after witnessing how he met his death with song—" He stopped, turned away his face for a moment with a hard breath. "With *song*. I have seen others in similar circumstances, and sometimes there is anger and cursing and sometimes calm. But the way he sang?" His eyes came back to hers. "If his faith was true, then he is with God. Aye, you may sorrow—but you must keep sight of that."

She took another bite, chewed, swallowed.

"Aye, that is it. Eat. Live. For Henry."

He rose and moved away, and with her thoughts settling into a curious flatness, she finished the bread.

Come evening, Ginny sat draped in one of the untanned deerskins and watched as Felipe built a fire. He'd found a sheltered hollow by a stream amongst the slightly rolling country they traveled through and gathered materials. A fallen bird's nest, a stick he handily sharpened on a stone, a chunk of tree branch with a hole to fit the end of the stick. With the bird's nest surrounding the hole, he rolled the stick between his hands until a curl of smoke arose, then bent and blew a little, repeating the process until tiny flames erupted. Clearly, he had much practice at it.

He handed her another piece of the bread and munched on one himself as he fed the fire.

She chewed half of the round, once more battling tears, then stopped and looked at it lying in her hand. "Why did he do it? *Why?*"

"Henry?"

She nodded.

Felipe's gaze was steady upon her. "Do you not know? I comprehend it well enough."

A strange heat spread through her. She huddled deeper in the deerskin—for cover rather than warmth—and glanced away. "It should have been me. 'Twas my fault we were out and taken to begin with."

He finished his bread, frowning, and brushed his palms across each other. "I think that is not how he saw it. Or if he did, it was of no consequence in the moment. He thought only to see your life spared." He reached for the other deerskin and worked it between his hands. "Just as you did, for me."

"As I tried to do, and failed."

He shot her another glance. "Do not despise the fact that you yet live and breathe." He gestured at her hands. "Eat."

She returned to nibbling the bread.

He tucked his head, seeming to examine the deerskin more closely. "I am very grateful you yet live and breathe—even if you are not."

She nearly choked on the last bite. He must have heard it, for he reached for the cup he'd fashioned from a piece of bark and handed it to her. While she drank, he kept working the deerskin. The firelight skimmed his strong cheek and jawline, the side of his head that he'd kept shaved, and dimmed to a bare glimmer in his dark hair, still oiled and caught back in a knot.

An owl hooted, and the thrum of cicadas filled the silence.

Just this morning, Henry still lived and breathed. For a moment, the tiny fire before her evoked a raging bonfire—one he'd willingly submitted to, to keep her alive.

Aye, she knew why, and her own heart bled at the knowledge.

For love.

Henry had loved her, plain and simple. And she'd loved him—though not in the way he'd hoped.

Do not fail to honor that, Felipe had said.

"You should sleep," he said now.

'Twas a simple matter of just lying on her side and tucking the skin more comfortably about her. "So should you."

"I will, in time."

Chapter Thirteen

Felipe thought through all he must do over the next few days. He'd need to make weapons. One of the other streams had provided a piece of flint, big enough to knap into a knife blade or spearhead. A bow and arrows would require time but also be welcome, especially if they hoped to have fresh meat. There were streams aplenty to fill the waterskin.

For a moment he let his gaze trace the firelight playing across the top of Virginia's head. Considering all the anxieties this day had brought—from thinking he'd have to watch her become Blackbird's wife, to witnessing the sudden flare of Blackbird's jealousy and expecting to lose his own life by horrible means—to find himself here, alone with her in deep forest, still seemed beyond belief.

And as she had asked earlier, what now? Where were they to go? It was more than the obvious question of bodily location, although he supposed it must begin there. Return her to her people.

But then—what?

He continued to work the deerskin then turned it skin side out against a curve on the stream embankment and leaned back. He'd keep the fire going as long as possible but watch the dark around them. The wild forest held many predators—not least of all, the two-legged kind.

"How many great rivers did we cross after the boys and I were taken?"

A half night's sleep was not enough, but Felipe bore her questions the next morning with patience. He too would want to know.

"Two," he answered, scanning the forest.

She'd at least kept her voice quiet. Had eaten without complaint—two rounds of bread, even.

"And they flow farther south than we need to go," she said. "The maps of the English show this. Sees Far—my mother's Suquoten husband—has told us that is why when he was returning Mama to our people, he could not merely take a kanoe the entire way, though 'twould have been faster."

"That is a story I would like to hear," Felipe said, and meant it. "But aye, that is also why, when the Skaru:re struck the Kurawoten and English, they went by foot over land and not by water."

" 'Tis a long walk," she said.

"Aye." Now they were only filling space with meaningless talk. But perhaps it helped counter the horror of yestermorn.

While they walked, she kept a deer hide loosely draped around her, skin side in this time. He'd traded her this morning for the one he'd spent much of the night working, and she'd exclaimed at its softness. She carried the other hide under one arm, rolled up, and held the basket in her other hand. He'd passed it off to her while looking for likely arrow and bow shafts. Of those he had a small armload himself.

She still wept, but not with as much force as yesterday.

Silence fell, and they kept moving, with the ground becoming marshier. "When we reach the river," he said, "we'll need to swim."

"I can swim. We all learned, because of the Kurawoten."

He peered at her again. Those golden locks and blue eyes, so misleading. It was no wonder the Skaru:re women praised her. She truly was well skilled in anything a young woman of this land should be.

And it was no wonder Blackbird wanted her. The sweetness in her face. . .

He turned and kept walking.

If they were no longer with the Skaru:re, and Blackbird's will would no longer prevail, did he have the freedom now to admit how he felt about the girl? Perhaps even to speak of it to her and consider whether his path lay with her, or no?

Freedom. It was something he thought he'd enjoyed well enough since becoming an adopted member of the Skaru:re people. And yet, he had not been free at all in regard to her—until now.

He did not know what to think about that. Would she welcome his advances? And did it even matter before he had her safely back to her people?

They stopped earlier on this day, about halfway through the afternoon. Felipe bid Ginny rest while he settled in to sort through the various sticks and things he'd collected.

She curled up and fell asleep almost immediately. When she awoke, the sun was significantly lower, and he'd not only cleaned several arrow shafts and at least one spear, but also knapped a chunk of flint into a workable spearhead and several small arrowheads.

"May I look?" she asked. He nodded and set the largest in her hand. "That is astonishing," she said, turning it this way and that and gingerly testing the edges.

He smiled but thinly as he fitted one of the arrowheads to a shaft.

"Aye, I know—you are Skaru:re, so what else should I expect?" She offered a wry laugh in return so he would know she was jesting, but he kept his chin tucked this time. She sighed. "I am grateful. You have done so much already."

He shook his head a little, fingers still busy. She reached out and laid a hand on his forearm. He went completely still then gulped a breath.

"Why?" she whispered. "You showed such faithfulness and loyalty to Blackbird and the others, even to the point of submitting to being put to death for my refusal."

No response for a moment, then— "It was more than that," he rasped.

"What do you mean?"

He set down the arrow and covered her hand with his, shifting toward her. His face lifted, his eyes glimmering. "He blamed me for turning you

149

against him. For—desiring you for my own."

Her heart gave a leap. "But you didn't—nearly your every word was to nudge me toward him!"

His throat worked. "At first, aye, when it was of no account to me whether you chose him or not. I had only begun to realize—" He shook his head. "It is too soon to speak of this."

He began to pull away, but she gripped his arm harder. "To speak of what?" To his widened eyes, she cried, "Say it! For all that is holy, say it."

Several frantic heartbeats—she could feel his pulse as well as her own—and then he subsided. "Very well. That day I walked away from the two of you, after you spoke of love, I realized I could no longer bear having to mediate. Having to watch him woo you and you become his wife." His lashes—very long lashes they were too—fell slowly then rose. "Though I knew it impossible, rightly did he accuse me of wanting you as well."

Her mouth had fallen open—she could not help it.

"But how? Why?" she asked finally.

The corner of his mouth turned upward. "As Redbud said, everyone loves you."

"Redbud too?"

The weeping overtook her. Once again he gathered her into his arms, and once again she sank into his embrace. 'Twas a comfort she could not deny, at least not in the moment.

And comforting it was, even as the tears continued. How strange as well that his admission did not fill her with alarm or dread—or even dismay, as Blackbird's attentions had, as well as Henry's declaration days ago.

"I do not know how to answer you in this," she said at last.

He smoothed a hand across the deerskin covering her shoulder and seemed in no hurry to release her. "I do not expect one yet. I would not even have spoken, except you needed to know that Blackbird's anger was not wholly on your account, but also mine. Your refusal was indeed a blow to his pride, but—" He drew in a long breath. "He would not be persuaded that I had not betrayed him by stealing your affections."

Ginny pulled away enough to peer into his face. "What was he to you?"

Felipe's blue eyes were grave. "Nearly an adoptive father. An elder brother, certainly. He made it possible for me to become a Skaru:re warrior and not remain a mere slave."

"Ah." She sat farther back and tugged the deerskin more tightly about herself, despite the day's heat, then thought of Granny Dove's last gesture. "Which is also why Granny Dove held such tenderness for you."

He nodded.

"What did she say? I mean. . .I know you did not tell me all of it."

Felipe studied her face then reached up to touch a tendril of her hair. "I asked her whether they would punish her for helping us. She said that she was old, and you and I are not. That we should go, and live. Both of us."

For some reason, that brought another surge of tears. Of course, everything made her cry at the moment. "We should not waste her kindness either."

He tipped his head and gave a little nod. The backs of his fingers brushed her cheeks. Lingering. Stirring a longing for—just what did she long for, anyway? 'Twas as if a sea storm raged across her soul.

"You should know," she said, "I may not be able to give you an answer yet. . .but mayhap 'tis not so impossible as you think. Or—once thought."

His eyes widened then darkened. He leaned in, and before she could even wonder what he was doing, he pressed his lips to hers, soft, warm, and utterly astonishing.

He sat up, gave her a swift, sharp smile, then rose and walked away.

Well, that was not what he had planned at all.

Felipe strode beneath the pines, still within earshot, but far enough, perhaps, to get his breath back and not completely give himself away. This girl—how could her softness and blue eyes call to him so? And that single, brief kiss—so sweet, and yet not enough.

Not nearly enough.

But she needed time. The awfulness of having to witness the death of her childhood companion, and knowing it was on Felipe's behalf as well as her own, would doubtless throw her feelings for Felipe into question sooner or late.

He glanced back. She'd gotten to her feet and was wandering in the opposite direction. Just as well. He needed to finish the weapons.

Virginia had gone just out of sight and he'd but settled in again when her cry split the air. He leaped to his feet and was running, flint blade in hand, without thought.

"*Redbud!*" she shrieked—and indeed it was he, laden with various items, staggering back a little as she reached him and flung her arms about him.

Felipe ignored a sudden barb of jealousy. After all, had it not been in his embrace she'd lingered only moments ago? And indeed, she stepped back quickly enough, wiping away tears.

"You two," Redbud said, looking between them, "make it very difficult to follow. And I was not far behind, or so I thought."

Felipe eyed all that he'd brought—a waterskin, a bow, a handful of arrows, and an additional deer hide, this one well tanned. "But you did track us."

"I did." He hefted his armloads. "Granny Dove sent more provisions."

"Good. Do you know if any followed you?"

Redbud shook his head. "It was a near thing, getting away without being seen. And Blackbird was still in a rage once he found you both were gone." He glanced at Virginia then leveled a look at Felipe. "Did he say the truth regarding you?"

"And what did he say?"

Redbud's dark gaze narrowed. "That you had influenced her against him because you wanted her for yourself."

Felipe flicked the leaves of a nearby bush. "I did everything I could to encourage her to choose him. But as far as my feelings for her—you already knew that aye, he spoke truth."

The Kurawoten lad sniffed. "I didn't see how it could be otherwise." He turned back to Virginia. "And your thoughts on the matter?"

She glanced between them, lips parting and cheeks going crimson, then turned away. Redbud snickered. "So there is at last a warrior to discompose the fair White Doe."

"Do not call me that!" she cried, even as a chuckle worked its way up through Felipe's chest. With both of them laughing, she cast her hands into the air and stomped back toward their makeshift camp.

Felipe beckoned for Redbud to follow.

"Are we for Cora Banks, then?" Redbud asked as they walked. At Felipe's questioning look, he amended, "Our town, over on the Pumtico River."

"Ah." Felipe nodded. "We are resting for a time so I could make a few things we will need." He showed Redbud the larger flint blade in his hand, and the lad expressed his admiration.

Virginia sat huddled in her deerskin, back turned to both of them as they approached. A corner of Felipe's heart crumbled, and he itched to reach for her.

Such a strange impulse.

He knelt beside the arrows and spear he had ready to tip and showed them to Redbud, who nodded approvingly as he set down his own things. "I see you have deerskins as well—from the two you took that day I hunted with you?"

Felipe nodded. "I couldn't see leaving them behind if I could help it."

"How many more days of travel, do you think?"

"I expect to cross the first wide river tomorrow. Perhaps six days beyond, seven at most? Now that we will both have bows, we can hunt along the way, although that will take time."

"Aye." The Kurawoten lad let out a long sigh and put his hands on his knees. "So. . .Henry."

With a sniffle, Virginia swiveled back toward them. "Did you. . .see?"

Redbud seemed to go pale beneath the bronze of his skin. "Not as closely as you two. But I was made to watch as well."

Virginia bent her forehead to her knees.

The next morning, without discussion, it fell naturally that Felipe led, Redbud brought up the rear, and Ginny walked between them.

Boys—men—whichever they were, creatures of the male persuasion—were an odd lot. One moment Felipe behaved in the most tender of ways, holding her close, revealing the softness of his own heart to her—and then to kiss her! In the next, he was sauntering away as if none of it mattered, and when Redbud showed up? They both were laughing at her, or at least at the idea that she harbored any affection for Felipe—as if that were a weakness.

Nay, to be fair, it was that she—a girl who in Cora Banks had not found any prospective suitors appealing in the least—was succumbing to the charms of a formerly captive Spaniard, now Skaru:re warrior, who had not even tried to win her.

Except for that one night, when they had danced together and talked long into the night. . .

She shook off the thought, snatched again at the petulance. Last night and this morning, Felipe behaved as if there was nothing at all between them.

Of course, how would she expect him to act, with Redbud present?

'Twas fitting enough for the three of them to be journeying together now. With Henry gone—oh, and his memory still made her very breath a knife in her breast—what else was there, besides stay with the Skaru:re?

She did not wish to remain where Blackbird could possibly change his mind and force her to be his wife.

"Will we be hunting?" Redbud asked.

"Not until we cross the river," Felipe said.

"Good. I wished to know if we should be quiet so as not to let our food know we are coming."

"We should regardless, in the event others are tracking us."

Ginny's eyes burned. The entire exchange reminded her of Henry, who always chattered too much by half. But she would not bring it up in the moment.

"You truly think Blackbird would pursue us so far?" Redbud asked.

"Aye. If his rage was enough of a thing to fear for Grandmother Dove to send us away—"

Redbud nodded thoughtfully.

"There will be time enough later for talk," Felipe said.

They'd risen with the sun and eaten some of the bread before setting out. About midmorning Felipe stopped for a brief rest and divided the last of the rounds between them. "We shall be crossing the river soon, and the bread will be ruined if we do not finish it."

Thunder rumbled in the distance, to the west.

"Rain would help cover the signs of our passing," Redbud said.

"Ehqutonahas!" Ginny snapped.

Redbud snickered.

Felipe looked over his shoulder at the two of them and smiled. Her heart gave a little leap.

One kiss, and she'd become one of those simpleminded maids? How much more ridiculous could she be?

I thought mayhap you would wait for me. . .

Her cheeks were already wet. "Oh Henry," she whispered, "I am so dreadfully sorry."

'Twas easy now to ask the question, she supposed, but—could she have ever come to love Henry in that way?

Felipe could smell the river before they saw it—a rich, heavy scent of waterlogged wood and rotting vegetation. They worked their way through the brush and emerged at the top of an embankment with the brown surface of the water swirling lazily beyond. A dry stretch, from the embankment to the river's edge, stretched between. "We could go upstream and try to find a ford," he said quietly, once Virginia and Redbud had gathered closer. "Or simply swim across here."

"It looks calm enough," Redbud said. "Although we know that is not always the case once you go in."

Felipe nodded. Perhaps that accounted for his disquiet. . .

A shriek—no, a war cry—split the air behind them. All three of them turned. A war party ran toward them through the brush.

"Blackbird!" he hissed, recognizing the pattern of war paint on the foremost warrior.

Redbud rounded on him. "Take Ginny and go! I'll stay behind and try to delay them."

"What? No!"

The Kurawoten lad gave both of them a shove. "No time! Just *go!*"

Then he ran back to meet the Skaru:re.

Did none of them regard their own lives?

Virginia seemed frozen with dismay. Felipe seized her arm and tugged her down the slope with him.

"Leave the basket," he said, and once she'd dropped it, he pushed her toward the water. "Get in—swim and do not look back!"

He went in after her—not fast enough—oh, not fast enough!

Gracious God, if You see us, if You hear us—

Once in, she went with strong, sure strokes. He kept pace with her and glanced back once, just in time to see Blackbird come to the crest of the embankment and lift his bow.

"Faster!" he said, and with a gulp of air, she did so.

Something hit the water next to him—and again. Virginia cried out. He lifted his head and looked. An arrow protruded from her shoulder.

And she was floundering.

God—oh God—I beg Your mercy! For her, if not for me—but help us!

He hooked an arm around her waist. "Lean into me," he said, shifting her back against his chest then making for the shore.

More arrows hit the water but landed short of them. Felipe cast a glance toward the near bank then behind, where Blackbird lowered his bow and stood watching them.

Would he come after, or did hitting the girl satisfy his anger at last?

His feet struck mud, and he scrabbled to haul himself—and her—out of the water. Blackbird did not move, and Felipe stopped for but a breath or two, staring back at the Skaru:re warrior-priest before lifting Virginia into his arms and carrying her the rest of the way up the bank and into the forest beyond.

Part Two

Interlude

Redbud

P *lease, oh good God, be with me—and with them! And ready my soul to meet You, if that is Your will.*

Redbud pushed Felipe and Ginny away and turned himself to go meet the coming Skaru:re.

Blackbird was in the lead, teeth bared against the red and black of his war paint. He motioned to the others. "Take hold of him!" he snarled, blowing past Redbud completely.

Protect them, oh God!

He braced for the onslaught of the others and was not disappointed. He bore with patience being shoved to his knees and stripped of all his weapons and gear.

At least he was not immediately slain, though they did not spare him a few cuffs.

God, help me. . .

On his knees, hands bound behind him, he waited. Blackbird returned shortly.

"Did they escape?" someone asked.

"One of my arrows struck the girl," Blackbird growled. "If it is deep enough, she will not survive."

"And Guh-neh? Shall we go upstream to ford across and pursue?"

"He is no longer worth my effort." The warrior-priest fastened his glare upon Redbud. "You, however. Do you wish your blood to flow with honor as your companion's did? Or shall we leave you for the beasts to consume here in the forest?"

Redbud thought his command of Skaru:re good enough to comprehend most of that. "I would ask, oh great one, that you would listen to my words before I am given to either end."

Chapter Fourteen

A flash of pain—and her arm would not work properly. The cool of the river swallowed her for a moment before a band of iron caught her about the middle and a warbling shout penetrated the haze with words she really ought to understand.

More pain—she was supposed to be swimming—why all the yanking about? Then—dry ground, and she was lifted—

The world tipped about her, and the forest closed in once more, rushing past. The bouncing hurt. She fought for breath.

Finally—mercifully—all went dark.

Felipe ran until his lungs and limbs burned. Even if Blackbird did not take up the chase again, they needed distance—and better that his legs accomplish that for both of them while they could.

At last, however, he stumbled to a stop and scouted for a likely patch of earth. He found it—a tiny stretch of mossy ground overlooking a clear stream—and lowered Virginia, still limp in his arms, carefully arranging her face down. He turned her head to one side and lifted the wet, loosened locks of her hair away from her cheek and wounded shoulder, which happened to be the one not covered by her tunic, then straightened the edge of her skirt across the back of her thighs.

He had tried not to jostle her unduly, but a certain amount could not be helped. Tucking the edge of her tunic under itself to further expose the wound, he bent closer. The wound still seeped around the arrow shaft. Impossible to tell how deeply the point had penetrated—but it must come out.

With a deep breath, he stepped back and untied the thong he'd used to bind his own newly made bow and arrows to his back. Awkward as it was, he was glad now there was something left of the past day's efforts. The spear shaft he had lost, but the knapped head was still, incredibly, tucked into his waistband.

He looked at the tip of the spearhead, then at the arrow protruding from Virginia's shoulder. A crude enough tool, perhaps, but it offered more leverage than his arrowheads.

At the stream, he washed his hands and the spearhead then returned to kneel at Virginia's side. His stomach threatened for a moment to give up its contents, but he shoved aside the feeling and gingerly probed the area around the wound with his fingertips. Pulling back the flesh at the opening revealed nothing. He sat back. It had to come out. There was no other choice, short of leaving it to fester.

He slipped the tip of his smallest finger into the wound, again ignoring the sickness welling up. Was that the edge of an arrowhead? Perhaps it wasn't buried as deeply as he feared. Perhaps—

He took hold of the arrow shaft with both hands, positioned himself for the best angle. Snapped closed his eyes and gulped a deep breath.

It must be done.

Gracious God, guide my hands!

Another breath, and then he pulled—hard and swiftly. With a little catch it came free, and blood welled from the hole. "*Dios—Dios mio*," he panted, looking about for something—anything—to stanch the flow. Yet perhaps it was better to let it bleed, at least a little. It appeared a steady stream and not pulsing, which he knew to be more dire. On impulse, he placed both hands on either side of the wound and gently pressed inward. That helped somewhat.

He held the position so long, Virginia began to stir. "Lie still," he told her softly.

Her lashes fluttered, and her lips worked then pulled back in a grimace. "Where—what—"

"We are past the river, but you are wounded. One of Blackbird's arrows struck you."

She swallowed. Her eyes came completely open. "Only one?"

He gave the ghost of a chuckle. "Aye. I have pulled it out, but you must not move yet."

"I think—I am content with that."

He did laugh then, and a tiny smile curled her mouth.

Just as quickly, he sobered. "I am holding the wound closed but will be letting go. Lie still."

When he eased his hands away, there was no significant increase in the bleeding. With a huff, he sat back and swiped a forearm across his brow. "I need to find something with which to pack the wound. I cannot seem to recall what Grandmother Dove would use, but I must go search."

Her eyelids rose and fell. "I shall be here."

He smoothed her hair back from her face then bent and gently kissed her temple. "Are you well otherwise?"

"Aye, tolerably well." She barely breathed the word, but another smile lingered. As he went to move away, she half reached for him with her unaffected arm. "Felipe?"

"Aye?" He crouched at her side again.

"Where is Redbud?"

He caught her hand and laced his fingers with hers. She craned her neck enough to meet his eyes, but the words stuck in his throat. He could only shake his head.

As he knew she would, she dissolved into tears again. He bent to put his forehead to hers and gave in to the burning of his own eyes.

After a little while he rose, with another quick press of his lips to her temple. "I shall return soon."

He glanced around to make sure they were still alone and to make note of landmarks—the peculiarities of the trees, which included a stand of lovely, sprawling oaks, and the lay of the stream—then wandered first in a rough circle. Soft sniffling and the cadence of her breaths told him she continued to weep, but he had delayed long enough in dressing the wound.

The forest lay tranquil in the heavy afternoon sunshine. Birdcalls, the buzzing of bees—was there a hive nearby? Grandmother Dove had made poultices with honey. Could he obtain some without arousing the bees?

Another thought came to him as he crossed the stream for the second time, and he turned aside to follow the chuckling trickle, keeping watch as he went. Though he had let down his guard to comfort Virginia, it was yet possible that Blackbird would pursue and attack.

Not just Henry, but Redbud too.

Both of them, gone.

Even if she made it back to Mama and the others, how would she face them, knowing she was to blame for the entire matter? And then being the only one to survive?

Simply breathing was an agony at the moment.

God. . .Lord God of heaven and earth, why have You let me live? Why not take me as well?

Like the softest whisper came an echo. *Do not waste their sacrifice.*

She sobbed harder at that.

And then there was Granny Dove's admonition. *Go. Live.*

'Twas not fair. Not to the boys, certainly not to their families and the entire community. Henry and Redbud were much loved. The men had been in the process of planning their huskanaw.

Come to think, if the men and boys had been away for that, how might the attack by the Skaru:re have gone differently?

But she could not ponder that. Could only return time and again to that last carefree run through the forest to her favorite spot on the creek bank. The soft, good-natured squabbling between herself and the boys.

Might it even have been better to give herself as wife to Blackbird? Henry and Redbud would have fumed, but they'd have been alive.

There was no going back, however. 'Twas impossible to do anything but take the path stretching before her.

I want to die as well, oh Lord.

Nay, child. 'Tis My will that you live.

In this moment, living apparently meant enduring an arrow wound and searing loss—both of which kept her pinned to the forest floor, watering the earth with her tears.

Soft footsteps told her that Felipe had returned. At least, she hoped it was him. A jolt of alarm forced her eyes open and lifted her head.

He crouched beside her. Never had blue eyes in a warrior's face been so reassuring. Ignoring the twinge in her shoulder, she bent her arm so she could encircle his ankle with her fingers.

"No—lie still," he admonished her, but softly. "You will start the bleeding again."

He didn't push her hand away, though, and it seemed when he shifted, it was to accommodate her touch. Out of the corner of her eye, she watched him tuck a fragment of reddish material into his mouth and chew. Finally he extracted the wad. "This might sting."

Sting it did, as he applied what she presumed was the masticated bit before standing up and moving away again. When he returned, there was a tickle and then a cool weight over the whole area.

"What—did you find?" she asked, still gritting her teeth.

"*Anéhsnaçi*, then the fluff from *una:kwéya* and mud over all. But you must remain still."

"I will—need to get up at some point."

He swiped his arm across his forehead, looking as if he had not thought of that. "Stay still as long as you can, then."

He was up and gone again but came back shortly. This time he sat down fully, where she could see him.

"Now what?" she murmured.

His gaze swept across her. "Rest."

For an instant, she wanted to protest. But then, incredibly, she let her eyes drift closed and did just that.

She awoke later to the sun slanting low through the trees and Felipe stretched out beside her, hands folded over his chest and eyes closed. 'Twas difficult to decide which to give greater attention to—but the lean, muscled young warrior won out, and she let herself study him while he lay unawares.

The barest shadow of a beard outlined his jaw and chin, with a matching stubble beginning to fill in the side of his head. Worked copper ornaments glinted in his earlobe and around his neck, studded with bits of pale pink and creamy white shell and glimmering green gems. His chest rose and fell with deep, even breaths, with not an ounce of spare flesh in sight anywhere on his form. The skin markings on his arms and legs begged to be traced with a fingertip.

Cheeks flaming, she dragged her gaze back to his face, to the long lashes gracing his cheekbones, the high, arched brows, the full lips, slightly parted. If she were not lying here wounded, perhaps she'd be the one to bend over him and press her own mouth to his—

She snapped her eyes shut. She was indeed wounded, and her bladder pained her most insistently. She needed to get up, but for nothing so frivolous as a kiss.

Gingerly, sucking in her breath as silently as she could against the aches that sprang from everywhere, she rolled to her good side and eased up to her knees, bracing with one arm while holding the other to her chest. Up now, carefully staying half bent so as not to dislodge the work he'd done. . .

She was halfway to her feet, braced on one knee, trembling with the effort and trying not to make a sound, when Felipe stirred. "What are you doing?" He sprang up and reached to steady her.

"I—need—" she gritted out, and he nodded.

"Come." He helped her up the rest of the way, making sure her arm stayed bent at the proper angle.

"The wound hurts less," she said.

They walked a little way, and then he turned his back, reluctance lining his face. He let her proceed by herself and take care of her business. 'Twas awkward and slow, but not as impossible as she'd expected.

"Back to resting with you," he said when she was done.

Felipe sat awake long after sunset had made the western sky brilliant and the first stars came out. Dare he sleep? Bears and wildcats prowled, and this girl lay in the open with a fresh wound in her back. He built a fire, stoked it, then lowered himself to Virginia's side.

He'd not touch her, yet stay within arm's reach. She lay half curled, facing the fire, her good arm bent beneath her head and the other positioned to accommodate the wound. His dressing was holding up well.

He reached out and very gently lifted a loose lock of her hair, winding it around his finger, marveling at the silky softness of it. He'd promised not to press her for an answer—how could he, given the circumstances, with the certain loss of one childhood companion and the possible loss of another? Just the thought of it reawakened the old ache in his chest. Papá and the others falling beneath the cudgels of Native warriors, their own martial training all for naught.

He leaned close enough to lift the lock to his nose and inhale. A fresh ache bloomed.

Wait. He must wait. For her sake. For his own.

It wasn't as if he didn't still quake from the sundering of his loyalty to Blackbird. To the Skaru:re as a whole. These people had been his family for—for too many years to count.

And now what? Would Virginia's people accept him? Or would his being Spanish prove too insurmountable? He recalled well enough how Papá and the other men spoke of the English.

He rubbed the lock of hair slowly between his fingers. Let his gaze trace the curve of her shoulder and hip. Virginia, however, was simply herself. Of no particular country, unless that be this one. Truly a child of this land, as much so as any winsome Skaru:re maiden and every bit as lovely. No, more.

He lowered the lock of hair and stretched out beside her. He was asleep nearly before he closed his eyes.

Sometime in the night, she began to shiver and mumble in her sleep.

Felipe rolled toward her and touched her shoulder. Her skin was fiery. But when he gingerly draped his arm across her waist, she burrowed back against him and seemed to settle.

Fever. He should have expected it with the wound. After the exertion of their flight, however, and the distress of Henry's death, she was likely more susceptible.

The night was already warm, and his body heated even more where hers touched, for reasons that had nothing to do with her response to the wound. But he'd not deny her comfort and warmth. He slid his arm more firmly about her and tucked her closer.

Morning found him bathed in sweat. To his memory, though, she had slept more soundly, and she did not stir as he detached himself from her, carefully, painfully, and rolled away. With a last look, he stepped down to the stream to wash. The handfuls of cold water he sluiced across chest and shoulders were bracing, refreshing. He followed with more, over his head, until his hair was soaking and his entire upper body satisfyingly clean.

He looked back over at Virginia, still slumbering. Red patches marked her cheeks, but white edged her complexion beneath.

She'd need something for the fever and the pain. Willow? Had he seen some nearby?

He set off downstream.

She woke feeling heavy. Her entire body hurt in ways it had not since. . .

Since the Skaru:re had first taken her.

Her eyes opened to a sky flocked with small clouds beyond the treetops. She went to rise, and a flash of agony across her back made her instantly sorry. A cry escaped her before she could stop it.

How had she managed this yesterday, the getting up? That's right—arm against her chest, roll to her knees, brace with her good arm.

Breathing deeply against the pain and effort, she managed it at last. The world tipped around her, and she waited for it to steady before shuffling away to find a suitable place to tend her needs.

And where was Felipe?

She managed what she needed then made her way to the stream, where she knelt and scooped a handful of water to splash on her face and another to drink. The chill in the water made her shiver, but her skin felt warm to the touch, even to herself.

Was she feverish? And what would Mama do in such a case?

She made herself take another drink then sat down, very carefully, on the stream bank, leaning over her knees.

She was so, so tired.

He returned with several strips of fresh willow bark. She would need to chew a piece, since they had nothing with which to brew an infusion.

His heart dropped at finding their small campsite empty. He scanned the area and at first found nothing—but then spied her, half sitting, half slumped over, on the ridge of the stream bank. He strode over and crouched beside her. "Virginia?"

Her eyelids fluttered then squeezed shut. "So tired," she whimpered.

"Come lie down over here, where there is more room." He patted her arm, which brought only a shaking of her head, and he contemplated just lifting and carrying her.

This was the worrisome part. How long would the fever last? Would weakness from the wound prevent her from walking on her own? He had known of strong warriors dying from infection from such wounds, if not tended properly, or even being maimed. And the summer days may be hot, but with the fever making her feel chilled, how was he to warm her? A fire and his own body heat again? He'd nothing with which to cover her after losing both of his deerskins.

There was the option of hunting, of finding at least a small deer. Or. . . He grimaced. They could not be too far from another town. Any

Skaru:re would gladly show him hospitality—as long as they had not already heard the news of what took place with Blackbird. But if word reached them of Virginia being an escaped captive, then what awaited them might be worse than before.

And he sometimes forgot, after being with the Skaru:re for so long, but with his blasted blue eyes, he could not pass as one of the People.

He looked at the willow bark in his hand then at the girl lying asleep on the stream bank and tucked the strips away into his carrying pouch. No sense in waking her just yet.

Raking his hands across his head, he walked back and forth. What should he do? The impulse washed through him to reach out—upward—for divine assistance.

But what would prayer avail him? He recalled too well the dying pleas of his father and other men, some interspersed with curses. God had not intervened on their behalf. Did He even hear?

And yet, Felipe had nothing else left. Nor could he face the hours ahead without so much as trying.

Dios. . .Dios mio. . .

His hair loosened under his fingertips, and he jerked away the thong holding the length of it back, finding a sliver of relief in combing through it and massaging his scalp. How was it the priests and bishops had prayed? "*In nomine Patris,*" he muttered, "*et Filii, et Spiritus Sancti. . .*" No, no, that was the close of prayers. He tried again. "*Gloria Patri, et Filio, et Spiritui Sancto.*"

He huffed. Nothing he could recall felt of use. How *did* one properly speak to the God of heaven and earth? Was it only with chanted verses committed to memory, accompanied by song and incense and flickering candles? Was it in the way of the Skaru:re, with cries of passion and tobacco tossed in the air or thrown in the fire? Or worse, with blood and fire?

Or—like Papá and the other men, with the name of God on their lips even as they perished?

Show me, oh Lord! Show me how I approach You in this land so far distant from that of my birth, where I first learned of You. Was it You who preserved my life after taking those of Papá and the others? And for what purpose? Am I to be shown more sorrow, or is there joy on this path?

He pushed aside the swirl of anger and despair and looked once more at the slender girl slumbering a few paces away. This was for her sake, not his.

The thought of a world without her in it—the hollowness came roaring back.

Lord—oh Lord God, whose hands shaped the earth and sky, help me! Help us. Let her live. Oh God, let her live! And—if it please You—help me to be what she needs. To be the sort of man she would choose.

The strength of his feeling rose up and caught him about the throat.

If she does not live, neither do I wish to continue breathing. If that is cowardly, so be it.

And to think she nearly gave her life, just days ago, in exchange for his. *My faith is settled*, she had said.

How did one accomplish that?

He paced again, scanning the forest about him. Perhaps—perhaps more of an attitude of humility was required. Feeling vaguely foolish, he sank to his knees, but to his shock, his eyes burned with the motion.

So many years it had been since he had knelt within the cool shadows of a church. . .

Show me, oh Lord. . . Show me what more I must do. I am but one soul, adrift in this land and so far from those who instructed me in Your ways. But if You see me, if You hear me, then I beg You to restore this girl to health.

His breath caught in his throat.

Please. Restore her. And—if I may ask—grant me to know You better. Settle my faith—as hers is settled.

He sank farther, head bowed, arms outstretched and resting on the ground, palms upward.

In the name of the Father, and Son, and Holy Spirit. All glory be to You, oh God.

For the first time in his memory, those words did not feel rote.

Chapter Fifteen

H ow long he stayed there, he did not know, only that he was stiff and not a little sore when at last he stirred and climbed to his feet. Virginia still slept, although she mumbled and shifted when he laid the back of his hand to her forehead. Slightly less warm than last night.

He dared not move her yet, not with the wound so fresh. He'd need to change the dressing soon, however. And in the meantime, he wasn't sure he could bear simply sitting and doing nothing.

He examined his bow and arrows—all dry now after their swim, and thankfully undamaged. Another glance toward Virginia. He should not need to hunt far.

If You would also send me a deer—or whatever would meet our need—I would be most appreciative.

Something prickled across his awareness. He froze, looking around— and there, past the oaks, a yearling buck picked his way across a glade carpeted with ferns.

It surely could not be that easy. But he crouched, fitting an arrow to the bow as he stepped a little closer. Then he drew himself up and the bowstring back—

And shot. The arrow sailed true and caught the buck just behind the shoulder. The creature leaped and then fell dead there in the glade.

Ginny woke chilled and thirsty. Favoring her shoulder and arm, she dragged herself to the stream's edge and dipped several handfuls of water.

Did she smell meat roasting?

She crawled back up the stream bank to find—aye, a small deer on a spit over a fire and Felipe a short distance away scraping the hide. His back was to her or he'd surely have marked her being awake and moving already.

Well, "being awake" was a bit of a stretch. So was "moving," come to think of it.

Trying her voice, she said, "You've been busy."

It came out as a croak, and he whirled, the flint blade gripped in his fist, half lifted. The arm lowered a little once he saw 'twas her, relief and concern flooding his eyes.

"Did you speak?" he asked.

She repeated the words, and after a moment's hesitation, he gave a single exhale—a rueful laugh—then, to her astonishment, grinned.

"Indeed," he said.

Would he explain what was so amusing?

But no, he shook his head and came toward her. "Be you well?"

She shivered and scooted herself closer to the fire. Ah, blessed warmth. "Remains to be seen."

His gaze lingered on her, then he nodded and returned to his task.

Well, then.

She poked at the deer. A bit longer before 'twas ready. A wave of weariness overcame her again, and she lay down, close enough to enjoy the heat but not so much she'd scorch herself.

After a bit, Felipe went to the stream and washed then returned to the fire to also check the meat. He took the flint blade, still dripping, sliced off a strip, and offered it to Ginny.

It might have been the finest venison she'd ever had. But then he ruined it by handing her a strip of something that looked suspiciously like a wood shaving and bid her chew it. "Willow bark," he said, "for the pain and fever."

She did, though 'twas bitter as anything, and her jaw ached with the accomplishment.

When she'd borne it as long as she could and at last spat it back into her hand and tossed it into the fire, Felipe smiled and cut her another piece of venison. Then a third.

"I did not realize how hungry I was," she said, accepting the last piece.

Afterward she slept some more, woke to eat and drink again, then fell back asleep.

Despite the willow bark and the fresh dressing on the wound, her fever climbed again that evening. The fire offered little comfort at that point, so after he'd finished cutting up the meat, he hung it up in a tree a short distance away, using the deer's own washed-out intestines, and returned to lie at her side again. This time, no matter how he tucked her against him, she remained restless, crying out now and again. At times her words were incomprehensible; at others. . .

She rose half up in the middle of the night, screaming Henry's name, thrashing. Trying to be mindful of her wound, he tightened his arms about her. "Shh," he murmured.

With a wail, she collapsed against him. He drew her closer, stroking her hair, pressing his lips to her forehead. "Virginia. I am here. You are safe."

"No—nooooo. Not safe. Never again. . ."

He closed his eyes, absorbing her shudders. What could he do that would calm her?

Dios mio. . .

"Most gracious God, be with us." The whisper came from his lips nearly without thought. "Shield us, protect us." Then, "*Pater Noster, qui es in caelis, sanctificetur nomen tuum. . .*"

As the long-forgotten words poured from him, gaining strength with each phrase, she quieted. Her body still trembled, but somehow she understood and echoed the closing *Amen*.

Two more times during the night she woke, in the grip of whatever nightmare afflicted her. He repeated the prayer over her, adding his own words as seemed fitting in the moment, and each time her distress subsided. The second time, as she went limp in his arms, cheek pressed to his chest with her hair spilling across both of them, he thought of the strangeness of holding her so closely. He perhaps better understood Blackbird's ire at Felipe touching her, however thoughtlessly or innocently. Not that he hadn't comprehended it then, but to be so careful about it before, and now be forced to hold and comfort her? It almost seemed too much.

And yet, he realized he'd not trade it for anything. And whether, at the end of this path, she'd consent to being his wife or whether she'd send him away—that mattered not in this moment. He'd savor what he was given.

Even holding her while stretched out on the hard ground, feeling too hot at the touch of her feverish skin, letting her be draped across his chest so as to put no pressure on the wound.

Gracious God, if You hear me and it is acceptable for me to ask this, I would like very much to be the one she chooses as husband. Or, if I am once again preparing and preserving her for another, help me to bear it. But I love her. God help me, I do.

She woke with the barest memory of a dream of ice and fire. Her back and shoulder ached with the moving of an arm, but all else was pleasantly warm.

A steady heartbeat drummed beneath her ear.

Her breath caught, and she pushed up—oh, too soon, it hurt—and Felipe's eyes opened sleepily into her own.

Oh. *His* warmth. His heartbeat.

For a moment she could not move. Then, with a hiss at protesting muscles and torn flesh, she somehow got a knee and elbow beneath her and pushed off of him.

Her cheeks burned, though it was not as if she could have helped the situation. But still she looked away and put all her effort into getting up.

He rolled quickly in the other direction and scrambled to help her. "You suffered nightmares last night?"

She nodded cautiously.

"Henry's death?"

"Mmm—and the pain of my wound. The fever in general, I suppose."

She stood, feeling a bit shaky. Her hair hung half loose, and she swiped at it. Would she be able to braid it if she brought it forward over her shoulder? She looked up to find Felipe standing before her.

"What do you need?" he asked.

Half a laugh escaped her. "Besides a long soak in the river?" She batted at her drooping, tangled locks again. "My hair—"

He nodded once and, stepping behind her, lifted the entire mass back over her shoulder. "I shall try to be gentle," he said.

She felt herself flushing even more. Then, for lack of anything better to do, she closed her eyes. Despite the tug on her sore scalp, his finger-combing efforts were obscurely comforting.

Much like the dilemma of waking up in his arms this morning.

"Which of the peoples along the coastlands are friends with your people?" he asked suddenly, while working with her hair.

"The Cwareuuoc. Manteo married a woman of their towns. And the Newasiwoc. Those are the only ones I can think of to the south and west of Cora Banks." She peered at him from the corner of her eye. "Why?"

"I am thinking. Perhaps it would be faster to go there first, especially if you have difficulty traveling as quickly as we would like."

"That may be a good plan." The longing to see Mama and Papa Sees Far and the rest of her family, though, stirred an impatience within her.

He gave a last series of small tugs to her hair then released it. "There. I have braided it as well as I could." He brought the length of it forward again for her to see. It was surprisingly clean and smooth. "I thought that easier than trying to tie it up in a knot," he added, somewhat apologetically.

"Thank you. This is wonderful." She fingered the end of her braid where it hung near her hip, slightly curling, and angled a look at him again. His own hair appeared somewhat mussed, and on impulse she asked, "How long is your warrior's lock, and how long have you been growing it out?"

The corner of his mouth lifted in a wry smile, and he reached up to loosen the thong holding the knot at the nape of his neck. The glossy, dark brown mass fell across his chest to his waist, slightly wavy, not as deep black as that of the People but nearly so. "Four or five years now, I think," he said.

Her fingers itched to touch it. What hindered her? He'd had no such hesitation when it came to helping with hers. But she could not help him, and they were not yet so familiar with each other that she felt she could do so without good reason.

Although, if he could hold her while she slept. . .

That was only because of her wound.

She did not recall reaching out, but her fingers wound through the smooth, heavy, oiled length. It was finer, softer, than her brothers' hair or what she remembered Sees Far's feeling like when she'd played with his as a small child.

Felipe shifted closer, and she was suddenly aware of his quickened breathing. He also reached up, brushing the backs of his fingers against her cheek. "The fever seems to be lessened this morning. You should still chew some willow bark for the pain."

Ensnared by the deep blue of his eyes, she gave the barest nod. Her own heart fluttered madly, and when he bent to press his lips to her fore-head, she could only lean into it.

He pulled away, and disappointment swirled through her. But then he kissed the tip of her nose and nudged her chin higher before settling those velvety lips full against her own. And she melted—into his arms, against his chest, into the kiss itself. Once, twice, three times, each one lingering a little longer than before.

She felt like a blossom of the great magnolia tree opening for the first time under the warmth of the sun.

He broke the kiss but still cradled her close. "Virginia," he breathed against her bare shoulder.

Why did she so love the way he said her name?

And why did she find herself so pliable in his embrace, when they'd settled no more between them of spiritual matters than she and Blackbird had? And the thought of that one holding her...

Yet here she was, feeling like she'd be happy to spend half an eternity being kissed by this wild Skaru:re-Spanish warrior. Because she'd no illusions, having grown up with English and Kurawoten boys alike, that he was anything resembling tame on the average day.

Time was when that repelled her. With Felipe, it only added to his appeal.

With a deep sigh, he straightened, set her back from him, and gathered up his hair. But his gaze did not leave hers, and a strange little smile played about his lips. "Do you think you can walk a bit today?"

"I will certainly try."

A sudden chill made her fold her arms about herself. He finished tying his hair up then drew her back into his embrace. "We will rest when you need to."

She could not resist laying her head against his chest again. "We also need to cover as much distance as possible."

"I am only mindful of your well-being," he said.

She smiled.

"Virginia," he said softly.

"Aye?"

His thumb smoothed across her shoulder. "I have asked this already, but this time, it is for myself. What is it you wish in a suitor?"

The sun itself surely blazed inside her in this moment. She pressed her cheek a little more firmly against his chest, and a chuckle escaped her. "My answer to that has not changed."

His arms tightened, yet she could tell he was mindful of her wound. "So. Love."

She nodded.

"And a man who is a Christian."

She lifted her head and looked at him—so close she could kiss him again. "Not just a man who calls himself a Christian, but one who truly endeavors to follow Christ."

He gave the barest nod. "Even as a child, I could tell the difference between those who took the name of Christ but cared only for their own interests, and those who did try to obey what is right."

"'Tis the same among the English."

"Then. . ." Felipe's arms loosened, and he turned her to examine the dressing over her wound. "Were you—how do you say it?—*bautizo* when you were born?"

"Christened?"

"Aye, that is it. Were you christened?"

"Aye—the Sunday after my birth. I was the second to be baptized a Christian here in the New World. Manteo was the first." She swallowed, softened her voice. "Henry was the third."

And then she was weeping. Felipe pulled her back into his arms.

How could she forget, even for a moment? To stand here so blithely and—and let Felipe kiss her, with Henry gone in such an awful way? After he'd so recklessly declared himself that morning not so many days ago?

Why could she not have found it in her heart to answer him, to at least try to return his love, even if only in word? Surely he'd deserved more regard from her than that.

And how was it not dishonoring to his memory to so easily let herself be drawn to another?

Not that she could find it in her to move, even now, as Felipe's hands smoothed across her back, oh so careful to avoid the wound, seeming not to mind as her tears once again wet his chest.

It was almost worth her tears to be able to hold and comfort her—but they dared not linger much longer.

As her weeping subsided and she pulled away, wiping her face, he cupped her shoulders. "If you can face walking a while, we should go." She nodded, so he went on, "The dressing is still sticking well enough for now. I will gather what we need on the way."

He strapped on his bow and arrows, took down the bundle of meat, and scanned the area to find a direction. "Stay close," he said.

She looked lost and distressed but trailed after.

"You asked about christening?" she said finally.

He glanced back, watching to gauge her strength. "Aye. If you were christened, and so was I, and we were both given a religious upbringing, where then is the difference between us?"

She drew in a long breath then let it out in a sigh. "That is a good question." Her gaze drifted back to him. "Perhaps the difference lies in a counterquestion. What is your present commitment to Christ and to His ways? It matters not if you were born and reared a Christian, if you abandon your faith upon reaching your majority."

He gave her a thoughtful nod. His prayers of the past two nights. . . Did that qualify as more commitment? Yet he would not say that aloud or tell her. Some things were between him and God alone, and he was still doubtful that God would even hear him.

Except, there was the matter of the deer. . .

He kept watching her, and she kept trudging, and soon they came to a creek surrounded by marshy ground on either side. Felipe led her upstream until he found a place to ford, and then they went slowly through the amber water, his arm about Virginia's waist to steady her and give her strength.

Afterward, she rested while he gathered more fuzzy heads of the una:kwéya, which he tucked into his carrying pouch before they set off again.

Sometime around midday, he took special note of the paleness of her face and the unsteadiness of her step. Would she not call halt with the weariness? Or would she indeed keep driving herself until she fell with exhaustion?

Pretending it was for his own hunger, he stopped them, built a fire, and set some of the meat over it to cook. She stretched out nearby and was asleep in an instant.

Unease swirled through him as he tended the meat and checked his weapons. Had something shifted within her that morning, to make her suddenly so distant? Perhaps he should not have given in to the impulse to kiss her. He had little enough experience in such things, but she certainly had not seemed offended by that. It was not until mention of Henry...

Of course. She was mourning Henry and likely would for some time. He thought of how long it had taken him to stop feeling as if whole limbs were missing after the deaths of Papá and the others.

Did that mean he had erred in kissing her, or no? He did not mean to make it seem as though he did not care. But he could not resist in the moment.

Patience. He must have patience with her.

"Tell me the story of your mother's captivity," Felipe said.

Ginny lay on her belly, wound stinging and sore after washing in a stream. Her head ached, and so did the rest of her. But talking was a welcome distraction as Felipe once again packed and dressed the wound.

"There was a feud between Wanchese and Manteo," she began. "They both crossed the sea to England, then returned. Manteo continued helping the English, but Wanchese disappeared into the wilderness, determined to be their enemy.

"My mother came on—oh, 'twas the third voyage of the English to this country. Her father had been commissioned to take notes and paint to life the people here and all else that he witnessed. On this third voyage, when they brought women and children along to begin to populate a new colony, he was appointed governor. During the first week, one of the men wandered too far alone, hunting for crabs, and was found cruelly slaughtered by—well, they knew not who. After inquiring with Manteo's people, on Kurawoten, they learned it was the Suquoten.

"The English had made enemies of the People on the mainland already. Eventually, my grandfather the governor was made to return to England for more support. My mother and father and others had been left on Roanoac, where there were few resources for them to live for long, and after a bit of time, the English moved south to live with the Kurawoten for safety. My mother had even been confronted in the forest by a lone Suquoten warrior, who all but vanished into the fog when she looked away." Ginny smiled, knowing the identity of that warrior, but she was spinning a story for Felipe.

"So they lived on Kurawoten for two or three years, but a particularly bad sea storm caused them to seek a new place to live, on the mainland. Thus Cora Banks, near the Coree people, was born.

"Meanwhile, Wanchese and his friends kept watching the English, seeking an opportunity to afflict them. One of those friends was Sees Far, son of the Suquoten weroance Granganimeo, who died of a strange sickness spread from the English before my father and mother's coming. He saw my mother—indeed, he was the mysterious warrior who appeared to her and then disappeared—and during an attack the year I would turn three, he took her as his captive."

She peeked back over her shoulder as Felipe packed mud across the cattail fluff dressing. He saw her looking and nodded.

"I heard whispers of this," he said. "Go on."

"My mother and the other captives were taken to Okisco, who decided they should be sold farther inland. 'Tis one of the great trading towns where all the eastern peoples meet—the Suquoten, the Weopomeioc, and I suppose the Skaru:re and others."

"Aye. I know of it."

"Well, on the way, Manteo and my father and others caught up. As my mother and the other men tell it, my father acted hastily upon seeing her used very ill by Wanchese, who could not contain his anger toward the English. My father went in to rescue her and was killed on the spot. Sees Far and Wanchese escaped with Mama and the rest of the captives.

"They were then taken and sold to a weroance who wanted to keep them for working copper at Ritanoe. Sees Far followed on some pretext, having decided that my mother was his to look after. In some time, he earned and hunted enough to buy her back for himself.

"When he tells the story. . ." Ginny giggled as Felipe sat back, finished with his task and listening. "He says he had not yet decided where to go or what to do. She had recently discovered herself with child—my little sister by my father, Ananias. Thus Sees Far would not take her as wife. He told us that Mama's continued sweetness and gentleness won him over, however, and so even without her requesting he do so, he started the long journey of returning her to our people."

Felipe was looking at her in a most inscrutable way, one brow lifted slightly.

"What?" she asked

At first he only shook his head, but then he said, "I wonder. . .whether I might have met him." His glance strayed then came back to her. "Shortly after we returned to our town, a band of warriors came seeking you and the lads."

Her breath caught in her throat. All this time, and they'd not known. "Were Henry and Redbud aware?"

"No." His brows now knit, he went on, "They told us they were Kura-woten, but one of the men had flaxen hair, like yours, and blue eyes."

Ginny nearly came off the ground with excitement. What a task it was to stay lying flat! "Why—that must have been Georgie."

He bent another questioning look upon her.

"He is son-in-law to Manteo. And the one whose father was killed their first week upon Roanoac."

Felipe gave a slow nod. "He offered to take your place as captive, but Blackbird refused him."

She could only stare, mouth agape. Oh, that was a part of the story she wished to hear once they returned to Cora Banks.

If they did, indeed, return.

"Pray continue," Felipe said. "Sees Far had begun the journey to return your mother. . .?"

"Aye. So he returned her. I well recall the day. And after speaking with Manteo and the other men and securing their promise not to instantly slay Sees Far, Mama invited him to stay." Ginny smiled. " 'Twas at the same time that Georgie and Mary wanted to be married, and the whole town was in an uproar because the elders would not let Georgie go huskanaw and Mary did not yet want to follow Christ. Sees Far helped Georgie prepare for huskanaw while himself learning more about Christ." She stopped, thinking. " 'Tis said that Sees Far was one of those who helped in the slaying of Georgie's father, but I know not what to believe about that. If so, 'twas truly a miraculous change, from hardened enemy who stole Mama away to a trusted member of our people."

"And he did become your mother's husband?" Felipe asked.

"Oh, aye. The council raised a flap about the fact that he insisted on staying with Mama and me and hunted to provide for us since bringing her back—but his baptism and their marriage all took place on the same day. And"—she drew a deep breath—"their love for each other is so apparent even now, they—they are part of why I wish for the same."

His mouth curled softly. "I can understand why."

"How was it in your family?"

He sighed, looked away, resettled his limbs. "I recall affection between my father and mother, but it was expected that she respect him and little more." He stared at the ground. "She begged him not to take me along when he sailed, but he insisted I should come and share the adventure and learn what it was to be a man and a soldier." He sniffed. "I had grand dreams of becoming a conquistador, as in legends of old."

She stretched out her arm—slowly and gingerly—but could only brush his mahkusun. "Adventure you have had, of a certainty."

Felipe shifted closer and slipped his hand under hers. "So Sees Far has proved himself a good man?"

"Aye." Ginny blinked. "I still remember my papa, Ananias, but Papa Sees Far is wonderful. I cannot imagine Mama's life, or mine, without him." She flashed Felipe a smile. "That is also why it was not merely being

Skaru:re that made me refuse Blackbird. Were it only that—" She shook her head.

The corner of Felipe's mouth lifted. "He is also—old."

She laughed. "Not so very old, surely."

"Do you think so? Perhaps I am also too old."

She studied him. Nay, the creases of his face were not as pronounced as Blackbird's. "That cannot be so," she said at last. "You told me you've been growing out your warrior's lock for only four or five years."

His eyes sparkled.

"Now, if you also had a wife, or wives. . ."

The sparkle vanished. "You know I do not."

Another laugh escaped her. "You are remarkably easy to tease, for a fierce Skaru:re warrior."

"Hmm." Something shifted in his expression—a slow smile that drew the heat to her cheeks and made her wish to turn away. "Were you not laid out, letting the mud on your dressing dry, I would show you the meaning of 'tease.'"

She suddenly could not breathe and shut her eyes. There was a whisper of sound, and when she opened them again, Felipe was settling alongside, facing her, not quite touching. So close she could see the lighter flecks of blue against the darker in his eyes. He bent his arm under his head.

"What are you doing?" she said. When he did not reply, she snorted. "Is this what it would look like for you to not be courting me on someone else's behalf but rather on your own?"

The smile deepened. "As I said, were you not lying there wounded. . ."

Fire lit along her veins. It was moments such as this one that made her long to be kissed—again—and held.

She closed her eyes for another moment. *Not yet. . .not yet.*

Would it ever be the right time?

A touch settled on her head, smoothing her hair back from her face, and she dared open her eyes and meet his gaze again. The tenderness there nearly undid her.

"I remember," he said, "the stir caused by the English seeking to settle

185

on these shores. It was nearly all my father and the other men could talk about." He huffed the smallest laugh. "Passing strange, it is, to think of your grandfather being governor—and the same man who sketched plants and animals as they traveled through the Carib. And come to think—" His hand skimmed her shoulder and arm and found hers. "I also remember mention of the two tall Indians who traveled with them, who spoke English."

"I imagine 'twas quite the wonder."

As ordinary as Manteo seemed to her, having known him only as part of the blended community of the English and Kurawoten, she tried to picture him in a society that was all only English. Wanchese, now—she still held the dim memory of a tall, swift, painted warrior swooping down upon Mama—or was that only the description of Mary and others, who insisted Ginny had hidden in a thicket and seen none of it?

A shiver coursed through her.

"What became of them?" Felipe asked.

"Of Manteo and Wanchese? Manteo is still one of our weroances— our chief man, especially of the English. His mother is the weroansqua of the Kurawoten, but he was declared lord over the English colony before my grandfather sailed away, right after I was born. And so he remains to this day. His eldest daughter married the son of the man killed by Wanchese and Sees Far and the others.

"Wanchese, now—they and his men renewed their attack on our town and people, and he was killed—by Manteo's daughter, no less—when he tried to take Mama again."

His thumb smoothed the back of her hand. "What an ignoble end for such a strong warrior."

"To be killed by a woman?" She chuckled. "Do you know the story of Jael's wife, in the Holy Scriptures?"

A frown drew his fine brows together. "I suppose I do not."

"'Tis in the book of Judges. The leader of the Israelites, Barak, said he would not go to war without Deborah the prophetess and was told that the actual victory over Sisera, the enemy king, would go to a woman, since he lacked the courage to obey God on his own. During the battle, a great rain fell, and Sisera fled first in his chariot, then on foot when that became stuck in the mud. He took shelter at a random encampment, where the wife of one of Israel's leaders recognized him but invited him to take refreshment and sleep. While he slept, she took a tent stake and drove it through his temple. Thus the victory of Israel went to a woman."

A triumphant smile stretched her lips, and Felipe answered it in kind. "I would say she deserved that victory, with such cool in the face of the enemy." His brows ticked upward. "Manteo's daughter as well."

"Hmm, aye. She was, furthermore, near to her time with her first babe. And 'twas her husband Georgie's bow she wielded."

His eyes widened. "You were raised among a strong people, it would seem."

She made a sound of satisfaction in the back of her throat. "I was, indeed."

"The Skaru:re speak of them as mild and weak."

"Mild they are, and happy with simply living their lives. But they are fierce to protect their own—which now includes us English."

"So different from the ways of the Spanish with the Native peoples."

"So we have heard."

They studied each other's faces for a moment, then Felipe disentangled his hand and pushed up on his elbow. "Virginia. Will they—I mean, your people, the English especially—would they even accept me among them, with the Spanish being such bitter enemies?"

She frowned. "Why would they not?"

"When was the last time your people knew of what was happening in the wider world?"

" 'Twas the year I was born, 1587."

He nodded. "There was an entire war between Spain and England in the span of years after—and before I sailed with my father." He watched her closely. "Spain did not wish to admit it, but England pushed back our armada. Blood between the two has been bitter. Very bitter, indeed."

"I think. . ." She thought back on conversations she had overheard regarding the Spanish. Most focused on their poor treatment of the Native peoples, and yet to the south and inland, trading was still taking place amongst them all.

'Twas always emphasized that the Spanish were to be avoided at all cost.

"I do not know," she said at last.

Chapter Sixteen

Night fell and Virginia went to sleep, but once again Felipe lay awake. Were she not lying there wounded. . .well, he might have made her his wife already. And by the way she melted into his arms, perhaps she would not have objected.

Perhaps. . .she would be more than willing by the time he could face her mother and stepfather and the rest of her people and properly ask to court her.

But whether *they* would be willing, that was another matter entirely. He was not at all sure they'd not rather slay him on the spot.

How much of the story of Virginia's mother and her Suquoten husband was missing? How much did Virginia not know because she had been a small child? The Kurawoten had given shelter to the English, but surely they did not simply take in one who had been an enemy not only in name but also in deed.

In no wise did he expect the path to end with ease for himself.

She slept a little better that night and walked a little longer the next day, and so for the night and day after that. 'Twas rough going, with the ground so swampy and one or two deep creeks to cross each day, but she pressed on.

Felipe spent an afternoon drying and smoking some of the remaining deer meat, and they debated the merits of heading a little south, toward the Newasiwoc and the Cwareuuoc, or angling farther north, adding a day or two, to make directly for Cora Banks.

The closer they were, the more impatient she was to see Mama and everyone else. No delays.

Please, oh Lord, no more delays!

When her strength ran out each afternoon, however, the exhaustion felt complete. She could wring no more effort from her body.

On the third day of actual travel after being shot by Blackbird—or was it the fourth? she'd lost count—she lay resting on the deer hide, her thoughts swirling when she ought to be sleeping. Felipe busied himself setting up camp and preparing food.

The last two nights when she closed her eyes, all she could see was fire. Henry's voice permeated her dreams. First his anguished shout, then his defiant offering of his own life, and lastly his voice rising reedy but firm in song.

She had offered her life for Felipe's. Henry had then given his for her.

What did that mean for her? Felipe had been firm that she honor Henry by choosing to live. But did she betray his memory if she came to love another, indeed, gave herself as wife? Or was that also a facet of living her life to the fullest?

She knew what Henry would say, were he here. At least, she thought she knew. Perhaps she was wrong. Because, what if he had lived? Would he eventually have accepted her choosing another? Surely he would have. And she'd have had to break his heart sooner or late, because there was no shred of feeling in her for that sort of relationship with him.

The tears welled, and she turned her face into the soft hair of the deerskin beneath her.

Could she have brought herself to marry him, if the choice had been put before her? If Henry's life had depended upon it? Without a doubt. However ill she might feel now at the thought.

But that was no longer a choice. Henry had given himself—for her. Ultimately for Felipe as well.

Was it wrong of her to think of returning Felipe's affections? To find comfort in his embrace? To. . .crave his kiss?

He'd not kissed her since that morning they'd begun traveling again. Hadn't spoken of it. He slept near her, soothing her with his hand and voice when she suffered more nightmares, but otherwise closely observed all propriety, as if he too were only a brother.

It should be a relief, she supposed. Perhaps he was but giving her room to ponder it all, but the thought nagged at her that perhaps he'd decided he did not want her as much as he thought he did. What if the burden of caring for her, after having to choose her over his loyalty to Blackbird, proved too much for him to accept after all?

And. . .what if when they did reach Cora Banks, it was not Felipe they were angry with, but Ginny? For leaving Redbud and Henry behind? For putting them in such a situation to begin with? Mama might be happy to see her, but facing Henry's and Redbud's families? And the rest of the community.

There was a rustle, and Felipe's hand smoothed across her head and good shoulder. Strange how she knew it was him now simply by touch—although, of course, no one else was present.

"What is it?" he wondered.

"Perhaps," she said when she could find her voice, "perhaps I should not go back at all."

"And why?"

"What if—" And she spoke aloud her fear of the people's anger over Henry and Redbud being lost.

Felipe bent close, brushed aside her hair, and kissed her cheek, just in front of her ear. Likely 'twas all he could reach, with her face muffled by deer hide.

"From what I have heard from the boys," he said, his voice low and gentle, "you are loved. They will be glad to see you, even as they sorrow for the boys. And"—he drew a deep breath—"your mother and family will welcome you. Their mothers would want to know their fate."

Was he thinking of himself? Ginny rolled to her good side and peered into his face. "How have you borne it all these years? Seeing your own father killed and then carried away by those who did it?"

"The Skaru:re were not the ones who killed them."

"But—oh. Then who?"

"Another people. I do not know who. They took me, carried me away, and sold me to the Skaru:re."

"To Blackbird," she guessed.

He nodded.

Well, that certainly explained much.

"I am sorry," she said.

"For?"

"Bringing trouble to you as well."

"Virginia." He gave her a long, hard look, then lifted his head to scan their surroundings.

"Do not say I have not," she growled, pushing up on her elbow. "If we had not been taken during that attack—"

He sat down next to her. "How do you know whether God did not bring you to us for a reason?"

Her eyes burned again. "What, so Henry could die?"

Felipe leaned toward her. "Henry made his own choice. And had you not come to us, then I'd not have found the girl I am coming to love above all else."

She looked at him, suddenly unable to breathe.

"Aye. I love you, Virginia of the English and Kurawoten. And I care not whether you feel the same, yet. I—"

He swallowed, then rose to his feet again and took two swift paces away.

"I do not understand how you can value your life so little," he said, almost a snarl.

She pushed to her feet as well—not as painfully as a few days ago—and went to him. Set her palm against his back. He shivered.

"I would only have spared you—"

He rounded on her, chest rising and falling. "Spared me what? The chance to hold you? To. . .love you? No, *mi amor*, do not spare me that."

Then he stalked away, into the forest.

"Felipe!" she called, tears clogging her throat again, but he kept walking.

She went back to the deerskin and lay down, sobbing, though she did not understand why.

She woke to twilight and the smell of roasting fowl. Flickering light outlined Felipe's form and features on the other side of the fire. Seeing that she was awake, he tore off the leg of what looked like an already half-eaten duck on a spit and brought it to her. She sat up and took it, thanking him softly.

He nodded once and retreated but watched her eat.

"My apologies if I have caused you more distress," he said when she was about half done with the chewy but flavorful meat. "I had determined I would be patient and give you time to mourn your companions. Instead, my heart spilled over." His gaze remained steady. "But I do love you. However foolish it may seem."

He did not wait for her to respond but rose and vanished again into the dark.

She finished the leg and tossed the bone into the fire. Felipe was back again in a moment. "Do you want more?"

"Aye, please."

Her heart broke a little more at his attentiveness, as he tore off bits until she'd had enough. Then he returned to the other side of the fire with the rest of the bird and finished it.

Afterward, he stretched out, hands folded across his chest, and closed his eyes.

She'd no choice but to do the same—on her side this time. It had become so tiresome to lie on her belly. And her eyes would not close for a long time.

He loved her. He'd said so—and not only once.

Oh Lord. . .

It felt like she'd ceased knowing how to pray days ago. How long had they been traveling? And how much longer?

How could she not tell him she loved him in return? He was the one her thoughts continually drifted toward at the end of her time with the Skaru:re. Every time she contemplated having to marry Blackbird and wondered if there was any other choice, 'twas Felipe, with all his swagger and intensity, who came to mind.

He said he'd not tried to win her for himself. But 'twas him at every turn, questioning, teasing, admonishing, at times even bullying. . .yet always careful with her well-being.

Watching over her, ostensibly that she might not escape, but also that she might do herself no harm.

Intent that she at least try to accept Blackbird, that she see the Skaru:re warrior-priest fairly.

Until—yes, the night of the Green Corn Festival, when he'd not only challenged her to dance but danced beside her. And talked with her long into the night. As if they were any young couple, free to linger in each other's company.

So much talk about the church and faith. Even if she did not know where he was with his faith at the moment, it behooved her to exercise patience and let him make that journey at his own pace.

How do you know whether God did not bring you to us for a reason?

Felipe's question, spoken in the midst of her distress, surfaced abruptly. As if it were just now registering.

Him, exhorting her to think of God's overarching will in a terrible situation.

What if Felipe was not so far from true faith as she thought?

And what if, despite her bitter reply in the moment, God had indeed brought her and the boys to the Skaru:re for a purpose? Dare she even begin to think that might be possible?

The tears flowed again. Was the God she had heard the elders speak of—Mama and Sees Far, for that matter—not mighty enough to bring something good out of something so awful?

Mama had thought so, even with her own captivity. Even with Papa Ananias' death. And she'd found the courage to keep living. To accept Sees Far as her husband.

At least Ginny thought it courage and not mere desperation. For the first time, she understood how easy it would be to simply lie here and refuse to go on.

Oh Lord, give me courage like Mama's.

She was awakened in the middle of the night by falling drops of water.

Just a few at first, then with a rush of sound through the forest, the first wave of rain came.

The wound in her shoulder protested, but she seized the edge of the deerskin and rolled so that it was covering her, skin side up, and curled as small as she could beneath it.

Where was Felipe?

She peered out from under the deerskin. There he was, on the other side of the dying fire, similarly curled but with an arm over his face. On impulse, she rose and went to him, carrying the deerskin, and lay down behind him, pulling the hide over both of them.

"What are you doing?" he mumbled.

"What does it look like?"

She folded the arm on her wounded side between them then settled closer. Oh, he was warm, despite the glaze of wet from the rain.

He sighed. She pressed her cheek against his back, between his shoulder blades, and dropped back into sleep.

This girl.

How was he supposed to sleep?

And how many more days until they reached her people?

Father in heaven, I beg You. . .

He could not even find the words.

The cadence of her soft breaths across his shoulder told him she was already slumbering again.

Help me to honor her. Help me to honor You. But I also beg Your mercy. Let us reach her people soon so that this question may be settled.

'Twas still raining come morning.

The deerskin lifted, and Felipe rolled away from her. Ginny cracked her eyelids to find the forest wreathed in mist. By the time she'd coaxed sore and weary muscles to move, he'd scattered the evidence of their fire and was gathering his bow and arrows.

"Go tend your needs, then let us be going." He motioned toward her. "Put the hide over your shoulders. You should keep the wound dry as long as possible."

Once they were ready, she followed him, trudging through the ferns and brush and trees stretching high above, as she had for days now. The ache in her body made her long to just lie down and sleep again, all the wet notwithstanding.

"How do you know which direction to go with the sun hidden?" she asked.

He shook his head, and she thought he wasn't going to reply, but then he said, "I took note of direction before the sun went down last night."

She should not be surprised. He was Skaru:re. He was Spanish. He was. . .

Her eyes snapped shut. How had he come to be the most intriguing male she'd ever known?

Her foot caught on a root, and she opened her eyes. Dangerous to let herself become so distracted. And yet—she most certainly was. Her gaze traced the lines of his shoulders and back swaying with his gait, then she looked off into the forest. There was a word she'd heard the elders use. . .*wanton.* Did that describe her? And what she felt about Felipe?

Tears burned her eyes. She was always weeping these days, and she could no more cease than she could bid the rain above her not to fall.

Before the morning was half over, they encountered a path. While Felipe stood, looking one way and then the other, Ginny drew up beside him. They'd avoided paths, for the most part, and anything that might lead them to towns or other people.

But now, coming up the right branch and already catching sight of her and Felipe, were three warriors.

They already had discussed how to handle such a meeting. Ginny folded the hide about her, best as she could with its stiffness, stepping up behind him and tucking her head while Felipe held himself firm. As the other men approached, he called out a greeting. They answered, and then one broke out in—

A gasp tore itself from her throat, and she found herself surging forward. "Who are your people?" she asked in Kurawoten, the words spilling out of her as if it had just been yestermorn when she was taken.

The warriors stopped and looked at her. "We are Cwareuuoc," one said.

"I am friend," she said, "of Manteo's people, the Kurawoten!" And she lowered the deerskin to show the color of her hair.

"Ah! An Inqutish! Why are you so far from your home?"

"I was—" She shot a look at Felipe and translated quickly. "They are Coree—Cwareuuoc! All friends of the English and Kurawoten. May I tell them who we are?"

He nodded, despite looking stern.

She turned to the other men. "I was one of three youth taken when the Skaru:re struck in the spring. I am returning home. This one is helping me. He is also friend."

They eyed Felipe with no small amount of suspicion. "And what is he?"

"His story is his to tell," she said. "But please, first tell me what news of the Kurawoten and Cora Banks?"

One of the other men stepped forward. "The Kurawoten and Inqutish removed to the island a moon or two past. A few remain."

Her heart sank, and her throat closed. "The island? Do you know who went and who stayed?"

"Mahta." He motioned behind them. "If you continue down this path, you will come to our village. Tell them that you have met us as we went out to hunt, and you will be welcome." He seemed to assess all they carried with them—or did not.

She repeated his words to Felipe. He dipped his head. "We thank you for your hospitality."

The three warriors moved on, and Felipe looked at her. "Is this what you wish?"

She could hardly breathe. "I would like more word of my people, if I can get it."

He tipped his head in assent then set off down the path. She followed, her heart still in her throat.

How strange to be walking a marked trail now. Stranger still to know that within a short time, she would be among those with whom she could speak freely and whom she had not seen for half a year.

How was Felipe feeling in this moment?

Chapter Seventeen

S he truly was loved by everyone, even here.

The women surrounded her the moment they arrived at the town, and once she'd explained exactly who she was among her people, many seemed to know her. Not surprising, if Manteo had married a woman of this people and the neighboring towns had visited back and forth. They touched her hair, fussed over the arrow wound, admired the workings around the edges of her skirt. Pointed at Felipe and asked questions, to which she flushed prettily and shot him a smile before replying with a giggle.

Did he even wish to know?

Almost immediately the women had pressed both him and Virginia to sit and offered them food. She handed Felipe a round of bread and with a little smile said, "Apon."

He repeated the word and took a bite. While they ate, one of the women cleaned Virginia's wound and, after clucking over it, slathered it with ointment but otherwise left it open. Afterward, they were shown to a house where the sides were rolled up to let in the breeze, and they were encouraged to lie down and rest.

Virginia took a spot on a raised platform that had been cushioned with three or four mats, and Felipe dragged a pair of mats over so he might lie on the floor next to her. She watched him with what seemed a sort of amused affection.

"When the men have returned from hunting," she said as he set aside his bow and arrows and settled in, "they wish to hear more of our story, and they will tell us all they know."

"And we are safe to sleep in the meantime?"

She smiled, though weariness edged her face. "I think no one will come and put a tent peg through our temples here."

He laughed then yawned. She did the same. "Stop that," she said.

"I am more wearied than I thought."

She put a hand on his arm and looked a little abashed.

"Who did you tell them I am?" he asked softly.

Her lips curved, blue eyes sparkling. "They asked if I was your woman, and I said not yet."

Lightning—from the center of his chest through his entire being. "Not yet, meaning that you wish to be?"

Her smile deepened. "Aye," she breathed.

"Truly?"

"Truly."

He sat up and kissed her. Were they more alone—but the walls being rolled up gave them no privacy, and so he kept it reasonably quick. At least, he meant to, then her hand caught him around the back of his neck. When they did break the kiss, she pulled back only the slightest bit, brushing the tip of his nose with her own. "Thank you for bringing me thus far."

He nodded and sank back to the floor, lest he be tempted to make both of them more of a spectacle than they already were.

'Twas a town meeting that had started it all—and here she was, center of attention at this one.

She gave, while not the complete story of her time with the Skaru:re, enough that the Coree people could gain a fuller picture of what had taken place and of Felipe's part in helping her, both among the Skaru:re and in getting home. They were much shaken by the news that he was

Spanish, which took her more aback than she expected.

How ill would the Kurawoten and English take that news?

An almost unreasonable annoyance prodded her—and not a little anger—at the thought. Yet she tucked that aside as the weroance told what he knew of the aftermath of the attack on Cora Banks. "Your mother's man, Sees Far, did lead a war party to find you and the other two youth. They tried to treat with the Skaru:re but were refused."

Though she knew of this already, her eyes burned afresh at the thought. Papa Sees Far and others had indeed come for her and the boys.

She nodded for him to continue.

"Manteo also sent to us and the Newasiwoc to ask us to go to war with them against the Mangoac. We considered it, but agreed at last that the Mangoac are too numerous for us." The weroance looked truly regretful. He cast a glance at Felipe. "And this one, is he to be trusted?"

All her distress crowded up into her throat again. "He broke loyalty for my sake with the man who bought him as a captive and then helped him become a warrior." Her voice trembled, and she fought to steady it. "He faced death for my sake and willingly would have given himself as that sacrifice."

She tried to ignore Felipe's gaze upon them both, steady and intent. She'd explain it later, but for now—

"I will let Manteo hear and judge on this matter," the weroance said. "Meanwhile, with you still recovering from the arrow shot, we can carry the two of you by water, at least to Manteo's town on the Pumtico, and then to the island if need be."

That was more than she had dared hope for. "Thank you. I will not forget your kindness."

Afterward, they were feasted by the Coree, and she translated the gist of it to Felipe. Then he was asked to share his story, and she translated into the tongue the Coree shared with the Kurawoten.

Music and dancing followed, but she was still too weary, despite their afternoon rest, to do more than lean on Felipe. He seemed not to mind, but quietly slipped an arm about her. Even with his unspoken claim upon her clear, a parade of young warriors seemed intent upon presenting themselves to her, inviting her to dance, but she refused each one.

At last she could bear it no longer and rose, tugging on Felipe's hand for him to follow. They would be returning for their overnight stay to the house where they had rested earlier, but she craved a quiet moment alone with him.

She led him down by the river, under cover of the trees but still within sight and sound of the town. Content at last that no one else was near, she sighed and, weaving her fingers more tightly with his, laid her head against his shoulder. A crescent moon and stars reflected in the ripples of the river. Fireflies flickered in the trees on the far bank.

He brought his hand up to smooth her hair. "I prayed last night that we would soon reach your people."

She lifted her head to look up at him. "You did?"

He nodded, gazing out over the river. "And then, before much of the day had worn away, we found that path and met those three warriors." He was quiet a moment. "It is not the first time in these past few days that a prayer of mine has been so speedily answered."

Her eyes burned, and she released his hand only to slide both arms around him.

"I have many questions," he said, "but I know I must wait for answers."

"There is nothing wrong with questions. I've had many in my life."

His hand still slowly combed through her hair. "Well, here is one. Are you certain you wish to be my wife?"

She pressed her cheek into the muscled curve of his shoulder. "Aye."

His embrace tightened a little. "And when did you decide this?"

"I was thinking, after you told me you love me, and realized"—she leaned back a little to look up at him—"when we were yet with the Skaru:re, 'twas you my thoughts always went back to. You I grew to miss when you were absent. Your voice—and your banter—that I looked forward to hearing." She slid one hand across his belly and chest, up and around his neck, and a tremor coursed through him. Her thumb traced the emerging stubble of his beard, which had oddly caught against her skin when he kissed her earlier, but not unpleasantly. "When the Skaru:re elders asked me who I would choose, had I the freedom to do so, I wanted to say even then that it was you. But I knew with Blackbird so angry, I dared not. And then all was made confusing after we lost Henry and Redbud. 'Tis you I'd have chosen, however. You are the one I wish to give myself to now."

He gazed down at her, brows together, all fierce. "You heard the concerns spoken by the chief man here. What if your people do not consent to our marriage?"

Tears threatened at the thought. " 'Tisn't theirs to consent to. If Mama and Sees Far are unhappy, that's one thing, but there is no reason they should be, given their own circumstances. And if I have already chosen you—"

His eyes held hers a moment longer, then he swooped in, his mouth taking hers, altogether different than before. This was a wild summer storm, all thunder and lightning and the wind tugging at her—not merely lingering but possessing and consuming.

For the first time in her life, she fully understood what brought a man and a woman together. Oh, she had thought she understood before, and had laughed, sometimes scoffing outright. But now, to find herself so utterly stripped of reason...

Felipe broke the kiss and bent, his face against her neck, his arms tight about her and yet somehow still tender. "I want you as my wife, make no mistake," he said, breathing hard. "But I will not simply take you. Not until I have faced them with the honor a man should have."

He straightened slowly, and she framed his face in her hands, letting the tears run as her heart broke a little with the moment's disappointment. She ached for him in ways she never thought possible, and yet...

"And that," she said, her voice cracking, "is what makes you the man I have come to love."

He gave a single hard nod, pressed his lips to hers for a breath or two, then released her—but only to take her hand. "Come. We should sleep. Tomorrow may be long and difficult."

How did she go from being sweet and unassuming to setting him completely aflame? And yet—he could not.

He could not.

The night sang about them. Cicadas buzzed in the trees above and a night bird gave its lonely three-note call from away in the forest as he led her silently back to the town. They found the house where they were to lodge and bedded down as before on the mats provided by their hosts.

That is what makes you the man I have come to love, she'd said. Ah, but it had cost him every ounce of restraint—still did—to not give lie to what he had just vowed and take her regardless.

But for love of her and the honor he wished to prove to her family and her people, he would not, until it truly was time.

Fingers woven with hers as she lay on the platform above, he fell asleep and did not wake at all until just before dawn.

Ginny woke to find Felipe gone. A flutter of panic beat at her—but likely he had just gone down to the river to wash. After greeting the women already at work cooking, she inquired where they customarily went to bathe, and they pointed the way. "Your man has gone with the others to their spot," one said with a smile.

She thanked them and proceeded down to the river. Mist sifted through the shrubbery and trees as she made her way to where a few women lingered, some of them singing to greet the morning.

Quickly she undressed and went into the water. Though they'd been in and out of rivers and creeks the past several days, this felt different. She bent her knees to dip under, letting the water sluice over her face and shoulders as she came up again, gaze fixed on the sunrise glowing golden through the mist.

Lord—oh Lord—I thank You for bringing us thus far! For keeping Felipe and me safe. If—if 'tis Your will, and is not already too late, I ask you to

*preserve Redbud as well. And help us not waste what Henry gave. Thank You
for giving us favor thus far. . .and please give us continued favor and the words
to break the news to Redbud's and Henry's families.*

A thought speared her, and she added, *Help me be truthful and humble
about my own part in this terrible hap. I ask Your mercy in it. . .but give me
strength to face whatever You will.*

She felt washed clean within as well as without and as ready as she
ever would be to face her own people.

She returned to find Felipe in the midst of a cluster of men, paying
attention to their talk as if he understood, munching a piece of apon. She
turned aside to offer help to the women in their meal preparation, but
they cheerfully refused and bade her sit and wait to be served. Ginny did
so, laughing a little. She'd forgotten how warm and welcoming the coastal
peoples could be.

Felipe came to sit beside her just as one of the women brought a
platter of fresh, hot apon, and they each took one, juggling it in their
fingers. Felipe lifted his. "As good as Skaru:re bread."

She shot him a saucy smile. "Better."

He laughed, his blue eyes vivid and bright. "Sleep well?"

She nodded, chewing, drinking in the sight of him as well. "And
yourself?"

"Well enough." He scanned the gathering and reached for another
apon. "Are you prepared for this day?"

"I am," she breathed.

"I am as well." He took a bite, chewed, and swallowed. "We will see
what God wills, shall we not?"

"Indeed," she said, looking into his eyes and feeling a little lost.

They ate well, possibly too well, and shortly after were escorted to
a kanoe outfitted with supplies. Two men accompanied them, one a
youth just past huskanaw, were Ginny to guess. Was he one of those who
attempted to coax her to dance the previous night? He gave no sign of
untoward attention as they readied at last to go. She stepped into the
kanoe, Felipe behind her, with the older warrior in front and the younger

behind. Then, with many shouts of farewell and her own thanks, they pushed off.

Ginny did not realize how she'd missed being out on the water. She turned her face into the breeze and leaned to trail her fingers in the light waves. Felipe laughed at her then gazed off into the mist, apparently caught up in his own thoughts.

What did he recall about his own journey to this land?

It was the first time he had been out on such open water since they'd sailed from Spain.

He thought of all the places he'd been since then—the warm Caribbean, with the islands of Dominica, Hispaniola, Santa Cruz, Jamaica, Cuba. The long-forgotten shock of seeing Native peoples strolling about as bare as God made them. The initial thrill of landing in La Florida at San Augustin, the adventure of marching inland through awful heat.

The horror of battle, and Papá's and the others' deaths. The terror of being taken deeper inland, and the humiliation of being stripped naked and scrubbed the first time. Learning to be content with wearing but a skin kilt as the other men did—sometimes not more than a deerskin apron.

Some of these things he'd not thought of in years. Was it merely the wind and waves that made him reflective?

The men in the front and back paddled with sure skill. Before long, the river widened to a small bay and then widened again. They stayed fairly close to the left-most shore the entire time, bearing first southeast then rounding a long point and turning northeast. The river bay kept widening, until at last the land to the right fell away and there was nothing but open water to the east.

"Kurawoten Island is that way," Virginia told him, pointing.

About midmorning, they stopped onshore to rest and stretch then were on their way again. Felipe asked to help paddle, and the men laughed but let him trade with the young man and sit in front. It took a bit, but he got the rhythm of it and was soon doing as well as either of the Coree.

He glanced back and found Virginia grinning, her entire face alight, and the older man laughed and nodded in approval.

Their path bore them back westward, into the mouth of another fairly wide river, but the shadows began to stretch long behind them before the older man indicated they were near. They rounded the next bend and nosed up a creek to find a vessel larger than the kanoe yet of a shape that Felipe knew from more than half a life ago.

A pinnace, half burned, listing and sunk into the water—handiwork of the Skaru:re.

Virginia gave a cry and rose to her feet. The older man spoke to her, and while she did not sit back down, neither did she fling herself headlong into the creek as she looked ready to do a moment ago. As soon as the kanoe bumped the bank, however, she leaped over the side and was away.

The older man gave Felipe a sympathetic look and shook his head.

She could wait not an instant longer. Running, hallooing the town. A dark head appeared over the lookout when the palisade walls came into sight. She waved with both arms. "'Tis I—'tis Ginny!"

And then she made for the entrance.

Voices cried out and townsfolk ran to greet her—but too few.

Far too few, and neither Mama, Papa Sees Far, nor her siblings were there amongst them.

Or Henry's family.

Those who came, however, embraced her, exclaiming and some weeping. And suddenly, there was Netah, Redbud's mother.

She peered past Ginny. "Where is Redbud? And Henry?"

Ginny crumbled at that. She fell to her knees and seized the woman's feet. "I am sorry—'twas my fault. All my fault."

She could not look—dared not—but Netah bent to her and lifted her upright. Those tearful brown eyes, the round face—'twas both Redbud and not—his mother looked at her and said, "Whatever it is, you are ours,

Ginny, and we are glad to see you!"

Her breath caught. She did not deserve such grace—yet she was but one of two mothers Ginny must face.

"Are Mama and Sees Far still here?"

Netah's expression grew grave. "Mahta. They went to the island with the others. We stayed, awaiting Redbud's return."

The tears overcame her again, but Netah's arms gathered her in again for a moment.

"Go. See to the house, and we will prepare food."

"Tell my companions where I have gone," Ginny said.

She found her way, though half blinded yet with tears, and hesitated on the threshold. Flowers still grew about the front door, as if she were still there. *Lord God, if You are still here and listening—*

She could not finish. There were no words.

With a deep breath, she unlatched the door and stepped inside.

It smelled musty, of dust and disuse. Much of the furniture remained—table, chairs, shelving, though anything that would have been stored there was gone. How strange to see it so empty, when time was, she'd thought the house too small and cramped by half, with her little brothers running about. 'Twas a good part of why she often sought the outdoors.

Slowly she climbed the stairs and pushed open the door to Mama's room. Why was the bed still here? And the chest, so lovingly carved by Papa's hand? She crossed to it and lifted the lid. A few clothing items and bed linens remained inside.

Why would they leave so much behind?

She sank to the floor, one hand inside the chest and fingertips brushing the fabric. 'Twas likely because of the pinnace—they could fit only so much into a kanoe, even the big ones.

On her knees, she lifted out the topmost garment. A shift, very like what she had worn and lost after being taken captive. A simple green gown below that. A linen sheet, a worn woolen blanket—that she knew only because of Mama explaining about a creature called *sheep* and how its hair was woven into clothing, bedding, and other items.

She carried an armful to the bed and laid them out then returned for the rest. A man's shirt and doublet. Those she knew had been Papa's. She could not believe Mama still had them, much less that she'd left them behind.

She fingered the shift. 'Twas tempting to put it on, but she should bathe first. And mayhap she shouldn't cover the arrow wound yet.

What if Mama left them here, hoping Ginny and the boys would return?

Felipe could only stare at the incongruity of tall, blocky English houses next to the rounded ones of the Kurawoten. To stand witness to that which so many of his own people had coveted finding—the "lost" settlement of Ralegh, not lost at all, merely hidden.

The town must be able to house at least two hundred, likely more, but fewer than fifty remained. "The rest are gone to the island," he was told by a man not much older than himself, clearly English with brown hair and grey eyes, yet dressed as the Kurawoten, much as Felipe himself. He eyed Felipe's attire and no doubt puzzled over the blue of his gaze. "Surely you are not also English?"

Felipe shook his head, glancing about for Virginia. He had not reckoned on having to make explanation without her at least nearby. And the Coree warriors were of no help.

The man's brows drew together. "Are you looking for Ginny? Were you a captive with her?"

"I am, and. . .I was indeed a captive once. I do not mind telling my story, but I must find her first."

"She went to her old house," said a Kurawoten woman cooking nearby. She beckoned to him. "I show you."

The Englishman came along, no doubt as much for escort as for curiosity. Felipe did not blame him.

A snug, tidy house it was, in good repair. The woman went in before him and called out softly.

Seeing the downstairs unoccupied, Felipe ran up the stairs. The door above was open, and Virginia stood in the middle of the floor, clutching a garment to her chest. She turned, eyes full of tears. For a moment they only looked at each other, then he stepped forward and offered his embrace.

Why did it stir such sharp relief that she came to him and sank into his arms? As she sobbed against his shoulder, he cradled her close and kissed her forehead.

"And what is this?" the Englishman asked behind him. "Are you two married?"

The Kurawoten woman, coming through the door, had the same question on her face.

Virginia did not stir, but Felipe shook his head. "Not yet."

Amazement glimmered in both their eyes. " 'Twas of much comment that Ginny had not yet settled her affections on anyone, despite having completed huskanasqua more than a year ago."

Felipe just tucked her in closer. Her weeping continued unabated.

Their expressions shifted to that of shared sorrow, and for the man, a sudden understanding as he studied Felipe. "Truly do you love her." When Felipe shot him a glance, he added, "It warms my heart to see it."

"As if you've any room, Rob Ellis, to say thus," Virginia said, lifting her head.

The young man's cheeks darkened, but he smiled. " 'Tis good to have you home, Ginny."

Felipe felt he had missed some vital part of the exchange, but at least he saw no true hostility there. Virginia wiped her eyes and turned back toward the bed, where Felipe now saw lay several items of apparel and linens. While she folded a shift and kirtle, he fingered the embroidery on the doublet.

Ten long years it had been since he'd seen such a garment—close enough to touch, anyway.

"I must return to cooking," the Kurawoten woman said.

"We'll be along anon," Virginia said, tucking the women's garments into the open chest.

The Englishman stayed to watch, confirming Felipe's suspicion, but Felipe kept his attention on Virginia. "This seems a curiosity," he said, indicating the chest and its contents as she followed the apparel with the bed linens.

"Indeed." She reached last for the man's shirt and doublet then hesitated. "I puzzled over Mama and Sees Far leaving so much behind, then thought surely 'tis because of the pinnace."

He held steady beneath her questioning gaze, but the Englishman answered for her. "Aye. The Mangoac burned it when you were taken."

Virginia stilled, and Felipe nodded. He still would not falter under her regard. "It is as he says. We—the Skaru:re—set fire to it."

"So you are of them," the Englishman said, his voice sharpening.

Virginia held out a staying hand to him. "Hold, Robby. He is a friend. I will explain more later."

The Englishman looked unconvinced but at last gave a terse nod. "So—as Sees Far, when he brought your mama home."

"Somewhat, aye."

He looked no happier at that.

She knew—she had known already—that Felipe was part of the attack on Cora Banks and the capture of her and the boys. But somehow it had not seemed real until they stood here again, in her old home, and she heard it from his lips.

She could only look at him. She should be beyond shock by now, but to have seen that lovely vessel, so familiar and steady, lying burned in the creek, and then to be here—it all transported her back to that day in the spring, when life as she knew it altered without remedy.

Felipe appeared so fierce and stern in the moment, yet she knew he was not the same as he'd been then either. She certainly would not let the likes of Rob Ellis act as if she needed to be protected from Felipe.

After putting away the clothing and linens and closing the chest, she led the men back downstairs and out into the town's common area. The food was not yet ready and the women declined her help, so she showed Felipe about the town.

Rob still trailed along, as if he expected Felipe to set fire to something besides the pinnace.

At last the food was ready and everyone sat down to eat. Afterward, Ginny gave as much of her story as she could. They all grieved Henry and Redbud, and deeply, but there was none of the anger she'd feared.

As the day ended and darkness fell and evening prayers gave way to modest singing and dancing, once again she felt too tired to join in, though 'twas good to be present for it again, where she knew folk and understood their tongue.

Just one more day.

Felipe tugged at her, and she realized she was falling asleep on his shoulder. They said their good nights, and she led him once more to her old house.

He stood back and looked at the bed for a long moment as she spread out the linen sheet she'd found. "I shall sleep on the floor," he said.

She could not suppress a laugh. "Papa Sees Far did that until he and Mama were married."

She pulled the wool blanket out and went to hand it to him, but he smirked and said, "I am not sure I know what to do with one of those anymore."

Rolling her eyes, she shook it out and refolded it in half, lengthwise, then laid it on the floor beside the bed. "There. 'Twill at least cushion the hard wood for you."

He said nothing, and when she straightened and looked at him, her pulse gave a leap. In the moonlight, it seemed his entire heart was in his eyes.

She took a step toward him, but he held out a hand, much as she had to Rob earlier. "Do not—press me."

Just the tone of his voice made her unable to breathe. "Why?" she managed.

"Is there anyone here who could speak a marriage service over us?"

She shook her head.

"Well, then."

"You know I simply want to be yours," she whispered.

"And that is why I must sleep on the floor."

With a stiff nod, she swallowed then turned and crawled up onto the bed. With a bit of rustling, he lay down on the blanket, then all was still.

How lonely it seemed, not having him directly beside her.

Chapter Eighteen

The next morning dawned clear and fair, and practically before the sun cleared the horizon, they climbed back into the kanoe and set off. Two of the townsmen—Redbud's older brother and John Prat—would go along in a second kanoe, partly to give company and partly because they wished word of those on the island.

Partly too, Ginny knew, because they wanted to see through the matter of Felipe and what Manteo and the other weroances would decide. Her stomach felt so twisted she could hardly eat. Today she would see Mama and Papa Sees Far again, meet her youngest baby sister, and hold her brothers and Sunny.

And today she would bear the awful news of Henry's death to his family and the rest of the community.

Help me, oh Lord. . .help me.

'Twas all she could pray as they skimmed over the water into the rising sun.

Felipe started out this time paddling in front, and she sat just behind him. Between her and the younger Coree warrior sat Mama's carved chest. She had nothing else with which to carry the clothing and had decided she would not leave it behind if she could help it.

After a few hours on open water with no land in sight, they stopped paddling and took turns swimming a bit, just to stretch and refresh themselves. Ginny still could not fully extend her arm or flex her shoulder, but she could tread water beside the kanoe.

She watched the clouds building on the horizon. Was that a sea storm in the making? She thought not. The cloud patterns were usually different.

If they were overtaken by rain—and none of them minded much, unless there was lightning as well—then she'd lay the untanned deerskin over the chest to shield it. But they all should otherwise be well.

Closer. . .and closer. She could hardly stand the waiting.

Then—a smudge on the horizon. She stood, only to be laughingly told to sit again. But it was definitely land.

Her heart pounded, her throat closing. Though the likelihood was strong that this was not Kurawoten but Wococon or one of the other westernmost islands, she held on to hope.

Felipe turned his head to survey the growing shoreline. The tightness had returned to his expression. Was he nervous? She could not blame him if so—her own gut had tied itself in several knots.

Sure enough, John Prat called out from the other kanoe and waved an arm, directing them more east. Ginny stuffed down her anticipation.

Shortly, however, they skirted an inlet, and as they paddled up the shoreline, other kanoes came into sight, with men standing and pushing them about with poles or spearing fish.

And beyond, the outline of a town, up the slope from where children splashed in the shallows.

A flurry of memory awoke, and Ginny could hardly keep still until the kanoe got close enough for her to leap out and run to shore. A shriek of pure joy ripped from her throat as she splashed through the shallows and raced up the slight swell of beach, for there, silhouetted on the ridge, were shapes of men she knew.

Georgie. Cousin Chris. Towaye, Master Roger Prat, and others. They turned at her cry—and as she hoped, one man of the People, tall and strong, pushed through the others and came running to meet her.

Papa Sees Far himself.

He caught her in his arms and swung her about. The wound twinged, but she minded it not in the moment. He swept her back to look at her, his gaze devouring her face.

"Ginny!" 'Twas Georgie, and she let herself be caught in that one's arms as well—older brother that he'd always been to her.

"Send for Elinor," Papa Sees far said to someone behind them, and Cousin Chris made no hesitation but sped toward the town.

"You are here!" Georgie said. "Fare ye well? Are Henry and Redbud with you?" He searched the beach behind her as the Coree warriors, Redbud's older brother, and John Prat drew the second kanoe up onto the sand.

And about halfway up the strand stood Felipe, still and watchful. The quick rise and fall of his chest was all that betrayed his unease.

Sees Far and Georgie also went still.

"Papa Sees Far," she panted. "Georgie. This—this is Felipe. He helped me."

The shadows in their eyes deepened. They remembered either meeting him before or the significance of such a thing, in light of Mama's own history.

Or possibly both.

She backtracked and took Felipe's hand, tugging him closer. Then—

"Ginny?"

A breathless feminine voice rang out, and a slight form pushed through the crowd of men.

"Mama!"

She threw herself back up the beach, where Mama caught her and clung, both of them crying, then laughing, as Mama leaned back to smooth both hands over Ginny's hair and cheeks, then seized her again in a wild embrace.

Home! She had made it home. She drew away and surveyed the faces around her—beloved, every one. "There is so much to explain—"

"Begin with that one." Georgie jutted his chin at Felipe.

Ginny let go of Mama's hand and retraced her steps to Felipe's side. "This is Felipe." She found her voice was shaking. "He began as a captive, when he was a child, then was adopted as a Skaru:re."

"You mean Mangoac?"

"Skaru:re," Ginny said firmly. They stared at her as if she'd taken leave of her senses.

Were none of them familiar with what their enemy people called themselves?

"And what sort of captive?" Cousin Chris asked. "Not English, surely?"

Ginny shook her head. How to explain without simply saying it...

Chris took a menacing step down the beach. "Tell me, Virginia Dare, that you have not brought the Spanish among us!"

Without thought, Ginny flung herself in front of Felipe, pressing her back to his chest, reaching both hands behind to seize his. "Virginia," he protested, his voice rumbling through her, but she held on to him.

"Nay," she said, "let me do this!"

She straightened, blinking back the tears as she surveyed the gathering.

"He is mine! Whatever he is—whatever he *was*—and aye, he came from the Spanish, but his father and all his company were slain and he was taken captive—but now? He is mine."

A tremor passed through Felipe, at her back. Mama stood stunned, hands covering her mouth, and many of the others gaped at her. Sees Far's look was the most inscrutable. Was he remembering when Mama first brought him home?

"We will explain all as soon as we can, but know this first. Henry and Redbud are not with me, because they gave themselves—their own lives—to save ours. That I might get away and mayhap come home." She was sobbing now. "But whatever wrath you mete out for that, let it fall on me, because 'twas my fault from the start. I am the one who left the town meeting to run the forest, and they but followed."

Mama dissolved into renewed weeping, face fully covered now. Heads bowed amongst the men. Sees Far stepped forward to put his arms around Mama. Even Cousin Chris looked stricken.

"I cannot believe I am asking this," Ginny said, "but I would like to call for another town meeting so we may tell all to everyone."

As she was speaking, a new face appeared at the edge of the crowd—several, actually. Mary, her lovely round Kurawoten face alight, her arms cradling a baby. And at her shoulder, a slender English girl with hair as fair as Ginny's.

Shifting her hold on Felipe, she tugged him along with her just as Sunny broke from the group and came running.

Virginia relinquished her grip on Felipe to greet the younger girl who appeared nearly as her own reflection, and he took the moment to survey the crowd. Every feeling was displayed on their faces. Their apparel, a strange blend of English and Native. And the Kurawoten themselves—they were both like and unlike the Skaru:re, and there was no doubt that his and Virginia's presence together stirred all their protective instincts. They were indeed fierce if the occasion warranted—the English as well, despite all the mockery of them he had heard during his childhood.

The young Kurawoten woman coming forward with the baby was nothing short of beautiful. Virginia's mother also—a slightly older version of her daughter. The warrior who shadowed her did so with an intensity Felipe immediately recognized and related to.

"Another baby sister!" Virginia exclaimed, taking the infant from the other woman. So it was not the Kurawoten woman's child?

Then there were two young boys, the older wearing the briefest of kilts and the younger naked, who ran from down the beach amongst a group of other children to fling themselves against Virginia. Her brothers, clearly—although the other children surrounded her with wild abandon as well.

Felipe looked up to find Virginia's mother gazing thoughtfully at him. He dipped his head ever so slightly in respect, and she nodded gravely in return, though her lips flattened for a moment.

The crowd parted again, this time for a dark-haired Englishwoman. This must be Henry's mother. Felipe's own heart stuttered as Virginia handed back the baby and went up the strand to meet her. They fell into each other's arms, sobbing.

The others stepped back to give them room. Virginia's mother and the tall warrior came toward Felipe, the fair-haired young Englishman with them. "I am Elinor," her mother said, "and this is Sees Far and Georgie Howe. Georgie's wife, Mary. And my four younger children, along with Mary and Georgie's." She spoke mildly, but her gaze was sharp. "We are indebted to you for accompanying Ginny home and are most desirous to hear how that came to be."

He nodded again, more a half bow this time. "I am Felipe. I was Guh-neh of the Skaru:re."

Speculation shone in her blue eyes. "Felipe, is it? Named after King Philip of Spain?"

He thought he could see where Virginia had gained her spirit. "The same, mistress."

Elinor's lips curved a little. "Interesting."

While he was attempting to interpret that, she turned to Sees Far and said something softly in the Kurawoten tongue then looked back to Felipe, eyes narrowed. "Is she well?"

He drew a deep breath, gathering his scattered thoughts. "Well enough. She suffered an arrow wound to the back several days ago, but heals."

"An arrow wound." Elinor's face paled, and her eyes sparked.

"Aye. We will tell it more fully, but a certain man wanted her as wife and became angry when she refused him."

As they murmured over that and exchanged glances, he let his gaze skim their faces. "She has spoken much of you—all of you. It is an honor to meet you at last." He waited until their attention returned, then met Elinor's gaze again as unflinchingly as he could and said, "You will ask, so I tell you now. I love Virginia and will go to any length you deem necessary to prove myself worthy of her."

Widened eyes—and smiles—in response to that. "Well. We shall see, young man," Elinor said.

And then she too returned up the strand to put her arms around Henry's mother and Virginia.

Both Sees Far and Georgie looked troubled, and tears stood in Mary's eyes. None of them seemed to have words for the occasion.

Virginia straightened and beckoned to him. "Come. Tell her how bravely Henry gave himself for us."

The gathering shifted, breaking up, although some lingered to hear. The horror of that day stole through him afresh—yet to bear the news of it was part of his burden, and Virginia's, and their purpose here.

He made his approach, half bowing as he had to Elinor. "You are Henry's mother?"

"I am Margery Harvie, aye," she said, her tears still flowing. A man stepped to her side, gripping the handle of a garden implement, glaring at Felipe. She reached for his arm. "This is my husband, Dyonis, Henry's father."

Felipe offered another bow. "He comported himself well amongst the Skaru:re. Quickly he learned their tongue, and diligent he was at nearly any task set him." Felipe released a sigh. "And aye, he died bravely."

"He was singing a hymn," Virginia added, her voice breaking. "To the very end."

Henry's father covered his face with a hand, and his wife put her arms about him, weeping afresh. Virginia and her mother embraced each other again, but Felipe held himself still. It was their place to comfort each other in this moment.

A brush of unease touched him, and he scanned the crowd. A handful yet watched him—men of the English in particular but also some Kurawoten. Were those part of the hierarchy of their warriors? He supposed he would find out in time.

Were he given enough time.

Virginia and her mother drew apart at last, and to his satisfaction, Elinor turned her around and pulled back the edge of the tunic to inspect the arrow wound. After hissing and exclamations all around, the older woman fastened Felipe with a look. "How did you treat it?"

"After stopping the bleeding, I packed it with anéhsnaçi and then una:kwéya, and clay mud over all."

He pulled fragments from his pouch, though the fluff had come apart and now blew away. Elinor took a thin piece of the reddish bark and sniffed. "Ah! Sassafras and cattail." She nodded. "Very good."

"Then I made her lie still for the next day or so, to rest."

Elinor's brows arched. " 'Tis an accomplishment all its own, that."

"Mama," Virginia protested.

Laughter rippled through the onlookers, and mother put her arm around daughter's shoulders and drew her up the shore. Felipe glanced back—the Coree warriors were already carrying the chest and following Sees Far.

Georgie hefted one of the children into his arms and, without a word, positioned himself at Felipe's side. He could not fault the man's protectiveness.

Most of the houses were built Kurawoten style, and they turned aside at one, where the Coree were bade to carry in the chest, and then Felipe was nudged inside after the Coree had left. Mary handed the baby off to Elinor, and she and Georgie shooed out the children so that only Virginia, her mother, and her stepfather remained there with Felipe.

Elinor sat on one of the sleeping platforms and set the baby to nurse. "Before we go for a town meeting," she said, her gaze alternating between Virginia and Felipe, "we wish to ask a few more questions."

Sees Far stood, arms folded, looking stern but nodding. Virginia sank to her knees beside Elinor and stroked the baby's hair. For a moment it seemed tears would once again overcome the older woman, but then she firmed her mouth and said, "Ginny, when you said he is yours—are you already wed?"

"No," Virginia said, flashing a glance at Felipe. "But we wish to be."

Another look between them. "Have you already given yourself to each other in body?"

"No," Felipe said quickly, but Virginia said, just as quickly, "Aye."

Heat rushed through Felipe as Elinor stared at her daughter. He could see the defiance edging Virginia's expression. Sees Far's countenance changed not at all.

He stepped forward, his own anger rising. "Why would you say thus to your own mother, Virginia, and lie?"

Her face whipped toward him, and she turned completely crimson—and then he saw her fear.

"It profits nothing to force the issue," he said more quietly.

Her tears welled, her mouth flattening.

"Virginia Thomasyn Dare, tell me true," Elinor said very softly.

"No," she said, rising and half stumbling back to Felipe's side, twining her arm about his. "He has behaved with perfect honor toward me, though I wish—I wish I were wholly his already."

Her mother's expression was as thunderous as Sees Far's. "What then did you think to accomplish, claiming otherwise?"

But she only shook her head and leaned her cheek against his shoulder, weeping outright now. He pulled her more completely into his embrace, pressing his lips to the top of her head.

Elinor gave a noisy sigh, and she watched the two of them with resignation. " 'Twill be hard enough to convince others of your innocence in this." Her gaze narrowed on Felipe. "Yet I believe you—and commend you for it. Know this, that we wish to be on your side, for our shared history if naught else." She reached her free hand for Sees Far, and he took it, relaxing his own stance and nodding.

"I too was an enemy," Sees Far said, the cadence and resonance of his voice reminding Felipe of Blackbird. "Elinor's people did not all accept me easily—for good reason, as I had part in the death of Georgie's father." His eyes seemed to take measure of Felipe. "But the good God had His hand upon me. We will trust He has done the same with you."

"I thank you," Felipe said, his own voice unsteady.

He had not expected this—this graciousness, not from her mother and stepfather.

Virginia straightened, drying her eyes. "I'm sorry, Mama. I think I must tell you, however, before the meeting—" She shifted, still leaning a little into Felipe. "A few days before the events that led to Henry's death, Henry told me. . .that he'd always hoped I'd wait for him to be old enough to marry me. I didn't feel the same for him, although he was my dearest friend." She swallowed. "Even Margery whispered to me that she'd wished for me to become her daughter-in-law." A tremor went through her. "Might I share that—with everything else—during the meeting, or should I not? I wish not to cause her and Dyonis more pain."

Elinor's eyes glimmered. "I think it worth sharing. That way there will be no question of how things stood between you and Henry—but that you never wished him ill."

Virginia sniffled. "Very well, then."

She was home—truly home, at last. And yet her heart and spirit still would not settle.

She should be happy that the initial wave of difficulty surrounding her return was past. The awful news broken to Margery and Dyonis. Now it remained only to tell their story before the town. And when had they failed to be fair while hearing matters out and offering judgment?

Upon emerging from Mama and Papa Sees Far's new house—which Mama owned she was still growing accustomed to but did find more pleasing in some ways than the old one—Ginny was greeted and embraced by the other half of the town that somehow had not made it to the shore when they'd first arrived. Mary's auntie Timqua and Master Johnson, their minister, her grandmother the Kurawoten weroansqua, and then—at last!—Manteo himself, catching her up as if she were only a child again, laughing and crying with joy. He greeted Felipe with his usual grave courtesy and showed them to where they were to sit during the town meeting.

As everyone else flocked to the open area and found seating or simply stood, she feasted her eyes on all the familiar faces. Most were happy, welcoming—but not all. Her heart sank a little. Dyonis Harvie and several of the other Englishmen appeared profoundly discontent, and she could not blame them if it was for the sake of Henry and Redbud.

Please God that it not be because of Felipe.

He also surveyed the crowd. She'd not noticed before, but he appeared worn and weary. He sat calm and alert, however, his hands resting on his knees. He'd left his bow and arrows and the bulk of his gear, such as it was, back at the house. Was he uncomfortable amongst all these strangers without the accoutrements a warrior should carry?

And. . .how must he appear to those she'd known all her life? She eyed the growth of hair at the sides of his head and the short beard that had, it seemed, sprung overnight and gained a goodly length in the days of their travel. He didn't look quite English—but she didn't know what the Spanish looked like either.

Judging by how they were greeted on the shore, clearly he looked Spanish enough to the elders to raise some alarm.

To her he was simply Felipe, and beloved.

His eyes came to hers. His chest rose and fell with a deep breath, but he held himself calm otherwise.

The council and weroances were seated in their places, with the exception of Manteo, who waited but a breath more and then began to speak.

"We are gladdened this day to receive back from captivity Virginia, daughter of Elinor and Ananias Dare, but sorrowed to learn of the loss of Henry, son of Dyonis and Margery Harvie, and Redbud, son of Netah. Ginny has requested this meeting so she may tell the fullness of what happened to them all."

He gave her an encouraging nod and smile, but a wrench in her gut stole all thought and breath and ability to speak for a moment. Then the air returned to her lungs, and she stood to her feet to be better seen and heard.

"'Twas a town meeting that began it. You all know that Henry and Redbud and I had known each other since infancy and often ran together—but in all innocence. And as Mama often admonished, after huskanasqua I should have. . .regarded my life with more soberness and left off the running about. Especially with the boys. Yet I did not, and on that one day, 'twas not only myself to bear the consequences, but also two of my dearest friends." She hung her head a moment then forced herself to straighten and face them all again. "And you—our families and community.

"And so, the three of us were taken by the people we have called Mangoac, but who call themselves Skaru:re. While on the journey back to their town, there was a moment when the warriors were inspecting us as captives. I did not appreciate their attempts to look under my skirt and resisted, and my shift became torn. One of the men covered me with a woven rabbit-skin cloak. I thought he had merely taken pity on me but discovered later that he had, according to their customs, claimed me as his own."

Ignoring the burning of her cheeks, she waited for the murmuring to die down. "From that moment on, I was treated reasonably well. I believe the boys were as well, although I cannot be completely sure, because I was kept mostly apart from them. 'Twas discovered that Felipe, a Spanish captive who became a Skaru:re warrior, understood enough of the English tongue to both translate and instruct us in the Skaru:re." She sniffed a dry laugh. "Henry was brilliant at it. Redbud as well. I, however, struggled, and 'twas a constant vexation on all our parts.

"Then came the day when the man who gave me his cloak thought to make good on his claim. I had learned by this time that he was one of their prominent warriors, indeed a priest of their religion. The women washed and dressed and ornamented me, and I was led to him as his bride." The breath she drew felt like a knife cleaving her lungs. "When I learned what was taking place, I refused. Their elders intervened on my behalf and decreed I would have time to be courted and to decide. Unfortunately, Henry also pitched a fit and, being a mere captive, was punished for it. More diligently then did they keep us apart.

"Some time later, I did improve in my knowledge of Skaru:re, and the warrior-priest pressed me for a decision. 'Twas all very sudden, and I thought I'd have more time—they'd given me the choice between becoming his woman or remaining a slave for the remainder of my days. He already had two wives and was very resistant to hearing anything about Christ. I could not willingly marry a man who was not, at the least, a Christian."

Across the audience, heads nodded and expressions were thoughtful and sympathetic.

"In the meantime, Felipe and I had many discussions regarding religion and the difference between the Roman faith in which he was reared and our view of God and His Holy Scriptures. Blackbird, the warrior-priest, found our arguments very entertaining."

She let herself smile a little, then it faded.

"So the day he pressed me for a response, I again refused. This time he became furious and turned on Felipe, accusing him of turning me against him. This was most untrue—Felipe did all he could to encourage me to consider Blackbird's suit." From the corner of her eye, she saw Felipe tuck his head. "What neither of us could deny, even then, was that the two of us had begun to feel drawn to each other." She lifted a hand and let it fall. "How could I not, when for weeks he was the only one in the entire town I could speak with without great difficulty? I vow, however, that I did my best to see Felipe as naught but a dear brother—as Henry and Redbud were to me."

She swallowed. "And—where Henry was concerned—just days before all this took place, he slipped away and caught me in secret, out in the brush, and begged me to escape with him and Redbud. 'Twas impossible—I was watched too closely, which Felipe also helped accomplish"—she slid him a wry smile—"but in another burst of feeling, Henry told me he had hoped—" She struggled again for breath and stumbled over the words. "He had hoped when I did not immediately choose a suitor after huskanasqua, I would wait for him to be old enough. I had not time to tell him that I truly saw him as a brother and friend and nothing more. Though I loved him dearly as those."

Margery's head went down, and even as Dyonis pulled her against him, the look on his face hardened. Was that sorrow or anger? Or perhaps both?

"So then, when I refused Blackbird again and he accused Felipe, the elders gathered and insisted my choice be respected. I explained that I knew it meant I would have to remain a slave. 'Twas not enough to soothe his anger, and when they asked him what he wished, he said he wanted to see Felipe burn—as a sacrifice."

A shudder went through the Kurawoten, who understood too well, but the English were also discomfited.

"Felipe would have submitted to Blackbird's will and given his life. But after all our conversations about religion, I knew Felipe was not settled in his faith, while I was. And so I offered myself in his place, since 'twas on me the matter rested, and 'twas on me that we were in such a situation to begin with."

Her eyes burned, and she let the tears fall. "As I was being dragged away, Henry once more intervened. He—he offered himself for me— for both of us, really." She released a broken laugh. "I seem to recall the suggestion being made that they slay all three of us, but Blackbird chose Henry. I think it was in his mind to force me to be his, after, regardless of what the elders had decreed about my having a choice. But in the moment, Felipe and I were made to watch as Henry died. I will not tell the horrible details of that here, before all the children, but know this: he died bravely, with a hymn on his lips, confident that he would shortly be in the presence of the Lord."

The weeping overtook her—and many of those listening. Dyonis and Margery leaned into each other now, faces together. She took a few moments to gain enough mastery over herself to continue.

"How Blackbird's fury would have expended itself upon us, I know not, but the old woman I had served while there took us aside and sent us away while the others were yet occupied. She promised to help Redbud escape as well, and so Felipe and I fled the town.

"It took Redbud two days, tracking us, to catch up. And we had just come to the first great river that lies between their town and Cora Banks when Blackbird overtook us, leading a war party. Redbud insisted Felipe and I go on without him and went back to meet them. Felipe and I set ourselves to swim across the river and might have made it unscathed, but Blackbird shot arrows after us—and one hit me."

She turned and bared enough of her back to show the healing wound. Gasps rippled across the gathering.

"How we escaped from there, I know not, save by the grace of

God—and mayhap the impulse of Redbud." Her eyes burned afresh. "Felipe tended my wound until I was strong enough to continue traveling. At the last, we came across a Coree hunting party and turned aside to the nearest of their towns. There, they offered to bear us by kanoe to Cora Banks, and after abiding there one night, we came here—this day."

She let out a long breath as they all continued to look at her.

Chapter Nineteen

G inny turned to Felipe. " 'Tis your turn."

He rose, all grace and sinew, and faced them with no hint of hesitation. "I was born Felipe Menéndez de Alvarado, son of Juan León de Alvarado, and at the age of nine left my mother and sisters and sailed with him and his men to San Augustin in La Florida. From there we were sent on a mission to the interior. My father and all his company were slain by the people there, and I was taken captive and sold to the Skaru:re. The Blackbird of whom Virginia spoke took my education upon himself, and I was trained to be a Skaru:re warrior.

"All that Virginia related of their capture and time with the Skaru:re is true. Henry and Redbud did well in learning the tongue and accomplishing the work they were given, although it is also true Henry was punished more than once for failing to obey. I was tasked with teaching them the ways of the Skaru:re and their tongue. I tried to obey those ways as well and told them if they did what they were told, they would live, but if they caused trouble, they would die." He hesitated. "I did not intend a hap such as this. Henry would have made a fine warrior, and I grieve his loss."

The response to his short speech appeared a mix of polite interest and dubiousness. Ginny stopped just short of releasing a growl. Felipe remained standing, his own expression a study of impassiveness to rival weroance or warrior. She lifted her chin and turned a little to include them all in her next statement. "If anyone wonders—aye, I choose Felipe as my husband, and if the town will not bear his dwelling among us, then I am prepared to leave again with him."

That did break the quiet. While Felipe shook his head, Dyonis rose to his feet. "What, having brought him among us, you think we should allow him to leave again and take word of our colony back to his people?"

"Which people?" Ginny asked. "His father and such are slain."

And Felipe called out, "I have no remaining loyalty to the country of my birth—"

Before anyone else could speak, Manteo stepped swiftly to Ginny's side and, laying one hand on her arm, lifted another to the gathering. "Peace! The council will meet and talk. In the meantime, let food be prepared and everyone fed." He turned to Ginny. "Will you come with us? We wish to question you both."

She exchanged a quick glance with Felipe. "Of course," she said.

Manteo's gaze swept the gathering as people slowly unfolded themselves to stand or otherwise shifted. "Before we recess," he called out over the rising din, "are there any questions?"

Dyonis rose. "Aye, that of his loyalty." His eyes went to Ginny. "And hers."

Manteo inclined his head. "Any others?"

"Should we prepare for another attack by the Mangoac?" came a voice from the back. Ginny could not see who it was, but the voice was male and English.

And yet another—"I wish to know if we have another Georgie-and-Mary situation here."

Her heart sank further and further.

Should they have returned at all?

Felipe had determined to see this through, whatever the cost. Not that he did not appreciate the sentiment, but could she not see that her belligerence would do no good?

At least Manteo seemed to be possessed of calmness and wisdom. Felipe found himself honestly impressed at how quickly the man took charge of the gathering, directing their attention to specific matters and not so much the feelings stirred by Felipe's identity and Virginia's defiant statement.

He and Virginia were led to one of the larger houses, and a mat was spread for them to sit on the floor. A few of the men he recognized already as they filed in—Sees Far, Virginia's cousin who had met them on the shore, and an older man with abundant silver in his dark hair who had likewise greeted them. Manteo's mother, the elder chief woman, settled herself nearby on a sleeping platform and gave both Virginia and him a genuine smile. He returned it with a small nod.

Virginia was distracted with watching those filing inside, still quietly weeping, still looking furious.

Manteo sat down next to his mother and leaned toward Virginia, waiting until he had caught her attention. "You are beloved here, daughter of our hearts. Why would you speak thus, and set yourself against us?"

Oh, such tender words! Felipe's own heart was smitten.

Virginia's head went down, and a sob broke from her. "I am sorry, Manteo."

Felipe longed to comfort her, but the older man stretched a hand to her, resting it on her shoulder. "It will be well, little one. Only remember we are not your adversaries. And you are no longer a child."

She bobbed a nod.

His mother gave a sniff. "Would that Mushaniq had been so biddable."

Manteo smiled. "Mushaniq is your granddaughter. How could she not be strong of mind?" He sat back as the others found places inside the house. "And this one—being the daughter of an English warrior, with his own strength. Perhaps 'tis not to be wondered at if she is so led by the heart, even to plunging ahead without proper thought."

The smile turned wistful but remained full of affection, and Virginia lifted her head to look at him, wiping her eyes.

Pipes were passed about, and cups with strong and sweet drink.

Virginia accepted a cup but passed on the pipe. Felipe took it and sniffed. "Tobacco?" he asked.

"Uppowoc," said Sees Far, who had sat on Virginia's other side.

Felipe drew a few puffs of the fragrant smoke before passing the pipe to Georgie, on his other side. "It is good," he said.

Quiet reigned inside the house for a few minutes, then one of the pipes came back to Manteo, and after a puff, he rested the hand holding the pipe on his knee. "I would remind you all that we are committed to live, not by passion and impulse, but by the rule of law—both English law and the higher Law of God Himself. We are also committed to live in love, under the bonds of our shared faith in Christ. Let it be known that this young man is a guest of our people, until we have decided otherwise or he has acted in such a way that violates our hospitality.

"I would also remind you all that when the youths were taken during the attack, there was always the possibility one or more would not return. A greater wonder it is, perhaps, that even one has returned. Let us not lose sight of the joy of that, and our gratitude to God for it, in our sorrow for the others."

A murmur of assent rippled through the group.

"I suppose whether this is a Mary-and-Georgie situation is as good a question to begin with as any," Manteo went on, his gaze resting again on both Felipe and Virginia.

Virginia straightened, her mouth firming. Felipe slanted a quick glance at Georgie, who returned the look with mild curiosity but otherwise seemed unperturbed.

"If by Georgie and Mary you are referring to the babe arriving before the marriage is accomplished," someone said, "well—'tisn't as if there haven't been other such situations over the years. Young people tend to take matters into their own hands when carried away by strength of their feeling for each other."

The unease prickled through Felipe again. He had no way of proving he had indeed behaved with honor toward Virginia.

"True," Manteo said. "I mention it in particular, however, because theirs was the first situation where, with him being English and her Kurawoten, the expectations of each people for the marriage to take place had not yet been met before the two took matters into their own hands." His mouth twitched.

"I think it more a matter such as mine with Elinor," Sees Far said. "All presumed I had claimed Elinor as my wife when 'twas not yet the case—and I came to your people as a former enemy."

"So you are saying that these two have not yet—?"

"They say not."

More murmurs.

"I actually said aye," Virginia said, very low, her voice saucy. Under the renewed stares of the others, she went on, "Besides, what does it matter if we say no? Who will believe that we have not, journeying together alone all those days?"

Felipe only shook his head, but some of the others chuckled at her words.

"What is it then, Felipe?" Manteo asked, his voice quiet and steady.

Virginia slid him a glance, her cheeks reddening again.

He blew out a long breath. "God knows the truth of my heart. I confess I have kissed her, but no more." He hesitated, then added, "I will not deny I wish more, or—as I already said to Virginia—that Blackbird spoke the truth when he accused me of wishing she could be mine, even as I pushed her to accept him." He held Manteo's gaze. "Nor will I deny that I might not have held back had she not been wounded."

Manteo gave him a grave nod, but Felipe could almost hear the silent growls from some of the men. Virginia bent a longer look upon him. He offered her the barest smile before continuing.

"I do wish to marry her, to be her husband, with all that entails. To be part of her people. I have no more ties to Spain, and in leaving the Skaru:re, all bonds with them have been sundered as well."

The older Englishman sitting on the platform shifted. "The Spanish still have holdings in Florida, particularly—where did you say?—San Augustin. 'Twould be simple to sail down the coast and find them."

"I have no wish to return there. I have lived with the Skaru:re and heard and seen what they have done to the people of this country. And now, my home—my heart—is with Virginia." He huffed. "I know not how else to assure you. Or to prove my intent."

Beside him, Georgie lifted his cup of tea and muttered, "Just let them marry already."

Manteo smiled a little before sobering. "The question of whether or not we should expect attack has merit, but we will hold that until we have eaten."

As the others began to rise and leave, Virginia made no move to do so, and Felipe stayed where he was as well. Manteo, Sees Far, and Georgie also lingered.

"Have you yet told them," Manteo asked suddenly, looking at Sees Far, "of our decision after we had gone over to get them back?"

"Mahta."

Virginia turned toward Sees Far, and Felipe could nearly read the questions in her bearing. Sees Far regarded her with a softening in his face. "Since the day your mother first reached her hand out to ask me to stay with her, years ago now, you have been as my own little daughter. We did not lightly leave you without a fight. But we saw this one"—he nodded toward Felipe—"with the warriors who came out to talk with us. We rightly guessed he must be Spanish. But I had a knowing in my spirit that the good God had a purpose for him in all this—that he would be used in an important way in your life." Sees Far drew a long breath through his nose and released it. "We did not know it would mean Henry's life. But we felt if we carried out any attack on the town—however much we wished to, and hated returning without you—then it would interfere with whatever God intended to do in the situation."

Virginia sagged anew with the weeping, and the warrior gathered her in his arms. He met Felipe's gaze over her head. "So take heart. God will not fail to continue to work here."

"But Henry," she wailed.

"Aye. But Henry."

Felipe felt a nudge at his shoulder, and he turned to find Georgie tipping his head toward the doorway. "Come," he said.

Most of the others were gone now. Felipe rose and, with a last glance back at Virginia, followed him out.

"Walk with me a bit," Georgie said. "She'll be fine with those two."

The smells of food cooking filled the air, and Felipe's gut cramped with sudden hunger, but Georgie led him back toward the water, past where dishes were already laid out on mats and others were gathering. The gazes of many followed them, lingering in particular on Felipe, but Georgie acknowledged very few.

They passed the last of the houses and stopped, overlooking the sound, where one of the most glorious sunsets Felipe had ever seen spread before them, gold and purple and pink, reflecting off the rippled surface.

"We have the best sunrises and sunsets," Georgie said.

Felipe could only smile.

The young English warrior swung to face him. "The beard is new, aye? I don't recall you having it before."

He coughed another laugh. "No. I kept it plucked, as the Skaru:re men do." He ran a hand across the stubble on the sides of his head. "And this they shave, with sharpened flint."

Georgie nodded. "So do the Kurawoten." He grimaced, scratching his chin. "Sees Far plucked my beard, sparse though it was, when he first outfitted me for huskanaw. I later decided to grow it, but otherwise, as you can see, I favor the Kurawoten mode of dress." He smirked. "The elder English grew accustomed to it."

Felipe grinned briefly. "Sees Far trained you, then?"

Georgie nodded. "He took me under his wing and prepared me for huskanaw, even before he was fully accepted by the town himself." He glanced at Felipe. "Has Ginny told you this story yet?"

"Some, perhaps, but I mind not hearing it again."

"Well, then. When Elinor was taken, she tasked me with carrying Ginny to safety. She was but a tiny child—two, if I recall correctly—and I took the responsibility very seriously. I'd no proper mother since my own died in England, and Elinor was the closest to that for me.

"Mary was known then as Mushaniq, the wild daughter of Manteo who also had no mother but often helped Elinor. Her aunt, Manteo's sister Timqua, now married to our minister, took up caring for Ginny, and Mary and I helped look after her. Over the next months, Mary came of age and. . .set her affections upon me." A slow smile curled his mouth. "Wild lad that I was with no firm guidance, I could not resist her. She promised to wed me as soon as we were allowed."

Many pieces of what had been spoken in the council meeting suddenly took new meaning. "But you were not allowed," Felipe guessed.

Georgie shook his head. "Nay. They wanted Mary to become a Christian, and she resisted, even though most of the Kurawoten had by then gladly received Christ. The Kurawoten, in turn, wished me to undergo huskanaw—their coming-of-age rite—but the English thought it heathen. 'Twas quite a time before a compromise was struck.

"In the meantime, Sees Far returned with Elinor, who soon discovered that Mary was with child. Finally, the English agreed to let me go huskanaw. Manteo and Sees Far promised 'twould not be a heathen affair, merely a test of my ability to be a warrior—to be a man, and thus acceptable to the Kurawoten though yet a youth. I survived the ordeal well enough but then felt the Lord leading me, on my last day out, to carry out an additional task which kept me from returning home for another month." He slid Felipe a thin smile. "By that time, Mary had given birth to our oldest son and she had at last surrendered to Christ and been baptized, so there was no longer any hindrance to our marriage."

Felipe closed his open mouth. "Virginia had not yet told me all that. I wonder if she knows the whole of it."

Georgie laughed. "Well, I thought you might appreciate knowing what you two are being compared to." He patted Felipe's shoulder. "Tomorrow I shall take you over to the ocean side of the island. 'Tis another sight not to be missed."

How she had missed the warmth, the sense of belonging. The *love*. 'Twas true, both Sees Far and Manteo were as papas to her, and it felt like she had been on her guard for so long, out of necessity, she nearly did not know how to simply *be*.

But would the tears ever not spring forth at every little thing?

She roused to find the meetinghouse empty, save for Manteo and his mother and Papa Sees Far. Sitting up, swiping at her eyes for the thousandth time, she looked around. "Where is Felipe?"

She winced at the plaintive note in her voice.

"With Georgie." Sees Far smiled. "He will not immediately slaughter him. Or let anyone else do so."

She huffed a dry, humorless laugh. " 'Tis a relief to know."

They all rose, and Manteo's mother gathered her into an embrace. "As Manteo said, you are beloved, little one. We thank the good God for bringing you home."

"Thank you," she said. Then she peeled herself away and ran out to find Felipe.

Weaving her way through the town, she kept being stopped by those who had not yet greeted her or who wanted to discuss some part or another about what had been shared. Neither Felipe nor Georgie was anywhere in sight—and Georgie at least should be easy to spot. She forced herself to contain her rising impatience and alarm. 'Twas Georgie, after all, whom she loved and trusted with her own life. With a deep breath, she gave herself as much as possible to each person who delayed her search.

At last she could bear it no longer and asked, "Has anyone seen where Georgie and Felipe have gone?"

Someone pointed vaguely in the direction of the sound—but there they were, carrying between them a spit from which dangled several broiled fish, each as long as a man's arm, making their way to the serving mats. There they carefully lowered their burden and laid the fish out on the mats.

She stood watching, a little dazzled by the way Felipe worked with

Georgie as if the two were already old friends, and Felipe's shy grin alongside the other man in response to others' thanks for their help. There was some hesitation in both the giving and receiving, but they were trying.

Perhaps her fears were unfounded and they could—would—truly make a home here. She'd grown to womanhood hearing continually how gracious the Kurawoten were in welcoming the English. Surely they could do no less for Felipe.

'Twas some of the English, however, she yet worried about.

Please, gracious Lord, let it be that they in turn offer grace. That You bring comfort and healing to the Harvies. That Felipe and I be a blessing to all.

The band about her chest, which she'd not even realized was there until now, began to ease. As she took her first free breath since before she was taken, the smell of the fish and other good things awakened ravenousness.

And Felipe looked over and saw her. The gladness and relief on his face nearly undid her again.

He came to her side, not quite reaching for her but leaning a little as if he wished to. "All is well," she said in response to the question in his eyes. Then she drew him with her—oh, where should they sit? She chose a space yet unoccupied along the mats and bade him sit beside her.

"The Kurawoten do also as the Skaru:re in community dinners," Felipe observed.

"As all the peoples of this country, so I have heard," Ginny said.

They both scooped pieces of broiled fish. She hummed with appreciation of the first bite—oh, how she had missed this as well! Felipe was nodding as he chewed.

They ate, glancing at each other, watching those around them. "There are many children," Felipe said.

"Aye, and I suddenly find myself not sure I recognize them all." Ginny laughed, but weakly.

"Well, you'd better recognize me!" piped a young male voice. A wiry form with a shock of dark hair, arching brows, and snapping black eyes dropped to sit across from them.

A genuine laugh erupted from her this time. "Waboose! Of course I do. Where have you been all this time?"

He waved a hand. "Running the island, of course."

"Of course."

As her sister Sunny took the seat next to him, windblown and laughing, they were suddenly surrounded by the rest of his family—Georgie and Mary with three other children in tow. The younger ones piled over each other to hug Ginny, and Mary waited until they were finished before sliding in for a quick embrace as well. "How we have missed you!" she exclaimed. Then, eyes sparkling, "Good work on keeping the elders hopping." She flashed a little grin at Felipe. "We are all for you two."

"Thank you," Ginny said. "I do understand their hesitation. And their sorrow over the boys."

"Of course," Mary said, scooping bits of food for the smallest child, on her lap. "But they need not be so foolish about other things."

"They are protective of the town," Georgie said, "as they ought to be."

Mary only firmed her mouth.

Felipe tipped his head and whispered to Ginny, "Jael's wife?"

A giggle escaped her. "Aye."

"What was that?" Georgie said, his gaze sharp upon both of them. But she laughed again while Felipe grinned.

" 'Tis naught. A story from the Scriptures I was relating to Felipe while he tended my arrow wound." And she laughed again, taking new measure of her old friend, clearly not tamed in the least by her motherly duties. When both Mary and Georgie continued to eye them, she amended, "I told him how she was the one to slay Wanchese when he tried to take Mama again."

"Ahh." Smiles now. Mary's brow lifted. "Did you tell him how I sent you into the bushes to play 'waboose' while I went back to help Elinor?" She nodded toward her eldest son devouring food as fast as his hands could scoop, watching them all, listening to every word. " 'Tis why I used it as that one's milk name."

Both she and Felipe laughed. "I did not recall that," Ginny admitted.

"He has a proper English name," Georgie told Felipe, "after myself and his grandfather—but we felt one Georgie in the town was enough."

"Mama gave my younger siblings English names as well," Ginny said. "Sunny is Johanna Elizabeth Dare, but Sees Far called her Sunlight, which eventually was shortened. The boys are—"

Mama and Sees Far and her siblings joined them at that moment, Mama giving Ginny a quick but heartfelt embrace before she settled over on Felipe's other side. "The babe desperately wanted milk and sleep, and then more milk. I think she may be about to grow again. Oh—Sunny! There you are."

"Sorry, Mama!" her younger sister said. "I was with Waboose. 'Tis such fun to explore the island."

The boys fell upon the food as if they'd not eaten in days. Ginny's eyes stung. It was all so achingly normal.

Felipe must have felt something of the same, for his expression seemed to sober as well. She reached over and put a hand on his forearm. His head lifted, his gaze meeting hers, and a slight smile flitted across his lips.

It had been a full day, for certain.

Nearby, a fiddle lilted a few notes, stopped for plucked tuning, then began again. Ginny's heart took flight, and Felipe's gaze lit with an answering surprise and joy.

As other instruments joined and some left the food to form a circle, he put his free hand over hers and leaned toward her. "Dance with me, White Doe of the English and Kurawoten?"

"With gladness," she said in return.

Chapter Twenty

S o, how likely is it that the Mangoac—or as they call themselves, the Skaru:re—will return to attack again?"

The meeting had been put off until the next morning and, as near as Felipe could tell, included only the chief men of the English and Kura-woten. Manteo's mother and sister both sat in attendance, and a much longer time had been spent passing pipes about to take the smoke of the tobacco—uppowoc as the Kurawoten called it—before anyone spoke.

It was one of the English elders who now questioned Felipe. He alone had been invited, leaving Virginia to most reluctantly attend her mother for the morning. But it was he who, by dint of ten years with the Skaru:re, could best advise her people.

And he did not take the responsibility lightly.

"It is difficult to say," he answered. "By custom, Blackbird should have been content with a death—a sacrifice, regardless of whether or not the one whose life was given was the one to offend. But it is clear he saw Virginia's refusal, and then my accompanying her away, as a very grave offense indeed. And he had not been convinced even by their own chief men and women that neither Virginia nor I intended any offense, which was why I knew it futile to protest his taking my life as the sacrifice to begin with."

He hoped the words were understandable enough.

"The grandmother Virginia served believed Blackbird's wrath would not be eased with Henry's death. This proved true, although why his arrow finding its mark in Virginia then was enough, I do not know." He was quiet for a moment. "He should have followed us, however, if it was not. Either he did not follow, or he could not find us."

"Clearly, God protected you," the elder English said with awe in his voice. The others murmured their assent.

Felipe tucked his head. Why them and not Henry? And why again had that lad chosen to take their place? "Virginia and I have recognized that as well. I exhorted her not to waste her companion's sacrifice, but to take heart and live henceforth."

"Words of wisdom," the older man said.

"You mentioned that Henry died singing a hymn," Master Johnson said. "Which one?"

Ginny had been sweeping the house while baby Berry slept, and Mama was off doing something when the minister stopped by. She'd stepped outside so as not to wake the sleeping infant and braced herself for whatever he might wish to say.

This she had not expected.

Eyes burning, a lump in her throat, she told him.

He nodded slowly. "Thank you. We cannot bury him properly, but I wish at least to hold a memorial service."

She started to speak, could not, and dissolved into tears.

Master Johnson stepped closer and set a hand on her head. "Oh child. You must not blame yourself."

"But I do," she whimpered. "How am I to not, when 'twas my foolish actions the day of the attack—"

"Ginny. Sweet girl. Listen."

She tried to suppress the tears and could not, but peeked up at him.

"First, Henry and Redbud were not small children. They followed you that day of their own will. No one compelled them."

"But—I led—"

"True, and one must learn to be a good leader. But second, do you think our God so small and weak that He cannot bring good from our foolish actions? Or from tragic hap?"

That did stop her. Another sob, then stillness descended upon her.

"I know you have been better instructed than that." He smiled gently. "But you must trust Him. If"—he raked a hand through his hair, caught back at his nape—"if 'twere easy to trust, then where would be the need for faith?"

" 'Faith is a sure confidence of things which are hoped for, and a certainty of things which are not seen,'" she quoted, suddenly recalling the verse.

"Aye."

She sighed. "I think my faith must be very small."

"Then we shall help it grow." Another soft smile. "You had enough faith to bring your young man here."

She choked again. "I credit his growing faith with that more than mine. Which—he will wish to talk with you."

"Oh?"

"He was raised in the Roman Church, as you know, but he has questions. I was not able to answer well enough on the differences in our own mode of faith or even our interpretation of Scripture itself."

"I look forward to that," Master Johnson said.

When he had gone, she went inside and sat down near little Berry, watching the babe sleep. Her own slumber last night had been troubled—another dream of fire and blood. It had been so strange—wondrous, but strange—to fall asleep in the same dwelling as her family, tucked in on one of the sleeping platforms, with Felipe on the floor at her side. Ignoring Mama's glances at the way she lay with her arm over the edge, resting across Felipe's chest, she'd fallen asleep fairly quickly after all the food and dancing.

But then came the nightmare, and she woke to the strangling sensation of a thin scream trying to force itself through her throat and Felipe's arms about her, his low, soothing voice near her ear. Words that she did not

243

understand with her conscious mind but somehow knew were a prayer.

Felipe—praying over her. *For* her.

Oh aye, his faith was greater than hers in this moment.

Papa Sees Far had whisked him off before she'd even properly awakened this morning, first to the sound to wash and then to the council meeting they were supposed to have finished last night.

She should be happy. She was home. Mama had pronounced her arrow wound healed as well as could be expected thus far, though it still hurt to use that arm or reach above her head. All of her family were glad to have her back.

No one had yet slain Felipe, although it had not yet been a full day, and the question of his presence here remained to be settled.

Still, an ache hollowed out the inside of her. A gnawing restlessness. Something was not settled. Not. . .right.

Had Mama struggled with this after returning from captivity all those years ago?

Little Berry stirred and let out a cry. Ginny swooped her up, cuddling the infant to her shoulder and patting her back. The babe continued to squirm, rooting about against Ginny's neck. She giggled. "There now. No, I am sorry, but I have no milk for you. Mama will be back very soon."

And then Mama did walk in. "I knew it must be close to time," she said and, taking Berry, sat to feed her.

Ginny noticed for the first time that Mama was dressed in a tunic of supple deerskin. "Mama—your dress!"

Her mother flashed her a grin. "Aye. Sees Far has his wish at last to see me in doeskin. 'Tis surprisingly cool and comfortable." She eyed Ginny's apparel—the doubled doeskin skirt and the ragged tunic she'd been wearing over it, then smiled. "Mayhap you would agree?"

Ginny laughed. "I do. Although I must admit that while with the Skaru:re, I didn't always wear the tunic." Heat crept into her cheeks.

"One does what one must in the moment," Mama said. "None of the People think it immodest for a woman to wear only the skirt."

Another wry smile. "Which has been a point of much discussion—and contention—over the years."

Oh, she recalled many of those discussions.

Mama's grin widened. "I remember when your grandfather first returned from exploring this land and showed me his drawings of the people. So scandalous! And yet I was fascinated—their faces were so alive, so beautiful to me, even then." As Berry continued nursing, she traced a fingertip across the baby's cheek then caught the tiny hand resting against her belly. "To think my own bloodline—and Papa's—is now a part of these people. 'Tis a wonder."

Ginny was quiet, thinking about the implications of mingling one bloodline with another. Of her, an English girl, with a Spaniard. "Mama. Is it wrong for me to love Felipe?"

Mama blew out a long, soft breath. "Do you love him? Truly?"

Her thoughts snarled. "Aye! I mean, why would I not? Have I made it seem that I do not?"

Mama shook her head, very slowly. " 'Tisn't that. But there is a concern. Is it truly love, or do you simply feel an attachment because, as you said, he was the only one you could speak to while a captive? Because he was something familiar to fix your eyes upon."

Heat rushed through her, then cold. Her mouth opened, but she knew not what to say.

Was everything about these past weeks, all that she felt for Felipe, built upon nothing but an illusion?

A slight smile curved Mama's lips. "Some made that assertion where Sees Far and I were concerned."

"But—nay! You and Papa Sees Far do truly love each other, do you not?"

"Indeed. But love is as much a choice as it is a feeling. Mayhap more."

Her throat ached and her eyes burned. "I want to be his wife, Mama. I never met anyone else I felt that for. As much as I loved Henry and Redbud—" She shook her head, slowly at first then with more force. "No.

Henry's declaration only made me feel a little sick and angry at being pushed."

Mama's brows arched, and she nodded. "I simply want you to consider and be sure." She lifted Berry from her breast to her shoulder. "Now, I understand Master Johnson intends to hold a service for Henry. Did you bathe this morning?"

Another wave of something like shame swept over her. "I did not."

"Well." To her surprise, Mama smiled again. "Let us go now."

Her brave, beautiful daughter! How Elinor had missed her. How she still ached at the time lost—at all Ginny had endured. Yet mayhap, because of her own journey, she could help Ginny navigate hers.

Before leaving the house, Elinor took the shift and kirtle from the storage chest Ginny had brought from Cora Banks. "I would have thought you'd have changed before coming," she said as Ginny watched.

"I didn't wish them soiled by travel and didn't have time for more than the briefest wash before we left yestermorn."

"That's reasonable."

She led Ginny down to the section of sound shoreline allocated for the women's bathing. Ginny did not hesitate, but slipped out of tunic and skirt and waded in. Unlike other portions of the shoreline, it was only a short distance before being deep enough to submerge.

"I seem to remember having done this as a child," Ginny said, "but the memory is fuzzy. I remember the water being colder."

Elinor laughed. "The Kurawoten women so made fun of us English and our aversion to the cold, but we soon learned to enjoy it."

Ginny splashed about, unbraiding her hair and scrubbing it under the waves. At last she returned, wringing out the dark golden length of it. Elinor helped her with the shift. She eyed the kirtle. "Must I?"

Elinor sighed. "For the funeral service?"

"Aye," they both said at once, and shared another chuckle.

After setting Berry down on the sand for a moment, Elinor drew and tied the laces so Ginny would not have to strain her arm and healing back muscles. "I bathed this morning," she said when Ginny gave her a questioning look.

"Everyone was awake before me," Ginny complained.

"Given that you seemed to have more trouble sleeping soundly, I am not surprised." She gave the lacing tie a last tug. "Do you recall the nightmare?"

"Aye," Ginny whispered.

Elinor waited.

"I dream oft of Henry. The blood and fire."

Oh. . .my darling child. "So 'twas not the first time Felipe has soothed you thus."

Ginny shook her head, still looking haunted. "The first time was after I took Blackbird's arrow. The fever from the wound, apparently."

Alarm coursed through Elinor and intense gratitude that Ginny had survived, and so relatively unscathed.

"I'm sorry for disturbing everyone," Ginny added.

"Sweet, dear heart. We're simply happy you're home."

A horn sounded from the town. Ginny startled, and Elinor put a hand upon her shoulder. " 'Tis only the call for meeting—likely the service."

She swooped up a cooing and gurgling Berry and beckoned to Ginny, now braiding her hair over one shoulder.

"Mama."

Elinor stopped. "Yes, dear one?"

Her daughter's blue eyes were sharp, narrowed against the bright sunlight. "How long must Felipe and I wait to be married? I mean, am I expected to delay until we have properly mourned Henry, or—?"

"I wish I could say. Much will depend upon what is decided by the council. How quickly the town accepts him." She held out a hand. "Mayhap it will depend even upon Dyonis and Margery."

Virginia's hands stilled on the braid. "So the Harvies have the power to prevent us from being wed?"

Elinor grimaced. "Not exactly. But we are all part of this community, aye?"

Ginny finished the braid with slower movements, tied it off, then retrieved her deerskin garments from the ground and shook them out. Her expression was strangely shuttered.

Quite unlike the girl Elinor had always known. Her heart squeezed. *Oh my daughter.*

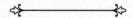

Felipe sat down on the dune and watched the motion of the waves as they rolled onto the shore, then out, then back up again, then out again.

Utterly mesmerizing. And soothing, the rush and crash of the water.

Georgie settled beside him. "I used to come here and do exactly thus—watch and listen to the waves. It helped with the sorrow of my father's death. And Mary would often find me and sit with me." He nodded toward the knot of children running down the beach, screaming and chasing each other or stopping to look at shells. "She was still a child then herself."

"An enviable childhood, it would seem," Felipe said.

"Indeed." Georgie smiled, but Felipe could see the shadow that yet lingered.

"How old were you when your father was slain?"

Georgie sobered. "Twelve. And yourself?"

"Nine."

"At least I had a community to see to my care," Georgie said at last.

"The Skaru:re saw to mine, though I was a captive at first," Felipe said. "It was not so terrible. I learned to avoid trouble and grew strong."

Georgie tipped his head. "That sounds very much like my own experience, given the circumstances."

They continued to watch the sea and the children, and suddenly there came a sound from over the dunes and hills behind them, faintly. "Was that—"

"A trumpet? Aye." Georgie called to the children, who heartily protested having to leave already. " 'Tis another meeting. Although I am not sure why."

Concern sparked in his eyes and drew lines in his face.

They made their way back over the island, running lightly. Past a fort the English had built nearly twenty years before, as Georgie explained, when they had first landed at Kurawoten, overlooking the ocean side. Through the low-growing forest, full of gnarled oaks that were nearly miniatures of the ones on the mainland, cedars, and other curious yet familiar-looking flora. The trumpet sounded again just before they reached the town.

They arrived to find everyone gathering in the town center. One of the elder Englishmen stood at the head of the crowd, where mats were laid out for the chief people and the infirm, and some English-style chairs behind those. "That's Master Johnson, our minister," Georgie said, nodding toward the Englishman. "He's the one you'll want to talk with on matters of faith, although he's done well over the years in making sure each of us is secure in Christ."

There was that phrase again, the one Virginia had used. From their vantage point at the edge of a rise, he scanned the crowd, looking for her. A golden-haired woman dressed in the Kurawoten manner and carrying a babe caught his eye—but no, that was Elinor—was it not? Behind her, the slender figure of another English woman, turned half away from him and clad in shift and gown, yet tugging at him with a strange familiarity.

Frowning, he glanced elsewhere but found his eyes drawn back. . .

She pivoted, speaking to the other woman. The curve of her cheek, the angle of her profile—his heart nearly stopped. There. That was Virginia, looking like a proper English girl.

He wove through the crowd toward her. Her head came up, and her expression lit with relief and gladness.

Both reflected his own feelings in the moment.

She reached for his hand as he neared. " 'Tis a memorial service for Henry and Redbud—Henry, at least, since we know of his death." The sorrow flooded her eyes again.

His chest squeezed. A memorial.

Had such ever been held for Papá and the others? Perhaps for him as well?

The minister called everyone to find places so he might begin. Virginia clung to Felipe's hand for a moment longer. "Mama wishes me to come sit with her up front. You should come as well."

He considered how it was the elders and likely family and nursing mothers and such taking the chairs and mats laid out. "No, but you go. I will be near."

She gripped more tightly, swaying toward him as if she wished to say more—or kiss him, but this was not the place—then with a nod, released him and slipped away after her mother.

Glancing about again, he located Georgie standing off to the side with Sees Far and some of the other men, all of whom had the young boys sitting on the ground before them, facing the minister.

"I have gathered you all," the Englishman began, standing behind a simple pulpit, "to commemorate the life of Henry Dyonis Harvie, and to commend his soul to our God and to heaven. This cannot properly be a burial service, since we have not his body, but we shall honor him before our Lord as best we can under the circumstances. Please rise and speak with me as you are able."

A rustle followed of the whole company getting to their feet.

The minister went on,

I am the resurrection and the life, saith the Lord;
he that believeth in me, though he were dead, yet shall he live;
and whosoever liveth and believeth in me shall never die.

I know that my Redeemer liveth,
and that he shall stand at the latter day upon the earth;
and though this body be destroyed, yet shall I see God;
whom I shall see for myself and mine eyes shall behold,
and not as a stranger.

For none of us liveth to himself,
and no man dieth to himself.

For if we live, we live unto the Lord.

and if we die, we die unto the Lord.

Whether we live, therefore, or die, we are the Lord's.

Blessed are the dead who die in the Lord;

even so saith the Spirit, for they rest from their labors.

"Let us also pray for all who mourn, that they may cast their care on God, and know the consolation of His love.

"Almighty God, look with pity upon the sorrows of Your servants for whom we pray. Remember them, Lord, in Your mercy; nourish them with patience; comfort them with a sense of Your goodness; lift up Your countenance upon them; and give them peace; through Jesus Christ our Lord. Amen."

He looked around at the gathering. "I would like us to begin with a hymn—a particular one, I am told, that Henry indeed sang with his dying breath. And so, to honor him, let us all sing."

He led, and indeed, within a few notes, Felipe recognized it. Chills rose across his skin. He could see Virginia's head bowing, her body shaking with weeping. Nearby, Henry's father put his arm about his wife's shoulders.

Felipe would only make a spectacle of himself if he pushed through the crowd to embrace Virginia as well, but he longed to. Oh, how he longed to.

Instead, he put his own head down and shut his eyes as voices rose and swelled around him. It was truly beautiful and moving.

When the song ended, the minister leafed through the pages of the great book lying open before him. "This is not a verse customary to a funeral or memorial, but I thought it fitting for Henry. In the fifteenth chapter of John we read, from the mouth of our Lord, 'This is my commandment, that ye love together, as I have loved you. Greater love hath no man, than this: that a man bestow his life for his friends.'"

The minister lifted his head to survey the gathering. "Hear again these words. Greater love has no man than to give his life for his friends. Henry indeed gave himself thus. Let us then take comfort that his life bespoke love above all—and that in Christ, such an expenditure is by no means in vain."

The minister looked at Virginia as he said this last bit.

"All our hope is in Christ. If we had no hope in Him—if indeed, Christ has not risen from the dead—then as said in First Corinthians chapter fifteen, we are of all people most miserable, for even in our labor for food and clothing and shelter in this life, all we strive for finds its final satisfaction in the life to come. We all hope for length of days, and yet if, as in the case of Henry, our days are cut short when they are hardly begun, all is not lost, all is not laid to waste, if we are in Christ. We trust that all who commit themselves to Him will rise again on the Last Day and will shine forever like the stars in the heavens.

"Even so, we will sorrow in this life for the parting from those we love—many of those taken too soon by our own reckoning. Yet who can say whether God might have some sovereign purpose in such loss, which we cannot see in this moment?"

Half the gathering wept now, Felipe among them.

Did God truly have a purpose for the cruel slaughter of Papá and his men? Or was that, as similar events had been regarded by their countrymen, merely the actions of devilish savages who knew nothing but to cause hurt? Felipe had lived among the peoples of this land and tasted of both their generosity and ruthlessness.

Perhaps it was true, they did not know all they should of the God who had made them—but his countrymen were no angels either.

Still, what did that mean for Papá? He had sought glory—professed it for Spain, for God Himself, perhaps a little for the family of Alvarado, that they might be remembered for generations to come.

The minister read again. "Out of the deep have I called unto thee, oh Lord. Lord, hear my voice. Oh let thine ears consider well the voice of my complaint. If thou, Lord, wilt be extreme to mark what is done amiss, oh Lord, who may abide it? For there is mercy with thee, therefore shalt thou be feared. I look for the Lord, my soul doth wait for him, in his word is my trust. My soul flees unto the Lord, before the morning watch—I say—before the morning watch. O Israel, trust in the Lord, for with the Lord there is mercy, and with him is plenteous redemption. And he shall redeem Israel, from all his sins."

He turned further toward the end of the book. "Behold, I show you a mystery. We shall not all sleep: but we shall all be changed, and that in a moment, in the twinkling of an eye by the last trump. For the trump shall blow, and the dead shall rise incorruptible, and we shall be changed. For this corruptible must put on incorruption, and this mortal must put on immortality. When this corruptible hath put on incorruption, and this mortal hath put on immortality, then shall be brought to pass the saying that is written: Death is swallowed up in victory. Death, where is thy sting? Hell, where is thy victory? The sting of death is sin, and the strength of sin is the law. But thanks be unto God which has given us victory, through our Lord Jesus Christ. Therefore, my dear brethren, be ye steadfast and unmovable, always rich in the work of the Lord, for as much as ye know, how that your labor is not in vain in the Lord."

Next he turned nearly to the end. "And I saw a new heaven and a new earth. For the first heaven and the first earth were vanished away, and there was no more sea. And I, John, saw that holy city, new Jerusalem, come down from God out of heaven, prepared as a bride garnished for her husband. And I heard a great voice out of heaven saying: Behold, the tabernacle of God is with men, and he will dwell with them. And they shall be his people, and God himself shall be with them, and be their God. And God shall wipe away all tears from their eyes. And there shall be no more death, neither sorrow, neither crying, neither shall there be any more pain, for the old things are gone."

Both hands on the corners of the pulpit, he straightened and looked at them all. "This is our hope and our confidence, that we will indeed share in the resurrection of Christ. We shall stand, as say the words of Job, and in our flesh behold Him—our God indeed, and no stranger. And so we trust that God holds Henry—and Redbud—indeed, all of us—and what we have committed to His hands, He is strong to keep.

"Please rise and pray with me the words taught us by our Savior.

"Our Father which art in heaven, hallowed be thy name. Let thy kingdom come. Thy will be fulfilled, as well in earth, as it is in heaven. Give us this day our daily bread. And forgive us our debts, as we forgive our debtors. And lead us not into temptation, but deliver us from evil. For thine is the kingdom and the power, and the glory forever. Amen."

Voices swelled around Felipe again, thrumming through him, burning his throat and eyes with the words he knew so well but had never heard spoken in such a rude tongue. And yet it seemed never so full of strength and power—except perhaps in the dead of night when he had whispered it over Virginia.

It ended with a firm, echoing "Amen," and the minister lifted his head. "Peace be with us all," he said.

The crowd began to move but slowly, as they all seemed caught by some unseen force. Virginia, still in tears, half turned to her mother, who gathered her into her arms. The embrace soon included Henry's mother and father and others.

Felipe eased toward the other edge of the gathering, tucking his head and keeping his gaze downcast as had been his habit for so many years, to avoid notice by those who would mark him as not Skaru:re and trouble him for it. In truth, he fit no better here than there. No return was open to him—yet neither could he go forward.

Up on the rise that he and Georgie had crossed on their way to and from the island's ocean side, he tucked himself beneath one of the gnarled oaks and watched the gathering. Virginia and her mother still had an arm about each other as they talked with those around them. The minister laid a hand on Virginia's shoulder, and she seemed to glance about.

Was she looking for him? Yet Felipe could not bring himself to move.

After this, there would be cooking and more of the amazing food they'd enjoyed the night before. More talk amongst the elders and warriors concerning the Skaru:re—and the problem he, Felipe, presented. He had watched their faces. Some, Virginia's family and close friends, were gracious and willing to accept him. But others' expressions were rimmed with doubts and fears, perhaps even hatred.

How was he to overcome that? To prove himself? He had become Skaru:re by training and feats of strength and cunning—but to be born Spanish was the sin the English could not forgive.

He shall redeem Israel from all his sins.

Redemption. Felipe knew the word—to buy back. To transfer the deed of ownership from one to another. It was in essence what Blackbird had done for him all those years ago, purchasing him out of captivity—or rather, from ownership of one people to another. The debt he owed Blackbird, the Skaru:re overall, was one Felipe believed he'd never be able to repay.

And in a moment—because of Virginia—all that had been undone. He was free, and yet unfree, in ways he knew not what to do with.

The Holy Scriptures spoke of God redeeming Israel from sin. Was Felipe likewise redeemed? If not, could God redeem him—or, a better question, would He?

None of that answered what he should do in this moment, however.

To force a community to accept him was impossible. Even should the elders declare him trustworthy, some would not see it thus. Certainly, there was nothing Felipe could do to force such trust. And if he and Virginia were to marry before such acceptance took place, what would the response be? It might be worse for her. And he would be nothing more in the eyes of Henry's family than a reminder of Henry's death as a captive. . .

The first inkling of an idea trickled through his thoughts.

Henry had indeed offered himself in Virginia's place, and Virginia in Felipe's. Redbud had turned back and offered himself for them both.

Perhaps there was a way to at least begin making this right, after all.

He rose from his place and, ducking beneath a low-hanging branch, started back toward the gathering, now eddying about. Virginia had stepped clear of her mother's embrace and was scanning the crowd, but her back was half to Felipe as he neared.

His chest squeezed. This would not please her—not at all.

Felipe angled for Henry's father and mother, still standing near

Virginia and her family, accepting the condolences of their fellow towns-folk. About three paces away he stopped so as not to interrupt their present conversation, and waited.

Henry's mother glanced over and saw him first, her eyes widening. The conversation faltered. Henry's father's gaze followed quickly, shock and alarm melting into hostility. "What is it you—"

"Felipe!" Virginia's voice, full of gladness, cut across the man's snarl. "Oh, thank the Lord. I was about to go looking for you!"

Chapter Twenty-One

She was completely, utterly wrung out with sorrow and grief. For several long minutes, when she could not spy Felipe anywhere in the crowd, panic had thrashed inside her at the possibility he had slipped away, never to return.

But there he was, standing by the Harvies, as if waiting his turn to speak. A courtesy everyone performed at such events.

At her exclamation, he shifted, appearing startled for the sliver of a moment, then gave her a smile of such tenderness the tears sprang to her eyes again. "Virginia," he said, in that rich voice she loved. "Please pardon me. There is a thing I must do."

He faced the Harvies again, who stared at him as if—well, as if he would murder them all. Except Dyonis looked ready to try to murder him first.

Her heart thudded hard, painfully.

"You have already been told," he said slowly, "how your son Henry traded his own life for Virginia. And Virginia sought to trade hers for mine. This is a thing I know I did not deserve. It should no doubt be Henry here instead of me. So I wish to offer myself to you—to your family. Not as a son, for I cannot ever replace him as that, but a captive as he was. A slave."

Dyonis and Margery gaped—Henry's younger sisters and brother as well. Felipe glanced around. At Ginny's side, Mama stood with a hand over her mouth. And just past her, Sees Far watched, his gaze hard and bright. Then he nodded, very slowly.

Felipe reached up to remove the ornaments from his ears then took Ginny's hand and, turning it palm upward, placed them in her grasp. His necklace of bone and shell and copper bits followed. Then—was that a moment of hesitation?—he drew the knapped spearhead from his waistband, loosened his hair with one hand, and made quick work of sawing off the warrior's lock at his nape. A strangled protest escaped her throat, and his gaze came back to her, tender once more. "As they cut Henry's and Redbud's hair, so do I humble myself." He placed the oiled length, now strangely lifeless, and the flint blade, also in Ginny's hands. "These are yours to keep, or not, as you wish," he said. Then, turning back to the Harvies, he sank to one knee before them, hands outstretched, palms up.

"But we do not—" Dyonis cast about for the words, looking first at Master Johnson and then at Sees Far. "Explain to him that this is not how our people conduct matters!"

But Master Johnson only spread his hands. "If he wishes to make such a gesture, I think it unwise to refuse."

Dark eyes gleaming, Sees Far added, "It is dishonor to refuse."

As if that settled it.

Ginny could not breathe—could not move. What had he done—and what did this mean?

"But—but what are we supposed to do with him?"

Sees Far lifted a single brow. "Have him work for you. Carrying water or wood. Any task for which you would require a young man or do not wish to do for yourself."

Margery and Dyonis were still gaping, and Ginny did not blame them. She was as well. Felipe, her proud Spanish-Skaru:re warrior, had offered himself as a slave—and looked happy about it.

"You cannot do this!" she burst out at last. She turned to the others. "Can he? How can he do this?"

Mama unfolded her arms. "He can, dear one. He can, and he has."

Papa Sees Far gave another nod, although sympathy rimmed his expression and Master Johnson's as well.

Mama's arm went about her. "Come, sweetling."

She tried to dig in her heels. "But nay!"

Felipe looked at her once more. "I must do this, Virginia. Go. All will be well."

Something inside her settled and calmed under that blue gaze. Better 'twould be were his arms about her—how she had longed for him during the service. . .

"Trust your God," he said, and smiled.

She could not breathe. Her lungs were heaving, but she could get no air. This time, when Mama's hands urged her into motion, she went, stumbling, for she could not see.

She clutched the handful of small treasures he had given her. She must not drop anything. He would want them back—would he not? Would there be a time he would take them back?

Somehow, she made it back to the house, where Mama led her over to the platform on which she had slept last night and made her sit. She released the handful of things into her skirt, spread across her lap, and with shaking fingers lifted the silky dark length of his warrior's lock.

A sob took her. And here she thought she'd no more tears after the service.

"What just happened?" she choked out finally.

Mama settled beside her, an arm about her again. Ginny let her head sag to Mama's shoulder.

"You'll never be able to tame that one," Mama said, with a curious note in her voice. Was that. . .amusement?

"What do you mean?"

She did chuckle this time. "Some men are willing to be bullied about by their women, whether openly so or not, never truly standing for what they themselves feel is right—if they even have an opinion on such. This one, however. Everything he does is guided by what he sees as honorable and proper." She cuddled Ginny closer. "Your father would greatly approve, I think."

How could Mama be saying all this?

Ginny shook her head, the slightest roll against Mama's shoulder. She lifted Felipe's lock and brought it to her cheek. It smelled richly of woods and pine and something that was uniquely Felipe. And her tears kept flowing.

"Why?" she said at last. "Why would he do this?"

" 'Tis his way of honoring Henry. Of honoring you and Redbud."

"Will he go and do this for Netah and her husband as well?"

"I do not know. But if he does, God will use it."

Ginny tipped her head to look at Mama. Her eyes were closed, pinched a little at the corners, but her face was otherwise serene. "God is using this. He will not waste what Henry has given. He has not wasted the time you were with the Skaru:re." She sighed. "Just as He did not waste my own captivity or your father's death."

'Twas comforting on some level—truly—but she still could not stop weeping. "I had so hoped he and I could be married as soon as we arrived. As soon as he had opportunity to speak with you and Papa Sees Far."

Another tiny chuckle from Mama. "And he did so, nearly as soon as your feet hit the sand of the island."

Ginny pushed upright to stare at her. "What?"

She laughed outright at that. "While you were greeting Margery, he made his feelings and intentions quite plain." Her eyes sparkled. "I've no doubt this circumstance will run its course, and then he'll find his way back to your side, sweetling. But you must give him freedom to do what he feels he must in the meantime."

Ginny laid the warrior's lock over one thigh, then picked up the necklace and examined it. All the bits of this and that—beaten copper, shell and bone—random perhaps, yet as familiar as Felipe himself. She looped it over her head and settled it about her neck then rolled the ear ornaments across her palm. The copper, shell, and gems all caught the light in their own manner. She reached up and fingered her own earlobes.

"Do you wish to wear those?"

She nodded. "I am not sure the piercings are still there—although they did put in ornaments when I was first taken to Blackbird."

She leaned up and let Mama see to putting the ornaments in place, working the copper wires through the holes and then bending them to make them secure. Not as much trouble as she'd feared and only the slightest pinch. "There," Mama said, and Ginny tipped her head this way and that at the unfamiliar weight. Mama smiled. "They look lovely on you."

They did not know what to do with him, but he would remain as long as needed.

And they did need the help, he could see that from the moment he stepped into their dwelling. The stack of firewood not nearly as high as for others, although it still was summer. Daylight shining through portions of the roof.

"Where do you wish me to work first?" he asked, addressing Henry's mother, who still looked at him as if he would turn upon her at any moment. "I can repair the roof. Or do you wish smaller tasks done?"

She chose carrying water first. Afterward, while she looked around helplessly, he went back out, gathered wood, and found a hatchet with which to chop it. He took a moment to heft the tool and admire the curve of its iron head before setting to the task. Then it was up onto the roof to inspect and assess what needed done.

The younger children—two girls in thin deerskin tunics and a pair of boys with eyes that reminded him of Henry—trailed along, watching. The mother also watched—the father as well, once he'd returned from some task, hands on his hips, the English shirt and slops he wore tattered and stained.

Felipe kept his attention on his work. Walked around the house to examine its structure. They had taken materials found on the island and worked them into a very English-looking house—or as near as he could tell, from seeing the town across the sound and those he remembered from his childhood and in San Augustin. He quietly pointed out where they might improve the structure and offered to find more materials and provide the labor. Henry's father waved a hand, a sort of reluctant assent.

Dinner was once more communal, which Felipe was thankful for, or they might have forgotten to feed him. When night came, the family all stared at him as he found a patch of floor, not blocking the doorway but near enough to act as a guard, and stretched out to sleep.

He closed his eyes. They were but two houses over from where Virginia and her family dwelt, but he'd done his best to avoid looking for her the rest of the afternoon. At supper, he'd caught a glimpse of her watching him through the crowd, open longing in her eyes and his necklace adorning her breast.

Something inside him burned, and after a wistful smile in her direction, he had to force himself to turn away.

He thought about the funeral service and the minister's closing words. *Peace be upon us all.*

A quiet sigh escaped him. *Even so, Lord—let Your peace be upon us, but especially this household.*

In the middle of the night, a sound awakened him. A cry.

He blinked in the dimness and realized a heartbeat later that he knew that cry. He was on his feet without thought, out the door into weak moonlight, and running.

Thankfully Virginia's family had not latched the door to their own dwelling, so he was able to slip inside. At the end of the sleeping platforms, where Felipe himself had lain the night before, Elinor crouched over someone on the platform. "Ginny—Ginny, wake up, 'tis only a dream!"

Felipe swooped in next to her and gathered up the thrashing, wailing young woman. "Peace, Virginia," he said softly. "All is well. You are home. I am here."

The wail lessened to a mere whimper. Elinor sat back on her heels, staring at the two of them. Beyond her, small faces lifted from their beds, similarly regarding him.

Felipe tucked his arms more securely around Virginia and began reciting the Pater Noster, as he had during every instance before. Virginia sighed and curled closer to his side. He also sighed, but quietly, and leaned back against the wall, savoring her warmth and weight against him.

Elinor rose and padded back to her own bed, behind a matted screen at the other end of the house.

Ginny could stand it no longer. Days and days of hardly seeing Felipe, much less speaking with him. Simply pushing through, trying to find her rhythm in the daily life of the town she had once known so well.

How long was she expected to endure this?

She swept the floor of the house so often, she'd nearly dug grooves with the broom. Mended clothing and mats and anything else she could find with the slightest sign of wear. Helped Mama with preparing food and tending the younger children. In short, kept herself busy enough that she'd not be tempted to go run the island.

Heaven forbid, after all, that she'd give anyone grounds for saying she was less than responsible now. And 'twasn't like she didn't give thanks with every other breath that she'd returned to her family.

But Felipe. . .

At last, on a day when the sun shone and lovely clouds built on the western horizon, she propped the broom in the corner, made some excuse to Mama, and fled the house. Barefoot she ran, down the shore toward the eastern inlet, then up through a strip of forest leading to higher ground, stopping only to pick a few sand burrs out of her feet before speeding on.

She'd heard talk of a fort over this direction, built by the first English to land at Kurawoten, but fallen into disrepair, especially after the sea storms that drove Mama and Papa and the others to the mainland. 'Twas not the fort she wished to see, however, but yapám.

The great, wide sea itself.

The exertion pinched at her lungs and drew an ache from her shoulder, but she kept going until she'd cleared the high ground and begun her descent to the dunes beyond. And there—an endlessly foaming, curling sheet of the deepest blue and green edged in cream and white, stretching as far as her eye could see.

She slowed, picking her way through the dunes more carefully. Emerging onto the shore, she stopped. Breathed in the salt air. Let the wind tug at her shift and hair, and the crash of the waves wash away all the tangled thoughts.

Fifteen years ago, Mama and Papa had crossed this great expanse. Made a home first at Roanoac and then here upon Kurawoten. The town of Cora Banks claimed the greater part of her memory, but mayhap she could find as much contentment here as Mama and the others seemed to.

But Felipe. . .

The ache returned to her chest. Tears blurred her vision, spilled over, then were dried by the wind. Here in the privacy of the beach, she let the tears flow—for Henry, for Redbud, for herself and Felipe.

What, oh Lord? What am I to do with this relentless longing for him?

They had left the Skaru:re and reached her people, but she felt no sense of peace.

When the weeping had spent itself, she gave a sigh and turned for home. The clouds now threatened rain, and she might as well find something else with which to busy her hands.

Chapter Twenty-Two

H er darling girl. Truly a woman full grown—and yet not herself.
Not at all.

Elinor was not sure whether 'twas lingering grief and shock from
Henry's death, her own wound, and the flight back home—or the continued enforced separation from the tall young man who held himself
aloof while he served the Harvies with unwavering focus and yet so
obviously loved Ginny with every fiber of his being. More than a week
it had been since his extravagant gesture after Henry's memorial service.
Thankfully, she'd not suffered nightmares every night. Also thankfully,
Elinor had not been so startled after the first time Felipe had let himself
in and come swiftly to Ginny's side to soothe her. But clearly, he heard
her cries every night that she did.

The fact that he heard and recognized her anguish for what it was,
and came—and that Ginny plainly responded more readily to his voice
than to that of her own mother—was very telling.

There was nothing for it that first time but for Elinor to return to
her own bed, though she lay awake long after Felipe had taken his leave
with a soft, "I love you—I shall return when I can," to Ginny's whimper
of protest.

During the day, he most studiously ignored her. The Harvies' house
had never looked so well kept, truth be told. But to have Ginny moping

about, with Felipe so close and yet out of reach, was a bit maddening, even to Elinor.

How would she have felt, all those years ago, had she been denied the simple comfort of Sees Far's presence and conversation?

As if her thoughts had summoned her daughter, Ginny came sweeping into the house, arms full of marsh grasses. "Shh, Berry is sleeping," Elinor whispered, "and so is Mouse for once."

The sullen expression on Ginny's face hardly altered, but she nodded, plunking herself down on a mat where the light was good, and began sorting the grasses into a pile. "I nearly had a basket completed the day we left the Skaru:re," she muttered, just loud enough for Elinor to hear.

Elinor peered at her more closely. "I'm sorry you were not able to finish."

Ginny sniffed. "I might as well not be home. There, I was the slave, pressed to choose a man I could not give myself to. Here, the one man I would gladly choose has for some odd reason made himself a slave—while I must carry on as if I do not care." She selected a few strands of grass and began working them with forceful, almost angry, movements. "In the meantime, I've had at least four young men just happen by and attempt to make conversation with me. Despite the fact that I'm wearing Felipe's ornaments."

Elinor was torn between distress on her daughter's behalf and amusement. "As it has been since you went huskanasqua."

The corner of Ginny's mouth twitched. Her fingers slowed, becoming more deliberate and sure as the beginning whorl of the basket bottom took shape beneath her touch. "You should have seen me with the Skaru:re, Mama. I was the perfect little woman of Tunapewak."

"I doubt that not."

" 'Twas a beautiful basket. I hope Granny Dove can finish it or perhaps still use it as is."

Elinor watched her for a few minutes. Ginny would never be the same girl she was before she was taken—no more than Elinor herself was unchanged after captivity. "Was Granny Dove kind to you?" she asked finally.

Ginny's head came up, and she laughed shortly. "Not at all. She was cross and demanding and often lost patience with me. But I tried to serve her well. And at the end—" Ginny sniffled. " 'Twas she who took Felipe and me from the middle of the gathering where Henry died, and with just a handful of provisions, sent us away from Blackbird's wrath."

Her hands went still, and she looked up, eyes glimmering. "Mama. How long did it take for you to feel you belonged again?"

"Oh darling." Elinor set aside her needlework and slid to her knees beside Ginny, who sank into her arms, weeping. "A long time. A very long time indeed, though I was so glad to be back with you."

The wave of tears passed, and Ginny sat up again. "I suppose 'tis foolish to think everything can be just as it was before." She shook her head. "I know I am different now."

"Aye, that is precisely true."

"And, of course"—she hiccupped, half a sob and half a laugh—"there is Felipe." She sighed, slanting Elinor a shy glance. "All I want is to be with him. To be held. To kiss him. Is that completely wretched of me?"

As she scooted away to take up her own work once more, Elinor marked the flush of her daughter's cheek. She smiled. "I take this to mean you've determined your attachment to him is not merely because he was the only one you could talk to with the Skaru:re?"

"Aye. 'Tis so much more."

"Well. 'Tis not wretched at all."

"But all those scriptures about fleeing youthful lusts—" Ginny blushed even more deeply.

"There are also scriptures extolling the joys of marriage."

"Truly?"

"Truly. In fact, an entire book—the Song of Songs—is devoted to comparing those joys to the union of Christ and the church. I've heard preachers say 'tis only that union to be considered, and not carnal pleasure, but I think if there were no such pleasure to be found between a husband

and wife, or were there shame in it, why would it be used as such a meta-phor? The very first line, in fact—'O that he would kiss me with the kisses of his mouth: for thy love is more pleasant than wine.'"

She could not hold back a grin at the way Ginny goggled, even though her face grew hot as well with the direction of her own thoughts.

"I think 'tis no shame, then, that you long to be fully his wife. He is proving himself to be a young man of honor. And he certainly is beautiful."

"Mama," Ginny said and ducked her head, fingers suddenly busy with her basket.

"What? Have I not eyes simply because I'm an old married woman?"

Ginny grinned at that, but even her ears were crimson.

"So," Elinor said, keeping her voice light, "he has kissed you and yet. . .no more?"

"Ma-*ma*!"

Elinor laughed, long and heartily. Ginny's smile remained, if shy again.

"He surprised me so, the first time," Ginny said. "I was used to think-ing of him as a Skaru:re warrior, though I knew him to be Spanish. And isn't it so, the people of this country do not kiss as we do, as an expression of love between a man and woman?"

A smile still tugged at her own mouth. " 'Tis so. Sees Far had to be taught." She giggled. "Although, not until after we were married did we kiss. 'Twould have been too dangerous."

Ginny's brows arched, then understanding flooded her expression. "Oh. . .aye." She sighed, a fresh blush coloring her cheeks. " 'Tis hard not to let it lead where it will."

The children at least no longer appeared afraid of him. The little ones often piled upon him when he sat down, and his work rarely went unin-terrupted after they discovered he could be induced to carry them about on his shoulders.

Margery—Henry's mother—looked upon him with less suspicion

after a few days as well. It helped, he thought, that he took time to entertain the small ones, but perhaps also that he'd approached her while she was using a pair of shears for something and asked her to finish the job of cutting off his hair more evenly. Though he'd cut the warrior's lock, the crest across the top remained. Not only did it look ridiculous, he was sure, but the gesture remained incomplete.

And so he explained before kneeling for her to accomplish the task.

She'd hesitated for a moment, and he had a wild thought of Jael's wife, with himself being in a most vulnerable position. Then her fingers took hold of his hair, and it was done quickly enough. Hold, snip, hold, snip.

"There," she murmured.

He stood up again, brushing his hand across his head—how strange it felt—and offered her a smile. "Thank you."

She returned the smile, though uncertainly. He could see Henry in her dark eyes as well.

After the first few days, it was becoming harder to find something with which to occupy himself. The roof was tight, which they seemed to appreciate all the more after a heavy downpour, and his additions to the house were nearly complete. He needed to search for more supplies, but rain clouds were rolling in from the west.

Felipe went in search of either Margery or Dyonis. He found the latter first. "I wish to go search for more building supplies, but also to speak with the minister."

Dyonis eyed him then nodded gravely. As Felipe turned to go, the Englishman cleared his throat. "Do you need the hatchet?"

He smiled. "It would be helpful."

Another nod, then Dyonis fetched the tool for him and he was on his way.

Despite the threat of rain, he stopped first to see if the minister was available—and indeed he was, sitting at a very English table at the back of a very Kurawoten house, with one wall rolled up to catch the breeze. His Kurawoten wife met Felipe with a smile and showed him in through the open door then dashed off to busy herself elsewhere.

The minister rose from his chair, offering a half bow. "Felipe, is it?"

"Aye, and you are Master Johnson?"

"Please, call me Nicholas." The grey eyes were calm, curious, even warm. His brown hair, tied back and slightly mussed, his beard askew as if he had been combing through it absently. And his clothing, of plain enough English cut, though a bit threadbare. He wore only slops and a simple shirt. "What might I do for you this day?"

"I would like to talk," Felipe said. "I have questions."

The man's face crinkled with a smile. "Ginny said you might—and welcome." He bobbed his head again then indicated a second chair occupying the space. "Sit, if you please. I am happy to attempt answering any question you might have."

Felipe settled gingerly on the chair and loosely clasped his hands before him, elbows on knees.

"How goes it with the Harvies?" the minister asked quietly.

He thought about how to reply. "They have not yet cast me out."

The minister—*Nicholas*, he reminded himself—gave a nod. "That is promising."

He drew a deep breath. "Blackbird, the younger priest of the Skaru:re town where I dwelt, had many questions about the faith of the English and how it differed from that of the Spanish. Virginia and I argued much." He smiled thinly. "Blackbird found that very diverting, I think. But she could never completely answer to my own satisfaction, beyond an overall difference in how we interpret the Holy Scriptures."

Nicholas nodded.

"She spoke of idolatry. I still do not quite understand that. And later, when Blackbird was angered at her refusal and blamed me for it, when he decided he would only be satisfied with my death, she intervened. I asked her why, and she said—" He hesitated, trying to remember the exact words. "Because her own faith was settled, and her eternal fate secure, whereas mine was not." He held Nicholas' gaze. "I wish to know how she could speak thus. Does Scripture truly teach such a thing?"

A slow nod, then with more strength. "It does indeed. Let me show you."

He turned the pages of the great book lying open before him on the table.

"You have your own copy of the Scriptures? And in English?"

Nicholas smiled. "Many of us do." He paused to look at Felipe. "I suppose I should ask first, where do you feel you are in your faith?"

Felipe blew out a breath. "I cannot say."

"You were brought up in the church, were you not? Baptized as an infant?"

"Aye to both. But I have been so long away, so far from benefit of the sacraments—" He spread his hands. "The Skaru:re view of religion—I suppose you may have some familiarity with it. And their faith seems as genuine as that of my previous countrymen."

He searched for the words, and to his faint surprise, the minister waited.

"During the funeral service, you spoke of there being no hope without the Resurrection of Christ. I can see how that would be. But the church where I was brought up, they teach of the Resurrection. And yet—"

"What do you believe?" Nicholas said, his voice still calm and even but his gaze unyielding. "You, young Felipe. Not them."

Felipe slowly closed his mouth then shook his head.

The minister hummed, glancing at the front of a page, then the back, before turning it and letting it lie. "Here. 'Wherefore, brethren, give the more diligence for to make your calling and election sure, for if ye do such things, ye shall never fall.' See here the words, 'make your calling and election sure.' 'Twould not say so if it were not possible, aye?"

Felipe nodded. Nicholas turned back several pages. "There is. . .so much. I would recommend at some point you read the entire book of Romans and perhaps Galatians." He laughed a little, as if enjoying a private jest. "The entire Scriptures, really, but we can start here.

"The third and fourth chapters of Romans discuss the faith of Abraham, how he was called and indeed believed God before his own circumcision and before the written Law, showing us that it is faith that justifies us before God, and not our deeds. So chapter five continues, 'Because therefore that we are justified by faith, we are at peace with God, through our Lord Jesus Christ: by whom also it chanced unto us to be brought in through faith, unto this grace, wherein we stand, and rejoice in the hope of the glory of God. Not that only: but also we rejoice in tribulations: knowing that tribulation bringeth patience, patience bringeth experience, experience bringeth hope. And hope maketh not ashamed: because the love of God is shed abroad in our hearts, by the holy ghost which is given unto us. For when we were yet weak, according to the time, Christ died for us which were ungodly. Yet scarce will any man die for a righteous man. Peradventure for a good man durst a man die.'"

Nicholas stopped, his fingertips resting on the page, his gaze far away. "Here is why 'tis such a curiosity that Henry gave up his life and Redbud turned back and stayed behind. It bespeaks their love for Ginny—and their regard for you. Yet we also must not discount their love for and confidence in Christ. As I read at the service for Henry, 'Greater love hath no man, than this: that a man bestow his life for his friends.'"

Felipe gave a slow nod.

"But this chapter continues, 'But God setteth out his love toward us, seeing that while we were yet sinners Christ died for us. Much more then now (we that are justified by his blood) shall be saved from wrath through him. For if when we were enemies, we were reconciled to God by the death of his son: much more, seeing we are reconciled, we shall be preserved by his life. Not only this, but we also joy in God by the means of our Lord Jesus Christ, by whom we have now obtained the atonement.'

"Do you hear the surety of language? The firmness? We that are justified by His blood. We were reconciled—*are* reconciled. And 'by whom we have now obtained the atonement.' Would there be such strength of wording were it not possible to be settled in one's faith?"

Felipe shook his head, marveling.

Nicholas leaned forward a little. "The great difference between how we walk out our faith and the Romish Church is that the Romish seems to have cluttered the simplicity of trusting Christ with a multitude of other things. Not that there are no genuine believers there, but—" He fluttered a hand. "We can talk of that in more detail if you choose to stay with us. But you see here, in the pages of the Scriptures, that it does indeed begin with us putting our trust in the blood of Christ to save us—and only that. There are things we must see to after, walking worthy of our calling and so forth, a continual dying to our fleshly ways and living by the leading of the Holy Spirit—but again, you can learn more particulars later."

"I do wish to stay," Felipe said. "I wish, more than anything, to be husband to Virginia. To be worthy of her affections and the trust of her people."

Kindness shone in the older man's grey eyes. "Is that why you so humbled yourself before the Harvies?"

"Aye. For good or for ill."

Nicholas nodded thoughtfully then turned a few more pages. " 'For if thou acknowledge with thy mouth that Jesus is the Lord, and believe in thine heart, that God raised him up from death, thou shalt be safe. For to believe with the heart justifieth: and to acknowledge with the mouth, maketh a man safe. For the scripture saith: whosoever believeth on him, shall not be confounded. There is no difference between the Jew and the Gentile. For one is Lord of all, which is rich unto all that call upon him. For whosoever doth call on the name of the Lord, shall be safe. How then shall they call on him, on whom they have not believed? how shall they believe on him, of whom they have not heard? how shall they hear, without a preacher? And how shall they preach except they be sent? As it is written: how beautiful are the feet of them which bring tidings of peace, and bring tidings of good things.'

"Again, see? To acknowledge with your mouth, to believe in your heart. That is the essential requirement. And the rest—that there is no difference among the peoples, that we all come to God on equal footing, but that the peoples must be told—" Nicholas rubbed his neck. "It is part of why we are here. To be a light to the nations. Or at least to try."

"Many of the Spanish clergy would say the same. That it is our obligation to preach Christ to the nations." Felipe thought back on all he had witnessed of his countrymen's dealings on these shores. "Some have faith that is more genuine, and others, not so much."

"Aye," Nicholas said. "So it is with the English."

"Virginia said something of the same."

The older man smiled. "Then she spoke well."

A rumble of thunder followed his words.

"I should go and complete the rest of this day's task," Felipe said.

"Which is?"

"To find more building supplies, to finish repairs and such on the Harvies' house."

Nicholas peered out at the gathering gloom. "Should you not wait until the rain passes?"

Felipe shook his head, considering the sky as well. "I am accustomed to weather and mind not the rain."

Chapter Twenty-Three

G inny rolled up all her basketmaking materials into a mat and set it aside. 'Twas too dim inside the house to see as clearly as she wished anyway, and the patter of the rain drew her to watch at the open doorway.

Inside, 'twas quiet. Once Berry and Mouse had awakened, Mama took both and went to visit a neighbor. She did not say which one, and Ginny was not sure she cared to know.

The walk over to look at the ocean had given her little solace. Mama saying it had taken a long time for her to feel at home again did comfort, yet the ache of Henry's death, Redbud's subsequent absence, and Felipe's current distance still gnawed at her. Questions howled from her innermost spirit—unspoken but flung at God all the same. And yet, in the midst of it all, she always returned to the impulse of prayer. Subsequent tears were but one more part of the day.

How weary she was of the tears.

Lightning flashed, a glorious display, and thunder pealed. The rain fell so hard, she could barely see the next house over. Her siblings and Papa Sees Far all doubtlessly sought shelter elsewhere. And—what of Felipe? Where did he shelter?

Help him, Lord! Help Felipe with whatever it is he is trying to accomplish. Keep him safe. . .and bring him back to me. Please—I pray You.

Felipe crouched beneath the boughs of an old cedar, the rain filtering down upon his head and bare shoulders, but as he had told Nicholas Johnson, he did not mind.

The minister, with his plain speech yet sincere faith, had given him much to think upon. Felipe still craved particulars on what Nicholas felt was added to faith by the Roman Church. As for what he believed. . .

Acknowledge with your mouth that Jesus is the Lord. Believe in your heart that God has raised Him up from death.

Could it truly be so simple?

We can talk in more detail if you choose to stay.

He felt at a crossroads here. Out in the wind and rain, wandering the island, glimpsing again the wild seas beyond, where both the English and Spanish had traversed in their ships. Somewhere across those seas were his mother and sisters and other family—who all believed him dead, he was sure.

The possibility of returning to the Spanish and revealing the location of the English colony had never occurred to him until spoken by one of the Englishmen. If he truly did so, it would secure his place among the Spanish as nothing else. But he had no desire for that, just as he had none for returning to the Skaru:re. Even there he was nominally accepted, but not truly.

Would that be the case here, were he to stay?

But if he did not stay. . .

The entire reason behind the journey of the past month was to bring Virginia back to her people—and he had done so. He'd marked the steady stream of young bucks sniffing about her since. She'd not lack for suitors who were more fitting than either Blackbird or himself. Yet could he let her go?

With a muted groan, he sat fully on the ground and bent forward, elbows on his knees, the rain dripping across his back.

He did not want to let her go. His heart was fully hers now.

"*Ah Dios*. God—oh God. I have done what I could. She is more Yours than she can ever be mine. And I cannot change the hearts of her people toward me. But You—I have seen with my own eyes how You gave Henry the strength to face death, even death at the hand of the Skaru:re. The Scriptures say You will raise him up again on the last day, as You raised up Jesú—"

He labored for breath, searching for the words.

"I—I believe, oh God. I believe You raised Him up from death. And I acknowledge You now as the Lord. Make of me what You will. I would be Yours as well, to know You as these people seem to know You."

Joy and peace burst within him, as if the sun itself had risen in the center of his chest. Driven by that strange, sharp elation, he crawled out from under the cedar and stood up, face tipped to the sky, letting the rain wash over him head to toe.

Elinor had intended to go directly to Margery but had been drawn aside by Alis Chapman, asking Elinor's counsel on a matter. The rain had begun well before that conversation was finished, but still she felt the urgency to continue on and visit Henry's mother.

"Come in, come in!" Margery exclaimed as Elinor ducked inside the door, laughing and brushing raindrops off of little Berry's head.

"Thank you! If you are busy, I could return later. . . ?"

"Not at all, although one of the boys is napping."

Elinor had pitched her voice a little low just for that very possibility. She glanced about, surreptitiously looking for Felipe, but the house was empty save for Margery, who chuckled. "The rest of the children are out playing in the rain."

"Mine as well," Elinor said, sighing, then laughed again.

" 'Tis good to see you." Margery's smile was a little tired. "Will you sit, or. . . ?"

"I would be glad to sit." When the other woman looked longingly at Berry, Elinor passed the babe over for her to dandle. "How do you and the family fare?" she asked after a moment.

Margery released a very great sigh. " 'Tis hard. Knowing for sure that Henry is gone ahead to heaven." Her eyes glistened. "And this unexpected addition to the household—" She glanced aside then met Elinor's gaze again. "How fares Ginny?"

"She struggles. Over many things, I think."

Margery's lips firmed, then her gaze strayed back to the baby, and her face softened. Elinor watched while she cooed and played with the infant for a few minutes.

"Regarding that unexpected addition to your household," she said finally.

Margery gave a dry laugh. "I did not know what to expect. We do not hold with keeping slaves here, after all, but he was so insistent. Dyonis and I have been on guard nearly every moment—at least at first. And when he whisked out and back in the middle of the night. . .well, we could not help but wonder if he planned to bring more enemies down upon our heads."

Elinor frowned. "You did not know where he went?"

Another ill-at-ease chuckle. "Oh, we surmised he must have eaten something wrong and needed the privy." Margery glanced up and froze at whatever she saw in Elinor's face.

She shook her head. "No. I mean, 'tis a reasonable assumption, but. . .no." She watched Margery's expression. "Ginny has been afflicted with nightmares. Presumably of Henry's death, although perhaps other things as well." She swallowed at the growing dismay on Margery's face. "Whatever, 'tis enough to make her cry out in her sleep. I could not soothe her. Then somehow Felipe heard and came—and only then did she settle."

"Merciful Lord in heaven," Margery whispered, lifting Berry to cuddle her close. "That dear, sweet girl."

"So I would not have you think ill of him for that."

Margery's eyes overflowed, and she shook her head. "He has been faultless in courtesy. Performed every task we have given and more." She waved a hand upward. "You see how tight and snug the house is, even with the downpour. 'Twas his labor. Dyonis is a man of many abilities, but somehow the fine points of building a Kurawoten house have escaped him." Another watery chuckle. "This Spaniard, though—he is quiet and terrifying and yet has won over the children. He went out before the rain came to gather more supplies for something else on the house, Dyonis told me, and asked for permission to go speak with Nicholas."

"That cannot be a bad thing," Elinor said.

Margery rubbed her cheek against Berry's downy head, and the baby bounced against her shoulder, giving a little chirp. Margery smiled then shot another glance at Elinor. "I know 'tisn't really my concern, but. . .are he and Ginny. . . ?"

The corner of Elinor's mouth lifted. "We had hardly been introduced before he made it known he wishes to marry her. Ginny avows he is her choice as well. She is most discontented about the present situation, although I have tried to explain his possible reasons for it. 'Tis hard for her to be patient."

Margery's eyes filled with tears. "He is. . .trying to prove himself. Is he not?"

"I believe so."

She tipped back her head, wetness running down her cheeks. Elinor moved to her other side and, as she did so often with Ginny, gathered Margery into her arms.

" 'Tis a sore trial to lose our eldest son," Margery whispered raggedly, "but I do not wish to cause more grief to Ginny. Nor to Felipe."

'Twasn't necessarily what Elinor had intended with the visit—she'd only sought word of Felipe's well-being and to offer comfort to Margery—but if the Lord saw fit to move this way, she would be grateful.

"He is so tall," Margery went on, "as are so many of the young people who have grown to adulthood in this country. I wonder how tall Henry might have been, had he not—"

She collapsed into full weeping against Elinor's shoulder.

The rain had stopped and the sun blazed once more in all its summer glory by the time Felipe finished gathering an armload of saplings, straight and true and yet slender, fit to be used for supports in a house, and carried them back to the town.

He angled first for the minister's house—again. This time Nicholas stood outside talking to—oh, that was Dyonis. The two men turned at his approach, looking oddly sheepish.

Had he been the subject of discussion?

No matter. He must speak. Resting the bundle of posts upright on the ground, he nodded first to Dyonis, then to Nicholas. "My thanks for talking with me earlier. I felt you would wish to know." He slid a glance at Henry's father then gave his attention to the minister once more. "In answer to your question—I do believe. What you read, from the Holy Scriptures, about acknowledging Christ as Lord—and believing that God has raised Him up. I do believe—and acknowledge."

The words came tumbling out haltingly. Felipe felt his face heating foolishly, as if he were a small boy again before his elders.

But he had to speak.

A grin spread across Nicholas' countenance. Dyonis' eyes went wide, his mouth slack.

"Well," the minister said. "Do you wish to be baptized again?"

Felipe laughed. "Is it necessary? Especially considering"—he laughed again—"I stood out in the rain for some time."

Nicholas joined him in the laughter. "This does remind me—do you not recall, Dyonis?—a certain night when many of the Kurawoten were so carried away in their enthusiasm to confess Christ that they ran out into the sound to dip themselves."

"I do recall," Dyonis said, shaking his head.

"I am very glad to hear it, young man," Nicholas said, beaming. He seized Felipe in a strong embrace.

"Thank you," Felipe said, for lack of any better words.

When he straightened, still holding his armload of posts, Dyonis eyed them and him. "Those are for our house?"

"Aye."

"Bring them, then. Margery and I would like a word."

Unease curled through his middle as he followed Dyonis back through the town. Passing Virginia's family's house, he thought he heard her voice for a moment—but he dared not stop.

"Set the posts there," Dyonis said, pointing to a place on the back side of the house, "and come in."

Margery was sweeping but set aside her broom as he ducked under the door lintel. "Sit, please," she said with a nod and a bit of a smile.

Now he truly was unsettled.

He sank to the floor and waited for both of them to find a place on a sleeping platform.

Dyonis sat forward, hands together, elbows on his knees. The greying length of his hair, tied back, fell across his shoulder, and a bit of the steel Felipe had glimpsed in Henry's face rested now in his father's expression.

"When you leave in the night," he said at last, "where is it you go?"

Felipe ignored the unsteadiness of his heart. Did they think he was up to some mischief?

And was it betraying Virginia's secrets to speak truthfully?

"Virginia dreams," he said simply. "I hear her cry out."

Dyonis bowed his head. Margery was instantly in tears.

Such immediate response?

"Elinor told us," Margery said unsteadily. " 'Twas the awfulness of Henry's death—aye?"

He nodded slowly.

"You—you both witnessed it?" Dyonis asked.

"Aye. We both were made to watch," Felipe said, trying to keep his face impassive. "Such a thing is not uncommon amongst the Skaru:re."

He rubbed his chin. The new beard was gaining a bit of length. So very strange.

"He died very bravely. And the Skaru:re would admire that," he added softly.

When Dyonis lifted his head, his gaze swam with tears as well. "This. . .gesture of yours. We are deeply grateful." His spread his hands, met Felipe's eyes. "But it is not a thing we wish to continue. Not with you behaving as a slave to us. Your abasing yourself will not bring Henry back."

There was no heat in his words, only sorrow and brokenness. Felipe nodded uncertainly. "It was not my intention to act as if it would."

"We understand. And we will not refuse further help if you choose to give it, but we wish to release you." The man grimaced. "Besides, 'twould seem you have your own house to give attention to building—that is, if your ultimate intention is what we think."

His heart gave a leap at that, but he held himself still.

"You do wish to marry Ginny, do you not?" Dyonis said with more force, tipping his head.

A smile tugged at Felipe's mouth. "I do."

They smiled as well—still tremulous but with honest joy. Margery extended a hand. "And though we do not seek to replace Henry in any wise, 'twould please us—nay, honor us—if at some point you came to think of us as a kind of foster mother and father. Or at least aunt and uncle."

"One has many aunties and uncles among the Skaru:re," Felipe said. "I suspect it to be much the same here."

Elinor watched Ginny sitting at the doorway of the house, her fingers busy with the grasses, at least a handspan of basket having taken shape beneath her touch. So intent, she did not notice she was being observed.

"Putting together a wedding is a small enough thing," Elinor said to Sees Far, who leaned close over her shoulder, both of them in the shadows where they could observe but not be noticed. "We've all been mostly taking meals together, so 'tis nothing different to make it a feast of celebration. But how quickly can a house be built?"

"Quickly enough," Sees Far responded, "with hands to help. But can it be done without Ginny catching wind of it?"

"Mayhap we don't have to," Elinor mused. "Mayhap we could go ahead with the wedding and then the house can be framed in the next day or so, while those two make camp somewhere on the island for the night." She laughed. "I think they'd not protest if we sent them off together."

Sees Far's mouth curved, and he nuzzled the side of her neck. "It is, after all, what they'd be doing were they given half a chance even without benefit of the wedding."

Another quiet laugh. "I would, were I them." She leaned a little more into his touch. "Can you slip inside to fetch that shirt and doublet without Ginny seeing? And ask one of the other men if they have any hose to lend. I gave all of Ananias' away years ago."

"Perhaps he would prefer to dress as Tunapewak," Sees Far said.

"No doubt 'tis more comfortable," Elinor said. Then they parted and each went to accomplish what they could in the next hour.

Ginny found that once she set to it, the basket came together smoothly and even more quickly than she expected. It also soothed her spirit somewhat—or at least kept her from wanting to run screaming through the town and away over the island. The edge was going to take the longest, but she'd decided to keep this basket just a few inches deep and tackle a taller one next.

She had the edge about halfway done when a trumpet sounded over toward the center of the town. A sigh escaped her. Another meeting. Well, she would not bestir herself. 'Twas not Sunday, and there was no matter she could think of that required her presence. Unless—mayhap— the Skaru:re had found them, but that would be an alarm call, not merely the call for a gathering.

Besides, she was nearly done—

"Ginny, are you not coming?"

She startled at Mama's voice, nearly dropping the basket. "Ah! You caught me off guard."

Mama laughed, looking at the basket, then inspecting Ginny's dress. She wore the shift but had laid aside the kirtle days ago because of the heat. "Come. Up—you are not dressed for the meeting."

"What? Nay, I need to finish this basket."

Mama fluttered a hand. "Finish later. You're needed elsewhere."

"Mama. . ."

She reached down and took the basket from Ginny's hands—gently but firmly. "Come, come."

Ginny climbed to her feet with a groan then rolled up the rest of her materials into the mat. Beckoning, Mama disappeared into the house. Ginny followed, dragging her feet.

Mama set the basket down on the end of the platform that had been Ginny's bed since returning, then flitted off toward the storage chest.

"I don't understand," Ginny complained. "Why under heaven would I be needed for yet another meeting?"

Mama ignored her question, lifting the kirtle from the chest and inspecting it. She turned to bend a similar regard on Ginny's appearance and clicked her tongue. "You bathed this morning, at least, and haven't been running about as you once did. Have you?"

Ginny huffed. "No, Mama, except for fetching materials for the basket this morning." And the quick jaunt to look at the sea, but that hardly counted. She rolled her eyes. "I am now the model daughter."

"Virginia Thomasyn," Mama said very softly. She stood still until Ginny met her gaze. "You always have been, and remain, everything I could want in a daughter. Your free spirit was given you by God Himself, and I have always treasured that. Even when mothering you is. . .interesting."

Then, of course, Ginny was weeping. Mama stepped close and drew her into her arms.

"If only I had not run off that one day," Ginny sobbed.

"Ah, sweetling." Mama's hand smoothed down her back. "Remember when I said that God will not waste anything? This as well, He will use."

" 'Tis so hard to believe that. To hold on to what He has said."

"Then 'tis a good thing He is the one holding us, aye?" Mama eased back and stroked both hands across Ginny's hair, framing her face. "What can separate us from the love of Christ?"

She swallowed. "Nothing. Neither death, nor life, nor—anything."

"Exactly so. We must trust that He is able to weave our past into good for us, and indeed does so. And we must trust Him with each day. *This* day. And then the remainder of our lives."

Ginny leaned her forehead on Mama's shoulder and simply wept—and Mama simply held her.

At last she straightened, trying to wipe her cheeks.

"Now," Mama whispered, "are you willing to trust Him, at least with today?"

Ginny nodded.

"Then let me help you with this kirtle, and perhaps braid your hair again."

Sniffling, she submitted to Mama's ministrations, suddenly realizing— "You're wearing one of your best kirtles as well."

"Am I?" Mama said mildly. "How curious."

"Mama."

But a chuckle was her only reply.

"There." Mama touched the ornaments at Ginny's ears and the chain about her neck, none of which she'd removed since that first day. "You are ready, except—you'll want your mahkusun too."

"Oh, for all the. . . Very well."

Ginny brushed the dust off her feet and shoved them into the worn footwear, gave a last tug to her shift and kirtle, then lifted a hand. "Lead on."

Mama laughed and did so.

She could hear the sounds of the crowd as they neared the town center. "What then is so important that I must be there?"

Mama flashed her a bright grin over her shoulder. "Someone is waiting for you. You will see."

Her mind flew with the possibilities. "Redbud?"

Sadness dimmed the smile. "No, unfortunately. He would be here if he could, I am sure."

They rounded the last corner, and Ginny halted, her gaze sweeping the gathering. Everyone was either sitting or standing off to the side, all customary to such a thing, but strangely, there was a pathway roughly down the middle. A knot of men stood at the other end—Master Johnson, Georgie, Papa Sees Far, and—

Her heart skipped a beat, stumbled entirely. Was that. . .*Felipe*? In an English shirt, doublet, and hose?

A very familiar-looking doublet.

"Is that Papa's—?"

Mama chuckled, and suddenly Mary, Sunny, and the Harvie girls were there as well. "Here you are," Mary said, and Mama took the handful of flowers, woven into a rough crown, and set it upon Ginny's head.

At the same moment, Felipe turned, seeing her across the crowd. He straightened, shoulders squaring and chest puffing.

Just looking at her. As if waiting for something.

The men around him turned and settled into similar stances. The crowd hushed as people noticed her presence.

"I ask again," Mama said, "are you willing to trust God for this day?"

She could not see for sudden fresh tears. "Mama. . .what is this?"

" 'Tis your wedding, my darling. If, that is, you are willing."

Chapter Twenty-Four

G inny sucked in a long breath, blinked to clear her sight. "Aye—
oh, aye."

Mary's laugh joined Mama's, and with one on either side of her, the
girls trailing behind, more flowers in their hands, they led her down the
cleared path in the middle of the gathering.

Felipe's face broke into the widest grin she'd ever seen. And as she
neared, her thoughts flew. She hadn't had more than glimpses of him this
past week, but oh, the beard had grown—and what else had he done to his
hair? 'Twas all cropped close, like Henry's and Redbud's by the Skaru:re.

Oh. Of course. 'Twas part of his offering himself as a captive.

But he looked very handsome. Very—*not* Skaru:re.

They stopped just a pace short of the men. Master Johnson edged
forward. "Who gives this woman to marry this man?"

"We all do," Elinor answered, and a laugh rippled through the gathering, then murmurs of assent.

A broken laugh escaped Ginny. His own smile undimmed, Felipe
stepped forward, extending a hand, and she placed hers into it. Mama and
Mary moved aside, herding the girls with them.

"Virginia Thomasyn Dare, this man has declared his desire and intent
to make you his wife. He has also, before me and Dyonis Harvie, confessed
the lordship of Christ and belief in His Resurrection, thus resolving any
uncertainty about his faith—and removing the main obstacle to your

marriage. Are you willing to take him as your husband?"

A wave of tears overcame her again. 'Twas a far different opening than she'd ever heard spoken at a wedding, but it certainly fit the circumstances—and 'twas all she'd dreamed of. "I am most assuredly willing."

"And he has also indicated his wish to take the name of Dare upon your marriage, so to further demonstrate his commitment to you and to your people, and that your father's name should live on in this country. Are you willing for him to do this as well?"

Felipe gave a tiny nod and squeezed her hand. She shot a look at Mama, who smiled and also nodded.

"If that is what he wishes, then I am willing." Her eyes came back to Felipe.

"Please, then, take each other's right hand and face each other."

They shifted, his right hand cupping hers, his left sliding over. She clung to his with her left as well, from beneath. They exchanged a quick smile.

Was this really, truly happening?

"Dearly beloved, we are gathered to witness the joining of this man and this woman in holy matrimony.

"Virginia, will you have this man to be your husband, to live together in the covenant of marriage? Will you love him, comfort him, honor and keep him, in sickness and in health, and forsaking all others, be faithful to him as long as you both shall live?"

"I will," she said, not taking her eyes from Felipe's. Oh, they were so blue today!

"And will you, Felipe Menéndez de Alvarado of the Spanish and the Skaru:re, have this woman to be your wife, to live together in the covenant of marriage? Will you love her, comfort her, honor and keep her, in sickness and in health, and forsaking all others, be faithful to her as long as you both shall live?"

"I will," he said, his grip tightening the slightest bit on hers.

As Master Johnson read the rest of the service over them, it finally soaked, drop by drop, into her weary, thirsty heart. This was indeed happening. Her Felipe—truly hers at last!—standing before her, promising himself to her in such a beautiful, deep cadence. But how had it come to be?

"And now," Master Johnson said, "I do pronounce you man and wife. You may now greet each other with a holy kiss."

A slow smile curled Felipe's mouth again, and he released her fingers only to gently cup her head in his hands. "My Virginia," he murmured, then pressed his lips to hers in a single, sweet, lingering kiss.

Applause shattered the quiet. Felipe straightened, grinning. She sank into his embrace, and he held her every bit as tightly as she did him.

"Oh, I have missed you," she exclaimed. "I have missed you so much!"

"And I, you."

The commotion began to die down and music trilled, but neither of them moved until family and friends surrounded them, pouring out their well wishes.

Felipe felt quite overcome. When the wedding service was complete, he and Virginia were led to a stack of mats and made to sit while the others prepared a feast. That was mayhap the thing he loved most about the ways of the people of this land—always so much good food, a feast upon the slightest pretext. The English among them seemed to have benefited much from that custom.

He was content to sit, arms around Virginia as she leaned upon his breast, his lips pressed to her temple and a thumb stroking the curve of her shoulder. What a day this had been—although he still expected one of the Englishmen to appear at any moment with a loaded and lit arquebus and send him into eternity.

A few cast dubious glances in their direction, but nothing more dramatic than that. Although he was not entirely sure whether Sees Far, Georgie, and others were not serving quietly as guards for Virginia and him. He would not be ungrateful if so.

Virginia tipped her face upward. "Did you plan this?"

Felipe laughed softly. "No. It was all your mother and Sees Far and Nicholas—and I think the Harvies and Georgie and Mary."

Her eyes were pale blue like the sky above. "The Harvies? What then of your arrangement with them?"

"They have released me from it."

She sat up a little, staring at him, mouth adorably rounded.

He smiled and kissed her forehead. "You are much loved."

Her gaze glittered. "You will have to tell me more later."

He nodded and tucked her back against his side. "Speaking of later. . ."

"Aye?"

"Would you very much mind if we spent a night or two out in the open again—alone? This came about so suddenly, I had not time to begin making a house for us."

Once more she peered up at him, smiling. "We're to have our own house?"

He laughed. "Of course. Did you wish to live with your mother and Sees Far?"

Her cheeks colored. "Well, nay. But—" Her gaze came back to his, shining with awe. "We truly are husband and wife now, are we not?"

"We are." He brushed a kiss upon her mouth. "And later I will show you just how thoroughly."

Her fingers tightened on the front of his jerkin. "Is it terrible that I wish we could just slip away now?"

He grinned. "No."

Stay they did, however, through the feast, where everything they were brought tasted like the rarest delicacies and the dancing began in earnest. When the music slowed to a tune both slow and sweet that stirred some of his earliest memories, he drew Virginia to her feet and led her in steps he had not danced since childhood—tentative and halting, their efforts were, but then after much laughter their feet found the rhythm.

The song ended, and Felipe gathered her into his arms again, simply savoring the moment. Then the musicians and drummers launched into something altogether wild, with a bit of the English but more of the Kurawoten, and they were joined by townspeople of both, leaping and whirling and stepping in place, as each seemed pleased to do. Virginia shook again with laughter against him then stepped back to take his hands, and they danced facing each other, carried away by the joy of it all.

As the sun was setting, a short blast of the trumpet brought everyone to a moment of attention, and Manteo stood up before them, hands lifted. "This day we welcome a new member of our community, the husband of our own little Virginia Dare. Her mother has asked to say a few words."

He stepped back and motioned for Elinor to take his place. She smiled at Felipe and her daughter then included the rest of the gathering with her attention. "I have been thinking upon the events that led to this one. Of the long journey of the English to this place. Of the very great hospitality of the Kurawoten in opening their homes and country to us, as if we were already their own. We understand there is yet some question concerning the trustworthiness of one who was born Spanish—the old enemy of both the English and Tunapewak—but let it not be said that we failed to extend the same hospitality given us—nay, more, the grace we are given by God Himself. Let this day mark a new dawn: not just English and the People living together in peace, but also the Spanish, even if 'tis only this one man, even if only symbolic. After all"—she smiled suddenly—"if no one else has marked this very great irony—just as my daughter is indirectly named after Queen Elizabeth, our Felipe is named after the king of Spain who once proposed marriage to Her Majesty. Some say Her Majesty's refusal was the very thing that led to the war between England and Spain, although others disagree. But whatever may take place in the outside world, let it not be said of us.

"And regardless, we are indeed pleased to welcome Felipe to our family. 'Tis irregular, to be certain, for him to take the name of Dare, and yet we appreciate his intent, which is to honor our family."

"So," someone called out, "he shall be known as Philip Dare?"

Amidst scattered chuckles, she waved for Manteo to step forward, and he released everyone to return to the celebration.

Elinor slipped through the gathering to stand beside Felipe and Virginia, with Mary, Georgie, Sees Far, and a handful of others, some carrying bundles and some merely there. She beckoned and drew their small company a little way from the gathering, to where it was quiet enough to be heard over the music without shouting. First she embraced Virginia, long and lovingly, murmuring in her daughter's ear, then she turned to Felipe, placing her fingertips on his cheeks. "Thank you again for bringing our girl home—and for all the times you've watched over her and kept her safe. We do indeed welcome you into the family."

And then she embraced Felipe as well.

The others took their turns—Georgie and Mary, then Sees Far, who gripped Felipe's shoulders and with a nod said, "The good God often works in strange ways. We believe it His hand that brought you to us, and whether just for our Ginny or for something wider remains to be seen. But we are glad she has you."

At last, Elinor had Felipe shed the borrowed doublet, and they were laden with the various bundles, which turned out to be rolled mats for bedding, their own more ordinary clothing, and baskets of food. Then they set out on the path leading over the low hills to the ocean side of the island.

"Do you know where we're going?" Virginia asked as Felipe led off. "Because I remember almost nothing of the island, and have only been outside the town once this past week."

"I think I know it well enough for us not to be lost," he assured her.

It was not so dark that he could not find the way to the old fort, and from there he cut to the south, where he found a likely little hollow above the dunes, exposed enough to the sea breezes that they would not be troubled overmuch with mosquitos, yet also sheltered from prying eyes. While Virginia tied the food baskets up into one of the oaks, he spread out the mats, found the linen sheet and wool blanket rolled up inside them, and made use of those as well.

He turned from that task and found Virginia watching him—the flowers still in her hair, her sleeves and skirts moving gently in the breeze, loose tendrils fluttering about her face. His heart nearly stopped.

"Ah—*mi amor*," he murmured.

Her lips tipped upward. "And what does that mean?"

He crossed the space between them in two steps and caught her into his arms, lifting her up and off her feet. She squeaked, and he grinned, brushing her nose with his. "It is 'my love' in my old tongue."

"*Mi amor.* I like it. And you looked very fine today."

He set her back on her feet but did not release her completely.

Mi esposa. Wife—she was his wife now—

She more than met his kiss, one arm encircling his neck, her free hand skimming his hair, his face and beard, body molding to his.

And this time, he need not contain the fire she kindled inside him.

He swooped her up in both arms this time, one beneath her knees, and carried her back to the pallet. Ever so gently, he lowered himself and laid her down then leaned to kiss her again. Her hands tugged him closer, and he sank down beside her.

He broke, briefly, to smile into her eyes. "Every young Skaru:re warrior was given instruction on how a man might please a woman. Now at last do I seek to put that to practice."

Her gaze flew wide. "You. . .truly never did. . .before?"

"No." Very gently, he kissed her cheekbone, then her earlobe, then along her jaw and down her neck. She shivered and tipped her chin to lean into his touch. "I do not know why, but I kept myself from all other girls. Perhaps"—more small kisses—"perhaps my heart was waiting for you."

A small sound broke from her. "I was so more than willing that night at the Coree town."

"I know." Another kiss, on her lips this time, but lightly. "And do believe me when I say I did want you—not only then, but many times before and since."

She swallowed, her eyes glittering in the twilight. "Then why do we delay?"

He gave a single, low laugh. "An excellent question." And he kissed her more deeply.

Chapter Twenty-Five

Spring 1603, Kurawoten Island

G inny loved spring. She always had, but this one seemed particularly meaningful after the terrible events of a year past. Today the sun shone warmly enough for her to shed all but her shift, and Felipe was dressed Kurawoten style, with only a deerskin kilt and furs about his middle, as they mended part of a wall on their little house after a particularly blustery night. Others worked about the town at similar tasks.

As she gave attention to repairing the weave on one of the mats covering the side of the house, a sudden little kick and roll from inside her belly startled her. "Oh!"

Felipe's gaze was on her in an instant. She laughed and beckoned him close then placed his hand on the rounding curve, pressing in a little. "Wait a minute," she breathed.

Patience was rewarded with another kick and turn. They both laughed.

"The babe wriggles like a little fish," she said.

"Or—" Felipe grinned. "Guh-neh."

She quickly translated his old Skaru:re name. "So, an infant eel?"

His smile held steady as she reached up to play with the edges of his hair, grown out now to about finger length. He'd been contemplating shaving the sides again, Kurawoten- and Skaru:re-style. He'd kept the beard—and she found that she liked it.

"Some called me 'mud crawler,'" he added, "ever reminding me that I'd begun as a captive and slave with them."

"Hmm. 'Eel' is hardly better than that."

He laughed again, softly, and slipped his arms about her. "It matters not now."

"Nay, Philip Dare, it does not." She pulled him down for a sweetly lingering kiss then giggled as the baby kicked again, against him.

A blast from the meeting trumpet broke the morning's quiet, three short notes to indicate the need for all to come to the town center, then a longer one to indicate urgency.

They broke the kiss, Felipe holding her gaze for but a moment before going for his weapons. They ran together to the meeting area.

Two younger warriors stood beside Manteo and Roger Prat, one Kurawoten and the other English but dressed as Tunapewak. 'Twas Redbud's older brother and Rob Ellis—both from Cora Banks.

Her pulse stuttered. Another attack upon the mainland town?

Manteo spied Ginny and Felipe and beckoned to them. The gathering parted but little to let them through.

Redbud's brother's eyes were wide, and both men were still breathing hard. "We left while it was yet dark and came as fast as we could," he said, dividing his attention between Ginny and Manteo. "But—Redbud is alive!"

A cry swept through the crowd. Ginny's hands went to her mouth, and she leaned suddenly into Felipe's embrace.

His brother continued, "He has brought a delegation of the Mangoac—the ones who call themselves Skaru:re—and they say they wish peace between us and to hear more of our God. They wish us to come—or some of us. They asked in particular for the one they called Guh-neh, who brought Ginny back to us last summer." He eyed her. "They call you White Doe?"

She laughed brokenly. "Aye."

"We are sure they intend peace?" Roger Prat said, brows still arched high.

Rob Ellis spread his hands. "There is always the possibility of not. But those who have come are not all warriors. There are women and aged among them, who in fact outnumber the warriors." His gaze sought Ginny's and Felipe's. "There is one—Redbud says she is called Grandmother Dove. She is most desirous to hear of your well-being."

"Granny Dove? She made the entire journey?"

"Oh, I forgot," Rob said. "They offered these as tokens."

From his carrying pouch he drew a scrap of some pale fabric and what appeared to be a warrior's shooting glove. Ginny took the fabric—'twas from the dress she'd been wearing when taken last year—and Felipe took the glove. He turned it this way and that. "It is Blackbird's," he said, then looked at Rob and Redbud's brother. "Is Blackbird with them?"

"One who calls himself thus is with them, aye."

Ginny exchanged a wondering glance with Felipe. Her heart pounded so, 'twas nearly painful. "I wish to go as well," she said.

"It is a risk," Felipe said. "If they mean to deceive us and attack when our guard is down. . ."

"There is always risk," Manteo said. "But we will assemble the council and make a decision."

'Twas no more than an hour that the men gathered, Felipe among them, while the women cooked and prepared for at least some of them to make the journey back across the water to Cora Banks. And sure enough, when they emerged, Manteo announced that they had decided, nearly to a man, that in this case they would take the Skaru:re at their word but bathe the matter in prayer and then trust God.

"Who knows but that this was His intent all along in allowing our youth to be taken—that not only should Felipe be brought to us, but that He would make our enemies to be at peace with us?"

The agony of suspense in the hours to follow, however, brought Ginny near to the point of illness. Borne in one of half a dozen kanoes skimming westward across the sound carrying warriors but also a handful of women, she watched the glitter of sunlight on the water and the far gathering clouds. Mama and Mary stayed behind, but Sees Far and Georgie had come, along with Manteo, cousin Chris, Dyonis Harvie, and others—and Master Johnson for the answering of questions regarding God. Were they racing toward their deaths—or another captivity?

'Twas eminently possible, the men had admitted, but also determined that as the English had chosen courage all those years ago in sailing to the New World, and then the Kurawoten had welcomed such pale, strangely garbed foreigners into their midst, so they would choose courage in this. They had not turned their faces from war these past years, with the Suquoten and others—why would they now turn their faces from the possibility of peace? But either way, they would go to meet this.

'Twas God, the Lord of every tribe, tongue, and nation, whether they owned Him or not, who held them in His hands, after all.

Hours later, as the sun slipped nearer the horizon, they sighted the shore and angled for the river leading to Cora Banks. Ginny breathed out an unbroken stream of silent prayer for God's protection and their own eyes to be open and watchful.

'Twas nearly dark when they arrived, all the kanoes sliding up onto the bank near the burned pinnace, hardly visible now above the surface of the creek. They disembarked, and Rob Ellis ran ahead to give word to the town.

Felipe took Ginny's hand to help her out of their kanoe and up the bank. How different from the last time they were here, six months or so ago, when she had scampered out and ahead. At the top of the bank he released her, but only to have his hands free in case of ambush, and she followed him closely.

Please, Lord. . .please.

Those were all the words she could summon.

Muted sounds of singing and dancing floated from inside the town. Welcomed most warmly, they were ushered into the palisade by a pair of guards and made their way to the town center, just outside the meetinghouse. There a mixed gathering sat, heads of silver shining among darker ones.

Ginny stopped, surveying the crowd. Her heart thudded and she could hardly breathe.

Lord in heaven! Mercy. . .oh, have mercy here.

And then a tall, lean figure popped to his feet and ran toward them. "Ginny! Felipe!"

It truly was Redbud, even taller than when last she saw him, throwing his arms around them with such exuberance she thought he'd pick both of them up. She clung to him, sobbing, but Felipe said with a chuckle, "Have a care with my wife, young one!"

Redbud released them, half laughing and half crying, looking them both up and down but Ginny in particular. "Wife—truly?"

She cupped her skirts around her belly to show him the growing roundness there, and his eyes widened. "Aye—nearly as soon as we reached Kurawoten Island," she told him. "But you—how can this be? We feared you dead!"

He laughed. "I thought myself so. But God had another plan."

A tremulous voice from just behind spoke a Skaru:re word that Ginny thought never to hear again, indeed never wished to hear again, but in this moment seemed the sweetest sound. *White Doe.* And there she was—Granny Dove, eyes glimmering and arms outstretched. Weeping anew, Ginny gladly embraced her, and Felipe stepped up to do so as well.

Behind Granny Dove waited others whom Ginny recognized—the elders from the Skaru:re town who had first argued in her defense with Blackbird—and then Blackbird himself, standing tall and silent and somehow much changed. They all nodded gravely at her and Felipe and motioned for them to come to the fireside.

Felipe and Redbud took up the conversation in Skaru:re—and a good thing, for Ginny had forgotten half of what she'd learned the year previous. They and the rest of the company from Kurawoten were gathered in and seated, and while they were fed, their Skaru:re visitors, through Redbud, spun out the story of what had taken place.

"That day Blackbird and his warriors overtook us at the river," Redbud began, "I turned back, hoping to deflect them from Ginny and Felipe.

At first I thought I had failed, when Blackbird kept going. But still I begged for them to hear me out, to not slay me immediately. And though it struck my heart sore that Blackbird boasted of having shot White Doe and hoped she would die so that Guh-neh, the name Felipe carried among the Skaru:re, could not have her either, I determined not to lose the opportunity to speak, if they would allow it.

"Then, to my amazement, they did allow it. So I told them how the English had come to us all those years ago. How their God had not only given them safe passage across yapám, but through Manteo brought them to us, to the Kurawoten, and how our two peoples had become as one. How their God had proven Himself true through many signs and circumstances—not the least of which, Sees Far's return of Elinor, then God making the way for the rest of the captives to come back as well. Though I was too young to remember those very well, I do remember. Then any number of small things after. The healing of the man left crippled by wounds given by the evil English who came before these.

"Above all, however, I spoke of how our trust in this God, who Himself became a man and died and yet came to life again as the sacrifice for all our sins, gives us peace and hope beyond death. How that peace was what led Ginny to offer to take the place of Felipe, and Henry in turn to take the place of both. How he could endure both the bloodletting and fire with a song upon his lips. And how I was not afraid to come back and face them, especially if it might mean freedom for my friends, because of my own trust in that same God.

"They did not wish to listen at first. They mocked and struck me—Blackbird in particular. And yet I was not slain on the spot. They brought me back to their town, though with much ill use. I prayed for God to make me strong and give me more words that they might listen to, that might change their hearts. And to my surprise, when we came back to the town, the elders did indeed listen, and consider."

As Felipe translated Redbud's speech back to the Skaru:re, the one who appeared eldest amongst the men lifted a hand and spoke. Felipe translated it back. "He says they were all sore wroth with Blackbird, for his refusal to accept the sacrifice of one as he said he would, and for continuing to pursue me and the girl, White Doe. Many of them had marveled in their hearts at the brave way the pale-skinned youth had faced his death. When Blackbird returned, not with White Doe and Guh-neh but the Kurawoten youth, who they suspected might be dull-witted since he had come back of his own will, they were angry enough to consider punishing him—an unheard-of thing for a priest of the Skaru:re. For one who claimed to hear from the spirits, he had made many rash and futile decisions."

Ginny peered over at Blackbird, who sat quietly, hands resting on his knees but head bowed as if he could not bear watching the other people's responses.

"They would have come at the end of summer." Redbud took up the telling again. "But it was time to prepare for the winter hunt. In the meantime, I told them all I could of God and His Son, Jesus, and they were gracious to listen. They asked many questions. So many that I knew it best to ask for our minister to come as well." He laughed. "In turn I went and helped with the winter hunt and did my best to serve them as if they were my own people—or, perhaps, serve them better."

An answering chuckle rippled through the group.

"So now it is spring, and they have been most desirous to come—to ask, and listen, and even to speak of peace between their people and ours."

Manteo rose and inclined his head to the assembled elders of those they had long called enemies. "We would be pleased to stay for a time and talk of all these things."

Ginny could not contain the swell of amazement, gratitude—and tears. Mama had said, and 'twas truth, that God would use all of it, even—and perhaps especially—Henry's death.

For the first several days, the Kurawoten and English remained on their guard, but then, with the Skaru:re eagerly devouring all that Nicholas Johnson and Manteo had to share, and most agreeing to confess Christ and be baptized, the realization sank in at last—and with it, joy. Even Blackbird, who had scarcely acknowledged Felipe or Virginia after that first night, came and on bended knee and with outstretched hands committed himself to God and to this new faith. The willingness of White Doe to die in Guh-neh's place, and then the death of the English youth, had shaken him beyond his ability to express or even admit.

Immediately afterward, he offered to prove his change of heart—and his people's goodwill—by surrendering himself as a captive and slave to the English and Kurawoten. Specifically to Dyonis, the father of the youth who had sacrificed himself.

Dyonis backed away from the kneeling Skaru:re warrior-priest, shaking his head and throwing a panicked glance at Felipe. "Nay—oh nay, not again."

The onlookers could only chuckle as Felipe and Redbud tried to explain to him, Felipe especially, that this was not necessary. Blackbird actually appeared crestfallen then offered the same gesture to Felipe himself. It was some time before they could convince him that they did not refuse because they despised the offering and all it symbolized, but that their own faith would not allow him to abase himself thus.

Besides, they had already tried to accept such an offering from Felipe and found it exceedingly distasteful.

After Manteo and the Skaru:re elders talked some more, the Skaru:re decided to build a town across and a little upriver, where the Suquoten had once dwelt. More discussion would take place between them and with the Cwareuuoc and Newasiwoc, concerning how they might continue to build peace amongst all peoples of the coastlands.

Felipe was asked to stay, to help speak between the Skaru:re and others, but he and Virginia both desired to return to the island at least until after their little one was born. It was determined Redbud might be the better choice for that, regardless, since he had the benefit of knowing Kurawoten more thoroughly than Felipe, though Felipe had applied himself to learning it as well.

On the last day, as Felipe and Ginny prepared to return with the others to the island, Blackbird did approach them at last.

The tall Skaru:re did not speak at first, only regarded Felipe gravely and glanced at Virginia, gaze hesitating on her rounding belly, before he turned back to Felipe. "You are looking very Spanish." With the barest smile, he touched one finger to his own chin.

Felipe let himself smile a little in return, with a slow nod, almost a half bow.

"You and White Doe are happy together? And she is recovered from her wound?"

"We are, and she is."

Blackbird studied her then, such conflict in his expression as Felipe had never seen in his years with the Skaru:re. "I regret the boy's death," he said at last, "and that it took such a thing to open our people's eyes."

When Felipe translated what he had said, Virginia placed a light hand on Blackbird's arm and said, "All is washed away now in the blood of God's Son. His was the only sacrifice that could atone for our sins—but what Henry did in laying down his own life will not be for naught. Nothing, in fact, that we have done, or suffered, is wasted, not if we truly belong to God."

Felipe relayed what she had said. His eyes wide and glimmering, Blackbird nodded. "I look forward to hearing more of this God, and learning His ways more perfectly."

Virginia smiled. "I could not be your wife, Blackbird, but I am most happy to become your sister in Christ."

Another look of wonder—and then even Blackbird allowed himself a smile.

ACKNOWLEDGMENTS

To Becky and her team. . .what an honor it has been to write for Barbour! Y'all are the absolute *BEST*. Special thanks to Becky for inviting me along, from Daughters of the Mayflower to True Colors and finally the Lost Colony concept. I'll say it again: I hope I've done your vision justice.

To Ellen. . .the most amazing, patient, encouraging editor I know. Thank you so much for being willing to work with my crazy process.

To Corrie and Lee. . .for faithfully reading in process. Y'all truly helped keep me going.

To Lee, Jen, and Beth. . .for prayers and encouragement and always checking up on me!

To Michelle. . .how crazy is it that we've been on this journey together for twenty years? I don't think I could do this without you.

To Kimberli. . .for pointing me to quick research on the Spanish, then agreeing to read and offering great feedback on all the historical context. (Not to mention the differences between Catholic and Reformed!)

To Lynne, Joan, Jenelle, and Naomi. . .thank you so much for agreeing to read for endorsement and/or feedback.

To all the ladies in my little influencer group. . .Jenelle, Paula, Jeanne, Jennifer, Teri, Tina, Susan, Kailey, Esther, Brenda, Vera, Carolyn, Andrea, Trisha, Brittany, and Nicole (in no particular order). A huge thanks to each and every one of you for your prayers, support, and promotion efforts over the past few years.

To my sons, daughters-in-love, daughters, and sons-in-love. . .for letting me have a front-row seat to your stories and for reminding me why I write romance—and try to write it well.

To Troy. . .it's only ever, always you.

And lastly—and most of all—to my Lord and Savior, Yeshua haMachiach, Jesus the Christ. . .for tenderly leading me through yet another adventure, even though I had nothing left emotionally or creatively after the past year and more, even when I was sure I wouldn't survive. You truly are most worthy of all our devotion. Only You are *THE* God.

HISTORICAL NOTE

With every single story I've written, I find myself bemoaning all the things I didn't know, the holes in my research, the things I misinterpreted. That was never more evident to me than with this story.

To begin with, I found bits of research I wish I'd had in the writing of *Elinor*. I'd already made liberal use of the excellent article by Roberta Estes on dna-explained.com (link in the bibliography), which includes a table listing all those associated with the Roanoke Colony and their profession and location of origin, both known and probable. Time and energy prevented me from developing that more thoroughly. Half a dozen other details fell prey to the same limitations—so if you find some aspect or another of the Lost Colony story missing, it's likely either I was not aware at the time or I just did not have the time to work it in. (Do also be aware, however, that many topics have been addressed in the historical notes of previous books, and while I revisit a few here, time and space prevent me from repeating them all.)

The overarching question of this story: Who are the Skaru:re, and how does their history intersect with that of the Lost Colony? The spelling I use is one of many variations for the name by which they refer to themselves, but the pronunciation amounts to sgah-*rooo*-rah. They are, of course, the great Tuscarora, most often associated in modern times with the Iroquois-speaking peoples of the northeastern United States but known to originally inhabit much of modern-day North Carolina when the Spanish, French, and English were exploring the southeast in the sixteenth century.

One of the earliest English primary sources we have on the Tuscarora people is the writings of John Lawson, around 1700. Lawson was killed a few years later by the Tuscarora, whose reputation as a fierce and unpleasant people was apparently well earned. Lawson reports that they were allies of several smaller coastal tribes and had a strong settlement near the present-day town of New Bern, North Carolina.

English explorations of the 1580s referred to the Tuscarora as the Mangoac—reportedly translated "rattlesnake." (I currently can't find my source for that, having lost a bunch of my online research links during a laptop crash just before the writing of *Rebecca*.) Essentially, we know they were enemies to the coastal peoples—at least to the Secotan and others—at the time of the earliest English explorations (Barlowe, Lane, Harriot) but during Lawson's time are reported to be allies.

So what happened in the hundred years or so in between? A few things could account for it: increasing encroachment by the English and the need for smaller people groups to seek protection from larger, stronger ones. We must not discount the natural tendencies of human nature in general to seek to subjugate and occupy the territories of others—and it's well established that the Indigenous peoples of America were busy pushing each other around and making war with each other for various reasons before Europeans ever arrived. (There is no such thing as an uncorrupted human society.) So here is where I use a bit of dramatic license and bend the legend of Virginia Dare into the realm of speculative—or at least alternate—history.

There is provenance for an Indigenous people to retain their belief in Christianity after being introduced to it by European explorers (at least one of the tribes converted by the Spanish is recorded as having done so). We have no idea how deeply the English colonists, who did migrate to Croatoan after being dumped on Roanoke Island, might have affected the peoples around them with an authentic faith in Christ. There is evidence, as I discuss in my notes for both *Elinor* and *Mary*, that at least some of them held such a faith, and that the Croatoan people adopted it.

John Lawson, my source for the earliest English interaction with the Tuscarora people in what is now North Carolina, complains of Native language being disorganized and inarticulate. After perusing the Tuscarora-English dictionary compiled by Dr. Blair Rudes, whose work is also one of my resources for eastern Algonquian languages, I am convinced that Lawson lacked either the patience or intelligence (or both) to see the fallacy in his assertion. Or perhaps he simply hadn't devoted enough time to studying. Either way, I went in hoping to simply glean a few words to add cultural flavor to this story and ended up completely dazzled by the beauty, complexity, and depth of language possessed by Indigenous peoples.

What you'll find on the pages of my stories, then, is the barest taste, and very imprecise. In southeastern North America during this time period, three distinct families of language existed—Algonquian, Siouan, and Iroquoian. The Secotan, Croatoan, and Powhatan peoples spoke variations of Algonquian and could generally understand one another, while the Skaru:re (Tuscarora) spoke Iroquoian. I have leaned heavily on Dr. Blair Rudes—not only his work creating Powhatan dialogue for the film *The New World*, which was only a side project, but also his years-long effort to preserve the Tuscaroran language. Honestly, I'm a little intimidated by the depth of his research and could have easily spent another six months geeking out and trying to get the word use in my story "just right," but publication schedules prohibited that. My readers are probably very thankful.

A note on my use of certain words, such as "kilt." One pre-reader questioned me on that, but I chose it (and have used the term throughout the series) because of its reference to a particular skirt-like garment for men rather than any association with woven plaid fabric. I also shifted to the exclusive use of Kurawoten for Croatoan, which is closer to the probable Native pronunciation. Someone questioned me as well on Ginny's difficulty with learning the Skaru:re tongue, but I drew on my own auditory processing issues there. Though I consider myself something of a language geek (I took two semesters of New Testament Greek in college just for fun) and can grasp the written forms fairly easily, I have a really hard time differentiating the spoken word—especially under stress.

Regarding locations: I've placed the Cwareuuoc/Coree town roughly where historical maps placed the Newasiwoc (previous spelling Neusiok), and I have them speaking a dialect of Carolina Algonquian, but some sources say they spoke Iroquoian or possibly even Siouan. There is also a location named Cora Banks—or Core Banks—but not where I've placed the fictional town occupied by the English and Kurawoten.

I had guessed the location of the original town of the Kurawoten—and almost certainly where the English settled after leaving Roanoke—to lay close to the modern town of Buxton on the lower part of Hatteras Island. This is corroborated by both recent archaeology and Lawson's map (see his reference to "Hatteras Indians," who boasted of English ancestry, and indeed many of whom had gray or blue eyes).

Manteo's copper necklace: it was common for Native peoples to wear ornaments of beaten copper, and one such piece uncovered during a dig on Hatteras Island by the Croatoan Archaeological Society, an organization headed by Scott Dawson, might have been from anyone. . .except for the faint etching—one barely legible squiggle—across the face of the copper. Dawson posted on his Lost Colony Museum page on Facebook that Thomas Harriot, who had traveled extensively with the English explorers and spent much time learning Carolina Algonquian from Manteo and Wanchese, had invented an alphabet for the language. (He had also compiled a list of words, which sadly does not survive.) The symbol for the letter *M* is what they found on the copper pendant, so he believes it very likely belonged to Manteo himself—he would have been the only one who knew that alphabet because, as Dawson says, "it never caught on." Speculation, perhaps—but I just had to work it into the story!

The Green Corn Festival, held when the first crop of corn comes ripe, seems to have been celebrated among all First Peoples in eastern North America. What we know of the customs surrounding it comes from contact dating around 1700 and after (Lawson etc.), so I can only guess at what went into preparation and execution. Sources say the festival itself could last up to four days, but I've shortened that time for the purposes of my story.

One of the things I enjoyed most about writing this story was the dynamic between Elinor and her daughter Ginny. As a bereaved mother myself, I have walked the road of grief—and tasted the bittersweet joy of helping my adult children navigate the waters of life through both love and loss. My last three, in fact, were all married while I was on deadline for this story. I am one blessed mama!

Alongside the blessings, however, came a parade of not-so-fun family events. I learned a heap about trauma responses and how very long the impression of a loss remains upon the soul and spirit. Nothing about Ginny's experience, or that of others, would be easy to recover from. Yet at the same time, life does go on.

One question I will revisit is this: Were the Roanoke colonists religious separatists? As I mention in the notes for *Elinor*, author Lee Miller offers this theory, which I found both intriguing and plausible. She suggests that if true, the colonists' religious separatism would have made them somewhat expendable to the Crown—although more effort was made to find and recover the colony than is popularly known. (See the article by Roberta Estes on dna-explained.com, listed in the bibliography.) I've written them as if they were, but since we don't know for sure, and there's precious little about what order of services the Lost Colonists might have used to conduct weddings, funerals, baptisms, etc., I borrowed liberally from an older online text of the Book of Common Prayer, especially for *Elinor* and *Mary*. This time I decided to go for something less structured for a theoretical memorial service. I was also deliberately imprecise in regard to how they might handle the specifics of someone converting from formal childhood Catholicism to Protestantism, or at least a more active and living relationship with God than they had previously enjoyed. One Reformed/Presbyterian pastor stressed to me that they would have insisted on baptizing Felipe again rather than accepting his christening as valid—but that they also would have called it "baptism" and not "christening." I looked back into John White's account, however, and the word *christen* was specifically used in reference to Manteo's conversion and Virginia's birth in August 1587. So, as I commented to my friend (the wife of said pastor), if the Roanoke colonists were indeed Separatists, then perhaps they weren't as "separate" as others.

We also don't really know how much hymnody carried over when Henry VIII established the Anglican Church. One source says that initially anything Catholic or Latin was thrown out, with many Reformers speaking in the harshest terms against even the use of musical instruments. They felt it distracting at best and an offense to the ear of God at worst—I suppose they never read the commands in the book of Psalms to use a wide variety of instruments in praise? I think it safe to say, however, that people carried with them the songs they had learned—that beautiful hymns of any tradition survived wherever people knew them. The lyrics of Elinor's hymn early in the story are attributed to William Byrd, first published in England in 1580, so I think it plausible she might have known it.

On choosing to use the Great Bible: One very perceptive reader asked me after *Elinor* why I didn't use the Geneva Bible, which was actually in widespread use at the time the Roanoke Colony set sail—but the research purist in me wouldn't allow usage of the Geneva when I could find no versions predating the 1599 edition. So the Great Bible it was.

A related note, however, about the Bible being available in the language of the common people. Where Felipe hears the Lord's Prayer in English for the first time and perceives it to be spoken "in such a rude tongue," my editor questioned the wording. I realized I unconsciously reflected here the historical practice of the Roman Catholic Church to conduct services only in Latin. In that time many people believed that Scripture was too holy to be read in common languages, and so only those who were properly educated, namely the clergy themselves, could read and interpret the Word of God for others. Thus rose the movement of the Reformation—led by Martin Luther, William Tyndale, and others—to translate the Bible into the languages of the common people, to make God and His Word more accessible to everyone. This effort was fought tooth and nail by the Roman Catholic Church—and initially by Henry VIII as well, who had Tyndale burned at the stake in 1536 but then later changed his mind and commissioned an English translation of the Bible. I researched a bit and found a similar effort to produce a Bible in Spanish, which was firmly squashed by the infamous Spanish Inquisition. Interestingly, the Spanish account that mentions Manteo's and Wanchese's presence with the English in the Caribbean in 1585 also makes note of the English offering a copy of the Bible translated into Spanish. David Beers

Quinn comments that this is a rare case of positive English propaganda by the Spanish.

Thus I was reminded of just how fresh these people were to the concept of God's Word in their own language. The English had a few decades to be inured to it, but the Spanish? No, the idea would have been very new and shocking. My next thought was, do we moderns even realize how privileged we are to have so many translations at our fingertips? Many bled and died to give us that luxury.

Also, if there's one thing I've learned while writing historical fiction, it's that I'm bound to offend somebody—especially if I'm trying to be fair to all sides. One of my early readers for *Virginia* complained that I paint the Tuscarora as "too nice." (She wasn't finished reading yet. I told her, "Wait for it.") I've heard lament over the anti-Catholic sentiment in this series. That may or may not have shaped the creation of a particular character in *Virginia*—although I am still bound by individual points of view. It remains an unalterable fact of this time period that people of different religious and political backgrounds spoke of each other in the most scathing terms—and yes, I might reflect my own Protestant-leaning upbringing and current beliefs in these stories. There isn't a single author who doesn't write out of their own faith. . .or lack thereof.

Which leads me to the point that the most offensive thing to some may be that I presume one religion to be superior to another, especially in regard to the First Peoples. It's something I struggle with, the apparent arrogance of Christianity to claim to be not only absolute truth but the *only* absolute truth. Can we not just focus on kindness and decency? Those are important things, no mistake. Our own Holy Book tells us we should speak the truth in love. Both, together. Love, but do speak the truth.

The vast majority of religions concern themselves with how frail, flawed humanity might be acceptable to God. Only Christianity claims a God who willingly took humanity upon Himself and not only gave His life as the answer to that question but shattered the bonds of death itself. God-as-Man said plainly that He is the way, the truth, and the life and that no one comes to the Father except through Him. We claim nothing that Jesus did not say of Himself. Also, while many religions speak of resurrection as a symbol, only Christianity claims it as a literal historical event—and thus the substance of all future hope for those who believe it.

So why don't more of us who claim to believe truly live it out? Why are we constantly at odds with others who also claim that belief? Very good questions. The answers have to do mostly with the limitations of still living in this flawed, damaged world—but we can always keep reaching for more understanding, more growth.

Here we are, then, at the end of my fourth and final installment of the Daughters of the Lost Colony series. (Third if you're coming by way of *Mary* and haven't yet read *Rebecca*.) I never dreamed four years ago that this story would eventually span four books. I actually had no plan in the beginning to write Virginia Dare's story, since it seemed so bound up in folklore already, but after finishing *Rebecca*, I realized that it would be too obvious an addition to the series to miss.

And so I offer a most heartfelt thank-you to all of you, my dear readers.

BIBLIOGRAPHY

Note: Many of these are specific to other titles in the series, but I include them because they have all contributed to my overall understanding of the times or culture.

Allen, Paula Gunn. *Pocahontas: Medicine Woman, Spy, Entrepreneur, Diplomat.* Harper Collins, 2004.

Axtell, James, ed. *The Indian Peoples of Eastern America: A Documentary History of the Sexes.* Oxford University Press, 1981.

Axtell, James. *The Invasion Within: The Contest of Cultures in Colonial North America.* Oxford University Press, 1988.

Custalow, Dr. Linwood "Little Bear," and Angela L. "Silver Star" Daniel. *The True Story of Pocahontas: The Other Side of History.* Fulcrum Publishing, 2007.

Dawson, Scott. *Croatoan: Birthplace of America.* Infinity Publishing, 2009.

Dawson, Scott. *The Lost Colony and Hatteras Island.* The History Press, 2020.

Fullam, Brandon. *The Lost Colony of Roanoke: New Perspectives.* McFarland & Company, 2017.

Fullam, Brandon. *Manteo and the Algonquians of the Roanoke Voyages.* McFarland & Company, 2020.

Harriot, Thomas. *A Briefe and True Report of the New Found Land of Virginia: The Complete 1590 Edition with 28 Engravings by Theodor de Bry after the Drawings of John White and Other Illustrations.* Dover Publications, 1972.

Hakluyt, Richard. *The Principal Navigations, Voyages, Traffiques, and Discoveries of the English Nation.* Google Books. Abridged edition, *Voyages and Discoveries*, Penguin Books, 1972.

Horn, James. *A Land as God Made It: Jamestown and the Birth of America.* Basic Books, 2005.

Horn, James, ed. *Capt. John Smith: Writings with Other Narratives of Roanoke, Jamestown, and the First English Settlement of America.* Library of America, Penguin Putnam, 1984. (Includes the texts by Harriot and Strachey.)

Hosier, Paul E. *Seacoast Plants of the Carolinas: A New Guide for Plant Identification and Use in the Coastal Landscape.* University of North Carolina Press, 2018.

Jamestown Rediscovery. *Holy Ground: Archaeology, Religion, and the First Founders of Jamestown.* Jamestown Rediscovery Foundation, 2016.

Johnson, Elias. *Legends, Traditions, and Laws of the Iroquois or Six Nations and History of the Tuscarora Indians.* 1881. Public domain.

Kupperman, Karen Ordahl, ed. *Captain John Smith: A Select Edition of His Writings.* University of North Carolina Press, 1988.

Lawler, Andrew. *The Secret Token.* Anchor Books, 2018.

Lawson, John. *A New Voyage to Carolina*. 1709. Public domain.

Lord, Suzanne. *Music from the Age of Shakespeare: A Cultural History*. Greenwood Press, 2003.

McMullan, Philip S., Jr. *Beechland and the Lost Colony*. Pamlico & Albemarle Publishing, 2010 (as a master's thesis), 2014.

Miller, Lee. *Roanoke: Solving the Mystery of the Lost Colony*. Arcade Publishing, 2000, 2012.

Moretti-Langholtz, Danielle. *A Study of Virginia Indians and Jamestown: The First Century*. Colonial National Historical Park, National Park Service, December 2005. (Available online, http://npshistory.com/publications/jame/moretti-langholtz/index. htm.)

Oberg, Michael Leroy. *The Head in Edward Nugent's Hand: Roanoke's Forgotten Indians*. University of Pennsylvania Press, 2008.

Perdue, Theda, and Christopher Arris Oakley. *Native Carolinians: The Indians of North Carolina*. North Carolina Office of Archives and History, 2010, 2014.

Quattlebaum, Paul. *The Land Called Chicora: The Carolinas under Spanish Rule with French Intrusions, 1520–1670*. Reprint Company, 2009. (Reproduced from a 1956 edition in the South Caroliniana Library, University of South Carolina.)

Quinn, David Beers, ed. *The Roanoke Voyages 1584–1590*. 2 volumes. Dover Publications, 1991.

Reader's Digest. *America's Fascinating Indian Heritage*. Reader's Digest Association, 1978.

Rountree, Helen C. *Pocahontas, Powhatan, Opechancanough: Three Indian Lives Changed by Jamestown*. University of Virginia Press, 2005.

———. *Pocahontas's People: The Powhatan Indians of Virginia through Four Centuries*. University of Oklahoma Press, 1990.

———. *The Powhatan Indians of Virginia: Their Traditional Culture*. University of Oklahoma Press, 1988.

———. *Young Pocahontas in the Indian World*. Self-published, 1995.

Rountree, Helen C., Wayne E. Clark, and Kent Mountford. *John Smith's Chesapeake Voyages 1607–1609*. University of Virginia Press, 2007.

Rudes, Blair A. *Tuscarora-English/English-Tuscarora Dictionary*. University of Toronto Press, 1999. (Online at archive.org.)

Rushforth, Brett. *Bonds of Alliance: Indigenous and Atlantic Slaveries in New France*. University of North Carolina Press, 2012.

Sloan, Kim. *A New World: England's First View of America*. University of North Carolina Press, 2007.

Strachey, William. *A Historie of Travaile into Virginia Britannia*. Hakluyt Society, 1612, 1849.

Straube, Beverly A. *The Arachaearium: Rediscovering Jamestown 1607–1699, Jamestown, Virginia.* APVA Preservation Virginia, 2007.

Townsend, Camilla. *Pocahontas and the Powhatan Dilemma.* Hill and Wang, 2004.

Ward, H. Trawick, and R. P. Stephen Davis Jr. *Time before History: The Archaeology of North Carolina.* University of North Carolina Press, 1999.

A handful of online sites have been crucial to my research as well:

Coastal Carolina Indian Center: CoastalCarolinaIndians.com

Virtual Jamestown: virtualjamestown.org

The Other Jamestown: virtual-jamestown.com

Roberta Estes, scientist and genealogical researcher, particularly this page: https://dna-explained.com/2018/06/28/the-lost-colony-of-roanoke-did-they-survive-national-geographic-archaeology-historical-records-and-dna/

The British Museum online, for its collection of John White's drawings and paintings: https://www.britishmuseum.org/collection/term/BIOG50964

CAST OF CHARACTERS

(For a complete list of Roanoke colonists and relevant historical figures of the time, please see notes at the end of Elinor *and* Mary. *All characters marked with an asterisk * are fictional.)*

Virginia Thomasyn Dare: daughter of Ananias and Elinor Dare, granddaughter of John and Thomasyn White, first English child born in the New World (middle name fictional)

Henry Harvie: son of Dyonis and Margery Harvie, second English child born in the New World (first name fictional)

*Redbud: son of Netah and unnamed Kurawoten father

Elinor White Dare: daughter of colony governor John White

*Sees Far: son of Suquoten weroance Granganimeo

*Sunny: Johanna Elizabeth Dare, given the milk name Sunlight at birth, daughter of Ananias and Elinor Dare, age 11

*Mouse: son of Sees Far and Elinor, age 8

*Owlet: son of Sees Far and Elinor, age 4

*Berry: baby daughter of Sees Far and Elinor

Dyonis and Margery Harvie: one of the original Assistants for the Cittie of Ralegh (the Roanoke colony) and his wife; father and mother to Henry

*Various young children

*Netah [nay-TAH]: Redbud's mother; means "friend" in Carolina Algonquian

Manteo [modern pronunciation MAN-ee-oh; historical probably mahn-TAY-oh]: declared "Lord of Roanoac and Dasemonguepeuk" at his baptism in 1587 as a reward for his faithful aid to the English; born on Croatoan Island and son to weroansqua of the same; accompanied Amadas and Barlowe back to England in 1584; returned in 1585 with Lane's expedition and stayed to support the English; returned to England in 1586 and part of White's colony in 1587; name means "to snatch"

(Manteo's Coree wife is not named in *Virginia.*)

Towaye [toh-WAH-yay]: Native man who accompanied the 1587 expedition back from England; nothing known about him besides his name being recorded on the roster alongside Manteo's

Georgie Howe: son of George Howe, one of the original Assistants who was murdered shortly after arriving on Roanoac Island in 1587; age 12 at arrival

*Mary, formerly known as Mushaniq [MUSH-ah-neek]: oldest daughter of Manteo; name means "squirrel"

*Waboose (George Howe III): oldest son of Georgie and Mary

*Unnamed boy: second oldest

*Firefly: girl, next to youngest

*Unnamed girl: youngest

Chris (Christopher) Cooper: nephew to John White and cousin to Elinor White Dare; one of the original Assistants

Roger Prat: one of the original Assistants

John Prat: son of Roger Prat, a boy when first arrived

Rob Ellis: about age 11 at arrival

Nicholas Johnson, historical member of the colony but fictional minister

*Timqua, sister to Manteo, now married to Nicholas Johnson

Edward Stafford: captain who helmed the pinnace in 1587; had been to the New World on previous expedition

Jane (was Mannering), midwife, now (fictional) wife to Edward

John Chapman

Alis Chapman: wife to John

*Tirzah Chapman: a little younger than Ginny

*Blackbird: Skaru:re priest and warrior

*Grandmother Dove: Skaru:re woman, actual grandmother to Blackbird

*Strong Oak: eldest priest of the Skaru:re

(Mentioned only)

Ananias Dare: Elinor's first husband, one of the original Assistants

Wanchese [modern pronunciation WAHN-cheese; historical probably wahn-CHAY-zay]: Native man, probably a Secotan warrior, who accompanied Amadas and Barlowe back to England in 1584; returned in 1585 and disappeared into the wilderness; name means "to take flight from water"

Okisco [oh-KEE-sko]: weroance of Weopomeioc, region north of Chowan River

Emme Merrimoth: taken captive and sold to the Powhatan

Libby (Elizabeth) Glane: taken captive and remains at Ritanoe [ree-TAH-noh-ay]

Granganimeo: father of Sees Far; weroance of the Suquoten; died in epidemic after earlier arrival of the English

REGIONS AND PEOPLE GROUPS

Cora Banks: fictional town on the Pamlico River, named after the Coree/Cwareuuoc people

Coree, Cwareuuoc [kwah-ray-yuh-wock]: a people located between the Neuse and Pamlico Rivers; probable source of the word "CORA" carved into a tree on Hatteras Island

Croatoan: present-day lower Hatteras Island; "the talking town" or "the council town"; in Algonquian, Kurawoten

Dasemonguepeuk [possible historical pronunciation dass-ay-mong-kway-pay-uhk]: the mainland peninsula nearest Roanoke Island. Spelled variously Dasemongwepeok, Dasemonquepeu, Dasemunkepeuc, etc.

Kurawoten [kuh-rah-WOH-tain]: see Croatoan

Mangoac: a strong people of the mainland

Newasiwoc: formerly "Neusiok" in *Elinor* (this spelling from John White), a people located between the Neuse and Pamlico Rivers, near the Coree

Powhatan: a people group in possession of present-day Virginia

Pumtico: Pamlico River

Ritanoe [ree-TAH-noh-ay]: inland Native town where copper was mined

Roanoac: present-day Roanoke Island

Skaru:re [sgah-ROOO-rah]: the Tuscarora, known to various Algonquian-speaking peoples as "Mangoac"

Suquoten [suh-KWOH-tain]: an Algonquian-speaking people group mostly residing upon the mainland but also apparently in possession of Roanoke Island at the time of the first English voyage in 1585; referred to previously as "Secotan"

Weopomeioc [way-oh-pom-ay-oc or way-ah-pem-ay-oc]: mainland region just north and east of the Chowan River

Wococon: island southwest of Croatoan; present-day Ocracoke Island

GLOSSARY

CA—Carolina Algonquian;
Tusc—Tuscarora;
hist—historical terminology

Ah!: Stop! or an exclamation of disgust (Tusc)

anéhsnaçi [ah-NEH-snah-jee]: sassafras (Tusc)

apon [ah-PONE]: corn bread (CA)

arquebus: a type of matchlock gun commonly used in the sixteenth century; also harquebus (hist)

a:we [ahh-way]: water (Tusc)

cunewahskri:yu [choo-neh-wah-SKREE-yoo]: common milkweed, also known as Indian hemp (Tusc)

doublet: a man's garment for the upper body; a type of fitted vest worn over a shirt, with or without detachable sleeves (hist)

ehqutonahas [eh-kwuh-TONE-ah-hahs]: Stop talking! Hush! or Be quiet! (CA)

ga:çi [gah-jee]: come (Tusc)

guh-neh: eel (Tusc)

gusud [GOO-sood]: grandmother (Tusc)

hose: see Trunkhose

huskanasqua: the coming-of-age rite for girls (CA)

huskanaw: the coming-of-age rite for boys (CA)

Inqutish [ink-uh-teesh]: English (from Blair Rudes' transliteration of the Powhatan pronunciation of England: Inkurut/Inku[d]und) (CA)

kahyeháhre [kah-yeh-HAH-rrée]: river (Tusc)

kanehúche [kah-neh-HOO-cheh]: corn bread, equivalent of apon (Tusc)

kanoe [kah-noh-ay]: canoe, dugout style from trunks of various types of trees, mostly cedar (CA)

kirtle: a woman's gown worn over a shift, having a moderately boned bodice and full skirts, with or without detachable sleeves (hist)

kupi [kuh-PEA]: yes (CA)

Kuwumádas [kuh-wuh-MAH-das]: I love you (CA)

mahkusun [mah-KUH-sun]: shoe (origin of the word moccasin) (CA)

mahta [MAH-tah]: no (CA)

nek: my mother (CA)

nohsh: my father (CA)

pegatawah [pek-ah-TAH-wah]: corn (CA)

quiakros [kwee-ah-krohs]: priest, holy man, spiritual leader (CA)

Suquoten [previously "Sukwoten," probably suh-KWOH-tain]: Secotan

shift: a woman's loose garment of linen, worn as an underdress or nightdress (hist)

slops: a man's garment, like trunkhose but not fitted to the leg, often worn by sailors or laborers (hist)

trunkhose: a man's loose-fitting garment for the lower body, rather like poofy shorts tied at the waist and gathered around the thigh, forerunner of breeches (hist)

Tunapewak [t/dun-ah-PAY-wahk]: the People ("the true, real, or genuine people") (CA)

una:kwéya [oo-nah-KWAY-yah]: cattail (Tusc)

unéheh [oo-neh-heh]: pegatawah, corn (Tusc)

uppowoc: tobacco (CA)

urí:'neh [oo-reeh-neh]: dove (Tusc)

ure:ye [oo-rreh-eh]: trees, forest (Tusc)

waboose: bunny, baby rabbit (CA)

wassador: precious metals, specifically copper (CA)

weroance/weroansqua: leader or chieftain over a town or towns ("one who is rich") (CA)

wutapantam [wuh-tah-PAHN-tam]: deer (CA)

yapám [yah-PAUM]: ocean, sea (CA)

Transplanted to North Dakota after more than two decades in the Deep South, Shannon McNear loves losing herself in local history. She's the author of four novellas, the first a 2014 RITA nominee and the most recent a 2021 SELAH winner, and six full-length novels. Her greatest joy, however, is being a military wife, mom, mother-in-law, and grammie. She's been a contributor to Colonial Quills and The Borrowed Book and is a current member of American Christian Fiction Writers and Faith, Hope, & Love Christian Writers. When not cooking, researching, or leaking story from her fingertips, she enjoys being outdoors, basking in the beauty of the northern prairies.